LEAH FLEMING

The
Girl Under
the
Olive Tree

SIMON &
SCHUSTER

London · New York · Sydney · Toronto · New Delhi

To Crete: island of my dreams and heroes. Long may you prosper.

First published in Great Britain by Simon & Schuster UK Ltd, 2013
A CBS COMPANY

This paperback edition published in 2018

1 3 5 7 9 10 8 6 4 2

Simon & Schuster UK Ltd
1st Floor
222 Gray's Inn Road
London WC1X 8HB

Simon & Schuster Australia, Sydney
Simon & Schuster India, New Delhi

www.simonandschuster.co.uk
www.simonandschuster.com.au
www.simonandschuster.co.in

A CIP catalogue record for this book is available from the British Library

Paperback ISBN: 978-1-4711-7858-0
eBook ISBN: 978-0-85720-407-3

Typeset in the UK by Hewer Text UK Ltd, Edinburgh
Printed and bound by CPI Group (UK) Ltd, Croydon, CR0 4YY

Part 1

DEPARTURES

There is no escape from Crete for those who have fallen
under the spell of the mountain heart of the island and
the hearts of the people who live there.

Lew Lind, *Flowers of Rethymnon*

Crete, 1941

At the sound of gunfire it was time to retreat to the back of the dark cave, time to flatten herself against one of the recesses, hoping it was just another false alarm. She pressed herself into the damp rock wall as the volley of shots grew louder and bullets ricocheted off the metal canisters. Suddenly the dim light from the entrance was blocked by the rush of troops shouting 'Raus . . . raus', storming through as only conquerors can do.

Flinging herself to the ground in one swift move, she tried to hide her presence, to play dead as they dragged out orderlies and the wounded to line them up on the rocks outside.

Every second seemed an hour as she lay prostrate in the gloom, tasting the salty sand, the grit and the stench of dried blood on her lips, trying not to shiver. She sensed it would be only minutes before discovery, so this was not the time to waver. Be British, be brave . . . Oh, be damned with all that guff, she thought. All she was feeling was a cold fury in her gut. How could she leave when there was still so much to be done?

Suddenly a pair of desert boots covered in mud appeared at eye level, a scarred hand jerked her upright. This was the test, the moment of truth and defiance. If she faced the enemy without fear, her bluff might just work . . .

Stokencourt House, Gloucestershire, April 2001

The nightmare woke me again. First the gun pointing at my head, then water was closing over me, my arms thrashing through the sheets to find the surface, ears bursting, lungs fighting for breath, struggling against bodies already sinking, grabbing at me for life, kicking out, tiring with the effort, my eyes opening in terror and then surprise. It was only a dream, but my heart was pounding in my chest. Each time it was harder to reach the surface. *How many more of these will I survive?* Nothing for it but to get up and face the day, I decided. Then with relief I realized for once I was not alone.

Opening the gold damask curtains, I peered out into the morning. The Easter weather was holding up, the April sun warming the golden Cotswold stones on the south wall of Stokencourt House. The daffodils were almost over but there was a hint of blossom on the cherry trees and the scent of new growth in the air. Time for a quick tour round the herbaceous borders in my dressing gown to see how much Oliver, the young gardener, had overlooked in his rush to finish the strimming and be on his way to meet his girl.

I was glad Lois was relaxing in bed, leaving Alex sitting in front of the TV, not demanding to be entertained. Later I'd order him to race round the small lake. My niece was still looking washed out after the trauma of her husband's desertion last year, and desperate for a bolthole. To be honest I was glad of their company over the bank holiday weekend. Bank holidays were not my favourite time: cars blocking the lanes, strangers peering over the stone walls, leaving litter and dog mess. Stokencourt always warmed to the echoes of children's noise along its rambling corridors and stone-flagged floors, its mullioned-window seats piled with discarded toys that Alex dismissed as babyish. The young grow up so fast these days.

He did like taking Trojan, the latest in a line of wire-haired fox terriers, for walks through the village where our family had lived for generations. When Lois and Alex disappeared back down the M4 to London, I'd soon feel the chill of their absence.

It was a couple of hours later that I looked up from my weeding to see Lois blinking into the morning sunlight, and I caught a glimpse of her mother, Athene, at that age, so tall and willowy, like all the Georgiou women who thrived in open air and sunshine with their olive skin and blond hair.

'Happy birthday, Aunt Pen!'

I paused, puzzled, and then sighed. 'Thank you but at my age birthdays are surplus to requirements. It's quite enough to wake up each morning still breathing.' I silently cursed myself. Why did I always sound so sharp and ungrateful?

'I knew you'd say that, but it's a big old birthday. You hate being reminded but you do so much for us, letting us stay here. Since Adam left . . .' She tailed off, still bereft by his desertion. 'My dear, you're the only living relative I have who is not stuck in some home away with the fairies. Why you bother with an old biddy like me, I'll never know.'

'Don't change the subject,' smiled Lois, standing her ground. 'Happy birthday with love from Alex and me.' She pulled an envelope from behind her back and shoved it into my hand.

'What's this then?' I was fishing in my gardening apron for my reading spectacles.

'It's a card and a brochure. I thought you might like to come on holiday with us. I've booked a villa in May when Alex is on school holidays.'

Instinctively I shook my head. 'That's a kind thought but definitely not . . . Lunch at the Royal Oak will be quite sufficient, if you must remind me how ancient I am now.'

'It's not what we're going to be doing this year. You've been more than a mother to me since Mummy died.'

'What does an old woman wish for but the company of the young? That's gift enough,' I replied. It was the truth.

I turned away, back to the kneeler pad to get on with the irresistible urge to tidy away all the winter's detritus. 'I'm sure you've got a friend you'd prefer to spend your holiday with, someone who can go at your pace.'

Lois was not so easily dissuaded and pressed the brochure on me. 'Look at it; you don't even know where I'm taking you. The villa I've chosen is on Crete. There's a Eurostar train to Paris, another down to Rimini and Ancona, ANEK ferries across the Adriatic. We can stop off in Athens and take Alex to see the Acropolis. You could revisit the Archaeological Museum, and we could take the night ferry from Piraeus to Crete.'

At the sound of those long-forgotten cities my heart lurched: Italy, Greece; I'd not been back since the war. 'Why should I want to go back?' I snapped, shocked by Lois's machinations behind my back. I'd lived too long alone to be able to hide my feelings.

'To show us around. I know it's a special place for you. Why else would this house be so full of pictures of olive trees, mountains, woven rugs and ancient bits of pottery? You ought to return and make your peace. Besides, I thought you'd like to go to the sixtieth anniversary reunion. There might be people there you know.'

I have never liked surprises. 'Not at all . . . For goodness' sake, the people I knew will be all dead by now,' I said sharply, hoping it would put an end to this discussion.

'Rubbish, and you know it. That time has always been a closed book – Grandma told Mummy when you came home from the war it was as if it had never happened, not a word about your adventures to anyone – and of course, I don't want to pry. I just thought you'd like to pay your respects, that's all . . . or we could just have a holiday under the Cretan sun.'

'Since when did I ever lounge about sunbathing? It'll be too hot and tiring at my age,' I replied, choosing to address the last thing she'd said.

Lois was prepared, batting off each of my excuses. 'Nonsense, you are fitter than I am. You can walk for miles with Trojan. And we won't be sunbathing all the time, just taking in the sights. I'd love you to show me the Palace of Knossos. Who better to guide us round? Holidays are a bit of a nightmare, if you really want to know.' she sighed. 'Alex misses Adam now he's in Saudi. I've got permission for him to leave early for half term to attend this historic memorial event. They are doing the Second World War in history . . .'

'You've got it all worked out, haven't you?' I said, eyeing my great-niece, whose dark eyes were now glistening with tears. I rose gingerly, hoping my hip wouldn't seize up, stunned by her crazy idea. I didn't want to upset her, but even after all these years I wasn't sure I was ready to return to Crete.

'Darling, I'm really not sure at my time of life this would be sensible.'

'When were you ever sensible, Aunt Pen? Granny used to say you always ploughed your own furrow, and I know you caused such a furore in the family when you bolted.'

'That's as may be, but it's such a long time ago. Look, if you must do this holiday, we could go to Scotland, take a trip to the Fair Isles. But all the way to Crete – I think not.'

'But Alex ought to know something of the Georgiou

heritage,' Lois argued, before changing tack. 'I never took you for a coward.'

I had to laugh at this direct assault. The young didn't mince their words and she had a point. If only Lois knew how old age was creeping through these creaking limbs and sapping my confidence to roam far from home, let alone revisit the dangerous past. 'Our Greek ancestry was back in the nineteenth century. My mother made sure we were as English as a cup of tea. This needs some thinking about. You mustn't rush me.'

'You do that and, talking of tea, I'll put the kettle on.' Lois darted off towards the kitchen door. 'Breakfast in the garden?'

'I only said I'd think about it . . .' I shouted to her back. 'And there's Trojan to think about, too.'

Lois stopped and turned back. 'There is such a thing as a kennel, or one of your friends might have him. It'll be for only two or three weeks.'

'*If* I go on holiday he goes to a pet hotel,' I said.

Lois's dark eyes were flashing in triumph as she pointed to the wooden hut in the corner of the lawn. 'I'll bring breakfast over to the summerhouse.'

Then my legs wobbled. I had to sit down on the old bench under the cedar tree that shaded the lawn and looked down to the lake. I could just see Stokencourt Place, the former Georgiou family house, across the lake, now developed into luxury apartments. All that was left of the estate was this smaller dower house, closer to the village boundary wall. I was the last of the three siblings to survive. Since my retirement fifteen years ago this was home, too large, too empty, too full of ghosts. *But it'll see you out,* a voice inside me said.

Dear Lois had no idea what this surprise gift was stirring up. But I couldn't let her down. Lois's mother, Athene, died far too young and now that Evadne, my own sister, was gone, she needed someone's support.

Alex was suffering too. The three of us were the last link to the George clan and Lois regarded me as a grandmother substitute. It seemed cruel to refuse and yet . . . How could I face going back to the island even though it was a lifetime ago? How could it be sixty years since those troubled times?

Even now, with the very thought of that place such fearful memories arose. The best and worst of times indeed: savage cruelty, suffering, hunger, and yet it was also the time of my life, a time filled with the exhilaration of danger and the overwhelming kindness of strangers. There were many things about that time that I could never tell anyone.

Lois was calling Alex from the TV, clattering a breakfast tray of cups and glasses as she trundled across the lawn, yet she did not entirely break my reverie. Why was my heart racing at the idea of a return to the island, that first reluctance to go back weakening by the minute?

Why shouldn't they know a little of my story? Who else is there left to pass it on to now? Who is there left to harm? Someone should know what really happened before all my precious secrets are buried in the ground with me for ever.

At my age each day was a bonus not to be squandered. Though I balked at the idea of sharing some of my past, a part of me knew it was time to let go of so much that had burdened my heart over the years. The young had a right to know just how it was then. We endured terrible times but embraced them too, and discovered parts of ourselves not known before.

Boys like Alex should learn that war was not all computer games, all swash and buckle gung-ho. It was a bloody, filthy affair. Men and women gave their lives so he could live free from fear; he ought to know that. So many of my friends hadn't lived long enough to enjoy the comfortable retirement I had. The battle for Crete was long forgotten now; just a page in dusty textbooks.

How can I go back and face all those ghosts and all the emotions locked within that sacred island? How can I survive the remembering, the nightmares and the dream?

Perhaps then, old girl, it's time you set them free? the inner voice niggled at me.

So I picked up the brochure and made my way slowly to the comfort of the old summerhouse chairs where Lois was waiting.

That night he came to me again, the bronzed man of my dreams in the shadowy half-remembered figure of his youth. He wore a black shirt, crisscrossed with a leather bandolier, cavalry jodhpurs, leather knee boots scuffed with dust. Round his forehead hung the lace bandana, and always there was that twist of his lips into a sardonic grin. His presence blazed through the morning mist and I smelled again the rosemary and thyme on the grey-white rocks of the White Mountains. I was running towards him with longing but then his face changed, the roar of the guns carrying my cry away. The dust and sand thickened, screening him from me. I couldn't reach him . . . Then I woke, my eyes wet and blurred, the only sound the sheep calling to their lambs on the morning air through the open window.

Who was calling me back to the island, back to those scents of sage and lemons, back to our Mediterranean nights? 'Didn't every love have its own landscape?' I once read somewhere.

But that was not where it all began, oh, no, I sighed, lying back on the pillow. To make sense of this journey one had to begin in another, far northern landscape of mountain streams and heather moors, recalling that first unpromising glimpse of what might be . . .

Blair Atholl, Scotland,
September 1936

Penny Georgiou sat on the damp heather, spying out the land with binoculars for a sighting of the old red stag that the laird's gamekeeper had earmarked for the cull. She loved being out on the moors, 'glassing the hill', as they called it, lying hidden in the heather with binoculars searching for the quarry, pretending she was one of the boys, stalking in the hills around Blair Atholl.

The sun was high and the hills sparkled purple, falling away in every direction like a vast sea of rolling waves as far as the eye could see. She loved the thrill of the stalk, the hikes on rough tracks, the scrambles over scree. The gillie said she was so fleet of foot, her long legs could outpace many a man, but when she'd told her mother about this compliment, it had not gone down well. 'I didn't breed you for mountaineering in breeches, get out of those nasty things and make yourself presentable,' she'd demanded.

Out in the mountain air Penny could forget all the daily restrictions of her life: the schoolroom, the dancing lessons, the interminable dressmaker's appointments. Here she was free to stretch her limbs, to breathe in the tang of the heather and forget that she was a girl. Even so, she was a crack shot, better than her brother, Zan.

Now she should be heading back; today was just a trial run. Most of the shooting party were out doing a Macnab, a challenge to catch a salmon, and shoot a brace of grouse and a stag all in one day, not that she was allowed to take part. It was the night of the Highland Ball and the women were busy dressing, preparing for the dancing and for showing her sister, Evadne, off to her prospective relatives, the Jeffersons.

It was Evadne's second season as a debutante and their mother, Lady Fabia, had stalked the ballrooms of Belgravia, sniffing out suitable quarry for her elder daughter in vain. The court was still in mourning for King George the Fifth, who'd died earlier in the year. Evadne had insisted on wearing black for the dance her parents gave for her. It was daring and sophisticated, and she'd bagged her own prize in the shape of Walter Jefferson, a young diplomat in the Foreign Office, well connected but with no title, much to her mother's disappointment. Their engagement was to be announced tonight.

At least no one was bothering Penny, leaving her free to roam around the magnificent house, with its staircase full of portraits of the noble Murray family down the generations. She'd found the library, its walls lined with leather-bound learning, books that were well thumbed and read, not like the showy tomes that passed for literature in Papa's study at Stokencourt. Why did they all think reading was such a waste of time, she mused. Papa read the *Financial Times*, Mother glanced through *The Lady*, looking for domestic servants, Evadne didn't read at all. She was always out riding with her friends and Penny was too young to enjoy all their girly chitchat. She sometimes wished, though, that she was more like her big sister in looks and temperament. Perhaps then Mother wouldn't be so hard on her for having her head stuck in a book.

Penny returned down to the big house, skiving off to the library where the magnificent busts of Milton and Shakespeare peered down at her. Her own scanty education had been imparted by poor Miss Francis, who had tutored her privately for a while, but now Penny was sixteen and a half and not expected to bother with anything other than flower arranging, drawing and ballroom dancing lessons. She longed to go to college, all because of a secret passion that none of her family would ever understand.

It started when Albert Gregg, the old gardener, gave her a knapped flint he'd found in the garden when she was seven. He'd pointed out how the flint had been worked in ancient times, an arrowhead for hunting. To be touching something thousands of years old thrilled her, sending her digging up the borders to find more treasures. Her mother had been furious when she'd turned up late for tea, covered in mud. Poor Nanny was blamed for this disgrace. It had not stopped Penny searching the ploughed fields for Roman remains, bits of tiles and pottery, which were later hidden in shoe boxes. Once she'd even found a coin stamped with an emperor's head. She wished she knew Latin so she could understand what it said. Her interest made every walk in the brown Cotswold fields an adventure into history.

At least Miss Francis let her clean her finds and draw them in her special jotter. That was one thing she was good at: line drawing, sketching in pen and ink. Miss Francis said she had a good eye for accurate representation but not for imaginary stuff.

Here in the castle library was a whole world of fresh books, including one on her favourite topic: *Digging up the Past* by Sir Leonard Woolley. It had pictures of digs in faraway, exotic places: Egypt, Persia and Greece. Penny idly wondered if she could borrow it for a day or two, but Mother would only snatch it away in disgust saying, 'You really are the most unnatural girl. I didn't bring you into the world to be a blue stocking.'

She sometimes wondered why they'd bothered to produce her at all. They'd got one of each, Evadne and Alexander. She was just an afterthought and the wrong sex. Girls were expensive to bring out and so they didn't get the education Zan took as his due. It was so unfair.

She'd managed to slip her chaperone one afternoon in London and found an exhibition in Burlington House showing details of the Palace of Knossos, with reproductions of frescos and what looked like a wonderful blue monkey. She persuaded Evadne to visit the British Museum, spending hours going through the Ancient History rooms, marvelling at the wonderful relics of past civilizations while Evadne yawned with boredom. This made Penny determined to get a library ticket in Cheltenham, the nearest town to Stokencourt, and carry on her studies in secret. She borrowed everything to do with ancient history.

Then there had been a mix-up over a library fine for a book she'd not been able to get back on time. Mother had torn into her in fury. 'What do mean, Penelope, sneaking behind our backs? What are we going to do to curtail all this silliness?'

'It's *not* silly. I want to go to college,' she'd snapped. 'I'm going to be an archaeologist.'

Everyone at the dining table had roared.

'Don't answer me back! Girls of our class don't do . . . they just *are*, future partners to the great and good of the country. Papa, tell her! I was married at your age, Penelope, and never read a book in my life. It's just time-wasting.'

Fabia turned to her husband, who slunk behind his paper muttering, 'This one's got a mind of her own. Let her use it or she'll make mischief.'

Penny knew Papa was on her side but no one stood up to Mother when she was on the warpath.

'Over my dead body!' Fabia exclaimed. 'She needs to learn obedience. Look at her, like a beanpole, and the way she slouches . . . I pay for all those dancing lessons and still she hunches her shoulders, plus her skin is too brown.' She paused, eyeing Penny with distaste. 'But I suppose one of our brats had to inherit your Greek colouring, Phillip. Sit up straight, girl, for once. You need fattening up.'

'I'm not a turkey for Christmas. I'd really like to go to college, take exams. I don't want a season. If it's the expense, think of the money you'd save. I could earn my keep. Miss Francis said there were courses—'

'No granddaughter of Sir Lionel Dellamane gets a job.' Fabia spat out the word as if it was poison and that was the end of the conversation. She stormed off, leaving Penny in tears of frustration.

Her father sighed. 'Bad luck, old girl, but she really wants the best for you.'

'She wants the best for herself,' Penny muttered out of earshot. Her mother was nothing but a snob. The titled Dellamanes might go back to the Conquest but their wealth came from banking, and the success of Lady Fabia's husband's Greek grandfather in trade, from shipping, something she chose to ignore, anglicizing his surname whenever she could. Penny was a reminder of that heritage; a dark-eyed blonde with walnut-coloured arms.

Yet the changing of their name was the one concession that Fabia had not been able to force through. Phillip was proud of his family and made sure his children learned to speak his mother tongue. It had helped Zan through his classics studies at Harrow. Penny had copied out lessons from his textbooks but it was hard to study without encouragement. Miss Francis taught the girls only French, ready for finishing school in Switzerland, should it be needed . . .

A bell rang summoning everyone to change and Penny reluctantly stuck the book on the shelf, making a vow to return. Up in their suite of rooms, everyone was fussing over Evadne's hair and make-up. She really did look beautiful in her white satin ball dress, and radiant with something no powder puff could create. Effy was clearly in love. The wedding would be in spring and Mother was already planning the trousseau and wedding dress. Penny would miss her big sister when she moved into her own home in London, but there was always the chance of visiting her and escaping Mother's regimented routines, a chance, too, to explore all London had to offer.

'Why aren't you dressed?' Fabia glared at her muddy daughter, still in her stalking gear. 'Who lent you those trousers? You really are the giddy limit, such a tomboy. You look as if you've been dragged through a hedge. How are we going to smarten you in time for the ball? Thank goodness you're not out for another year,' she sighed, pointing to the door. 'We'll have to lick you into shape or you'll end up a farmer's wife,' Mother continued her lecture outside the bathroom door after Penny had reluctantly retreated there. 'Tonight you'll sit with the other young girls and watch and learn.' Penny dunked her head under the water to drown out the strident voice. She didn't care what Mother thought. Her parents didn't know who Penny really was inside. It was Effy and Nanny who listened to her tears and troubles. Papa tried his best but was always busy or away. And what was wrong with being a farmer's wife? When she married it would be for love, not to satisfy her mother's social aspirations.

The magnificent ballroom shimmered with candlelight and polished wood, a riot of coloured kilts and black velvet jackets, ladies in their long white dresses and tartan sashes, swords and banners and portraits on the walls. The pipers drowned the air with their tunes and the smoke from pipes and cigars wafted up the stairs where Penny stood taking in the scene as if it was a painting come to life.

In the centre Effy and her fiancé were taking to the floor in honour of their formal announcement. On her finger flashed a cluster of diamonds and sapphires, matching the blue of her sparkling eyes. It was her night, her moment of glory, and

Mother stood still in her lavender velvet dress, her hair plastered into swirling waves, admiring her offspring and receiving compliments like a queen among courtiers. It was her moment too, her mission accomplished, one daughter engaged to be married.

Penny observed the scene knowing it would be Mother's last such triumph; there was no way she would go through all that rigmarole to find a mate. She'd read enough biology to know that it was all simply about breeding with the right sort to produce good stock for the future. There had to be more to life than weddings and parties and comings-out.

She sat with a line of other future debs, who were tapping their feet, itching to get on the floor with the dashing men with sturdy calves and broad chests swirling their partners around as the music quickened and grew wilder. There was a protocol and their turn would come later tonight. Penny thought it was unfair to be tethered to chairs and polite conversation when there was fun going on.

Mother stood behind her, pointing out a group of young men in the corner, laughing loudly, their whisky glasses glinting in the firelight. 'That must be the Balrannoch rabble . . . Good-looking specimens but wild. I hear Lord Balrannoch never could control his boys,' she added, sizing them up as if they were cattle. 'The tall one's just a friend. He sounds like he's from the Colonies,' she muttered. 'Expelled from Eton, so I am told.' She sniffed, eyeing him with disdain. 'The other brother, Torquil or Tormod, is in the army . . . Pity their mother died and left them to run wild. Still, they do cut a dash on the dance floor.'

A woman in a tartan sash, standing behind her chair, whispered, 'Fabia, have you got your eye on one of those boys for Penelope? She could do far worse . . .'

Penny anxiously strained to hear the reply.

'Not yet, but I was wondering if there was a sister . . .'

'For Alexander? Afraid not, just boys. There's a quieter one that might do for Penelope, though.'

Penny felt her cheeks flushing with fury. She was not going to be foisted on anyone, and she slipped out of the chair, saying she wanted the lavatory, desperate for fresh air. The torch-lit corridors were dark but she knew her way by now to the library. Here it was quiet and cool, the lamps were lit and the log fire was crackling and warm. Blissfully alone, she made for the book about archaeology that had so fired her imagination. She settled down into one of the deep leather chairs. No one would miss her for a while.

Her eye caught a copy of the *Scottish Field*, and a catalogue for an exhibition at the Ashmolean showing pottery from some recent excavation at the Palace at Knossos. Oxford wasn't far from home. If she was careful she could suggest a shopping trip with Effy and persuade her to see the exhibits. It was worth a try.

'Not bad . . .'

Penny jumped at the sound of the voice behind her.

'I've seen some of those artefacts for real. Over 5,000 years old, and they look as if they were made yesterday. You interested in all this?'

Penny turned to see who was talking; the accent was unlike any she'd ever heard before, deep and round. He was one of the crowd in the corner, one of Mother's wild boys from Balrannoch. 'Where did you see them?' She eyed the young man. He was taller than Zan, with black hair plastered down with Brylcreem, his lace jabot already splattered with gravy stains.

'On an island off the Greek coast, we watched them being brushed out of the ground. We washed the bits and pieced them, well, those who were trained up did . . . I just observed. I was a summer student in Athens, the British School of Archaeology, brilliant place.'

'Sounds wonderful. I'd love to do something like that,' Penny sighed. Why did boys get all the opportunities, the foreign travel to exotic places?

'They take female students. You can always apply . . . It's backbreaking work in the heat and dust, and you have to pay, of course, but give it a shot. Go next year.' He smiled as if it was the easiest thing on earth to do. As he talked she saw his black eyes flashing with enthusiasm, smelled the whisky fumes on his breath. No one had ever talked to her as an equal before.

'Where're you from?' she asked. 'You don't sound Scottish.'

'My parents emigrated to New Zealand but sent me to board here. It's where I met Torquil and Tormod, the mad twins . . .' he laughed, and she thought it sounded like a peal of bells. 'I'm at Cambridge. I want to be an archaeologist but my pa says I must join the forces when I've finished. Where're you at school?'

'I'm not,' Penny blushed, ashamed. 'Evadne's getting married next year . . . It'll be my season after that,' she muttered as if it were an apology.

'So *you're* the little George sister. We've heard about you . . .' Penny bristled. 'What?'

'You're the one who can hit a target straight out and outpace some of the older gillies. The mountain goat, they call you.' He was laughing, looking at her amused. 'I'm Bruce, Bruce Jardine, in borrowed plumes, I'm afraid.' He indicated his kilt. 'Jardines are Lowlanders, don't have a clan tartan so I borrowed one from Torquil's clan . . .'

'I'm Penelope George, but then you know that already,' she said smartly, suddenly feeling uncomfortable at the backhanded compliment. Was he mocking her?

'Old pots are not the sort of thing most of the debs I know go in for, but it figures,' he added, eyeing her book with interest. 'I'm doing a slide show about a dig in Greece tomorrow, if it's wet.'

'Where?' she asked, despite herself.

'In here, that's why I was doing a recce. You'll see what I'm talking about.'

'I'm not going to be a deb,' she announced suddenly.

'Good for you. What will you do then? University?'

'You must be joking! My mother would have a fit. And I'd never make the grades. But one thing's certain, they can't make me go into that cattle market.' She blinked back tears of frustration. Bruce sat down beside her, his eyes fixed on hers with a look of sympathy. He was really listening to her. He pulled out his pipe and began to fill it. She could smell the rich aroma of his tobacco. Nobody ever listened to her at home, not about serious stuff. It felt so safe with him next to her, the fire crackling in the hearth and the lamps flickering, a world away from the noisy ballroom upstairs. She sat back on the sofa, wanting this moment to go on for ever.

'If you want something badly enough, you'll make it happen,' my old nanny used to say. "Find what you love and do it well." That was another of her sayings. See you tomorrow!'

Then he was gone and the room felt empty as if a fire had gone out. Penny shivered. Time she too went back to the ball before Mother sent out a search party. But instead she sat back in the leather sofa, turning over their meeting in her mind. Why did she resent being called a mountain goat? Why did she suddenly yearn to be on that dance floor under the spotlight like Effy rather than stuck on the sidelines?

Find what you love and do it well: it's all right for you, Bruce, but what about me? How do I change my destiny, defy my parents' plans, get myself an education that will allow me to follow my dreams? There must be a way, but will I be brave enough to take such a daring path to freedom? There's just a chance, if you are on my side and believe in me. Then it might be possible.

Suddenly life didn't feel quite so bleak after all, and she jumped up to join the dance.

2001

I woke next morning, smiling at the memory of that first meeting with Bruce Jardine so long ago and those first longings wakened within me, but also the shame at being so uneducated, so ignorant of the wider world. I recalled how the following evening I'd crept into the darkened room where the shutters were closed against the autumn gloom, ready to devour his talk and slide show. A handful of guests sat staring at the white sheet on the wall, their cigar fumes spiralling like blue mist before the projector.

Bruce's slide show transported us into another world, a world scarcely glimpsed in the Pathé newsreels in the cinema. There were snow-capped mountains set against a tinted blue sky, a harbour full of ancient sailing boats he called caïques, men in strange costume, baggy pantaloons and knee boots and waistcoats, with thick moustaches on their rugged warrior-like faces. He'd taken shots of their team leaders, the Pendleburys, a couple who were the curators of the British School of Archaeology, with premises on Crete, a tall man who had a glass eye and his tiny wife, Hilda, peering across at the camera, blinking against the sun.

Then came that first glimpse of archaeologists in pith helmets unearthing ancient treasures, brushing the sand and dust, washing the pots. Girls in shorts, not much older than I was, sketching details of the discoveries. There were piles of wicker baskets full of finds ready to be labelled up and catalogued. Scenes from the tops of mountains, picnics by caves on Crete. Shots of the party all laughing and the men doing strange dances, and I felt the jealousy fired up inside me for their freedom to be out there doing something of such importance. It looked a wondrous place. But a place that was so far away from my humdrum life, it could have been the moon. It was boys who got to tramp round Europe, to travel without chaperones, to learn foreign languages. I'd hardly been down the street on my own. There was always someone by my side, giving me orders, checking the seams on my stockings. I'd never been on a bus or train alone, gone into a public house or hotel, or been allowed to stay out late. Permission would never be granted for a girl like me to go on such a risky expedition, even if Greece was in my father's ancestral homeland and I did possess a little nursery Greek.

A burning sense of injustice seized me at the unfairness of our childhood, privileged as it was, and now I laughed out loud.

But you did it, old girl. You did it in the most roundabout way. Oh, the single-minded arrogance of youth. This was going to be your destiny and you flew towards it like Icarus to the sun, regardless of others or the danger.

I sighed, shaking my head. If only youth knew and age could, went the saying. How true. Little did I know then that such a flight would demand a lifetime of service to pay back its dues.

The brochure for Crete was still lying on my bedside table, unread. Now I was going to return to that special place, perhaps to gather up the scattered bits of myself that had been left behind there, if they were still to be found. Perhaps only by facing the past would I find answers to the mysteries that still lay hidden on that island of heroes and dreams.

Stokencourt Place,
April 1937

Evadne's wedding had taken months of preparations. The fact of the King's shocking abdication and the coronation of the new King George in his place were merely minor events in Mother's calendar. Nor did rumours of war in Germany ruffle her determination to make this the wedding of the year. There was to be a grand reception in the grounds of Stokencourt Place, with London catering, after a service in the parish church.

Effy's dress was being made by the society couturier Victor Stiebel, whose team demanded endless fittings, making trips to London a regular occurrence. This gave Penny a chance to explore the capital with the help of Effy's chief bridesmaid, Diana Linsley.

Diane, as she preferred to be called, had just been 'finished' in Munich and kept the George girls in stitches with stories of her escapades in Hitler's Germany. She described the Führer and his ardent followers strutting down the streets like cocks in a barnyard. She'd been sent home early after speaking out too loudly at a party, making a joke about the Hitler Youth camp she'd attended with her hosts.

'It's not like our Boy Scouts, I tell you. I saw a nasty side to them: kicking old men off the street, chanting abuse at anyone forced to wear a yellow star on their coat, knocking their hats off and tormenting their children. My hosts tried to apologize for their behaviour but I could see they were worried too. We'll have to face them one of these days,' she warned, but no one was interested in such gloomy news, chattering instead about corsages and the wedding trousseau.

Diane was a kindred spirit with Penny's own sense of adventure, and she covered for Penny while she browsed in bookshops and spent her allowance on anything she could find that might help her to become an archaeologist. And it was Diane who sparked something in her when she kept reminding them that they ought to be doing something useful in case war came.

'The Red Cross are holding lectures and training sessions, we ought to sign up,' she announced, while they were being fitted for their bridesmaid's dresses, which were slinky slub satin, cut on the bias, in the latest shade of eau de nil.

Their mother was horrified to see Penny being fitted too. 'She should be in organza with puffed sleeves and a sash,' she insisted, but Effy stood firm.

'She's taller than Diane and Clarissa. This style is perfect on her. I want all six to look alike, not have one standing out like a sore thumb.'

Penny could have hugged her, but the George family didn't go in for shows of affection. She wanted to look grown-up and glamorous just in case a certain New Zealander was on the guest list. Since that meeting in Scotland she was hoping to see him again and tell him how much she was studying, but their paths never seemed to cross.

She'd not forgotten his encouragement, and dreamed he would be waiting for her to catch him up somewhere. It was a silly sort of infatuation, but she would never forget how he'd helped her. She was not going to let him down.

The ceremony was held on a perfect Cotswold spring day, the elm trees lining the route to the church decked in bright green foliage, and the new lambs prancing in the fields. Papa looked smart in his tails and Zan in his army officer's dress uniform. Mother had chosen to dress in a concoction of the palest of crocus-coloured silk.

Later, Walter made a half-decent speech of thanks. The best man, Angus Balrannoch, toasted the bridesmaids whilst making eyes at Clarissa. Penny heard someone say Bruce Jardine had gone off on another dig in Egypt or Greece somewhere, and she tried not to let it spoil the occasion for her. Trust him to be out of the country, she sulked.

The bombshell came later when Walter announced that after a honeymoon tour to a secret destination, he would be taking Evadne abroad for a new posting in the Balkans, to Greece.

Mother nearly fainted at this news, while Papa smiled and clapped him on the back. 'Wonderful place, well done, young man.'

Diane burst into tears. 'Oh, Evadne, so far away!'

Evadne looked sheepish. It must have been hard for her to hold onto this secret. 'I'm not going for ages yet. There's the coronation, and the house there must be prepared for us, but you can all come on the Orient Express to see me whenever you want to.'

Penny didn't know whether to laugh or cry. It was bad enough losing her big sister to London, where she'd imagined all sorts of schemes to foist herself on the Jeffersons so she could begin studies in earnest, but to Athens? She barely knew where it was on the map.

As the sun set over the lake and the clinking of glasses fell silent, couples retired to inspect the gardens and walk off the splendid feast. Penny and her parents sat on the bench by the lake, Mother disconsolate at the news of Effy's departure.

'How can he do this to us, take my daughter away like that?' she sniffed. 'Now Zan is at Sandhurst, he's just as likely to spring an unsuitable girl on us, one of his giddy types. Why are our children so disobedient?' she sighed. 'Evadne was so sensible, so reasonable, not with dizzy ideas like this one,' she added, glancing in Penny's direction. 'It's your turn next, young lady. Let's hope you can cast your net closer to home.'

'I'm more worried about things in Europe hotting up . . . Wouldn't like her caught up in anything nasty out there,' said Papa, gazing out over the water. 'Athens is no place to be if there's war coming.'

'Oh, I hope not. I don't want Penelope missing out on her due if all the boys enlist. Must get her out well before that. I shall speak to Lady March about renting her house for the season.'

We'll see about that, Penny smiled to herself. Mother might hatch her plans but she'd got ideas of her own. Diane's words at the dressmakers were still racing through her mind. Surely no one would deny her the right to do something useful, should the emergency arise.

As she looked around at all Evadne and Walter's friends relaxing in the sunshine, the flash of gold braid on Zan's uniform glinting in the light, she prayed there'd be no war, no more slaughter and heartache. No one talked much about the Great War but the village memorial had a long list of local names on it, including two of Papa's cousins. She hoped it wouldn't start up again, but what if it did and it affected where the newlyweds were going? Walter wouldn't risk bringing Effy into danger.

Yet even with this shock news there was a flicker of excitement coursing through her. That handsome New Zealander in the borrowed kilt had presented a memorable slide show, and he'd told her that the British School of Archaeology in Athens took girls. If Evadne was safely housed in that city, she could travel there even though a million objections would be lodged. Maybe her dreams were now beginning to find some reality at last.

But first she must gain some independence, and signing on for the Red Cross lectures was a start. Who knew where that might lead?

2001

It wasn't worry about the trip that had disturbed my sleep. It was the thought that I was returning to a place I'd deliberately shoved to the back drawer of my mind like a forgotten garment. How would I feel to see it all changed, like the face of a once-young friend ravaged by time?

Stop being fanciful . . . What does it matter, no one will know you or care. I flopped down, suddenly wearied, in my favourite armchair, gazing at a photo in a silver frame, a snapshot of Evadne and Walter smiling into the sun.

'It's all your fault, Sis,' I whispered. 'Little did we know Walter's diplomatic posting would change my life for ever, tipping my secure little world off its axis, spinning it out of control. Oh, those were the glory days, Effy. If only we'd known how precious and short-lived was the time we had together . . .'

Athens, 1937

True to her word, Diane signed up herself and Penny for Red Cross lectures on first aid, and even persuaded Penny's mother to grace the local committee with her patronage, organizing flag days and country excursions for sick children.

The lectures were thorough and more interesting than Penny had expected. She learned how to stem bleeding from a wound, to make splints from anything to hand for broken bones, to bandage elbows, and how to give resuscitation after drowning. Penny was always a willing volunteer when it came to both playing the role of patient and administering to the sick. She took notes, passed tests and got her proficiency certificate. Soon, she was being measured for a uniform and proudly stood by their ambulance at the County Show, hoping someone would faint and require her services. She particularly wanted to test her squeamishness should something really nasty happen.

There was talk of volunteering in hospitals as Voluntary Aid Detachments, giving extra support to local hospitals, should war come. No one could miss the growing sense that change was coming in Europe, unwelcome change that might one day affect their own country too.

Evadne flew out to Athens to join Walter after a tearful fare-well dinner where she made Papa promise that Penny and Diane would come to visit as soon as she and Walter were settled.

'Knowing they're coming will make me feel less cut off,' she pleaded, her big blue eyes directed imploringly at her father.

As the weeks went by, Effy's letters with colourful stamps arrived in the post with tales of diplomatic parties among palm trees and olive groves. There were snaps of them both reclining under huge sunshades, sipping exotic cocktails, riding on mules up into the hills outside Athens for picnics in the forests, on trips to the mountains and the sea. Effy's new villa, the Villa Artemisa, looked as if it were straight out of a Hollywood film set. But no invite was extended, no dates offered. Had she forgotten her promise?

Mother's plans for Penny's debutante season were well underway. 'If there's going to be a war, I want you out before the balloon goes up, so I hope Neville Chamberlain does something to stop that little Hitler man from spoiling our plans.'

Penny saw a lot of Diane; a link to her much-missed sister. Diane's new beau was joining the Royal Navy. Zan was on manoeuvres somewhere in Devon. Penny's summer meant being dragged round all the places Society attended until it was time to decamp to Scotland for the shooting season.

Just when she'd given up hope of ever getting to Athens a letter came that changed everything.

Penny will love to be out here to see all Athens has on offer in case, come next season, well, there could be war. Diane is coming for a few weeks so they can travel together and I promise to look after her. Please, Mummy, I could do with a bit of cheering up as I'm a bit off colour, awfully sick, I'm afraid, but the doctor here assures me by December I'll feel a lot better. Yes, a honeymoon baby is on the way! Don't worry, I'll be sent home to have it in England. Isn't it wonderful news?

The announcement sent Mother into a flurry of telephone calls and this invitation slipped smoothly into 'We've decided to finish Penelope in Athens. She's going to be supervised by Evadne, of course. Did I tell you they're expecting a happy event in December? Penelope will be such a great comfort to her sister . . .' It was as if the whole idea was her mother's alone. There followed a rush of dressmaking appointments to kit out Penny with a respectable tropical wardrobe of cotton lawn dresses, linens and sandals, and a suite of smart leather suitcases.

Evadne had also sent a list of must-brings, including a large jar of liquorice bonbons, for which she now had a craving.

They were to leave at the end of July before her parents departed for Scotland, and would be taking the Orient Express from Paris. Penny felt almost breathless with anticipation. At last, she felt, her life was finally beginning. She borrowed everything she could find to read about Athens and its history as well as asking Papa to help her with her rusty Greek. She wanted to be prepared for all eventualities – a new and interesting social life with Effy and Walter's friends, the chance to study archaeology or at least visit the famous sights, and maybe even the chance of bumping into Bruce Jardine again so for once she took a keen interest in her packing.

The journey from London was a blur of porters, steaming engines, the bustle of passengers and luggage. At the Gare de l'Est in Paris Penny looked up with awe at the deep-blue sleeping carriages, embossed with gold lettering. She felt like a film star, her heart leaping with excitement. Diane was still moping about leaving her new boyfriend, hoping his ship would anchor in Greece and they could meet.

Then they gazed out over the battlefields of the Great War. She caught a glimpse of the cathedral at Rheims, and eventually the jagged outline of the Alps came in sight. Names on station platforms whizzed by – Strasbourg, Karlsruhe . . . It was fun dining in the restaurant car in their best dresses by evening. These were wonderful days of luxurious living as the picture-book scenes unfolded before them, while the train rattled them across Europe, far away from the restrictions of Stokencourt Place. It was like waking up each morning in some glorious dream in their little bedroom with its wood-panelled walls and beds that folded back to make sofas and a sitting room, knowing that soon they would be changing direction at Niš for the journey to Athens, where another world was awaiting them.

Diane practised her French and German to great effect and was invaluable as a travelling companion. Penny continued to mug up on her basic Greek from the little Berlitz handbook she had purchased before she left. All the while the excitement kept bubbling up in her chest. Evadne had made it happen for her.

As they stretched their legs at their final destination, Penny felt the first blast of heat as if someone was blowing a hot-air fan into her face. So this was what Athens felt like! For a moment she was thrown by the noise and bustle, the colour and smells, as her eyes searched for someone familiar. Then she saw Evadne and Walter waving, and then Evadne rushed up to hug them both, kissing their cheeks, taking Penny aback.

'You have to get used to kissing in public. *Everyone* does it here. Oh, it's so good to see you both. I know it's the worst time of year. I daren't tell Mummy how hot it gets or she'd not have sent you. Don't get brown or she'll *kill* me. You know how she is about staying pale and interesting.'

Penny thought Evadne had never looked more sophisticated. She was wearing a white linen dress with three-quarter sleeves and navy braid trim on the cuffs and collar. Her face was hidden by an enormous navy-and-white straw hat with the brim turned down. The outfit all looked very nautical and cool.

It felt as if they'd never been apart and yet, as she looked more closely, Penny realized her sister looked pale and her cheeks sunken. Walter had stood aside to let them greet each other and now he shook hands formally. He was wearing a crumpled linen suit and a panama hat. He escorted them to an open-topped saloon car waiting at the station entrance as their luggage was strapped to the boot.

'Did you bring the liquorice?' Evadne turned to ask Penny. 'You can go back and fetch it if you haven't! I even dream about it now, I swear! We're going to have a spiffing time. Can't wait to show you the sights.'

'Now you watch her,' Walter warned Penny. 'Make sure she rests in the afternoons and no going out in the heat of the day.'

'Don't worry, we're both first-aiders, now,' replied Diane. 'Got our badges, haven't we?'

The first few days flew by as Penny and Diane gradually grew accustomed to the heat, strolling in the rosy glow of evening light and dining in the busy nightclubs, where all the foreigners chattered with their own cliques. There was an air of such wealth in these places, in contrast with the poorer quarters glimpsed from the back of the limousine.

Athens was a small elegant city shimmering white in the sunlight, its wide boulevards punctuated with squares lined with cypresses, orange trees and pink oleander bushes. The cafés opened onto pavements around Constitution Square where they could sit watching the rush and bustle on the streets, or else enjoy the indoor opulence of the Hotel Grande Bretagne, watching the wealthy at their leisure.

Penny soaked up the dusty heat as sights that had previously been only postcard pictures came to life: the Parthenon, the Acropolis, the noisy disreputable streets of the Plaka district, which they strolled along with Walter's trusted escorts from the embassy staff. They sat at tables sampling rich dishes, plates of *mezedes*: yogurt flavoured with pungent garlic and mint, strips of octopus, rich tomato sauces full of dried beans and herbs, creamy feta cheese drizzled with olive oil, and custard-filled pastries warm from the oven.

Everywhere a blaze of colour feasted the eye: blood-red geraniums hanging over wrought-iron balconies, lilac wisteria dripping from walls, the ink-blue of morning glory crawling over wasteland and the frothy bracts of bougainvillaea, rich in vermillion, purples and pinks. Long-forgotten phrases came into her head, and Penny discovered to her surprise that she could understand snippets of conversations rattled out like gunfire and raised voices shouting instructions, back, as if she'd always known them. Reading was another matter. If only she'd been taught a little formal Greek like Zan, she thought wistfully.

Evadne's house was delightful, a villa the colour of pink blancmange. It had cool marble floors and high ceilings, elegant wooden furniture. The shutters were kept permanently closed. The sun was the enemy in summer, bleaching fabric and wood. The fans in the ceiling whirled through the night to cool the air. Penny slept under only a sheet and a net, waking at first light, dying for the day to begin.

How different from their routine at home. If an excursion was planned, they rose early in the cool of the morning, wandered about town, stopping for strong coffee or freshly squeezed orange juice, before heading for the open market before it shut at noon. There, her senses were assaulted by the noise of the stall holders shouting their wares. Tables of fresh fish, most species she'd never seen before, shimmered in displays. The butchers hung skinned rabbits with furry paws, whole lambs and poultry from hooks. The vegetable stalls were a rainbow of new and exotic shapes. Evadne's housekeeper rose at dawn to pick only the freshest of produce; the girls were not here to buy, only to marvel at the variety, the

bustle of people and the contrast to their own sedate market
squares back home.

Often they had a late lunch with Walter and then the compul-
sory siesta. Afterwards, maybe a little shopping or visiting friends
in their lush manicured gardens, sitting in a grove of lemon trees
sipping lemonade or milkless tea. Then home to change for a
late dinner in one of the clubs with friends from the English
community.

There were British living all around the district, their social
life consisting of cocktail parties, pre-dinner visits, dancing in
the nightclubs. Penny wondered if Evadne would soon get
bored with this small circle of friends. She knew *she* would.

Their outings to the coast were a delight, picnicking looking
out across the peacock-blue Aegean under great parasols. The
change of diet and too many honey-soaked pastries caused
Diane to fall foul of enteritis, which most new visitors endured.
She was confined to the bathroom for an entire day, heaving
her guts out. Penny played dutiful nurse, trying to put into
practice her meagre knowledge of the affliction.

To her surprise she was good at bed making and brow spong-
ing, which was just as well, as poor Effy just wanted to heave at
the attendant smells. Walter escaped to his office, leaving Penny
to minister to the two invalids. When it was time for Diane to
leave, several pounds lighter than when she arrived, Penny was
not sorry to be staying on. She wanted to have time with her
sister alone. There were exquisite places to shop for baby linens,
intricate lacework to buy to take home, lunches, and strolls in
the wonderful National Gardens.

The extended stay would give her a chance to explore further.
Plus she had an ulterior motive.

'You know Mother did say I was to be "finished off" here?
Well, I'd like to take some art lessons. Do you know anyone
who would teach me?' she asked Effy one day when they were
sipping iced coffee and nibbling yet another syrupy pastry.

Evadne laughed. 'There are plenty of young artists who'd like to take you off my hands but none I would trust alone with you . . . I'll see what I can do. I realize you don't want to go back yet.' She paused, lifting off her sunglasses to eye her sister with interest. 'You've grown up, little sis, quite the gazelle.' Evadne smiled as she smoked her cigarette. 'All that Red Cross stuff's made you responsible. You did us proud when poor Di was ill. I couldn't have gone near her. If war comes, you'll know where to do your bit. I hope I can be useful too.'

'But you'll have the baby . . .'

'There's always Nanny. It won't change our lives so very much. Look at Mummy – when did three children ever stop her doing as she pleased?' Evadne sat back, relaxed by the thought.

'But we never saw her, it was Nanny who brought us up. I wouldn't want that for my child.' Penny leaned forward, sucking on the straw in her coffee.

'It didn't do us any harm. If you're that keen you can push my pram when we come home. We won't be here for ever, but Walter says it's quite safe. Hitler doesn't want southern Europe. He's leaving that to Mussolini, who's busy being Caesar.'

Penny shrugged. It was funny how Effy took everything Walter said as gospel. Was that what all married women did?

'I'll help you with the baby when it comes, but I'd like to see the British School of Archaeology before then. You remember your engagement party and the slide show next day? Someone I met that evening told me that there's a school here.' Penny didn't want to mention Bruce Jardine's name for fear that Effy would make something of it.

'Oh, yes, we know the Director and his wife and some of their students, a rum lot . . . The women students are so clever, keen types, very eager. They tend to keep themselves to themselves, always off digging up mountains or something dusty. Always look frightful in gumboots and short skirts!' Evadne hooted.

'I'd like to be an archaeologist,' Penny sighed. 'I suppose an assistant is more realistic at the rate I'm going. My drawing's not up to scratch yet, but I will practise more if I go to classes.'

'I'm certain Mummy doesn't have an academic career in mind for you. But let's not talk about that. Where shall we go today? I feel tons better seeing you, and full of energy now.' Evadne was already up and raring to go.

In her head, Penny ticked off each day that passed with mounting dread. Why did the beginning of a visit go so slowly and then, as the return loomed, speed up? She was now due to go home via London in September with the Boultons, a diplomatic family whose children were off to boarding school in Cheltenham. She was dreading the day when her suitcases would appear. How could she face dull Britain after city life here, the colours and smells, the Greek chatter? How could she return before she'd seen everything there was to see? Effy was often tired and didn't want to go far but Penny was not allowed to go out alone.

In desperation she begged Walter to find an escort and he came up with one of the embassy secretaries, Miss Celia Brand, who took her around the city, pointing out famous shops, and spent hours browsing through windows at the latest fashions, which was not Penny's idea of fun.

One afternoon, in desperation, she gave Celia the slip and, having wandered around a little, enjoying her independence, eventually found herself in the backstreets, caught up in a Nationalist demonstration. The street was full of young boys and girls dressed like Boy Scouts and Girl Guides, holding up banners, marching smartly as some of the passers-by stopped to give them the one-armed salute.

'Bravo! Bravo!' the crowd shouted but Penny didn't like the look on those ardent faces. 'What is this?' she asked and a woman shrugged. 'Fascist . . . General Metaxas's young army of thugs,' she spat on the ground. Suddenly men were shouting insults from balconies. Penny stepped back as black-shirted men peeled off from the march and raced up the stairs to the apartment. There were shouts and a scuffle. Suddenly a man was thrown off the balcony onto the pavement. He didn't move. Women were screaming as they rushed to shield him from further blows, and still those young people marched past staring ahead

Penny watched in horror as the gang of ruffians dragged out any protesters, beating them round the head and marching them away. She knew she'd seen something unspeakable, far away from her peaceful world in Artimisa Villa. She felt helpless and afraid knowing she'd made a big mistake.

As the crowd began to melt away she knew she must find her own escape route. It took all her courage and quick thinking. She covered her head with her silk scarf, swiftly bought a bag of oranges, bent her head down and, passing herself off as a busy Greek housewife as best she could, slipped down a side alley and back onto the main streets.

When, pale and shaken, she reached the embassy and described everything, Walter was furious with her.

'The sooner you're back in England, the better, young lady. Girls of our class don't wander around. It's not safe, not now. There're fascist groups on the march in the city since Metaxas's coup, trouble brewing. I'll be glad when Evadne returns home. Dark forces are at work and who knows where it will end?'

She'd never heard Walter so pessimistic but she was secretly proud that she'd made it back safely without any help.

Then, in the fourth week of her stay, something happened to change everything. On a September morning hazy with heat,

Evadne woke up grumpy with backache. As the morning went on Penny noticed how pale she was, and the pain had intensified. It was when Effy tried to get out of bed and Penny was smoothing the sheets that she noticed blood had soaked into them.

'How long have you been bleeding?' she asked, trying to look calm while her pulse raced.

'Am I?' Evadne lifted back the sheet in surprise. 'Good Lord!' She looked up at Penny, her eyes full of fear. 'What's happening? It's going to be alright, isn't it?'

Penny immediately summoned Kaliope, the housekeeper, to call for the doctor. By the time he arrived poor Effy was curled up in a ball, crying in pain. Penny found a case and packed some toiletries while the doctor examined Evadne briskly and then put her in his car to make for the private clinic.

Walter arrived stony-faced as Penny sat outside Effy's private room feeling helpless.

Suddenly there was no honeymoon baby, no explanation, no reason for such a late miscarriage.

'It's just one of those things that happen,' the duty doctor explained in broken English. 'We can never know why. Your wife is healthy and she should go on to have plenty of sons for you once she has recovered.' He meant to be reassuring but it sounded cold and heartless to Penny. If ever I was a nurse telling someone bad news, she thought, I'd sit them down in private and show some sympathy.

Later Penny sat with her sister, seeing the light had gone out of her eyes. She looked so small, like a frightened child, not the Evadne who was a fearless horsewoman, jumping high fences, who served like a man at tennis and won with a demolishing forehand. Now she lay helpless, uncomplaining, numb.

'Everything's been taken away . . . I never even saw if it were a boy or a girl . . . I feel so empty.' She didn't cry, just sat staring out of the window. 'Just get me home, Penny, please,' she whispered.

In those few hours it was as if a whole new world of suffering had opened up to Penny, a world of which she'd known nothing in her privileged life so far. There was nothing left of her sister's dream. Kaliope had packed the baby's layette away out of sight. Now there was only a terrible disappointment that no one could talk about. It hovered in the air unspoken, and all the more powerful for that. None of their crowd had been brought up to talk about feelings or intimate bodily functions. 'Bad luck, old girl,' was the best the men could manage in the days that followed.

Penny wanted to hug her sister better but she couldn't give back what had been so cruelly taken from her. They brought Evadne home and she lay in bed curled into a ball, not speaking. Penny knew then she'd not be leaving with the Boultons as planned, and she hated herself for feeling relief at this terrible time.

Walter was glad she was staying on and wired home to tell the family of the change of plans. It was strange how their sad loss would be Penny's salvation. Even Mother couldn't begrudge her extended stay, phoning every day to check Evadne's progress and threatening to come out herself if she were needed, but insisting they all be home for Christmas. Then, she promised, trying to rally their spirits, there would be preparations for the big coming-out dance in the spring, which Penny would be sharing with Lady Forbes-Halsted's daughter, Clemency.

It was a grateful Walter who insisted that Penny must continue her interest in archaeology and drawing at the British School of Archaeology, arranging for her to have private drawing lessons in the autumn term. She could stay on, using their villa as her base, living the life of an expat. Penny could barely believe her good fortune: to be treated at last like a grown-up and given freedoms unknown to her at home.

As Evadne recovered her strength, if not her spirit, they grew ever closer. Penny was discovering that suffering was a great leveller. It took no heed of age, status or wealth. She learned to be useful and to be independent, but how she wished she could have achieved her sense of responsibility and freedom some other way. But fate had dealt this cruel hand and she was here now, for better or worse.

2001

I woke with a start. Dozing off in the afternoon was getting to be a bad habit and thoughts of returning to Crete had brought the past so close in my dreams. *Dear Evadne, how much I owe you for my freedom and how relieved we all were when you eventually got your reward.* Effy and Walter's precious daughter, Athene, arrived after the war was over, a strange child, not unlike myself, who brought us such joy and, later on, sorrow when she contracted leukaemia and died young.

How those halcyon days stretched out before us. Athens had a vibrancy that seduced my senses and lured me to its heart. I thought that heady time of learning and independence would never end. But then came the dreaded day when I had to make the biggest decision of my young life, cutting for ever the silken threads of family loyalties, choosing to abandon everything I'd ever known in my bid for romance and adventure.

How on earth did I ever do it? I often ask myself and the answer is always the same. You were young and the young have no fear. Only that desire for freedom gave me the courage to change my destiny.

Athens, 1937–1938

Miss Bushnell arrived one morning at the villa to give Penny the once-over. She would not commit herself to taking on a student until she was sure she was serious about the subject. She herself was on a scholarship to the British School, seconded from a girls' grammar school in the north of England. She was tall, her fair hair bleached by the sun, and wore round spectacles. She was about the same age as Evadne and eager to make a new career in archaeology. She'd been recommended to Walter by the Director. She peered now at her new charge with suspicion and Penny tried to look enthusiastic. This was an important interview.

'What have you read? What experience have you had? How's your Greek?'

Penny shoved all her drawings of museum artefacts under Miss Bushnell's nose. *'Ela.'*

Miss Bushnell peered at them closely, then glanced up at her with interest.

'You've got an eye but *our* work is all about accuracy of line and shading. You'll need a better selection of pens and pencils . . . I can't provide equipment. I presume you have been to all the museums here?'

Penny nodded, taken aback by her sharp tone. This was not an encouraging start.

'If I take you on, I want no time wasting, no flitting off to cocktail parties on a whim. My spare time is precious and I'm not interested in excuses. Girls of your age can be keen one moment and then off onto the next craze once the assignments get harder. I won't give praise unless it's due,' she continued brusquely, but her eyes were warm, Penny noted. 'You've made a valiant attempt to impress, I'll give you that, but we'll have to go right back to basics if you are serious about archaeological illustration. Reputations are made or lost on how finds are represented on the page. Have you ever been to a stratigraphic museum?'

Penny looked blank.

Miss Bushnell smiled. 'Latin and Greek; it means layers and drawing. It's where discoveries are cleaned, sorted, recorded, drawn from many angles, then stored for reference and research. You must read John Pendlebury's work and, of course, Sir Arthur Evans on Knossos.'

'Papa once went to dinner in Oxford and he was a guest,' Penny chipped in hopefully.

'I'm not interested in your social goings-on,' Miss Bushnell snapped. 'You need to read all round your subject, and find out what's been going on here in the British School of Archaeology. I can get you a ticket for the Penrose Library but first, here are some ground rules for our sessions. I'll give you six and then I'm off on a dig. I will leave you a chunk of work while I'm away. If you make a decent shot at this, I'll give you some more. Oh, and you must make a visit to a stratigraphic museum and see what really goes on. I also want you to observe an excavation and learn how the artifacts are recorded. I'll be going back to Crete with the Pendleburys next spring. That might give you something to aim for.'

Next spring. Penny gulped – she and Evadne were due home for Christmas – but she nodded. 'That will be wonderful but I'll have to check with my parents, of course.'

'Why? How old are you?'

'I'll be eighteen by then.'

'And never done a day's work, I hazard a guess . . . There are children of thirteen full time in the mills where I come from. Surely your parents won't object to your studies, though it's dirty work. You won't keep those nails or those hands, and your skin will turn to leather in the sun,' she warned, inspecting Penny's smooth hands and painted nails.

'It's not that, it's just they have plans for me.'

'Don't tell me you're going to be one of those debutantes with feathers poking out of the back of your head, traipsing down to Buck House to curtsy to a cake? If so, we might as well stop right now.' Miss Bushnell turned to leave.

'No, please,' Penny pleaded. 'I don't want to be a deb. I'd rather stay here. I love Athens. I have Greek ancestry. Papa'll understand. I'll write to him and explain. I really want to have a useful career, something that interests me. Someone once said to me, "Find what you love and do it well" and I'm trying to do just that,' she continued.

'Couldn't have put it better myself,' said Miss Bushnell, turning back. 'No education then?'

'Afraid not,' Penny sighed. 'It isn't thought necessary for girls like me. We can't choose our parents, can we? They come from a different world and expect us to be just the same as them.'

'Fair enough,' Miss Bushnell replied, and her eyes softened. 'Forgive me for blaming you for something you had no control over. But now things can change if you take charge of your own life. Don't expect miracles, it takes years to train the eye to *really* see and interpret what is in front of you. You need confidence and reference books and patience by the bucket-load.' Miss Bushnell shot out a leathery hand. 'See you next week, Penelope. At least your parents gave you a good Greek name.'

'Thank you, Miss Bushnel, but I prefer Penny.'

'Then you can call me, Joan *or* Kyria Joanna,' she laughed.

As Penny watched her striding down the path she felt a surge of hope. With women like Joan supervising her studies, she might just succeed. She would not let her down.

Evadne suddenly appeared from the orchard of citrus trees. 'Goodness, what an old bluestocking!' she exclaimed as they watched Joan striding down the steps in her long skirt and floppy hat.

'Oh, don't say that,' Penny retorted, feeling oddly protective of her new teacher. 'She loves her work. I'm going to visit the British School of Archaeology and its library,' she boasted.

'She's very mannish. I hope she's not one of those . . . well, you know.'

Penny sensed what she was getting at. 'She's wearing an engagement ring. Stop now – I really like her. She's coming back next week and she's left me a list of things I'll need.'

'Goody, a trip to the shops, but rather you than me,' Effy smiled. 'Wait till I tell Mummy you've got a tutor . . . Come on, let's have an early snifter.'

'No, Effy.' Penny grabbed her arm. 'I'd rather you didn't tell them, not yet, not until I've got something to show them. It'll be a surprise. I don't want them to think I'm just playing at this. I really, really want it to be our secret. Promise?' she pleaded.

'As you wish, but don't forget we're going home for Christmas and then you'll be busy coming out . . .'

No, I won't, thought Penny, though that shocking thought gave her no comfort at all. If she stayed on here there would be all hell to pay and Effy would be blamed for leading her astray. Yet the rebellious seed, long planted in her mind, was now firmly rooted.

On that first visit to the British School of Archaeology Penny was allowed to make her own way, with strict instructions to talk to no one and to take the tram straight there. Evadne was playing bridge with friends and so arranged to meet her later at Costas for dinner.

The building was impressive, set high on the slopes of Mount Lycabettus, overlooking the grandeur of the city skyline. The Director's house was in the classical style, surrounded by immaculate lawns, orchards and even a clay tennis court.

Penny found her way to the student lodge at the side, built in the same style, and saw Joan waiting for her in the Penrose Library. Its walls were apparently lined with every book on ancient history known to man. How was she ever going to devour all this knowledge? For one agonizing moment she wanted to rush back outside, fearing her ignorance would make everyone laugh. Who was she to be attempting to join these serious students? What did she know that was worth knowing? But the students merely looked up and smiled at her entrance before turning back to their own projects.

One face, however, continued to fix her with a grin. 'Good Lord, it's "the mountain goat"! So you made it here after all. Thought you would. I could see that steely look of determination in your eye.'

Bruce Jardine smiled up at her, twice as large and handsome as she remembered him in Scotland.

All eyes were now on her, everyone waiting for her response. Penny felt herself flushing, but Joan leaped to her defence, holding an armful of books she'd been picking out from the shelves.

'Take no notice of our Kiwi friend; he's always on the charm offensive with new arrivals. Do you know this bounder?'

'We met at a ball in Scotland . . . he gave a slide show . . .'

'Glad to know he takes his studies seriously. Miss George is joining us for some tuition this term so don't distract her,' Joan barked at Bruce. 'Come on, Penny.'

Bruce jumped up. 'How's the family, Penny? Fancy a game of tennis some time?'

'She's here to work, not thrash around the court.'

'Slave driver!' Bruce whispered loudly, and even Joan laughed as she and Penny made their way to the corridor.

'He really is the limit. Has all the girls eating out of his hand, drooling over his muscular thighs in shorts, but it cuts no ice with me,' she said, looking down at her ring. 'My fiancé is back home and we're getting married when I finish my scholarship out here.'

They found their way to another common room with a huge stone fireplace and armchairs, the walls filled with yet more leather-bound books.

'This is where we relax in the evening.' Joan pointed out a dining room and stairs leading up to the study bedrooms. Penny was getting the full tour of the student quarters.

Joan's narrow room was as bare as a monk's cell. There was no space here for their lesson. The whole hostel had an aura of study and academia, and Penny felt her confidence slipping as she wondered how she would fit in. But she sensed the students had fun too. They seemed lively, older than she was – teachers, researchers, graduates on tight budgets.

'Everyone has their own project and digs to write up, finds to record, theories to argue. There are open meetings you must attend if you want to know where the latest excavations are heading. Our Director has one next week. Then we often go out for dinner later, somewhere cheap but lively. I think you might enjoy that side of student life but keep away from Jardine. He's like an overgrown Boy Scout. He'll have you racing over mountains as if they were hillocks. What's all this about "a mountain goat"?'

'Just a joke. I like stalking in the hills in Scotland. I'd enjoy a decent hike. I'm getting soft in the city.'

'You toffs live in a different world. It's all just a game to you, isn't it?' Joan sneered. 'I don't know why you're bothering to take up a profession. You don't need to work, do you? Jardine is just the same. Neither of you is made for the rough and tumble of life at all.' Joan sat moodily smoking, looking out of the window. 'You've no idea how hard it is for ordinary mortals to follow our dreams.'

'And you have no idea how many lies and evasions I've had to make just to be sitting in this beautiful building seeing a world I can never be part of,' Penny snapped back, waving her hands around at the books and pictures. 'We're not so different. At least you have an education and a world to go back to, whereas I am dependent on the whims of my family. I'm not even capable of striking out on my own. For me there is no prospect but of a suitable marriage, a gilded cage with the door shut.' Penny felt tears welling up and slumped down in despair.

'Steady on, I didn't mean to pry,' Joan whispered, putting her hand on Penny's shoulder. 'Sorry . . . Let's just do the tour and then go into town. Better if we do our work in the villa in private. You're going to have to toughen up, though, you know, if you want to join us in the real world, young lady.'

Penny tried to smile back. Joan was trying to be kind but she didn't understand how much Penny was envying her life, her freedom, her knowledge. She resolved not to waste one hour of this wonderful opportunity. This was what she'd always longed for, and such a chance might never come again.

Joan's lessons became the highlight of the day for Penny. Effy got quite jealous when she was too busy studying to go shopping or to the beach. Penny took every chance offered and often found herself in the company of other students as they sat drinking coffee in a fug of blue smoke, spinning out their ouzo and *meze*, putting the world to rights, planning how they would fund their next excavations, studying for exams in a world that was looking increasingly unsettled. Everyone borrowed English newspapers to read about Herr Hitler and Mr Chamberlain's attempts to find common ground. There was talk of appeasement and the rise of Fascism. Penny recalled the violence in the backstreet with the Blackshirts and their slogans. What if the unrest spread? She began to take an interest in the debates and read the dog-eared papers for herself. She looked around at the graduates, the teachers on secondment, the lecturers. What would happen to them if war came?

Bruce offered to play her at tennis to make up foursomes, to escort her home to say hello to Walter and Evadne, but Joan's words of warning rang in her ears. He was too old and worldly-wise for her. Now she felt shy in his presence, nervous and self-conscious. He was much darker, rougher than she recalled, with his jagged, rock-like features. In the cafés, he was often loud and half drunk, quick to argue and make jokes she didn't understand. Then he disappeared into some mountain in the Peloponnese on an excavation, leaving her wishing she could join the other students on a dig, but Evadne wouldn't hear of it.

'Look we've got to face the fact, it's time you went home. We must make plans, though I don't want to miss the Christmas ball at the legation. We must find you something decent to wear for that too . . .'

Soon enough Evadne was distracted by talk of clothes and the subject was mercifully dropped. But Penny was all too aware that she was living on borrowed time.

Evadne was never still, always out shopping, visiting friends, preparing to entertain. Penny noticed that as the time when her baby should have been born drew nearer Effy grew increasingly restless and snappy. Penny was outstaying her welcome but the thought of going home now was unbearable. She knew now that Joan's down-to-earth dismissal of her Society world wasn't sour grapes but welcome iced water thrown on all Mother's fanciful plans for the coming season. Sometimes her words were challenging – 'Who is she doing it for, you or her?' – and Penny loved it when she argued so hard on her behalf. Mother would be appalled at Joan's accent but she would be no match for her plain-speaking. Joan was becoming a close friend, one from whom Penny had so much to learn: how to interpret sculptures and art, how to study textbooks and write up reports, how to live on a shoestring, looking for bargains in the shops and markets. Life was never dull when Joan was around.

Penny challenged Evadne about why she had to come out as a debutante, but Evadne just dismissed her arguments with a wave of her hand. 'If I had to endure it so will you. It's not that bad and it got me darling Walter and away from Mummy's clutches. Just buck up and bear it.' However, Evadne wasn't rushing to leave either; there were so many parties and social events over the Christmas vacation.

At one of these gatherings, at St Paul's Anglican Church, Penny felt a sudden tightness in her throat, a blinding headache, and then the room began to swim. By the time she was taken home and put to bed she couldn't raise her head from the pillow. Within hours Walter lay prostrate in the other bedroom and soon Evadne was crawling through on all fours, feeling ill. They'd all picked up influenza and were in no fit state to travel anywhere. Christmas was cancelled.

As they lay pole-axed on their pillows, wishing they were dead, Joan called in with supplies, and Kaliope fed them fresh juices to keep up their strength. None of their fair-weather friends dared visit for fear of being struck down, though Bruce, who was up in the north, sent Penny flowers with a card promising to take her to see the Blessing of the Water in the New Year. This lovely surprise cheered her recovery. Here was something to look forward to, another chance to be in Bruce's company. Perhaps he cared for her after all?

A furious telegram arrived from England, saying how the girls had ruined all their mother's house-party plans and Penny must return by air or ship immediately. She was needed for fittings in London or she would have to attend her coming-out party in last year's frilly organza.

Penny couldn't even raise herself to reply, much less be concerned. For once in her life she was going to ignore the summons from Stokencourt. How could she go home when there was so much waiting for her here? If only she felt better. It was such a bore being sick and feeble with no appetite for anything but sleep . . .

If Penny felt wobbly and weak-kneed at the sight of all the jostling crowds gathered by the old harbour in Piraeus, she was determined not to show it. This was her first outing since falling prey to influenza, and she still felt washed out, her joints aching and her head fuzzy. At the edge of her mind was the fear that her time was running out here and she didn't want to miss anything. She was getting used to filling her days with what she wanted to do, not what was expected of her. How could she go back to the straitjacket that was Stokencourt?

Then there was the delicate matter of Bruce Jardine. He had called in to see how the invalids were coping, charmed Kaliope into laying an extra place for him at dinner. Walter and Evadne were glad of his company. They chatted away, ignoring Penny as they caught up on family news. Why did he make her feel so awkward and silly, as if she was still a schoolgirl? He reminded her of his invitation to join him and his friends to see the Blessing of the Water and Effy was happy to let her go. So now Penny was standing at the harbourside, feeling wobbly and looking less than her best, among the throng of onlookers.

'Watch your bag, put it under your arm, there'll be pickpockets everywhere in this rugby scrum,' Bruce yelled, grabbing her hand as if she were a child. Bruce guided her through the crowds as if she were his little sister, useful in the beginning when she was unsure of her bearings but strangely irritating after a while. She'd watched him flirting with all the other female students, teasing and joking, but with her he was always correct, polite and careful. Was it because he knew her world? Had Walter had a quiet word with him? Was he her chaperone, her protector from bothersome attentions? Oh, how demeaning!

The Athenian crowds were gathering in every nook and cranny, climbing on lampposts to catch a glimpse of the archbishop in his golden robes as, at the climax of the ceremony, he raised his great crucifix over the harbour basin while everyone crossed themselves fervently. There was chanting and singing, and then he threw the top of his precious silver cross into the water. A scramble of bare-chested boys and young men dived into the chilly water to retrieve it. The crowds cheered and shouted as an arm came up – like Excalibur out of the lake, Penny thought. The lucky swimmer came out to receive his special blessing, which guaranteed a run of good fortune for the whole of 1938.

'Cleansing the water of evil spirits is a very ancient ceremony, probably pagan,' Joan whispered. It was good to have her company. She was trying to take pictures with her box camera. 'Haven't you noticed how superstitious they all are here?'

Joan didn't attend St Paul's. She wasn't interested in organized religion. This had shocked Penny, who'd always gone to St Mark's in the village in Gloucestershire. It was what one did to show support for the village, to set an example, but the more she mixed with this metropolitan Athens crowd, the more she realized they didn't observe Sundays much, preferring to lounge about the cafés with newspapers, lunching under the mulberry trees or on the pavements, drinking and dancing till all hours while she had to be back at the Villa Artemisa before eleven. Walter's orders.

The Blessing celebrations went on all day, with dancing and singing in the restaurants to bouzouki music. Later she heard the guns rattling across the city, not guns of war but of celebrations as street parties and dancing got under way.

Penny wanted this day to stretch out for ever even though she felt exhausted. The plan was to go to Zonar's café and then on to a nightclub to meet up with the usual gang.

Alexis, a stocky Greek American, over for a few months on sabbatical, introduced a young woman called Nikki, who looked as glamorous as a film star as she shook hands around the table. Her English may have been halting but her effect on the men was immediate. They instantly straightened themselves up, slicked back their hair and vied to sit next to her. It was as if she exuded a secret but hypnotic perfume into the air.

She wasn't exactly pretty, though dark-eyed, with black hair rippling down to her waist, but there was something in the way she moved and conducted herself, the way she glided onto the dance floor with each of the men in turn, that made people watch her. Penny felt stabbings of jealousy when she saw Bruce responding with all his usual charm to great effect.

'Who *is* that?' said Joan, sensing the change in the atmosphere too. 'Quite the Mata Hari. She's very exotic, probably Italian or Turkish. Just look at the poor blighters all with their tongues hanging out,' she laughed. 'She must be a dancer with that body.'

'She's Greek, from a good family. If the boys step out of line there'll be trouble from her uncles. Her family have power in the city,' whispered Sally, one of the students who helped Penny in the stratigraphic workrooms. 'I didn't think they let their girls out alone, as a rule, so they must be quite modern.'

Penny didn't care who she was, she just wished she would go home, but she was also curious about this girl who lit up the room. She made to sit closer but her path was blocked by Bruce and the others. 'Like moths to a flame,' Joan observed.

Suddenly Penny felt gauche and abandoned amongst the crowd. The exertions of her first day out were catching up with her and it was time to go home but she didn't fancy walking back through the deserted streets alone. She had expected that Bruce would escort her home. Fat chance of that now.

'Got to go,' she announced loudly. No one took any notice as she rose to leave, gathering her bag along with her pride. Bruce was still engaged in deep conversation with Nikki, and one of the officers from the legation was muscling in on their party.

'I've had enough for one day. I'll walk back with you. Don't want Evadne blowing her top. She's a right mother hen where you are concerned,' Joan offered, standing to leave.

Penny couldn't wait to get away. She felt sick and furious that her exit went unremarked. Was she so invisible?

They walked back in the balmy night in silence. Joan could see Penny was suffering. 'A word to the wise . . . this isn't your usual cattle market. All the lads here are intent on furthering their careers or gaining some useful foreign experience, making hay before the rain pours. They'll be in the army before the year's out, if things go on as they are. Don't begrudge them their fun and games. You've plenty of time for all that . . .' Joan went on, but Penny was no longer listening.

I haven't got all the time in the world, she thought. You don't understand. I have to go home soon, and then what?

By the time they reached the villa gate she was exhausted and heart sore. It was all Bruce Jardine's fault. If only he looked at her like he looked at that Nikki woman.

As she lay tossing and turning in the darkness Penny realized that it was only quirks of nature that had kept her here so long: a miscarriage and a bout of influenza. Because of these unexpected events, she'd been able to fend off her return. But not for much longer. Evadne was organizing their travel schedule. Penny was going home for the season and to catch up with the family. They'd all be gone by February, just as springtime arrived, whereas the students would be off to Crete, an island of spectacular beauty, according to Joan. How could she leave all these plans behind: her studies, Joan's lessons and most of all her freedom? She couldn't rely on snow or storm to cancel their journey home. If she was going to do the unthinkable she must take responsibility alone for the thunderstorms ahead.

'What do you mean, you're not coming with me?' Evadne almost choked on her pasta soup.

They were sitting in the dining room when Penny announced her intentions in a croaky voice.

'I'm not going back. I want to stay in Athens and continue my lessons.'

'Don't be tiresome, it's all arranged. We leave in two weeks.' She tore off a chunk of thick bread.

'Then we can unarrange it. I can stay here with Walter until I get myself sorted,' Penny continued, seeing she had her sister's full attention now.

'Oh, no you won't. I can't have a single girl staying with me. When Evadne goes, so do you, and that's the end of the matter,' Walter snapped. 'It's not proper.'

'Who cares what's proper? I want to be a student not a debutante.'

'And just how do you intend to do that with no allowance? Live off thin air?' Walter slammed down his soup spoon in annoyance. 'You've never earned a penny in your life.'

'I know, isn't it dreadful at my age? But I'll find a way . . . I'm not going and that's that.'

'We'll see about that. I'm going to telegraph Mummy right now. She'll insist you return. We didn't bring you out here to make waves in the family. You have to do what is expected. Don't disgrace us,' Evadne demanded. 'I don't want to fall out with you. I thought you'd grown up enough to know when it's time to leave the party.'

'I'm sorry to disappoint you all, Effy, but is it disgraceful to want to earn my own living, to exercise my brain and be useful, not just an ornament?' Penny hated upsetting her sister but she had to make her understand how she was really feeling.

'So I'm just an ornament then, no use to anyone? Is that what you think after all we've done for you, you ungrateful madam?' Evadne was in tears now. 'What's got into you? It must be the influenza; they do say it can affect the brain. You're not thinking straight. We've given you all this freedom and you throw it back in our faces. How can I return home without you?'

'Can't you see I'm trying to be grown-up? You came here alone, and I have been useful here since . . .' she hesitated, not wanting to hurt her sister further, '. . . since you were ill. I didn't mean to stay so long but things happened. I just love being here. I belong and I've made friends. Why can't you see that?'

'It's that Bruce Jardine, he's at the back of this. He's filled your head with nonsense.' Walter banged his spoon down again as if trying to call her to heel.

Penny felt her cheeks flushing. 'No, it's not,' she replied, but they were not convinced.

'Look I understand, you've got a pash on him,' Evadne leaped in, sensing a chink in her resolve. 'Oh, Penny, it's what happens at your age. You've led a sheltered life. He's the first boy who's shown an interest but he's an adventurer and not likely to settle for anyone less than a countess when the time comes. I've seen his type: handsome, sporty and a bit of a daredevil; the sort that breaks your heart. Don't throw it all away drooling after something that's never going to be yours.'

Penny shook her head. 'You've got it all wrong. Bruce isn't interested in me one bit.' Somehow saying it aloud suddenly made it more true, more real and it hurt. 'I'm staying because this is where I want to be, not parading round some stuffy ball-room in London.'

'We'll see about that,' said the couple in unison as they looked at each other.

'You are in no position to argue any more,' Evadne added. 'Let's just finish dinner in peace.'

The atmosphere in the villa was fraught for days afterwards as Evadne made preparations for leaving and Penny refused to budge at first. She spent as much time as she could at the student hostel, reading, drawing, making herself useful in the museum, washing pottery, anything to keep her mind off what was about to happen. She told no one of her coming departure, especially not Joan, because if she did it would become real. Every morning she secreted some clothes and personal bits and took them in a shopping bag to her locker in the hostel. She made an outward play of asking Kaliope to wash her clothes ready for packing and took them off the line, a few at a time, bundling them into her college bag, leaving all her art materials at the hostel. Each day she siphoned off a few things she might need: her papers, address book. It was madness but she had to escape before it was too late. On the night before their departure, she pretended to go along with their preparations and said she would have an early night while Walter and Evadne went out into the city for a last dinner, assured that she had come to her senses at long last.

As soon as they had left, Penny sat down and wrote a letter to her parents.

Please don't blame Evadne for my decision to stay on in Athens. She has had no part in my actions and knows nothing of my plans. I know you will feel let down by me but I want to make you proud of me in another way.

Papa, your forefathers were humble tradespeople who, through hard work and luck, and maybe some cunning made their fortune from this very city. I feel I have roots in Greece.

My language has come on well. My archaeology teacher says I have the eye and aptitude to succeed in my own right, not because of connections in high places.

Please forgive my disobedience to your wishes: we have but one life to live and I want to live it my way.

I am not taking the easy route. I will be penniless for the first time in my life, but deep in my heart I know this path is the true one for me wherever it may lead.

I am still your loving daughter though you may wish to disown and reject me after this act of what you see as treachery. Try to understand my decision.

Ever your loving if disobedient daughter,

Penelope Angelika Georgiou

Later that day Penny left a note for Evadne, gathered up her new carpetbag and suitcase and made for the British School, leaving her luggage with the concierge there. It was still light as she made her way for the first time up the high mount of Lycabettus towards St George's Chapel at the summit. It was a long, slow climb, every step distancing her from home and family. Half-way she halted in panic, knowing she ought to go back and say goodbye to Evadne and Walter, who would be confused, angry and frightened by her leaving. She'd drawn close to her sister in these past months and she'd miss her company. But the only way was forward through the brush of thyme and sage and buzzing insects, on and on to the little white chapel. Once there she stood in awe, watching the sun set on life as she'd known it. The palette of sky as it slid to the west was streaked with lavender, ochre, pinks and apricots. The sight of it brought tears of relief and wonder at such beauty. How could she even think of leaving such a majestic place?

She found a quiet corner to sit and watch the city lamps slowly light up as evening turned into night.

Early in the morning she arrived at Joan's bedroom door,

dishevelled and exhausted, having spent the night sitting in the chapel, knowing there was no going back.

'Where on God's earth have you been? They've been out searching for you. Honestly, Penelope, I thought better of you. Your sister is so worried. You can't just walk out on people like that,' she scolded. Then, seeing Penny's stooped figure, her look of exhaustion and fear, she relented. 'Don't suppose you've eaten a thing. We'll get something from the kitchen. You'd better go and explain yourself to Bruce while you're here. He's had Walter at his door thinking you'd eloped with him into the hills.'

Penny sat down on the edge of Joan's bed. 'Have they gone?' she asked anxiously.

'I don't know. None of my business, or it wasn't. What were you thinking of, roaming the streets? You could've been robbed, or worse. There are some wild folk in Athens these days . . .'

'I climbed Mount Lycabettus for the view and just stayed up there until dawn. The sunrise was so beautiful. I needed to think what to do next. I'm not going back,' she cried.

'What's brought this on?' Joan asked softly.

'You did,' Penny replied, looking up through tear-stained eyes. 'You told me my life was useless and I ought to be working, earning my own living.'

Joan flung her hands in the air in protest. 'Hang on! I never said anything of the sort. Don't pin all this at my door. I may have pointed out the contrast between your situation and others less fortunate. You just don't walk out on your family after all they've done for you, especially your sister.'

'If I return to England, that's me finished. There is no way will they'll let me return.'

'How do you know? Don't be so dramatic. You have to face them and stand up for your decision. Running away solves nothing.' Joan sat herself down beside her. 'In my book, it shows you are still a kid who can't face up to the disappointment and anger your parents must be feeling. They let you come here on trust and you will let them down.'

Penny jumped up, making for the door. 'Whose side are you on?'

'Yours, of course, but if you're going to do this, do it properly and don't burn your bridges. Families are important, meet them half-way . . .'

'I've written them a letter explaining my decision. I am not going back.'

'Then ask them to trust your decision, ask them to visit you to see how you are making your own way. And you'd better apologize to Bruce for putting him in a difficult position.'

'It's got nothing to do with him,' Penny snapped.

'Hasn't it? I think he adds a little to the attraction of the city. I'm not blind, you follow him around like a lovesick puppy.'

'I do not . . . Oh, shut up, Joan!'

'Don't be so touchy. I'm trying to be reasonable here. Come on, let's get you some breakfast; see if we can repair a few burned bridges.'

Later, Penny found Bruce bashing tennis balls over the net. He laughed on seeing her peering round the wire netting. 'So the Prodigal returns,' he said, whacking another ball across the court. 'You've caused quite a stir. Half the British legation were out looking for you.'

'I'm sorry you got involved, but there was no need for them to panic. I just needed to think things through. Now I feel so foolish.'

'Walter seemed to think I'd carried you off into my lair,' Bruce laughed, but his eyes were concerned. 'As if I'd dare? You're a sweet girl but I'm not in the market for romantic entanglements, not with war on the horizon. I'm returning to England, finishing off my course and going to join up while I have choices. Things will shut down here if it comes to a fight so enjoy your stay while it lasts. John Pendlebury's team is off to Crete soon. Come on, let's go for coffee. I expect you've been up all night. Can't have you wilting away.'

He found a perfect spot in a pavement café under a mulberry tree in Kifissia village. Penny was feeling exhausted but relieved he was still speaking to her after he'd had to brush off her romantic attachment to him. They settled down to share a huge slice of sticky baklava. Penny was trying so hard not to get the syrup all over her lips, Bruce burst out laughing. Then he looked her straight in the eye with those piercing dark eyes.

'Look, if you're determined to stick it out here, you'll have to work hard. Joan will keep you up to scratch. Not sure they'll let you on board yet for an excavation but try to learn the mountains while you're here and keep yourself walking-fit, go hill walking. Archaeology is not for sluggards. Have you met Mercy Coutts and her friend Marion Blake? They're superb at what they do. Mercy is so agile she can even outstrip John on their mountain treks. Ask their advice and you'll not go wrong.'

'You're not cross with me then?' Penny asked.

'Why should I be cross? What you do is up to you. You're following your dream, good for you. I just hope we get enough peace for the school to get on with its business. I'd hate anything to happen to all the excavation work we've done in Egypt and Greece.'

As they sat in the shade they looked to passers-by like any young couple out for a stroll, but Penny knew as far as he was concerned she was a nuisance, just a kid who behaved as mixed-up girls often did. He'd befriended her and she'd let him down, and now he was letting her down gently. He was off to follow his own destiny and she wasn't part of it.

She suddenly felt flat and despondent, especially with Joan's accusations still ringing in her ears. It was true that Bruce was the first man to excite her imagination and interest, but she realized now it was all a silly childish fantasy. He was confident, handsome in a rugged sort of way. She'd imagined she was special to him but she wasn't and never had been. He'd burst that bubble and she must hide her disappointment. How could something be over when it hadn't even begun?

Better make the most of this moment alone with him, save it up to chew over on a rainy day in the future, she sighed as she tucked into the last of her cake.

Only one thing mattered and that was her chosen career; the chance to do something interesting and be useful too. She would make the most of her opportunities and show her family that Penny George would succeed.

Penny braced herself for a tearful reunion with Evadne and a telling-off from Walter, but no one was at home when she called. Kaliope said they'd left as planned, then shut the door in her face. She was in disgrace and on her own now.

Funny how the next few weeks seemed to be full of farewells. Everyone was disappearing into the hills, across to Crete or returning home on vacation. Joan left for England and Penny found lodgings with Miss Margery McDade, a retired teacher who taught music and sometimes helped out washing and cataloguing artefacts in the stratigraphic workroom.

The Pendlebury expedition did not need her services so it was back to washing dirty artefacts from recent digs, and drawing practice and trying to remember all the things Joan had drummed into her. Money was tight and she was glad to have learned all Joan's little schemes to stay afloat, but she sold her pearl necklace to fund her stay.

Athens was hot in early June and it was a relief to find coolness in the wooded groves of Mount Lycabettus whenever she could. She toured sites with Margery as her guide, just like any tourist: first to the sacred groves of Delphi, north of Athens, in the steps of pilgrims thousands of years ago who had come to hear the Oracle's prophecies. Then they visited the Temple of

Apollo high in the hills of the Peloponnese, built 2,000 years ago, through the rough winding tracks, down to the finger-lines of coast at Mani. Later they found the ancient city of Mycenae where the School was doing excavations, and it was Penny's turn to show Margery around the site. The party invitations from Walter's friends dried up on hearing about her disgrace. She was left to fend for herself, much to her relief. There was always a book to read, a museum to visit and lots of time for reflection, but life on a shoestring was not easy. Thank goodness for pupils wanting to learn English, and cheap food from the markets. Margery would always make her meals stretch for two. If she went hungry sometimes, it was the price of this new-found independence.

The silence from Stokencourt Place was deafening. Some-times she felt she'd made a terrible mistake, doubts creeping in as she floundered around the fringes of the shrinking student community, hoping for distraction from her guilt, but without Bruce and Joan and the familiar gang, it wasn't the same.

There was one young man who seemed as apart from the crowd as she was. Steven Leonidis had an English mother, who came from a landowning family in Wiltshire, and a father in the Greek diplomatic corps. He'd been studying at Oxford and had been schooled by private tutors and at public school. He was interested in all things Greek and the philosophy of the ancient Greek society. He liked hiking and sunbathing on the beach in the briefest of bathing trunks. The other students avoided him, for some reason. Once he started on political theory, the groups scattered and Penny was left clutching her coffee, not knowing how to make her exit without causing offence. He was lonely and so was she, so it made sense for them to go about together.

Steven was from a large Catholic family with many brothers and sisters, and was expected to join the army soon, but so far he, too, was reluctant to return home. He and Penny got into a habit of lazy lunches and swims, and trekking into the hills. At first it was a companionable sort of friendship. But Steve was very serious, and when one day he clutched her hand, suggested she return to England to meet his family, and asked if she would consider becoming a Roman Catholic, Penny knew it was time to cool things down.

At least someone thought her attractive enough to declare himself, even if he wasn't Bruce. She found those slate-blue eyes hard when he started spouting how marvellous Germany was in recovering from such an insulting treaty. He was pleased the Greek Minister, Metaxas, was following this Hitler's lead, transforming their economy by instituting public works. It was as if he were standing on a platform giving a speech and it hardly mattered if she were there at all.

'Don't you feel excited at how Nationalism is rising up all over Europe?' Steven argued, and she gazed out over the beach, wishing she was back in the pink villa reading a book. 'I don't know how you can hang around with all those types at the BSA.' He dismissed her friends with a wave of his hand.

'You were happy enough to let them buy you drinks,' she snapped. 'They're my friends. What's wrong with them?'

He shrugged. 'They have all the attributes of decadent fops and mix with the wrong type of Greeks, Jews, dagos . . .' And you are boring, she thought. She'd had not forgotten the Nationalist march and the terrible scene she'd witnessed. How could he admire such people?

This friendship was now a bore to Penny. They made an expedition to the great theatre at Epidaurus with its perfect amphitheater and acoustics. It was funny whispering down in the epicentre, knowing you could be heard right out on the periphery. It was a wonder of construction and Penny felt such pride to know her ancestry harked back to such ancient times.

'How can you be so fair and yet be of Greek stock? I thought you were true English,' Steven said one day when they were sunbathing.

'I'm just like you are on my mother's side, but who knows where we British come from?' she laughed, but he was not amused.

'I wouldn't boast of anything other than your mother's family, if I were you. Mixing races is never a good idea. It's bad enough having a Greek name to live down. Still, we are lucky, it is always the mother's blood that is truest,' he sighed 'So we are both safe there.'

He really said the silliest things, but his attention soothed Penny's loneliness. They would climb the path up Mount Lyca-bettus to watch the apricot moon rise and the stars compete with the twinkling lights of the city. Steven made brief fumbling approaches, kissing her ardently, making her body flicker into life with unusual sensations, but her mind stayed distant and unresponsive. This was not what she wanted, not from him. She would have to let him down gently, but how could she throw ice on his ardour and walk away without hurting his feelings?

She began to make excuses to cancel their hikes and coffee meetings but he was not easy to shake off. He knew where she lodged and that she was related to one of the diplomats, that she gave English lessons to foreigners. He kept asking questions about who she taught, and also about Walter, and the staff at the BSA, especially about John Pendlebury, and where he was excavating.

'I don't know his plans, hardly know the man,' she replied. The summer had not turned out as she had planned and now Steven was boring her with endless and rather intrusive ques-tions. 'Why do you keep asking me all this stuff? Are you spying on them all?' she accused, but he laughed it off. She even thought of warning Walter about his curiosity but since their falling-out, she took great trouble to avoid him. She was still embarrassed by her flight.

As the summer heat grew more oppressive, so her spirits sank to their lowest. She was in her bedroom taking a siesta when the downstairs bell rang. If this was Steven coming to call again she was ready to give him an earful. Miss McDade was out, so Penny went down herself and flung open the door with a curt 'Yes?' to see a man shadowed by a panama hat.

It was her own papa on the doorstep. She fell into his arms, no thought of English reserve, just relief to see a familiar face. 'Oh, Papa!'

He clasped her to his chest. 'Penelope, at last! If the mountain will not come to Mahomet . . . Are you well?'

She burst into tears and he hugged her again. 'Wipe your eyes. Whatever have you been doing to yourself? Put something decent on,' he ordered, staring down at her bare legs in shorts. 'I'm taking you out to lunch.'

They entered the cool, hallowed portals of the Hotel Grande Bretagne in Constitution Square. Penny was dressed in her Sunday silk dress with matching straw hat and sling-back sandals. She hadn't worn anything so formal for months. They dined in style as if they were in London in the season. Papa was on a short cruise.

'Now tell me just what has been going on,' he asked. 'I can't get any sense out of your sister.'

Out it all poured about Evadne, the British School, Penny's life in Athens, all the frustrations of months of being left on her own . . .

'So you want to come home?'

'No, not for a season and all that stuff,' she confessed. She had never talked so openly to Papa before, and he was staring at her in surprise as if he was taking in how much she'd changed since she'd come to Athens.

'You've grown into quite the young lady here. You are looking very Greek,' he said, admiring her golden skin and hair
bleached by the sun. 'Your own mother wouldn't recognize
you,' he added with a twinkle in his eye.

'How is she?' she asked anxiously. 'Is she very cross with me
for bolting?'

'Oh, she'll get over it,' he said, hungrily eyeing his soup. 'As
far as her friends are concerned, you're still being "finished" in
Athens. But she worries, we both do . . . Are you drifting?'

How could she reply to such a direct question? She nodded
and then shook her head. 'I know that's what it looks like, but I
feel I've just not yet found what's right for me. I know I have
something to do here but I don't know what it is. I thought it was
being an archaeologist. Don't get me wrong, I adore the School
and all the wonderful tutors here, but I'm not up to it, Papa.
Drawing, yes, but the rest of my education is too thin.' Penny
paused, stunned by what she'd just said. All through the summer
there'd been this growing feeling that she would never be like
Joan or Mercy Coutts or the other dedicated women. Now she
had spoken her fear out loud, but where did it leave her future?

'And your Greek? It is good now. I heard you talking to one
of the waiters.'

Penny smiled at the compliment. Weeks of bargaining in the
shops and markets, finding the cheapest goods, arguing with
noisy neighbours meant she had good street Greek now.

Papa's face was suddenly still. 'I have to tell you, Evadne isn't
returning here for a while. I'm afraid she's lost another baby.
There's a man in Harley Street who hopes to sort out the problem. She's coming back after she's had a rest, to be with Walter.
You two must make it up then.'

Penny bowed her head. 'I'm sorry. I suppose I didn't help
matters. I didn't know she was . . .'

'She says how you helped her when she was ill before. I
know you'll be kind. Walter is waiting to be transferred back

home for good. The climate here does not suit Evadne. Please visit her and help her, Penny. I'm counting on you.' He reached out his hand to her and she clasped it tightly.

'War is coming, Penny. Chamberlain is trying appeasement but it isn't working. I worry about you here. Not that Greece is much use to Hitler, but everyone is girding their loins. Zan has joined the Dragoons; his regiment is being stepped up. Who knows where it will all end, so you must promise me you will return; no histrionics when the time comes.' He gripped her hand. 'You always were a funny little thing with a mind of your own. Remember when you ran away on the lake in the dinghy, alone with all your toys in a pillow case, trying to make for the little island?'

Penny smiled. It was after a row with Mummy.

'No amount of persuasion would bring you back until you dropped the oar and had to be rescued.' He laughed and Penny noticed the pronounced dark rings under his eyes.

'I'm a big girl now, Papa.'

'Are you? I hope so. I'm counting on you to help Effy if . . .' he paused, '. . . when the time comes. Don't let me down.'

'I know it sounds strange but I feel this is my home now. The Greeks are our people too. If they had to fight, I'd like to think I'd be here to help. I can't explain, I'm sorry, but I promise I won't do anything hasty. It's been hard these past weeks, and I'm sorry about Effy, but I just had to hold on to my independence.'

'I think I understand. I want to know you are safe and that you've found a life for yourself. You are different from the others. My grandmother used to say, "Your children will all wear their heels out in different places." Your poor mother doesn't understand you, but I do. I know you'll make us proud of you.'

Penny wanted to cry but stopped herself in the grandeur of such a dining room. She'd always known her father loved her, but until now she didn't know how much. He'd defied his wife, sought her out hundreds of miles from home, listened to her troubles and recognized something of himself in her heart. He never insisted again that she return, after that conversation. Instead, each day they toured the city's sights and he proudly explained the history behind her Greek heritage. She cried when he left for his ship. She had his blessing and he trusted her to honour the family name. From that moment on she went by the name Georgiou.

2001

Somewhere a dog was barking in the field, stirring me back from those far-off days, rousing my thoughts as darkness surrounded me. Penelope Georgiou . . . I'd used that surname for many years. It saved my life on many occasions. Later, when the country was torn by political strife, I was advised to revert back to the English version.

How precious are the memories of that summer in Athens before war devastated its gracious heart and famine starved its citizens. It was only later I discovered that Papa was under observation for heart disease. If only he'd told me how sick he was, and that in coming to visit me he was in fact saying farewell, I would have gone home with him. I would never have insisted on my independence and my life would have taken a completely different path. I didn't hear of his death in 1942 until it was too late. My mother never forgave me for not being at his funeral, but I was by then in no position to return, had I even known he was gone from my life. It weighs heavy on my heart to think how he let me go on thinking all was well with him, and I was so self absorbed in my own plans.

We had so little time together, but every moment of that visit is haloed in sunlight to me, a precious meeting of minds. His memory never leaves me and I weep to think how stubborn and self-centred he must have found me then.

But now, I know that true love is wide enough to encompass

such failings, transforming them into strengths. Out of my furnace of stubbornness came courage and determination, perseverance and a strength of will to endure tortures of mind and body. How I needed these later in the dark years under occupation. But I'm getting ahead of my story here.

It was dark. I must have dozed longer than I thought, my arm was stiff but I sat back staring out of the window, reluctant to move. So many memories still whirling round my anxious mind. In that final year before the war I was drifting round the fringes of student society, flirting with archaeology until I realized I had neither the aptitude, discipline nor talent to stick to its hard course. I gave English lessons, attended church more for company than conviction, but couldn't help noticing more uniforms sitting in the pews as 1938 drew to a close. The hotels, cafés, parties were full of strangers with stories of expulsions and escape. Steven Leonidis disappeared back to his family or into the army; by then he was of no interest to me. He'd been a pleasant interlude in a hot summer, a distraction from my own heartache.

One by one the British men left to join up and I knew that I must redirect my life into something purposeful. I had indeed been 'finished', but playtime in Europe was over and it was time for me to join the real world. Once again, fate took the decision out of my hands one afternoon in the spring of 1939.

Piraeus Harbour, 1939

It was hard for Penny to wave her papa off from the harbour. For a second she wanted to jump into the ferry taking him out to the liner in the bay, but the stubbornness that was making her feet refuse to move, forced her to turn her back and head uphill towards the city. Tears filled her eyes. Now she felt more alone than ever.

As she was walking back uphill from the harbour she noticed a crowd jostling noisily around what looked like a fight. Penny edged nearer. A young man was raining down blows on an older man's head while some of the crowds jeered, though others were trying to drag them apart. Anyone could see it was an unequal fight. Under the onslaught the older man stumbled and fell, and there was a distinct crack of bone. As he screamed in pain, the crowd edged away, melting into the busy throng, leaving the injured man lying on the cobbles with only Penny to hear his cries.

'He stole my money! Please . . .' His Greek was heavily accented. He was gasping in pain.

'Don't move, don't move.' Penny bent down to see blood seeping from his trouser leg. The displacement of his leg was enough to show her that it was broken.

The man tried to rise, but fell back in a faint with shock and pain.

'We must find a doctor,' Penny said, glancing round for support, but there was no one listening. The crowd had dispersed. It was then that her old Red Cross lessons flashed into her head: *Page 14: What to do with a broken limb.*

She must bind the broken limb to the other leg and check to see if the bone was protruding. If she could make a splint out of a plank or stick . . . She looked around her. There was nothing to hand. She yanked up her skirt and unhooked her stockings from her suspenders; at least she had some stockings and the belt of her cotton dress that she could tie to his ankles, but she needed help.

She looked around again and saw a mother with two boys hovering, curious, and she shouted in her roughest Greek, '*Ela!* Come here, help me!' Hearing Penny calling for help, a man came out of a shop holding a couple of broom handles, which she used to bind the legs into splints. It was the best she could remember of her knowledge. *Keep the patient comfortable. Treat for shock.*

'*Efharisto poli . . . despinis.*' The old man was slowly coming round 'You are kind, *despinis*. He stole my money. He promised me tickets to sail to Egypt with my family. I came for the tickets and he laughed in my face. Now we cannot leave. I have papers and cannot leave.' His distress was clear, the pain making his skin grey.

Penny knew they must find a hospital, and soon.

'*Kyrie*, your leg is broken. You can't go anywhere but to a doctor,' she told him.

'But I must,' he whispered. 'My wife, my daughter, they are waiting. We are leaving.' He began to wail in a language she didn't understand and, seemingly, nor did anyone around her.

'Where do you live? I'll find them,' she whispered into his ear. He said an address in the poorest part of town. But first she had to find him transport, anything to get him off the dirty street before he passed out again.

'Help us, please . . .' She turned to the strangers. 'We cannot leave him to die!' What had happened to the famous Greek hospitality? This was supposed to be the land known for its kindness to strangers, famed for its courtesy, but no one wanted to get involved.

Then a shopkeeper and his wife, seeing the drama, shut their shop and offered their handcart for the old man to lie in. 'Where is the hospital?' Penny asked, but they shook their heads. They were immigrants with halting Greek. She asked again and someone pointed her up the hill to a doctor's clinic.

It was hard work pushing the cart uphill. The man was short but stocky, his constant groans of pain were distressing, but thankfully he kept passing out. The clinic was in a house, shabby and none too clean, but it was somewhere help could be given at least.

'Are you a relative?' the doctor who opened the door asked, eyeing Penny with interest after she had explained what had happened. 'His name?' Again she shook her head.

'*Pos sas lene?*' she asked the old man, smiling. 'I will find your family for you.'

'My name is Solomon Markos. Here see . . .' He pointed to his passport in his pocket.

'Another Jew on the run,' said the doctor with a sneer in his voice.

Penny was incensed. 'He was cheated. He bought tickets. His drachmas are no different than any others and here, look, he was born in Thessaloniki. He is as Greek as you are,' Penny snapped. 'All he did was come for his tickets and when the man refused to hand them over, Kyrie Markos protested and was beaten to the ground. I saw it happen with my own eyes.'

'You don't understand,' the doctor said patronizingly. 'Jews are not one of us. That is how it has always been. People want to leave, others take advantage. He will have to pay here. Does he have family? You cannot leave him without security.'

'You have his passport papers. And I have my watch.' Penny unstrapped the gold watch from her wrist, slamming it on the table in disgust. 'But I want a receipt from you. That is my security, but you can also ring the British embassy. They will vouch for me there. Penelope Angelika Georgiou,' she replied in her most imperious English voice.

'I would have taken you for Greek, *despinis*.'

'See to his leg and I will return.' She was in no mood to talk to the doctor.

As she made her way back into the city, she fervently hoped the man would get good treatment. She must find Othos Dimitris, the street where the Markos family lived, and break the news to them. She was glad it was still daylight as she followed a trail of dark streets through Kokkinia, a rundown area of the city where houses were divided up into rooms, and lines of washing hung across the road. There were fierce dogs barking, a stench of rotten vegetables and rubbish. This was a world away from the icing-sugar villas on Kifissia Avenue, where the diplomats lived. Where she used to live.

She asked some women sitting by their doors for the Markos family, but they just shrugged, spat and then pointed upwards to an attic. 'The Jews live up there.'

Penny wrinkled her nose at the stench coming from the stairs: stale fat, urine and the sweat of unwashed bodies. She struggled up the rickety staircase to the top where a battered door with flaking paint was shut. She knocked hard.

'Who is it?' a voice answered, but the door remained shut.

'I have news from Kyrie Solomon Markos. It is important.'

The door opened a crack and a pair of anxious dark eyes peered out at her. 'Who are you? What do you want with him?'

'Please may I come in? I have news of your husband. Mr Markos has had an accident.'

Penny moved to enter as the door opened wider and the woman cried out, 'He is dead. His heart has given up. I knew it . . .' There was a girl standing in the shadows, a pale face with hair braided high over her head, wearing an apron like a waitress or a maid in one of the diplomatic houses.

'Oh please, *Kyria*, you are wrong. He was quite alive when I left him. There was an accident in the street and his leg was broken. He is in the clinic at Piraeus, close to the harbour. They will set his leg,' Penny tried to reassure the mother and daughter.

'But we are sailing tonight to Egypt. It is all arranged. He went for tickets. Look, we are packed for our journey.' Mrs Markos pointed desperately to two large carpetbags on the floor. Penny saw now that the walls were stripped of decoration and the room was almost bare.

The girl stepped forward to comfort her mother. 'Don't worry, we can wait. Papa needs us here. Our journey can wait.'

'But the tickets – who will exchange our tickets?'

'I'm afraid there was a misunderstanding. There were no tickets. Your husband was cheated by a fraudster. There was a fight.' Penny didn't know how best to explain without alarming them even more.

'Oh, no! Solomon is no match for harbour rats. I warned him but he wouldn't listen, didn't I?' she cried, turning to her daughter. 'We have no savings now to pay for more tickets.'

'Shush, Momma,' her daughter consoled. 'We can still sew and mend, and I can work for Beulah Koen in the shop. We have friends who will help.' She held out her hand to Penny. 'Thank you for helping us. I don't even know your name.'

'Penelope Georgiou. I am a student – or rather I was. And you are . . . ?'

'Yolanda Markos.' She held her mother's arm. 'We arrived from Thessaloniki six months ago. Papa was hoping to teach at the university but it hasn't worked out. Many people, few posts. I was hoping to train as a doctor, but as you can see . . .' she tailed off. 'Poor Papa, we must go to him.'

'I'm sorry to bring bad news.'

'It's not your fault, Miss Penelope. We must bring him back here. There are doctors in our community who will help him. He'll feel more comfortable with his own people. We are Jews,' she said flashing her dark eyes, challenging Penny to respond.

'And I am English,' Penny smiled, holding out her hand again.

'So we are all strangers in the city. Strangers helping strangers. We will thank you for your kindness. Now we must leave.'

'I will show you the way,' Penny offered, hesitating whether to tell them about her watch. It had been a parting gift from her father and she didn't want to lose it. 'It is not the best clinic but it was closest to where he fell. I'm sure they will reset his leg. I made splints . . .'

'You are a nurse?' Yolanda asked.

Penny blushed. 'Not exactly, I did some first-aid training in England with the Red Cross, but that was a long time ago.'

'When we are settled I intend to do some training too. I fear nurses will be needed soon. Why are you not returning to England?'

As they sat on the bus back to Piraeus Penny tried to explain how she had come to Athens and how she was now reluctant to leave. She kept looking at Yolanda. Her skin had not that fleshy bloom of youth, and she was thin and drawn as if she had not been eating properly, but she was still beautiful in a graceful, serious way. It was lovely to see how close mother and daughter were, holding hands, chattering. A far cry from the relationship she had with her own mother. They had come down in the world; anyone could see that. Now their plans to emigrate had been thwarted by cruelty, greed and violence. She recalled Steven's extreme views about nationalism in the light of the way the old man had been beaten and cheated and what she'd already witnessed. This was the first time she had ever considered how dangerous it could be to be of the Jewish race and she felt ashamed she'd never even given their plight much thought before now.

She knew there were men in England who claimed Jews were behind all the woes of the world, men in black shirts such as those who had marched on Cable Street in the East End of London but were pushed back and defeated. It had been reported on the Pathé news and in the papers, but such political dramas had been a world away from her comfortable life in the Cotswolds and easily forgotten. Now it hit home that people like Yolanda and her family were vulnerable, even in such a cosmopolitan place as Athens.

She took Sara Markos and her daughter to the clinic. Solomon had been sedated and his leg set in plaster of Paris. He would be helpless now for weeks.

His wife cried at the sight of him. 'We have to take him home. We can't afford any more treatment here. Who paid for this?'

The doctor pointed to the gold watch and shrugged, looking at Penny as he shoved it back in her hand. 'She left this as surety.'

'I see.' Yolanda shook her head and shoved her hand down into her shirt, pulling out a thick gold chain on which was a six-pointed star. 'Take this,' she offered the doctor.

Penny protested, knowing this symbol must be precious. 'I can wait to redeem my watch, please, keep it!' But Yolanda insisted on paying the man herself.

'At least let me get you a taxi,' Penny offered. 'Your father is in no condition to travel any other way. Please, give him crutches,' she said to the doctor.

'Give the man what she asks,' the doctor ordered his nurse, looking at Penny with new respect.

As they made their weary way back to the shabby flat, Penny knew she couldn't desert the Markos family now . . . Then she had an idea. 'Kifissia Avenue!' she ordered the taxi driver. 'You are coming with me!'

She still had the keys to Walter and Evadne's villa. No one would mind if they used it for a few days. It was furnished and clean, with plenty of rooms. She could explain to Kyria Kaliope that she was staying there with friends for a few days. No one need know their business. In those hours since leaving the harbour, she'd been caught up in a drama and for once she'd known exactly what to do. In helping the Markos family she suddenly felt useful and determined once again.

All that mattered now was making this family comfortable, and she could also spend more time with Yolanda. She had admired how calm and caring she was to her parents, how determined she was to pay her own way. There was something about her that was worth knowing.

2001

How our lives are changed in minutes by collisions of incidents upon which we arrive as innocent bystanders. The encounters I made that afternoon pushed me into another world, into other viewpoints, and my life in Athens turned to a totally different direction. The discovery that I could think on my feet, take charge of an emergency and not panic was a strange revelation to me. Then, taking charge of Solomon's convalescence, I forged one of the deepest friendships of my life. Yolanda and I were from such different backgrounds and religions, yet in many ways we complemented each other, Yolanda being many things I could never be.

She challenged me to look at myself, my prejudices and assumptions, by her devotion and obedience to her parents. How I envied their tight little unit as they fussed over Solomon until he was finally back on his feet.

From those weeks when we squatted in Evadne's house, I learned much about the Jewish faith. It was fortunate for me that they were not Orthodox in their religious observances so that we were able to accommodate some of their customs and traditions in a Gentile home. They gave me a lifetime love of Jewish cooking: *pastela,* a wondrous lamb pie that Sara said came from her Italian ancestors in Sicily, and almond crescents they called *boskochs*. Every festival had its special foods. I tried to explain what we made for Christmas but as our cook had prepared all our meals at Stokencourt, I'd not a clue how to make even the simplest dish.

Sara was quick to put this right, making me chop and stir, measure out and watch how flavoursome dishes could be created from the simplest and cheapest of ingredients. What Kyria Kaliope thought of this new arrangement I didn't know or care, until the day when I received a curt call from the embassy saying the house was needed for another diplomat and we must vacate the premises forthwith.

When my guests left to return home, I missed their noisy, colourful, loving way of living, and I returned to my rooms at Margery McDade's, determined that my life would change.

Anything Yolanda could do, I decided I would do and better. Oh yes, rivalry was always there under the surface of our growing friendship. We made an incongruous pair in our Red Cross uniforms, me tall and fair, she so slight and dark . . . But once again, I jump ahead.

Training as nurses in the days before penicillin and modern surgical techniques was no easy feat. Discipline and menial work were hard pills to swallow for someone like me. At the end of a back-breaking day, collapsing in laughter with a friend makes anything bearable. In the years that followed, our friendship became the rock to which we clung for survival. There's hardly a day goes by when I don't think back to those times, scrubbing floors on our knees, finding quiet corners out of Sister's way to have a secret smoke. Why is it now that the past feels so close at hand that I can almost reach out and touch it? How can I return to Athens without thinking of Yolanda?

Athens, 1940

The two girls sat in the darkened lecture theatre watching the slide show in stunned silence. The new intake of Red Cross trainee nurses were layered up in rows behind last year's. Everyone was forcing themselves to watch the unwatchable. Their lecturer was a sturdy Irish sister called Teresa McGrath, who had nursed British troops in the Great War. She explained her mission was to prepare them for injuries they might have to face should the present conflict with Italy over borderlines develop into something more serious.

The interpreter struggled to keep apace of her strong accent. 'War is a filthy business. Guns take no prisoners, they mutilate soft tissue, bones, decapitate, disembowel whatever stands in their way.

'I don't want you to flinch from such injuries when they are presented to you. Better to see them now and be prepared than fail your duty of care. This is not a pleasant lecture – I know some will disapprove – but it must be done. I cannot prepare you for the smell of the battlefield or the sickly sweet smell of death in your nostrils. That you will overcome as best you can. A mask soaked in oil of lavender may help. Only experience and discipline will give you the confidence to withstand such sights as I am about to show you.'

She proceeded to illustrate how wounds left untreated became gangrenous balloons of rotting flesh. Penny was glad the photographs were not in colour. Then came clean amputations and bad ones, good stumps, infected ones, stomach wounds and entrails hanging from uniforms. Head and facial pictures next. There were faces all but destroyed, noses and eyes lost, men disfigured by burns. No one asked any questions at first. Penny shivered at the thought of her brother, Zan, being subjected to such atrocious wounds. She was glad that letters from home were still getting through and she knew he was safe.

'Each of these young men gave himself up to his country's cause. Some here are British, German, French. Guns make no distinction and neither must we. This is the principle that underpins the work of the Red Cross. We treat all who need our help, regardless of nation, race or creed. We feed the starving, we do not judge or take up our own national cause, only that of suffering humanity.'

When Sister McGrath had finished and the blinds were lifted, Penny and Yolanda stumbled out into the light, wanting to breathe fresh air.

In the six months since she had begun training, Penny found there was no hiding place from the eagle eye of the matron. The wards were inspected twice a day for any sign of slacking among the new trainees. The hospital had been founded by no lesser person than the late Queen Olga of Greece. The twenty-five beds had been expanded over the years and it was considered one of the best hospitals in Athens.

They'd started as the lowest of the low, scrubbing floors, emptying bed pans, mopping up vomit and blood. Yet Penny found herself taking to each task with relish, knowing it was a step closer to proper medical instruction.

Her back ached and her legs throbbed at the end of a shift, but she retired back to Margery McDade's rooms, satisfied that no one could ever call her a social butterfly again. The severe uniform, with its thick dark-blue cloak and stiff white headdress, was a bit like wearing a nun's habit, but she was proud of the Red Cross emblem on her chest.

It was Yolanda who had challenged her to sign up for training. She'd watched a film about Florence Nightingale in Salonika, and at first had wanted to train to be a doctor, but now, like Penny, she moaned after a hard day and they both wished she'd seen some other film.

Penny was glad when the Markos family left Othos Dimitris to stay with a rabbi friend in the Jewish quarter. They were hoping to ship out to Crete but Yolanda fought to stay and finish her training. She was lodging with another rabbi, Rabbi Israel, who lived nearer the hospital, helping his wife look after a handful of unruly children to pay for her board and lodging.

Now at last they were learning about wound management, how to stem blood flow, give injections, all the latest techniques. Penny was keen to get her hands on real nursing techniques, but after the slide show she knew she would have to start getting used to the the simpler tasks before they were allowed to do anything complicated.

There were lectures on hygiene, anatomy, and care of children, the elderly and the chronically infirm, but despite her studies Penny found time to read in the newspapers all about the war in Europe. The march of Italy to the Albanian border was causing concern throughout the Balkans, and there were letters from home once again, demanding she return.

Yet she felt safer here in the city doing a job she loved. There was nothing to spoil the glory of spring and early summer before the heat got oppressive. There were flowers in bloom everywhere, which cheered the two nurses one hot afternoon as they staggered out of their lecture towards the National Garden, trying to absorb all the horrors to which they'd just been exposed.

'Do you think we'll cope if we're faced with stuff like that?' Yolanda asked. 'I feel sick. How I ever thought I could be a doctor . . .'

'You still could train,' Penny said, but Yolanda dismissed this with a wave of her hand.

'Poof! I am a woman, a Jew . . . who will train me now? You know our situation. It's not an option, just a silly dream.'

'And it's *when* we're faced with stuff like that, not *if*,' Penny replied, sensing Yolanda's disappointment. 'You can feel the tension in the air. The legation has people coming and going like Piccadilly Circus. They've taken on extra staff to help with administration and registration. Margery is working there now. I saw John Pendlebury in his uniform outside the Hotel Grande Bretagne. He's only got one eye – I wonder how he passed a medical board . . . You know, while I was looking at those slides I kept thinking what if one of those pictures had been of my brother? He's in the army in France now. I hope he's safe.'

Yolanda peered at her with serious eyes. 'You ought to go back to your family. I don't know how you can stay away from them . . .'

'We're not like you, we go our different ways.' How could she explain how distant they all felt to her now? Effy's letters were full of news of who was married and enlisting, what parties she'd missed in London and how the season would be cancelled. It was a world away from her life now.

'I couldn't bear anything to happen to mine. I'm so glad they've gone to Crete. Uncle Joseph will look after them. My father fears for the future of our race should Nazis come here, and I promised him I will join them if there's trouble.'

'I suppose you have more to fear than I do,' Penny blurted out without thinking. 'Sorry! You know what I mean.'

Yolanda smiled, patting her arm. 'They say we Jews belong to no nation but ourselves, but it's not true. I'm Greek, these are my people,' she indicated the passers-by. 'I have to do what I can for my country. No harm will come to us here.'

'That's just how I feel too. I belong here now. This is my home and I'm not going to desert it.'

*   *   *

Penny was learning fast that no matter what emergency there was in the hospital, a nurse must always walk not run, must stay calm for the patient's sake, no matter what she was feeling inside. She mustn't flinch or frighten a patient by showing emotion, even when death was close at hand. She'd learned to wash and lay out bodies according to their religious rites, respect each patient and the hierarchy of hospital procedures. She was not to speak unless spoken to, to put the patient's comfort as a priority, listening to their grumbles and fears . . .

Not that the nurses didn't have fun after shifts. There were name-day parties with cakes and wine, flirtations with some of the young doctors, who tried to hook in pretty nurses with their smooth talking. She had no inclination to attach herself to any one in particular and understood, now she'd found her own vocation, why Bruce had backed away from any real intimacy with her. There was always safety in numbers and mild flirtations. He'd got his future to think of. She blushed every time she thought of how keen she must have seemed to him. She couldn't help wondering just where he was now and if they would ever meet again.

Yolanda was a good influence, her head forever stuck in the newspaper, gleaning information about the international situation with her own slant on politics, making Penny feel lazy and slack on current affairs. She'd not picked up a book for months; one glance at a page and she fell asleep.

Yolanda insisted they made tours of the museums and art galleries on their precious days off. 'When war comes, all this will disappear,' she warned.

Penny wished Yolanda's influence could be brought to bear in her revision. Penny had never sat an examination in her life before she began her nursing training and she found the tests hard. There was so much to mug up on: anatomical details, drug regimes and chemistry. Yolanda seemed merely to glance through her notes and passed everything effortlessly, blessed with a good memory. It wasn't fair. Penny, however, had more stamina for walking around the city. Yolanda was hopeless at hill walking, complaining about the steep paths, wanting to sit down and rest every five minutes. She'd never hiked or ridden a horse or swam in the sea. Her parents preferred to keep her close to heel and out of view. They usually met up in the city, never at Rabbi Israel's house.

'I'm sorry, but they are stricter in observance than my family,' Yolanda explained. 'They don't approve of unmarried women working out of the home, let alone working with Gentiles. They're kind but old-fashioned. Any time soon I expect them to produce a nice Jewish man for me to marry, but I'm not ready for the chuppah yet.' She laughed as Penny looked blank 'It's the canopy under which we get married in the synagogue. Perhaps one day, but not yet . . .'

There was so much for Penny to learn about Yolanda's way of life. One of the things she loved about Athens was the melting pot of different peoples, religions, costumes and languages in the bustling streets and markets.

It was a glorious hot summer, with languorous nights spent sitting under the stars watching the swifts wheeling over the rooftops. The news from England, according to Margery, was dire. France had fallen and the army had been evacuated from Dunkirk. The post was not so reliable now that war had come to the Mediterranean so Penny didn't know whether Zan was safe.

The expats had to register their presence with the embassy, then were given papers and instructions on evacuation procedures, but Penny, turning up in her uniform, found no one bothered much with her presence. Effy's news, when it came, was worrying too.

Zan's home at Stokencourt wounded. He shuffled in with a tattered uniform like a tramp, in shock from Dunkirk. Poor boy was stunned at how quickly they had been defeated and how

many men and arms they'd lost en route. He slept for three days
solid. 'Only the Channel and RAF separate us now from defeat,'
he keeps telling us. I've never seen him so cut up. So stay where
you are. At least one of us will be safe. You promised us you'd
come home but no one expects it of you now, though I do miss
you. Walter's been shipped out to Egypt for the duration and
Diana keeps asking after you. She's joined the FANYs, the nursing corps. No point you coming home unless you want to join
up too.

But Penny knew she *had* joined up in the fight for justice and
compassion by taking on further training. There were now
troops of every nation stationed around the city, the port was
heaving with ships and Greek troops were on manoeuvres
outside the city, gathered up as if waiting for something to
happen. It could be only a matter of time before she was needed
here.

2001

I felt myself shivering, and woke to find myself sitting in my chair, stiff, staring at the cluster of silver-framed photographs. How long had I been dreaming?

For a second I panicked. *Where am I? Have I packed? Have I missed the plane? Is this all still a dream?*

Trojan was restless at my feet, pawing me to open the French windows and let him out, so I pulled my limbs back into shape, stretched my arms out, feeling the night air cooling my cheeks, the scent of the night-scented stocks heady with allure. A fox barked from the spinney.

Now I was leaving I didn't want to move from the comfort of my own fireside. Here I was safe, known and relaxed. What would be waiting for me out there on the island? What ghosts from the misty mountain tops would come down to haunt me?

With relief I saw my cases were packed, everything in order. I mixed a malt whisky and walked down the path to call the dog back. It was so peaceful, so very English; flowers like silver ghosts in the moonlight brushed my arms. How could I have ever thought of leaving here on some wild-goose chase? But a promise is a promise, and I couldn't let Lois down at this late hour.

I sat under the cedar tree and sipped the whisky with a sigh. The last time I'd seen Athens it lay in ruins, a broken filthy place fit only for rats and cockroaches to live in. It would be good to see how it had risen from those ashes. Besides, what I learned there made me who I am today, taught me how to survive and showed me just how tough I could be. But more than that, it had given me one of the best friends of my life.

I made my way back slowly to the open door and resumed my place in the chair. Tomorrow I would sleep far away, but as dawn was breaking I would keep a vigil, relive those memories of olive days and remember.

December 1940

Penny shivered under her cloak, trying to forget the numbness in her fingers as she fumbled to cut away the frozen sleeve of the soldier's uniform. Infection was his enemy now. The bullets had done their worst, but the journey back from the field clearing station to the train, carrying the casualties on makeshift shelves full of stretchers, had taken so long in the snow that there would be only hours before gangrene would claim its due on his flesh.

She looked down on his ashen face, knowing his life was in her hands.

She sighed, recalling how proudly the Greek army had marched through Athens on its way north to defend the country from invasion. Was he one of the young gods paraded through the streets, girls throwing flowers at their trucks, waving and blowing kisses just as they had lauded Papa's troops on their way to the Somme all those years ago? Now this youthful soldier lay wasted by frostbite and shock as they worked on him, a pitiable sight with blackened fingers, in a flimsy uniform not fit for the treacherous terrain of the Pindus Mountains during one of the worst winters for years.

All those Athenians who'd danced until dawn, fired bullets into the air in joy at Prime Minister Metaxas's stand against Mussolini in October when he said '*óhi*' to his demands, would weep now. Death was gathering up the best of their youth. The bells might be ringing there for a string of victories against the enemy – and one as badly equipped as themselves, thank God – but the cost in lives was high.

It was a shock see what mud and ice could do to the human body on top of the injuries. Men frozen into a stupor were brought back to life with warm soup or hot drinks when they could find enough water to melt and enough fuel to fire up the stoves. Frostbite was eased with oil of turpentine, wrapping the wound in cotton wool and gently heating the limb. Infections were soaked in Lysol solution and liquid paraffin, the doctors amputating as best they could.

Yet, enduring this, the men would smile at the nurses, call them angels of mercy, grateful for any attention. Sometimes Penny wanted to weep with frustration when the light went out of a boy's young eyes. For weeks the medical teams struggled under makeshift light and heat, trying to keep their patients alive long enough to get back to one of the major hospitals. Many did not survive even the journey from the front to the clearing stations.

Now attached to the military wing of the Red Cross, Penny was glad of Sister McGrath's lecture all those months ago, though nothing could prepare her for the reality: those feelings of helplessness and fury when they ran out of dressings, ether and all the essentials of medical care. It was hard, learning to walk through the lines of stretchers, marking those who would get priority treatment, a chance of life, and those who could only be made comfortable and allowed to die. She knew the lucky ones would be patched up, given leave, perhaps, and then returned to this hell of bitter winds and barren unforgiving terrain.

Yet the intensity of each day's new challenges – cleaning the men, delousing them and preparing food – gave Penny an electric charge of satisfaction that she'd never known before in her young life. Here I am needed, saving lives, she thought. She was alive in a way she'd never experienced before, busy, exhausted, but satisfied that her existence was suddenly worthwhile.

Yolanda was out there somewhere doing the same work. It was so good to have a close friend who knew exactly what you were enduring. There was such a camaraderie within the team; doctors, nurses, aides and orderlies with no time for petty jealousies. They tried to snatch sleep when they could, lived on the most basic of meals, and tried to ward off the fleas by warming stone hot-water bottles under their covers. It was a losing battle but the chill had at least discouraged the larger insect life, which was a blessing.

Where they set up, villagers came out offering coats, socks and scarves for the soldiers at the front, thick blankets and food they could hardly spare. Everyone was making sacrifices in this war. Sometimes they were stranded by blizzards and ice on the tracks, but they kept on nursing, cleaning, feeding right through January and into February 1941.

It was good that there were fresh troops from the islands coming to relieve the poor Greek army, who battled on, overwhelming the Italians, pushing them ever backwards into Albania. But the price was high. There was a victory at Ioaninna, but then came the prisoners of war, streaming in for treatment, pathetic bundles of rags, starving, defeat etched on their faces. Some were grateful to be fed and sheltered in tents, others needed to be guarded. There was so little fresh food to go round that men began to suffer from lack of vitamins as they were shipped down to camps in the south.

There were no enemies in a Red Cross hospital, just frightened exhausted men at the end of their hope, grateful for any act of kindness. Penny learned that there were no winners in this campaign. Only losers.

It was with relief she was granted leave. The girl who had gone north in all innocence was returning to Athens a woman bloodied by battle. She arrived with only one thought on her mind: to find the deepest warmest oil-scented bath where she could try to soak away all the horrors she'd witnessed.

The city was buzzing with British troops being sent north to enforce the new borders, to show the Axis powers that Greece was not standing alone. There were boys in blue stationed at Royal Air Force bases in Tatoi and Eleusis. Once again the city was full of excitement and confidence that it had seen off the enemy for good. Yet Penny felt an outsider in all this celebration, knowing the people of Athens had no idea of the tensions in the north. If Italy had failed to conquer its neighbours would Germany come to its aid?

There was a course on theatre nursing that she must attend. In emergencies she'd been forced to give a helping hand when the hospital was short-staffed, but there were huge gaps in her knowledge. Now she knew she had the stomach for the work she felt good about learning more advanced skills for theatre surgery.

She kept asking around if anyone had seen Yolanda but no one knew anything until she met a young doctor who pointed her in the direction of a hospital ward. 'They've put her in there.'

'She's wounded? Oh, no!' Penny fast-walked down the corridor in panic, only to see Yolanda coming in the opposite direction with a bandaged arm in a sling.

'I've been looking everywhere for you. Praise the Lord, you're here, but I've just heard you're injured. What happened?' Penny greeted her.

'Nothing but a scratch that went septic,' Yolanda fobbed off her concern, but Penny noticed she looked more tired and drawn than usual. 'I've got a week off.'

'It's more than a scratch then.' Penny eyed her carefully. 'Let's go to out and celebrate your leave.'

'I couldn't . . . I'm broke . . .' Yolanda hesitated. Penny guessed most of her pay was going to her parents on Crete.

'The treat's on me. I've had a windfall,' she lied, though there were still some drachmas left in the kitty from when Papa shoved a wallet of notes into her bag before he left. She had kept this dwindling little reserve for emergencies. 'Come on, pastries at Zonar's and then onto the Argentina. I feel like dancing the night away. Time we had some fun.'

'But I've nothing to wear and, besides, what would I tell Rabbi Israel. I've only just returned.'

'What they don't know won't hurt them. Let's treat ourselves. We should dress up, forget our nun's robes and have a ball. If anyone deserves it we do.' Penny felt she needed to decide for both of them. They'd seen so much suffering of late, she just wanted to forget it all for these few precious days.

'Weren't you glad of Sister McGrath's slide show?' Yolanda began.

'No talking shop, I forbid it!' Penny shouted. 'We dance till dawn tonight.'

'You've changed,' Yolanda laughed.

'We've lived with death all these months, let's see a bit of life. Who knows where we'll be sent next? Come on, the shops are calling me . . .'

They arrived back at Margery's rooms laden with parcels: a dress for Yolanda and some pretty shoes for Penny, rose-scented soaps and toiletries and perfume. They lunched on *tiropita* – cheese pastries – and Sachertorte, giggling and relaxed for the first time in months.

'Let's try everything on again. This is so decadent,' said Yolanda, inspecting her new outfit with delight. 'What will Momma say to such a short dress?' It was long-sleeved, made of navy-and-white spotted silk and gathered in at the waist.

'You look better already,' Penny said, noting the flush in Yolanda's cheeks. 'Let me change the dressing on your arm first.' When she undid the bandage she saw how raw and blistered was the wound. 'What's this?'

'It's nothing, just a burn It's healing now.'

'Is there a story to this?' Penny asked, curious.

'Not really, just a soldier crazed with fever, who brandished a hot poker and lashed out at us. He didn't mean it, poor chap and he died later. They think it was rabies.'

The wound was deep and ugly and would leave a scar. Penny was angry that Yolanda would be branded for life by the madman.

'We're going out on the town tonight, Margery, don't expect us back until the heels of our shoes are worn down with dancing. I've got my key.'

Margery sniffed in response, settling down for the evening with one of her beloved Agatha Christies.

The Argentina was busy, tables taken by officers and their girlfriends, but Penny was a regular from her days as a student and was seated by the bar. She recognized familiar faces from the legation, old friends who waved the young nurses over and found them chairs at their tables. The band was on fine form and the officers were soon up to dance, swirling the young women round the floor. Drinks were ordered for them, especially when the soldiers found out they'd been at the front. Everyone wanted to know how bad it was. This was not on Penny's agenda so she suggested they find another table if they wanted to talk shop. Where had all this new-found social confidence come from? Months ago she wouldn't have dared to come into a place like this without a man to take her arm, but things were changing, and for the better. She was recognizing a little more of her own worth in surviving the rigours of life at the front. She and Yolanda deserved time off to relax and not feel guilty. Yolanda was not so easily convinced.

'If anyone recognizes me, I'll be in trouble,' Yolanda whispered. 'This is not what single girls do in my community. I hope no one tells the Israels and they write to Momma. We don't go out without a chaperone. I think I should go now.'

'No, don't. Why shouldn't you have a life of your own? If anyone deserves a break, you do.' Soon a procession of dashing young army and air force officers were again escorting them onto the floor. No one pestered them, but as the men got drunker they started holding the girls tighter, asking for their addresses. Soon it was time to head back to Margery's lodgings, weary but relaxed. Yolanda was to stay over so as not to disturb the Israels.

To Penny's surprise Margery was waiting up, a pained look on her face. 'You've had a visitor,' she announced as Penny flung off her new shoes with relief. 'One of the BSA boys . . . a Captain Jardine.'

'Bruce? Bruce Jardine? He's here in Athens?' Penny was stunned for a second. She'd been so busy, she'd not thought of Bruce for weeks.

'He heard you were still here and wanted to catch up with you. He's brought letters from your sister,' Margery said, plonking a pile of envelopes on the table.

'How long is he here? Which regiment?' Penny felt excited that he'd looked her up after all this time, but a little deflated now she'd missed him.

'Steady on, the young man was three sheets to the wind, but they all are, these days. He did leave a number. You can give him a call tomorrow, not now; it's one o'clock and I need my beauty sleep.'

'Sorry for keeping you up, you are so kind,' said Penny, now flushed with excitement.

'I couldn't sleep. There's been unsettling news on the wireless. Hitler's massing troops in Romania. It looks as if he's going to finish what the Eyeties couldn't . . . He'll be in Athens by Easter, mark my words. Time for us to pack our bags.'

'Looks as if we'll be on the march again then,' Yolanda looked to Penny with concern.

'That's why the troops are here. If Hitler thinks the British are a walkover, he's another think coming,' Penny replied with a confidence she didn't quite feel.

'So who is Bruce Jardine?' Yolanda quizzed, changing the

subject. 'His name had brought colour to your cheeks like rouge.'

'Oh, someone I used to know when I was a student,' Penny said, not wanting to go into detail about her girlish crush all those months ago. She was now a different person from the one he would think lived here with Margery.

Yolanda slept on a camp bed in the bedroom while Penny tossed and turned. Bruce had called. If only she'd stayed in she wouldn't have missed him . . . but she'd ring and arrange to meet him somehow.

Do I really want to see him though? she pondered. Do I want to raise my hopes all over again? She must thank him for bringing post – that was only polite – but was that the only reason she was glad he'd come round? It was pointless going over her feelings. She'd think straighter in the morning. One thing was certain, Penny Georgiou had important priorities these days, and the thought of Hitler's storm troopers marching south towards them was no comfort at all. Even so, she heard the owl hooting well into the night, and then the screech of the cock in the yard before she finally fell asleep.

The telephone, at the number Bruce had left, rang for ages until a sleepy woman's voice replied. Penny wanted to throw down the receiver with disappointment.

'You want Brucie? Darling, *everyone* wants Brucie . . .' The accented voice paused to shout upstairs, 'Where's he gone?' There were muffled voices, one of them a man's.

'Sorry, can't help you,' the woman told Penny. 'They've all been marshalled somewhere hush-hush. Who shall I say called?'

Penny hung up without giving a response, in no mood to listen to the drawl of Bruce's hungover mistress. Still the same Bruce, up to his old tricks with the ladies. She stomped out of the room, furious to have raised her hopes that his call was anything other than that of a polite courier, helping out Evadne.

Yolanda left early to return to the Israels, leaving behind her new dress and evidence of last night's excursion.

Penny heard in the bakery that the Greek General Papagos wanted his best forces to remain in Albania while the British were heading north to back up forces on the Bulgarian border. But then she heard a rumour in the grocery store that it was the other way round. She knew the state of the army in the west and just how brave and tired they were in trying to defend every inch of Greek territory, despite how poorly equipped they were and short of bullets. People in Athens had no idea how dangerous this conflict was getting.

Margery came back from her office in the embassy, hinting that there were big meetings going on in the Hotel Grande Bretagne. Even the King had been seen walking through the foyer with his entourage. It was all rather fraught there, she added, and plans were being made to evacuate troops and British residents from the southern ports, should the alliance fail.

Penny prepared for her recall to service with a heavy heart.

It must be a bleak prospect to engage with the best army in the world. As they headed north, this time she knew what was awaiting them. She took time to notice the wild beauty of the hillsides, the carpets of wild flowers, reds, yellows, whites, the blossom. Villagers flung biscuits and bread into the trucks, and wine, as if this were some celebration of certain victory. Their joy did not last for long.

Raiders began serious bombing of the city and Piraeus harbour. The *Clan Fraser*, a munitions ship, exploded, destroying every ship close by and most of the harbour, with a terrible loss of life. Then through a mountain pass came the fresh troops of the German mountain divisions, breaking the Greek line. Within days Salonika fell and the Greek Second Army surrendered. Only New Zealand and British troops were left to hold the defensive line.

For Penny, it was back to the trucks ferrying the wounded

south again as the news grew more worrying each day. The British were not holding out. There would be no relief from either east or west, and the morale of the divisions was flagging as they were forced to retreat over land once won at such cost. The Cretan 5th Division fought bravely at Aliakmon but the forces pounding them were overwhelming in fire power, strength and equipment.

Suddenly the nightmare of retreat began in earnest as bedraggled men headed south, strafed all the while by planes and bombs. Trucks were held up by huge craters in the roads, which took hours to fill in with dead animals and debris. Miles took days, not hours. Progress was painfully slow, the retreating soldiers bloodied, their uniforms tattered, the defeated look of exhaustion on their faces. The seriously wounded were hidden in villages or left to die where they fell for lack of men to carry them.

Penny's team pulled aboard as many wounded as they could. Yolanda, working close by, went out with a doctor to tend the walking wounded, and sometimes they carried men on their backs to get them to shelter.

One soldier begged Penny not to chart his temperature, wanting to get up and return half-healed of his infection. 'I'm fine now, let me go back. Those are my friends out there. How will I look their mothers in the eye if I don't go and find them?'

They were getting used to taking out makeshift casualty stations to help men on their way, everything easy to fold up. Beds, chairs, cases of medical equipment, gas stoves and pans, all were loaded onto mules to be taken to temporary respite centres.

When they came to a river it was a matter of ropes and pulleys, persuading the animals to forge across, and Penny rode at the helm of her convoy, confident that she could manoeuvre the mules as well as any man. She pretended to be back in the hills of Scotland, among the bracken and glens. How simple and luxuriant were those long-gone days. Here, they were in constant danger from German planes spotting their stations. At first she had felt sure that no one would ignore the big Red Cross signs on their uniforms and tent roofs, but some took no notice and then it was everyone into the ditches for cover. They were treating any wounded, friend or foe, but the soldier guards found that hard to stomach after such a raid.

At night the nurses sat stony-faced, saying little. How could Greece fall so quickly?

A doctor smiled and sighed. 'I expected to eat my Christmas dinner in Athens, and I did, but where I will eat my Easter egg, only the Good Lord knows!"

Yolanda looked sombre when she heard gathering rumours of Jews being rounded up across the borders. There was talk of them being singled out as hostages and even for execution.

While she had more reason than any of them to be worried, for all, it was a matter of one foot in front of the other when their truck broke down. Penny wondered if she would ever sit down again. She had never felt so filthy in her life, her scalp itched and her skin was flea-bitten, but there was no time for self-pity as the wounded piled in for help. When would this journey ever end?

One by one the lines of defence crumbled: the Aliakmon River, the Mount Olympus defences and then the famous narrow pass at Thermopylae, where King Leonidas and his Spartans held out against Xerxes and the Persian hordes. British and Anzac troops were flooding back south in retreat, and the Red Cross staff also moved back with the wounded as, one by one, the hospital bases were occupied or destroyed.

Penny went south to Kifissia, where it was utter chaos. She was trying to sort out accommodation for the wounded – hotels, tents, anywhere to give them shelter and where they could be treated. It took seven days for soldiers to return from the north, and by then the worst casualties were in a terrible condition. The makeshift wards in the grounds of the hospital were little more than open-air tents to give shelter from the sun and rain. The Greek troops were grateful but Penny was anxious. There was a constant struggle to find hot water, and with no sluices or bedpans, the place stank. The ever-present rumble of guns in the distance told of rearguard actions, desperately trying to hold off the onslaught.

The German POWs were restive, fearful that they would be killed before their army liberated them. There was bribery on offer, fear and unease around nursing them.

The nurses tried to keep hygiene routines but the Greek soldiers lay around in unwashed uniforms, unshaven, covered in lice and fleas, their morale so low that some shot themselves. The doctors were wearing revolvers on duty in case discipline should break down. It would only be a matter of time before the British nurses and others would be evacuated to Egypt with the most serious casualties that were fit to travel, but the constant air raids now made travel to the ports dangerous.

It was a very sombre Easter Day, everyone trying to make the most of that most holy celebration. There *was* no dancing in the city now, not when so many wives were widowed and children orphaned. Yet the retreating armies were shown only courtesy and concern. '*Nike! Nike!*' Girls throwing flowers wished them well. 'Come back soon . . . Take care. God be with you.' It was humbling to see them lining the streets in black. Surely they'd know this retreat was more like a rout.

In the midst of her duties, Penny received a visitor from the embassy, a Mr Howard, an official in a linen suit who had worked alongside Walter, before his departure.

'Time you were heading home, Miss George,' Mr Howard told her. 'Walter has made arrangements for you on the next ship out. I hope you have a suitcase ready and packed. It's highly irregular but we have transit papers ready for you to sign.'

Penny paused, lighting up a much-needed cigarette. 'This is news to me. You can see the situation here. I'm a nurse. How can I just walk away?'

'The British wounded are being evacuated and their nurses are going with them. The Greek nuns and nurses will hold the fort. You must be prepared to jump when called.'

Penny suddenly felt a rush of anger after all the Red Cross staff's efforts to help every casualty they could. 'So my Greek casualties are to be abandoned here, then?'

'That is *their* government's concern. Ours is to get our fighting men and essential staff and civilians away as soon as possible.'

Penny shook her head, having heard enough. 'Thank you for the offer but I have patients to see to now. I'll be remaining here.'

'Don't be a silly girl, do you want to be interned as an alien? You've got a British passport.'

'I have a Greek name. I can pass as a Greek nurse,' she insisted.

'Who are you fooling, Miss George? It says you are a minor.'

'Miss Georgiou, actually. Now I really must return to duty. I will go when I am ordered to by my superiors and not before.'

Mr Howard stormed off, muttering that she was lucky to be given preference. But Penny didn't want preferential treatment. It was only then that she realized he was wrong about her age, and her twenty-first birthday had indeed come and gone unnoticed, without so much as a bunch of flowers or a cake. She'd been so busy, away from the city for weeks, and the post now was erratic. How could she have missed that important milestone? She was free to choose for herself now, and she'd just made yet another momentous grown-up decision, in dismissing Mr Howard. How she had changed in the past months. She no longer recognized her former self, the debutante bolter, the lovesick adolescent, but to be twenty-one and forget such a milestone? Somehow she'd make sure they all celebrated her birthday in traditional Greek style with chocolates and cake, easier said than done in this chaos.

She found an orderly, who went in search of a local bakery and came back with honey pastries and wine to share with the ward. It was a welcome little treat in this crazy situation. '*Chronia Polla,* many years!' chorused the staff and patients.

Later, as they sat hugging their cocoa, watching the night sky lit up with a thousand stars, and listening to the distant crumple of bombs, Penny decided to tell Yolanda of her encounter with the embassy official.

'I promised my father I would come home if there was danger but how can I go now, after all we've been through?'

Yolanda looked out over the darkened city and sighed. 'I've been thinking the same. I promised my parents I would join them on Crete. When the enemy comes I am sure to be on some list, if the rumours are to be believed, and I've heard some terrible rumours . . . Should I leave now?'

Penny shook her head. 'You must do what is best for you, but I'll miss you. I'm going to hang on until the bitter end. They'll have to lever me out with a crowbar. Everyone is so disheartened. Today I had one boy refuse to eat or drink. He says he just wants to die. Others just want to go home. Who will help them if we don't? I can't help feeling they're being abandoned. I'd feel ashamed to be British, hopping onto the first ship to safety.'

'Promise me you'll keep in touch, whatever happens.' Yolanda smiled, patting her arm. 'Happy birthday. I'm sorry it's not much but I want you to have something.' She pulled out a little parcel from under her cloak.

Penny unfolded the tissue paper to find a beautifully embroidered white handkerchief with her initials intertwined with a purple Y and delicate flower.

'You did this? It's beautiful, so delicate. I had no idea you could do such work, and the lace edging . . .' Penny felt tears in her eyes. 'Wherever we land up we'll always be friends. I wish I'd got something to give you back.'

'It's not my birthday, wait until October.' Yolanda pointed to the violet flower. 'Now when you see those little flowers on your travels you can think of my name, of us; friends for ever,' she added.

'Thank you so much,' Penny whispered, giving her a hug. 'I shall treasure it always.'

Two nights later all the nurses were ordered to help the British nurses gathering up their wounded for evacuation in trucks, ambulances and anything that could pull a cart. There were tears as the British nurses parted company with their faithful aides and Greek staff, knowing they would be left to the mercies of the oncoming enemy, already only miles from the city. Wrapped in their cloaks, Penny and Yolanda sat with the stretcher cases, checking dressings and pulses as they made their slow journey down to the beaches under cover of darkness.

It must have been an orderly retreat at first, but by the time the hospital evacuees headed out there had been bombing, and the usual craters, abandoned trucks and lorries were blocking their slow crawl. The remains told their own story of hurried retreat: dead horses shot, suitcases ripped open and looted, scattered equipment, broken guns. There were queues all heading in the same direction, and in the distance the sad silhouettes of wrecked merchant shipping, warships and caïques, while other vessels sat uneasily out in the water at Nauplion.

The waterfront was bombed out of recognition, the stench of cordite and rotting flesh was everywhere. How would anyone get on board the waiting ships before dawn? It would be a miracle in this confusion of men and machines, but orders were barked, lines drawn up, the stretchers off-loaded with care.

Thankfully the sky was clear of raids that night and the moon was not too full.

Penny stared out at the ships in the bay with a heavy heart. How many of them would make it safely to their destination? What would become of them once the troops had left? Suddenly, one of her soldiers in front began to panic and fit. It took Penny and two of her colleagues to hold him down and inject him with a sedative. By the time he was calm, the queue to board the boats had shuffled forward and the evacuation at last seemed to be progressing smoothly.

Yolanda was far ahead out of sight, busy with the walking wounded, guiding them towards the waiting ferry boats in the embarkation area. Penny carried on with her paperwork, comforting the shaken men, waiting for Yolanda to rejoin them. 'Where's Nurse Markos?' she enquired after half an hour. It was almost time to return to base for another ambulance load, if needed. She walked around the crowds of men, searching for her friend. No one seemed to know or care as they went about their own duties. What was one nurse among so many?

It was only when they were heading back that Penny concluded with relief that Yolanda must have taken another truck back to the hospital. She ran up the steps to check the staff room, the washroom, the ward corridors and outside huts. But after dawn when there was no sign of Yolanda she began to panic. Why wasn't she back here? Surely she hadn't left without telling anyone?

Yolanda would never abandon her charges. Had something happened in the mêlée? There had been some desperate types, some drunk and despairing, on the beach, and Yolanda was petite and attractive. But surely no one would harm a nurse in Red Cross uniform. Had she slipped and fallen on the beach or into the sea? Penny's mind was racing with explanations as she combed the wards, back and forth, hoping to see her familiar figure propped up somewhere, half asleep.

By daylight she knew in her heart Yolanda was gone, leaving her abandoned and alone. Something awful must have happened. She gripped the hanky Yolanda had given her, knowing it would soon be her turn to go on board with the wounded. Where were they sending them? Would she ever see her friend again?

In the days that followed, Yolanda's disappearance puzzled and unsettled Penny. She felt isolated, suddenly bereft, her resolve to stay put, weakening by the hour. What good would it be if I was interned, she thought. At least if she returned home by sea she could continue nursing. Then the air raids were stepped up and ships en route out of the Aegean were sunk. There were few of the brave RAF pilots left who tried to cover the evacuation and the last rearguard actions. If Yolanda was aboard the *Ulster Prince* where was she now? Penny dreaded to think.

Then came news of the sinking of the steamer *Hellas* full of civilians, burned alive in Piraeus harbour.

'We will manage. We can look after our soldiers. You go and look after those poor young men from your country,' Penny's nursing friends insisted.

She lay awake all night wondering if they were right. She had promised Papa she would leave, so there was nothing for it but to humble her stubborn pride and register for evacuation. But she would go with a very heavy heart.

It was chaos in the embassy office when she arrived and she was not exactly welcome, having refused to go earlier.

'You've left it too late, young lady. They've all gone,' the official snapped at her. 'You should've come last night.' Mr Howard, when he passed her in the queue, seemed to take great satisfaction in seeing her there. His smug face was more than she could stomach. Running away was the coward's way. Hadn't she just celebrated being an adult and free to choose her own path? Gathering herself, shoulders back, Penny turned round and walked out of the door.

Blinking into the afternoon sunshine, Penny missed a step and went stumbling out of the embassy when an arm appeared and reached out to stop her fall. 'Steady on,' said a man in uniform. Then: 'Good Lord! What are you still doing here?'

She looked up into the sunburned face of Bruce Jardine. For a second she was overjoyed to see such a familiar face and beamed, but then, wondering if she'd get another lecture, flushed with annoyance.

'Looks like I'm stuck here for the duration,' she replied, in no mood for conversation.

'I told Walter they'd get you out ages ago. Where've you been?'

Penny gave him a look of utter contempt. 'I've been at the Albanian front since January with the Red Cross. I was going to call it a day and make for home but as usual I'm running a bit late.'

'Balderdash! I'll get you out, but you'll have to be quick about it, and hush-hush. Jerry is only a few miles outside the city. I called to see you . . .'

'I know and I rang you back but your girlfriend didn't know where you were.'

'That was Sadie, Dennis's little playmate. I've been about and around myself; can't say where . . . Come on, let me buy you a drink, you look as if you need one. You're terribly thin, but then you always were a bit of a beanpole. Pretty terrible out there, was it?' He had the decency to looked concerned.

'You could say that.' She was being prickly, unnerved by this unexpected encounter and the sight of that rakish face. As always, he picked up as if it hadn't been ages since their last embarrassing encounter.

As they sat in a pavement café sipping a cocktail with a *meze* of dried fruits and nuts, Penny couldn't believe there was a war raging around them. Everything on the surface appeared so normal: the clack of trams and shouts of street vendors plying their wares round the tables, vying with the donkey carts full of passengers queuing in line like taxis in the sunshine, the lull before the storm. Tonight she'd be whisked away to safety, all because she'd stepped out of the embassy at the right time. It was all so unreal.

'I ought to stay on. They need me,' she said with a sigh.

'The Greeks will manage their own affairs but they need us to fight on and return one day. You must have heard them shouting "*Nike* . . . Victory" as those poor defeated sods tried to march back through the city. Still, they'll not make it easy for the bastards.'

'Where are you heading?' she asked.

He shrugged. 'Who knows? Where we're most needed, wherever the ship lands us. That's not your concern. I'll find us a taxi and we'll go for your stuff. I'm not letting you out of my sight now. Evadne will kill me if I don't get her little sister back in one piece.' Bruce's face, leathery from too much sun, creased in a smile.

Why did she suddenly feel awkward and guilty? There was a time when she'd have welcomed him as her knight on a white charger come to rescue her, but now he was making her decision to leave too easy. Yet was this unexpected reunion a sign that it was time to leave the mainland? Odd that their paths kept crossing,and nothing was ever dull when Bruce was in charge, but did she want to embark on another adventure with him in control of things or was it better to strike out and make her own way? How could she do that now? Where would it lead and would she survive? The embassy had washed its hands of her so perhaps this was the best option, she thought, struggling to be grateful for his help. If only Yolanda was here as well. Oh, why did Bruce Jardine always make her feel confused?

The convoy of diplomats and their families with an escort of soldiers drove through the evening to the port of Monemvasia. The diplomatic families were sailing on a steam yacht, *Iolanthe*, while Penny's more subtle exit was to be made with some Greek political evacuees and diplomatic staff with their wives and children in a Greek caïque, hired from some seafarer who knew the remote islands in the Aegean.

'We must travel only under cover of darkness,' Bruce explained.

Penny shivered, glad of her Red Cross cloak and battledress khaki borrowed from one of the army nurses, who'd given her a tearful farewell and a medallion of St Christopher for safe travelling. How could she be deserting them? Yet she knew her own presence might put them at risk for harbouring a British alien in their midst.

As they bumped along the now familiar rutted tracks she stared out at the sheet of gunmetal that was the sea. It looked calm enough, but danger lurked from submarines and the ever-present dive bombers. She prayed she was not taking up someone else's precious space, but Bruce assured her that there would be plenty of room on the caïque for stragglers and strays. The *Amalia* looked seaworthy, which was more than could be said for its captain. He looked like a pirate with his black beard, and he was rolling on deck, drunk to the point of stupor. Bruce and his friends threw him down into the hold in disgust.

'Anyone know how to steer this thing?' he yelled.

Two bronzed Anzacs in tattered shorts, waiting for a lift off the beach, volunteered to get them started with the Greek crew, who looked nervous. It was going to be a motley bunch sailing the ship until they could sober up the captain.

Slowly and silently they edged through the water. The *Iolanthe*, sailing ahead, was now just a speck on the horizon. With the throb of the engines, Penny curled up under her cloak, trying to snatch some sleep. Danger lurked under the water and they all sat in total silence seeing the smoking wrecks of ships lurching down into the deep. Penny stared out at the black water, smelling the telltale fumes of oil and burning rubber with only her thoughts for company.

Everything had happened so fast: bumping into Bruce, collecting her case, her uniform and papers, saying farewell, all in one afternoon. As she left the mainland shore behind, she thought of Yolanda, wondering where she was and if she was still alive. Soon the numbness and stupor of exhaustion and a good helping of rough red wine settled her queasy stomach.

She woke at first light, stiff-limbed and hungry, knowing that they could easily be spotted by air. Bruce had ordered that no men, guns, helmets or uniforms be visible. There was a tarpaulin for the men to hide under should the worst happen. Penny felt she was holding her breath, looking out constantly for any sighting of the enemy in the sky and under the sea. No one spoke when only minutes later, they heard the throb of engines. The Fates were against them but no one panicked. Now they must put Bruce's strategy to work.

'Are you OK, Pen? You know what to do?' he asked as he ducked out of sight.

Penny nodded, trying not to shake as she whipped off her cloak and trousers and flung on a pair of khaki shorts, which she rolled up to reveal her long legs. The Greek wives were sitting in dresses and they spread out a tablecloth and lay down as if they were sunbathing. Penny could see the Messerschmitt swooping down low, and then it banked and turned, ready to strafe the deck. Heart in her mouth, Penny shook out her hair, showed off her tanned legs. 'Show your legs, ladies,' she ordered, hoping they would act out this desperate attempt to fool the pilot. 'Wave! Look as if you are on holiday!'

Penny felt as if her heart were leaping out of her chest as she looked up and waved a book in the air, trying to smile through gritted teeth, hoping their ruse would work.

Then, to their immense relief, the pilot swooped down, waved back to them from his cockpit, and sped off to look for other prey, leaving the girls staring up into the sky, shaking at such a close encounter.

'Well done, Pen. I knew I could rely on you in a tight corner.' Bruce smiled down at the prostrate women. 'Hold to your posts, ladies, we're not out of danger yet. We're heading for the nearest uninhabited island.'

Penny watched a lump of rock slowly emerge from the haze on the horizon and they sailed towards a shallow bay where the *Iolanthe* was already moored. It looked like a paradise island of white sand and turquoise-blue waters. There was plenty of shade from the trees on shore and it was good to feel terra firma once again.

I can climb any mountain but the sea unnerves me, Penny thought as she jumped ashore to join the party already spreading tablecloths and opening picnic baskets. The children were letting off steam playing tag and hide-and-seek, with strict orders to hide properly should any planes appear.

The *Iolanthe* had a Lewis gun on board, and ammunition, but it had suffered some damage getting out of the harbour, and the crew and some of the officers were busy trying to make repairs.

Penny joined Judy Harrington, whom she'd once met at one of the embassy parties with Evadne, sitting with the other embassy wives for gin and limes under the shade of the huge trees, lying back and wondering if she was in some bizarre dream. Then they heard a warning klaxon from the yacht ringing in their ears and the wives jumped up to gather the children and run for cover. This time there would be no play-acting on the beach as three heavy bombers thundered overhead. To her horror Penny watched the *Iolanthe* blown out the water in a ball of fire and the *Amalia* was rocked with the blast. Immediately Bruce and the Anzac soldiers were rowing out to the blazing wreck even though there was ammo still exploding. In the chaos of smoke and screaming, the wives yelled in terror for their children to take cover. Suddenly the calm sea was rocking with debris and burning oil, and the smell was of burning flesh.

The survivors were dragged from the water. It was a terrible sight on such a beautiful spot, but there was no time for delay. The children were rushed away from the shore, while women were screaming in horror, not knowing who had been killed.

Penny's mind went straight from gin as a drink to gin as disinfectant. What could she use to make a clearing station? Alcohol to cleanse, salt water, bandages, stretchers, wood for fuel.

'I'll need clean shirts, underskirts, anything clean, cotton, silk. You'd better rip them into strips,' she ordered. Giving the stunned women jobs might keep panic and shock at bay for a while.

The first to come out were beyond her help. The others, she examined, having read somewhere that salt water burns healed better than dry ones. She hoped this was correct as she tried carefully to peel fabric from skin.

There were nine dead men – crew, officials and two soldiers – six had third-degree burns and two were in shock. Shock played havoc with the body if not recognized so she put these men in the care of Marisa and Elpi, the Greek maids from the *Iolanthe*.

Bruce had superficial burns on his arms but no blast injuries. He was anxious to make repairs to their caïque now, take everyone off the island and hide somewhere else in case the Stuka dive bombers returned to finish them off. The captain, sobered now by the morning's tragedy, knew how to navigate to a safer port where they could get help for the injured.

At nightfall, everyone gathered to bury the dead. It was a sad party that limped across to Kimolos. Bruce stood on deck grim-faced, his arms bandaged with Penny's shirt.

'Sorry, Pen, didn't mean to bring you into all this, but it was a good job we had someone on board who knew what they were doing.' He was looking at her with admiration and Penny felt herself blushing. How strange they had once met in their finery in a Highland ballroom and now they stood ragged, burned and exhausted in this world of war.

'Perhaps I was meant to be here . . . What'll happen now?'

'We'll get picked up, not sure when, but there are too many important chaps on board for us to be overlooked. Don't know what we'd've done without you.'

'Where were we heading, before all this happened?' she asked.

'Over the wine-dark sea to the birthplace of Zeus, to the island where Theseus overcame the Minotaur,' he whispered.

She was too tired to take in his allusions and looked blank.

'To Crete, last outpost of the King of Greece now,' he continued. 'The show must go on and they're preparing for the next onslaught. You'll be shipped out on the first convoy with the diplomatic wives and children, of course.'

That's what you think, Penny thought, staring out across the blue waters. She'd made herself useful, saved lives because of her training here. Once again fate was conspiring to point the way forward. Surely there was a role for her here more than ever now? With a deep certainty in the pit of her stomach Penny knew she'd not be seeing England for a very long time.

2001

So there you were, old girl, stranded with a bunch of strangers, but not for long. Remembering, I smiled, then drained the last of the whisky as dawn rose. I stared into the crystal glass; whisky, like wine, is a great consoler of the lonely.

As the morning light beamed into the room, I heard my alarm clock ringing and I knew I must make an effort and rouse myself from this stupor. Time enough for reminiscing later, but I sat back for one more time, reluctant to leave those heady days when I was young and full of hope, even as the bombs rained down on us. How can you explain to the young how good it was then to be alive?

Steady the Buffs, old girl, stop your daydreaming. Wakey, wakey, rise and shine. There's still a list of must-dos before you swan off on your hols and you don't want to keep Lois waiting . . .

Part 2

CRETE

Red shines the sun, standby
It may not smile for us tomorrow.
There's no way back. Comrade, no way back
Dark clouds ahead, far to the west . . .

'*Rot scheint die Sonne*'('Anthem of the Paratroopers'), 1941

May 2001

An old man stood on deck with a bird's-eye view of Piraeus harbour, watching preparations for the ferry's departure, the clanking of the trucks into the hold, last-minute backpackers strolling up the walkway. He was a stranger among strangers, choosing this longer way to the island for this overdue return, rather than fly. His cabin was adequate, not luxurious. At his time of life his wants were simple: a firm bed, toilet close at hand, a private space to retreat to with a good book when the bustle on board got intrusive and his leg played up.

He'd enjoyed reacquainting himself with Athens. The great buildings hadn't changed much: familiar yet strange. Greece had its own history unfolding since the occupation, from civil war, *coup d'état*, rising slowly from the ashes of world war, coming to a different understanding of itself, as had Europe since the fall of the Berlin Wall.

After a few days in the city streets he felt layers of his own life unpeeling – the academic career, his retirement, his marriages – back to the kernel of those youthful glory days when he'd believed so utterly in the purposes they'd been given: to secure and defend the Mediterranean seaboards, oil supplies and shipping routes. How they had been deceived. How naïvely trusting in such faulty leadership. Ah, he sighed, the wisdom of hindsight and the arrogance of youth, so many excuses we've made over the years but nothing can change any of it. You have to

live with your actions, live with success and failure, he thought
now, distracted by watching a plane descending overhead.

*It wasn't all bad; those first heady days of victory, the comradeship
of men who made the ultimate sacrifice in the name of duty and honour.
How could I ever deny the bravery of my friends?*

He stood watching the lights of Piraeus harbour slowly fade
into the distance, a last sighting of the majestic Acropolis and
the mountains. Ahead was a long night's crossing. How could
he ever forget the last one he took during the war, that first
sight of the Aegean and the mission to follow? He sighed again.
That mission was a different matter. *Who was it said that raw
recruits had the courage of ignorance, little knowing what terrors lay
ahead when they jumped from the sky?*

May 1941

Rainer Brecht sat with the other officers in the ballroom of the Hotel Grande Bretagne, his eyes adjusting to the darkness as he focused on the screen with its huge map of Crete. He smiled, recognizing its elongated shape from visits in his student days. There was silence as General Student pointed out the three airports targeted for their drop on the north coast.

His regiment must take Maleme, close to the old Venetian capital, Chania. He would have preferred Heraklion, recalling a visit to the city and a trip to Knossos to see the excavations. The island was divided by a string of mountains, the ports were fortified with old Turkish forts and arsenals, and the rest was just olive trees, scrubland and glorious white-sand beaches.

'The British have retreated and their presence is weak – no more than 5,000 troops at the most. Most of them have gone to Egypt. They are exhausted, defeated and badly equipped. Morale is low. And as for the Cretans, we are assured they will be passive, even welcoming in places. Their hospitality is legendary.'

Rainer was puzzled. Were they talking about the same nation that had battled the Turks for their freedom, whose brigades had fought with such distinction in the Albanian campaign? It was not his place to argue with official intelligence on the ground, though, so he sat in silence.

He'd met swarthy hard-drinking Cretans on his travels, men quick to flare up, who held grudges into the next generations and whose idea of a wedding was to abduct their brides. A classical education had taught him much about the Greek peoples, and the Cretans were a race apart.

Once the briefing was over, Rainer went outside, blinking into the afternoon sunshine. Operation Mercury, as it was called, must be kept top secret from his men until the last possible minute. Young boys could be careless in their cups and overenthusiastic in their boasting. They were excited, raring to be in action after so many months in preparation. He was proud of their progress, these volunteers, hand-picked for courage, fitness and leadership.

After a stroll around the National Garden in its springtime glory – purple blossom still hanging on the avenue of trees, the roses, wild lilies and herbs sprouting even among the bombed, charred ruins, reminding him that nature was tougher than man – he sat sipping ouzo, watching the wary looks on the faces of passers-by as they noticed his uniform.

The street urchins hovered, hands outstretched. He liked to throw them coins and watch them scrabble like monkeys, scrapping amongst themselves. Life would be tough for them now; only the fittest would survive. This thought reminded him he must return to the tented camp at Topolia and make sure all their supplies were accounted for. They must be ready at a few hours' notice.

As he drove towards the base, catching glimpses of the blue sea, Rainer reflected that just 160 miles of sea separated them from their targets. The diving eagle clutching a swastika, on his sleeve, was a badge hard won with physical endurance, courage to leap from a plane and land with accuracy on a marked target. Many applied but few were chosen, and those who protested at the hardship were soon dismissed. He had left a cavalry regiment, volunteering for service, pitting his courage against his fears. Taking risks made him feel alive. He looked for the same traits in his men. Some were hardened from years in the Hitler Youth, hotheads, quick to flare up. He favoured the oddballs, the adventurers who loved to take risks, who led from the front. For all his twenty-five years he felt old compared to these boys of barely eighteen: students, farmers' boys and some sons of the old aristocracy.

Who would not be proud of this unit, with its distinctive uniform, a magnet for pretty girls? Not that it had done him much good. He was shy with girls. He was looking for an equal, not a *Hausfrau*, someone with intelligent eyes and keen wit, but so far he'd had no luck. Just as well since this mission was dangerous. Better to wait and see who would turn up when the war was won and he could return to his academic studies.

No more daydreaming, no more sunbathing; their brief holiday was now ending. It was forty degrees and late afternoon, his men were lounging in the shade of the olive groves, curious now about the preparations beginning in earnest.

It was time to check the wooden containers to be parachuted down with them. They had tried to think of everything: fresh bread, sausages, chocolate, caffeine tablets, cigarettes, sulphur tablets and glucose, medical packs in their own containers, a silk handkerchief with a map of the island imprinted on it. Each crate was coloured to denote its contents. Then there were the parachutes packed into plump bundles, two per man, in the hope that the second would speed them on their way eastwards towards Cyprus, once Crete was settled.

'Sir, is it Crete? asked his sergeant. 'We've taken bets it's Cyprus or Crete.'

Rainer smiled. It was too soon to tell them what he'd heard at HQ. 'You just make sure your parachute is fixed and ready, and call in the platoon commanders.'

He gathered his maps and aerial reconnaissance photographs, and placed them on a wooden crate.

His most trusted leaders, Schulze and Genz, squatted down beside him, staring at the pictures on the table. They looked at the map, then at Rainer. 'So it's true then?'

The night before the mission began the quartermaster issued extra beer and brandy, and as the boys relaxed over campfires, Rainer heard their mouth organs playing their battle hymn, 'Red shines the sun'. He found it hard to sleep, knowing that they would be taking off tomorrow.

In the morning he made everyone strip down his gun. A paratrooper was useless without his armaments.

He watched their faces, eager to please, excited and hopeful, and for a second his heart shivered. None of them knew what lay in store once they had landed. He wished they could be certain of a welcome from the Cretans.

Then before take-off came the last task. Each of them crated his own private belongings and effects, along with a will and a last letter home. Rainer filled his crate with his books: Plato, Thoreau, the plays of William Shakespeare and poems of Goethe. There were souvenirs he'd gathered for his brother's children, some lace for his mother and sister, Katerina, cigars for his father and that last letter home. Should he not return, this would all be sent to comfort them.

He thought then of the commandments of the regiment: be calm and prudent, strong and resolute in valour and enthusiasm. Be of an offensive spirit and this will cause you to prevail in battle. Would that it would be so easy? They were flying onto a fortressed island and God only knew how many of them would be flying back. It was his duty to keep his men as safe as possible, to lead the best way he knew. He prayed he would be up to the task.

He'd seen enough now to know that the emblem 'God with Us' was a joke. There was nothing of God in this war, but that was something he must keep to himself.

Early in the morning, he watched the first of the Junkers taking off on the dusty runway, blinding the planes behind them with sand. The sight of the wooden gliders being towed behind them filled him with unease, knowing a dozen men were strapped into these flimsy crates packed with equipment, chutes, and life jackets in case they should ditch into the sea.

Then a runner brought an order already two days old, which he read with disbelief.

Contrary to previous assumptions, enemy strength estimated around 12,000 has now been revised upwards to 48,000 men . . .

Rainer felt an icy chill running through his body. They were sending 4,000 of their finest troops, lightly armed, against an army entrenched and fortified with artillery pointing in their direction. He felt sick at the thought that if this information was true he was sending himself and half his men to certain death.

May 2001

The flight from London was straightforward and we'd spent a night in the Hotel Grande Bretagne in Constitution Square. How busy it all looked. The last time I was here there was a gun emplacement outside and queues of Brits hollering for papers and transit advice, keen to flee the city that had given them such a wonderful life.

I kept gazing out at the planes heading into Athens, silver birds full of happy tourists. How could I not think of the black hawks that dived down, spewing fire over our heads in those last days nursing in 1940? How had I survived such danger?

Then I recalled that very last time I had seen Athens. It had lain in ruins, as I did too, broken, a city reduced to rubble and filth, fit only for rats and cockroaches. I didn't want to think of that time. How lovely to see it now, risen from those ashes. But the past can't be ignored. What I experienced there made me who I am today, a survivor. Our ferry was waiting in Piraeus harbour, full of both tourists and locals: students in shorts plugged into phones and personal stereos, Cretan families returning from shopping trips. No one could miss those strong dark, almond eyes, babies nursed by *yiayia*s with cropped hair in shades of ebony and aubergine, widows in dark-spotted Crimplene suits, playing cards and chattering in that thick guttural accent I half-remembered.

There was a party of old British soldiers in blazers with regimental badges, reliving old times, no doubt, en route to the coming ceremony. Were their memories like mine – sepia snaps, faded and foxed with age? Already old images were beginning to rise in my mind.

It was hard to sleep with all the strange noises: the ship's engines, the rattle of pipework, children racing in the corridor. Better to rise early before the ship docked in Souda Bay.

I stood on deck, warmly wrapped as the midnight of the dark sea slowly merged into the rich turquoise in the shallows, the sun rising on the snow-capped outlines of the White Mountains, tingeing them like golden highlights on greying hair. Oh, yes, I felt my lungs opening to the scented air, seeing small cubic houses on the shoreline. I smiled. It was all coming back to me: the colours of Crete, which have shaded my dreams for years.

Chania,
May 1941

At first light the island slowly took shape out of the mist rising between sea and sky, a range of snow-capped mountain peaks and rocks falling down to the sea, as the *Amalia* limped past artillery batteries high on a fort jutting out into the bay. The sun rose, capping the mountain tops with a lemony light. Ahead was a harbour with a jetty hard-pressed on every side by warships and boats and yachts: a sorry flotilla of wounded vessels from the north carrying in the remnants of the British armies, the men hanging over the sides, staring blankly with tired faces. All around was the smell of smoke, burning rubber and cordite, evidence of recent bombing raids.

The children on their caïque were subdued, still shocked from their ordeal. The women huddled together, not knowing what to expect. The sea was calm but grey and muddied, echoing this picture of retreat and defeat.

'You will stay with us in Chania,' Judy Harrington insisted. 'You need a rest and the children respond to you. Gordon's made arrangements for us to stay in a villa. Thank God he went on ahead. Poor Angela is distraught losing Edmund like that and not able to bring his body . . .'

'I must stay with the patients, see to them first.' Penny didn't want to commit herself until she knew the score. She was betwixt and between, neither an official army nurse nor orderly, but someone might want her services.

'Is there a hospital?' she asked Bruce as they sipped mugs of welcome tea, shoved into their hands on embarkation. There was a mêlée of troops, dockers, local men, ambulances, carts, trucks. Judy fell into her husband's arms with relief, glad their ordeal was finally over. Angela hung back, gathering her children, white-faced. Her ordeal had only just begun, Penny feared.

'The field hospital's out west of the town on the shore. It's pretty busy. Not a place for a young girl,' said Judy's husband, Gordon, looking her up and down.

'Darling, she was Florence Nightingale out there. Half these men would be dead without her,' Judy rallied to her defence.

'I can be useful there. These men need attention,' Penny replied.

'You're not an army nurse,' Gordon continued. 'They'll be shipping them out soon.'

'I rather think I am now, Gordon. Do you think they'll refuse another pair of hands?'

'Is she being awkward again?' Bruce interrupted, walking over. 'Evadne will be furious if we don't get her out in one piece.'

'I'm not a child. Don't order me about like one of your minions. I will take these men for treatment and see you all later.' Penny stormed off.

'But you don't know where we'll be . . . I'll pick you up later and that's an order,' Bruce yelled back, but she wasn't listening.

They'd been glad enough of her services on the boat. She was not going to lounge in some villa, drinking cocktails, waiting for some ship to take them to Egypt when there was work to be done.

She jumped into the ambulance truck, looking out from the rear at the organized chaos in the port. There were exhausted men unloading crates, barefoot and shirtless in the sunshine. She felt filthy and sweaty, desperate for a bath, but her charges needed dressings checked and temps taken, first. She was sure two of them had infections. Being mucked up was one of the hazards of any nurse's life. Daily baths and changes of clothes at least twice a day were a luxury from the past, no longer a priority, but she could still dream of them at a time like this.

The nurse driving the truck was an Aussie in battledress, who knew her way around the winding narrow streets of Chania. Penny checked her carpetbag of possessions and clutched her cloak with affection. It had been, in turn, a screen, a blanket, a makeshift shroud, a uniform and a shield, and she didn't want to be parted from it.

She felt a strange sense of freedom driving through this foreign town, so different from Athens. It sprawled from Souda in the east in a straight line following the shore. The squat cube houses with flat roofs, by the side of dusty tracks, were shuttered against the heat, the lines of buildings broken by lush groves of oranges and lemons and olive trees. The streets were shaded by tall avenues of plane trees, and others she didn't recognize.

They crawled in a convoy behind donkey carts and mules laden with panniers. Everywhere cheery faces smiled at them – women in black headscarves, barefoot children running alongside them – and barking dogs snarled at the wheels. As they drew into the centre of the town, larger houses rose up, stuccoed, with balconies and painted shutters, smarter residences in classical style with elegant windows and wrought-iron gates. Then they swung left and climbed out of the main streets towards a high promontory, then down towards a rocky shore-line where huts and tents with a Union flag flying high announced their destination was close.

Galatas beach looked pristine, tents fluttering in the breeze, organized between road and sea with rocky outcrops sheltering it from some of the breezes. There was some shade from cypress and olive trees, but it was overflowing with new arrivals and orderlies were lined up giving instructions. Penny had only her passport, her uniform and badges, her gold watch and Yolanda's precious hanky, now covered in blood, but she wasn't above dropping a few important names – all Walter's connections at the embassy if need be – should they refuse her entrance.

Fat chance. They were waved towards a clearing station where Anzac nurses were taking name and rank, and siphoning off the wounded for treatment.

In other times this would be a beautiful spot for sea bathing, with its gentle slope, sandy beach and view right across Chania Bay. Penny wanted to strip off her torn khaki shorts and make-shift uniform, run into the glistening jade sea, and feel the cool salty water on her skin. There was work to be done, however. She must register her presence and get on with anything they needed done.

The sister took her particulars, and when she heard the name of Arta, and Kifissia Hospital and Penny's experience, she ordered her to find a clean uniform and a billet, assuming she would be staying until shipped off the island. 'We're holding a service of thanksgiving this afternoon. Do join us.'

'What for?' Penny asked in all innocence. She couldn't think of anything to be thankful for, seeing what she had these last months.

The sister looked shocked. 'We must be grateful to have evacuated so many gallant men to safety. We are all still stand-ing. My dear friend was on the hospital ferry *Hellas*, taking wounded men and civilians out. They never got out of the harbour; burned alive.'

Penny shivered, thinking of Yolanda, almost certainly dead by now.

For the service a rock was draped with the Union flag. The two jam jars stuffed with wild flowers set before it made her want to cry. They spoke of rock pools and freedom and mead-ows, not tents and death and disinfectant.

When twilight fell she joined Sally and her friends, and they found a secluded part of the beach, stripped off and ran into the chilly water, splashing and swimming. It was sheer relief to be off duty for a few hours.

'Let's enjoy this while we can,' Sally said. 'We'll hitch a lift into town. You have to see the harbour, or what's left of it. There's a place that sells the best ice cream in the world, just off the cathedral square.'

Penny had hardly anything left in her carpetbag that hadn't been torn up for bandages. The town was bustling with narrow alleyways running off the harbour. There'd been terrible bomb damage but people were strolling around, intent on their business, scrabbling over debris, and some shops were still open and stocked. Penny bought a pretty lacy blouse to replace the shirt she'd ripped up. They wandered through the covered agora, buying almonds and nuts, soap and oil, then Penny's friends took her to Leather Alley off Halidon Street, which smelled of hide and polish. Here, cobblers and saddlers hung their wares across the narrow passageway. This was where the Cretan soldiers bought their knee-high boots; boots she had often had to saw off to get to her patients' wounds. Penny haggled for a slim purse on a waist belt, big enough to hide her papers, some sovereigns she'd concealed in her shoes, a small silver brandy flask, her gold watch and her precious hanky. It was a 'be prepared' trick one of the older nurses had taught her in Athens, should she need emergency cash and courage.

The nurses found the ice-cream parlour off the square and watched the world go by as the sky darkened. For an hour at least they could relax in the warmth of a summer evening and share their nursing experiences while watching a sky full of swifts screeching and wheeling overhead. Penny explained about being trained by the Greek Red Cross and her journey across from the mainland.

'We'd've taken you for an officer,' Sally said, passing her

cigarettes around the group, offering one to Penny. 'And your Greek is so good.'

Penny shook her head; she didn't feel like smoking. 'I'm just a volunteer but we did see action on the Albanian front,' she added, wanting them to know she was no shirker from duty.

The nurses nodded in sympathy. Having come down with the New Zealanders in retreat they knew about the hardships there.

'They say all the Cretan fighting men are still stuck, up north. God help the poor civilians here when the raids come again. They've no idea what's coming their way. You've seen the state of our troops: hardly a gun or a pair of boots between them. It's a shambles. Glad to be out of it,' Sally sighed. 'And we're needed in Egypt. It's no bed of roses there either.'

'So who's to be left nursing here?' Penny asked.

'Just the male staff and orderlies. All the females are leaving. Orders are orders,' Sally replied.

But I've only just got here, Penny thought. Why must I leave? I'm not under their orders. I haven't seen anything of the island or its people, or any of its famous archaeology except in books. She thought of the School of Archaeology with longing and wondered where all the students were now. But she said nothing. Here, protocol was strict and military discipline tight. There was no mixing. She could see why the nurses would be whisked away from the front.

'Just remembered, I promised someone I'd visit, some women from the boat,' she said, standing up. 'Good luck! See you back at camp.'

Better not to linger here with these nurses in case she got caught up in their imminent evacuation to Egypt. She needed time to think. Perhaps she ought to head out to Judy Harrington's house in the diplomatic quarter of the city for a while. Better to lie low, bide her time and spruce up her Greek Red Cross uniform, what was left of it, just in case. Who knew when it might come in handy again?

She collected her belongings, found a horse-drawn cab and made her way up towards Halepa and the district where the Harringtons were lodging, paying off the cab and searching on foot for a villa called Stella Vista. She found a large elegant town house right on the top of a cliff, with a wonderful view across the Akrotiri peninsula and the whole of Chania Bay.

Just as she opened the iron garden-gate Gordon came rushing out.

'Good, you've arrived. Go and help Judy out . . . Angela's in such a state. Must rush . . . Things to do, things to do . . .'

Angela was sitting nursing a whisky glass, a blank expression on her white face.

'The children keep asking what happened to Daddy. How can I tell them? What will become of us?' She was rocking back and forth in her chair, shivering.

'I hope you made that a strong one,' Penny said to Judy, indicating the glass. 'She's still in shock. Where's she billeted?'

'Here with Nanny. We all are . . . there are ten bedrooms,' Judy replied. 'Might as well all stay put. We'll be shipped out in days so I hope you are packed and ready to go.'

Penny smiled, lifting up her shabby carpetbag. 'I'm afraid this bag is the sum of my wardrobe. How are the crew?'

'In a clinic. Bruce saw to them. Good chap in a crisis, isn't he? You two know each other, I gather.'

Penny could see Judy speculating. 'He's a friend of Walter and Evadne, my sister and her husband,' she told her, 'but I've no idea what regiment he's in. He keeps popping up out of the blue.'

Judy smiled, tapping her nose. 'We don't know so we can never tell . . . Part of some overseas outfit, all hush-hush behind the scenes. His Greek is useful here – not as good as yours, of course, and you're so brown you could pass for a native. How're things at the hospital?'

'They're getting ready to ship out the nurses and the worst cases. Sand is no place for wounds, the flies are unbelievable and the dust gets everywhere. It'll be a skeleton staff after that.'

Later, in the room to which Judy showed her, Penny stared out across the bay. It all looked so beautiful, and with the luxury of a bath and a bed with crisp cotton sheets under a net, the war seemed more distant than it had done for weeks. She lay listening to the night sounds: the wind, the hoot of an owl in the tree, the whimper of a child in an upper room. Suddenly her limbs turned to lead and she sank into the dreamless sleep of exhaustion.

She was woken by the roar of engines, the whistle of bombs and the crump of gunfire. Opening the shutters, to her amazement she saw a line of Stukas flying at window-level across the bay towards Souda, where anti-aircraft guns blasted out their riposte.

'There goes our wake-up call, on time as usual. Get the kiddies down to the basement for a game of ping pong,' Gordon ordered, making light of the raid.

Penny was worried about Sally and her nurse friends on Galatas beach. Surely the Germans wouldn't bomb a hospital? But no one was letting her leave to find out until the raid was over.

Somehow the morning was taken up with preparing meals, sorting out the children, while there were comings and goings to the British HQ in the old prime minister's residence.

Judy decided to organize a tea run for troops sheltering in the olive groves by the docks. 'They're softening us up for the kill, demoralizing the locals and the troops, making life difficult and cutting off supplies,' she said. 'I think we should gather up a few tins of our own and make a stash, just in case we're stranded here.'

Ever practical, Judy was trying to keep everyone busy, taking their minds off the danger. Even Angela was rising to the effort.

This was Penny's moment to pick her way back to Galatas beach and report for duty.

She had gathered her cloak, was preparing to leave, when Gordon returned with Bruce, both covered in smoke and ash dust.

'Been burning papers at HQ, just a precaution. Don't want Jerry or any quislings reading our reports. Bruce has got some good news. There's a ship out tomorrow so it's time to pack for a sea voyage.'

'Darling, there's nothing to pack,' Judy replied. 'But there may be time to nip into the town and buy a few bits for the children while the shops are open.'

'Better be off then,' Penny said, sidling towards the door, but Gordon barred her path.

'Not so fast, young lady, this means you too.'

'Sorry, but I'm under orders at the hospital. I must do my bit there.'

'You'll do as you're told,' Gordon snapped. 'You are under consul orders.'

She pushed past him, determined to escape, but Bruce strode after her and took her by the arm. 'This isn't some game we're playing here, Penelope. Things are hotting up. This is no place for women once the show starts.'

'Tell that to the Cretan women. Where do *they* hide?'

'Their families will take care of them in the hills. They are not your concern.'

She stood defiant. 'I'm Red Cross. Civilians are my concern too.'

'Don't be a martyr, this isn't your fight,' he said, his eyes blazing.

'Isn't it? I'm half Greek, a nurse by training and experience. The Red Cross takes no sides, remember.'

'Do you think any of that matters once battle begins? Grow up, Pen. You're a liability. *Women* are a liability . . .'

'Listen to yourself, you pompous ass! We weren't a liability on the *Amalia* or on the island, or have you forgotten who patched you up? I'm not leaving yet, not until I have orders. There's a job needs doing on the wards. I'm sick of running away. I'll go when there's no longer a job for me to do. You can tell Gordon to give my ticket to someone else. And don't you order me about any more.'

Bruce smiled down at her. 'You're magnificent when you're angry. Come on, let me at least buy you luncheon somewhere. I think you need to think this all through with a glass in your hand.'

'I ought to be heading back. I'm already late.' Penny hesitated, aware that duty should come first, but not knowing when she'd see him again. If she'd ever see him again. His company would take her mind off what lay ahead and she owed him for getting her out of Athens.

'Late for what? You're not really official, are you? Is there a record of your work? Come on, I know a place where we can get good local fish. Then I'll see you back safely; the roads are not exactly pristine. I shall be off soon, I expect, so a couple of hours won't make any difference.'

It was no good, when Bruce spun his silken web she was trapped. He'd always have that effect on her. A short break wouldn't do any harm. He led her to an open-topped two-seater truck and then she found herself bumping along up the coast, over the rutted tracks, her hair wrapped round her face like a scarf.

They were heading up towards the Akrotiri coastline, down narrow tracks and past guard posts, gun emplacements, winding through olive grove tracks and past golden stone monasteries, ancient turrets glinting in the fierce May sun. Then they were at a crossroads where some small houses jutted out and a little *kafenion* had chairs onto the street.

Here Bruce introduced her to Kyria Chrystoulaa, who showed her the fish which her husband had caught that morning before his boat was almost shot out of the sea.

She baked the tiny fish in a salty crust and served it with oil and lemon juice, and a plate of mountain herbs freshly picked from the fields. As she and Bruce washed down this simple and delicious food with a jug of village wine, Penny felt herself relaxing for the first time in weeks, as if there was no more war.

She looked across at Bruce and smiled. 'Thanks, but this changes nothing. I'm staying put. No one orders me about now.'

'Don't be prickly, Pen. It doesn't suit you.'

'What gives you the right to tell me what I must do?'

'I care about you. I feel responsible for bringing you into all this,' Bruce replied, his eyebrow raised in a challenge.

'Don't flatter yourself!' she said. 'When I refused to leave Athens with Effy and Walter's friends, I knew it was the right thing to do, to make something of myself. I'm not giving up now. I'm not afraid.'

'That's what scares me. You should be afraid. There's one hell of a storm coming and no one knows how it will end. I'd hate to think of you in some prisoner of war camp behind wire – or worse. It will be ugly.'

'It was ugly in Arta, or have you forgotten last winter? Believe me, I saw things there . . . I will cope. I know deep in here,' she said, patting her chest, 'this is what I was put on this earth to do, to help people who are sick. I can't explain, but coming to Athens just to be free from family changed when I started nursing. Suddenly it's a matter of life and death, and here now on Crete even more so. This is my journey, my vocation, my destiny, and I have no regrets . . . This is my battle as well as yours.'

They fell silent as if her outburst had shaken both of them. Bruce grabbed hold of her hand. 'Then good luck! You'll need it.'

'And you too,' she said, putting her other hand over his. 'We've come a long way since the Highland Ball.'

'I can see you still sitting in the library in that awful frock.'

'It was rather dreadful, so frilly . . . Where will you go now?' Penny asked, sensing the intimacy growing.

'Wherever I'm sent . . . can't say much, but now you see me, then you won't. Who knows where I'll be tomorrow? Be careful, Penny, don't trust any strangers if the worst happens and we're defeated. Your presence will be already registered here. They watch the ports and the cafés to see who is new in town. You're easy to recognize. Go native, perfect your accent. Say you're from Athens and you'll get by. Blend in, don't stand out, dye your hair, cover up and act Greek. You are taller than most women here . . .'

'What are you trying to tell me, Bruce?'

'Only that if things go badly, they'll need nurses in the hills with the *francs-tireurs*, the freedom fighters,' he whispered. 'Look to the hills. You're a mountain goat, use your legs and head into the mountains if the worst happens.'

'You don't think we can win this battle?' she asked in surprise.

He paused, looking around to make sure none of the other diners was in earshot. 'I don't know, I honestly don't think our men have enough stamina, arms or guns to see it through, but we won't be leaving the island in the lurch. That's all I can say.' He looked at his wristwatch and sighed. 'Time to get you back to base.'

The drive back was silent, both of them lost in private thoughts. Any romantic notions Penny had sensed had been quashed by Bruce's pessimism. He was heading into danger; whatever he was doing was clandestine, a secret mission he mustn't discuss. He'd told her enough for her to know she must make her own plans too, and she wondered if she would be more useful with the other nurses on board a hospital ship after all. It was one thing being brave and daring and willing to serve, but another matter to put others in danger should she have to flee again. If she was caught as an alien amongst the locals they might be shot.

Bruce dropped her off at the guard post on the beach. She stood waving to him, listening to the screech of the tyres as the spray of sand gritted her eyes, wondering just when he'd appear again. His company was always such a delight, she sighed. Was this the beginning of a new relationship between them at last?

There was something different about the place now. It was quieter, with not so many prostrate men on the shoreline. She made for the hospital barracks and bumped into Douglas Forsyth, her senior medical officer.

'Good Lord! What are you doing here?' he shouted.

'Reporting for duty, sir. Sorry I'm late. There was a raid . . .'

'Never mind that . . . why aren't you on the ship?' There was a puzzled look on his sunburned face.

'What ship?'

'They've gone without you, Nurse. They all shipped out under cover, took on board the worst cases and all the female staff for Egypt. God Almighty, you weren't on base, were you? You've missed the bloody boat.'

Penny's resolve shook at the news. Escape from the island was no longer a choice. She was stranded. Oh yes, it was one thing choosing to stay on but another when the choice was taken from her. Suddenly the reality of deliberately staying away hit her. You've done it now, she sighed, her heart thumping, and her courage failed for a moment but she swallowed back her panic and took a deep breath.

'I'm billeted with a consul family; I'm Red Cross.'

'You'd better leave with them. I can't have you here, one female, hundreds of soldiers, wouldn't be proper.'

'Sir, I can still assist; you know I'm experienced.' Nurses didn't argue with doctors but Penny was beyond such formalities. 'Surely a pair of hands is a pair of hands.'

'It's the rest of you that's a problem. It's against regulations. Where will you mess? Not with the orderlies . . . You're officer class. I can't have you singled out . . .'

Just at that moment the second in command arrived, Dr Ellis. 'Two more silly asses with sunstroke . . . Nurse George, can you deal with them? I've got five more cases of the squits need isolating or the whole camp with come down with it. Doug, have you a moment? There's a private who needs looking at; don't like the look of his back?'

Penny shot out before Forsyth could call her back. They would sort out logistics later. She went to collect the tubes to give the patients cold enemas, a transfusion of salt and glucose, and ordered lots of cold water from the well. These fair-skinned soldiers were suckers for the sun, lying about with no idea how dangerous it was in such shadeless terrain.

Penny sped on her way, knowing tomorrow she must formalize her position here with the authorities, irregular though it may be. They might protest, but she was Greek Red Cross; if necessary she could be transferred locally. The ship leaving without her was a sign. The decision had been made for her. This is where she was meant to stay, and stay she would.

2001

'I know, it sounds so implausible, Lois, doesn't it? Me being the only British nurse left on the island. "You've done it now," I thought. Part of me had always known the risk I was taking. Yet part of me couldn't believe it at first and kept searching round for Sally and the other girls. Surely someone else had hidden or forgotten the time, not heard the call back to camp, but no. I was the crazy one, left clutching little but my principles, and feeling my gut churning up,' I said as we drove up the new National Highway, heading eastwards in a hired car from the port in Souda Bay, following printed instructions on how to find our villa. 'I just stayed at my post and got on with the job, until things changed.'

'One woman and thousands of men, how did you manage?' Lois asked, while concentrating on driving on the right.

'They brought me my food and I had a room of my own. I never went out at first, just on my rounds. Then, once things hotted up, well, all that formality went by the board but that's another story.'

We turned off the main road, down towards the coast and the villages overlooking the bay, down a winding lane towards a village with a brightly coloured church at its heart. Then we turned down a winding drive to a fine two-storey stone house with a balcony on the first floor. It had an olive grove to the side, a courtyard in the shade and a gravel drive for the car. There was a sparkling swimming pool, which caught Alex's eye immediately, and he shot out to examine it. I didn't recognize any of it, though the name of the village, Kalyves, struck a chord somewhere in the back of my mind.

'Do you like it?' Lois was looking anxious for a positive response. 'I thought you'd like something with character.'

'I think it's charming. We can walk into the village for supplies.'

'You know it, then?'

'I'm not sure. I can sense the sea isn't far and there will be shops. I think we'll be fine here but I insist you and Alex must not hang about for me. Take him on trips. I can hire someone to drive me when I need it, but now I could do with a cool room and drink.'

Inside was chilly after the sun's warmth. The hall had patterned marble floors, and a fan rattled overhead. There were clean simple furnishings and heavy dark-wooded tables and chairs, lace drapes and tablecloths, wall hangings and old prints.

'You must choose your own room, Aunt Pen,' Lois insisted.

'The one nearest the bathroom will do,' I laughed.

'I counted twelve shrines on the way here,' Alex piped up. 'Why do they have pictures in them and lamps?'

'To remind us life is short and brutal sometimes, and memories are long. The lamp burns as a prayer for the dead to be remembered and a photo helps keep them alive. I think it is a nice custom.'

'When you die, shall we put one in the garden for you?'

'Alex!' Lois gasped.

'I would be very honoured but I think the people who bought my house might not want my ugly mug stuck in their flower borders.' I laughed.

'Can I have a swim?'

'Only if one of us is watching,' Lois warned. 'I'll take you exploring later and we can make plans. It says there's a sailing school close by, we could take lessons.'

'Cool,' he said, racing up the staircase to explore.

I, too, retreated upstairs and quickly chose my room. From the window was the most glorious view of the White Mountains of the Apokoronas, still snow-capped even in the heat of the late afternoon.

I felt tired but excited. After all these years of absence, why did I feel as if I was coming home again, back to those heady dangerous weeks in May sixty years ago? If truth be told, I'd felt a strange connection the moment we entered into the bay and I saw the harbour, smelled the diesel fumes and oily seawater, heard that loud guttural accent. I also had a strange feeling that my arrival was the beginning of something important. It was hard to explain what I was feeling deep inside.

I peered out of the front window. In the distance I could see people going about their business in jeans and black shirts, on scooters and mopeds, and tourists in sundresses and shorts. Part of me was expecting to see everyone in traditional dress: breeches, cloaks, lace bandanas and white boots. Customs had changed, Europe was closer now. Then an old woman, bent, with a stick, covered head to toe in widow's weeds with the full black headscarf covering her chin, came into view, taking me back instantly to those far-off days before the onslaught began in earnest on 20 May. That was the date none of us would ever forget.

I looked up into that ink-blue sky, half expecting to see what we saw then, and I shivered, hearing again the little girl shouting, '*Kyria*, look! Come and see! Men with umbrellas are falling from the sky!'

Rainer Brecht sat staring from his hotel balcony in Platanias, sipping a bottle of Mythos beer from the minibar.

The taxi, sent to collect him from the port, had rattled along the by-pass heading west of Chania, to a holiday resort still in the process of construction, judging by the concrete lorries blocking the main street. The driver tried out his excellent English and German after checking if his passenger spoke any Greek.

When the old man complimented him, the boy smiled and said his family had lived in America for a while. 'Now we are home.' Rainer was glad the boy didn't ask the obvious question, 'Were you here during the war?' but it hovered just the same. He was the right age to be a veteran.

Their journey took him through many familiar routes, though the olive groves had shrunk, replaced by harsh concrete buildings. Chania was still sprawling out towards the high hills, an outline that he hoped would never change, but the mule carts and donkeys had been replaced by battered cars and bikes and smart buses. There was investment beginning, but here and there he spotted familiar squatted shacks and old houses dwarfed by high-rise apartments, and homes with iron rods sticking out of the flat roofs, ready for another storey to be added. It was a world away from the one they had jumped into in 1941.

Out in the bay he could see a distant island rising from the aquamarine sparkling water. The sea never changed its appeal or yielded its secret store of bones. He'd chosen this hotel for its bland anonymity. It was rough round the edges still, three stars, spotless, soulless. There was a smell of fresh paint ready for the new season, newly laid paths to the shingly beach. It was quiet, suiting his purposes well enough. This was a personal pilgrimage, a time for reflection. He could smell barbecue smoke and music blaring somewhere. He hoped it wouldn't be intrusive or he would move on. He had not hired a car – his eyes were no longer reliable – but he would hire taxis for his trips into the interior.

The snapshots he'd collected over the years didn't do justice to the colours of Crete. He was too late for the famous spring flower meadows, the heat had dried them out. He had a wallet full of sepia shots of his old brothers in arms and lined them up on the bed. How relaxed they all looked, smiling in the sun in shots taken on some forgotten beach before they set out on their campaign, none of them realizing what lay ahead. He had nothing else to honour them by but flashes of memory, and their ever-youthful faces, these silent ghosts who haunted his dreams, brave young men who never saw another dawn. He had come to pay his respects and recall each one of them.

How could they have known what was awaiting them right here in the sea, in the hills, olive groves and ditches just down the road?

No one knew that they were rushing headlong into the swallowing jaws of hellfire, or that their sacrifices would change the course of military history.

20 May 1941

The transport planes flew out at first light towards Crete, in formation, skimming the water then rising over the mountains, heading west to their target, landing close to the western airstrip at Maleme. As they sat facing each other, Rainer had time to examine the eager faces of his men, wearing wool jumpsuits full of pockets, heads protected by new rimless helmets. Some grinned with confidence, others, grim-faced, kept checking their harnesses and kit, silently lost in the discomfort of the flight. How young they all looked with their bronzed features. He felt a stab of fear for them all.

Then came the guns roaring at their approach and he saw tension flash among them as the Junkers swerved but thundered on their course. The radio operator yelled, 'Get ready, Crete.'

Rainer saw its shape, familiar from their briefings, coming ever closer in the morning light. They juddered down low and then swooped up to avoid being struck. He felt his stomach turn over as their target position appeared.

Some of the men started to sing their anthem to steady the nerves. 'No road back . . .' rang in his ears. Now, primitive instinct and months of training kicked in as they stood ready to harness up and check their chutes. He must be first out, leading the way by example as they leaped into the cruciform shape in free fall.

It was a strange sensation to leap from the sky, full of such power and adrenaline. Then came seconds of panic, waiting for the first chute to open. He felt the jerk and the lightening relief, but he turned in horror to see one of his boys caught on the end of the plane, his harness ripped as he fell like a stone to earth.

Suddenly the lush green valley spread before them and he saw the lake. They were close to the prison compound that must be secured as their base. The ammunition crates were floating down, and supplies, suspended from chutes of different colours, and they must be found before the enemy got hold of them. They were out there watching, waiting for the right moment to pounce. He must get his men under cover and armed as quickly as he could.

Rainer landed without mishap, but he saw some of his men fall into the trees, and he heard the rattle of small-arms fire and a roar of angry voices. Suddenly all hell broke loose, and he watched in horror as his men were shot out of the sky like ducks. Their chutes were set on fire, ripped, and they jerked helplessly like puppets, brave handsome paratroopers shredded by fire before they had even reached the ground. For a second he was enraged at such lack of chivalry but he realized this was no ordinary battle in which you set up your lines and marched in. Once they arrived they were target practice for troops on the ground.

He yelled for them to hide in the olive groves and dry river beds. Everyone was scattered out of sniper shot, alone in a cat-and-mouse game with the enemy. It was hot and the jumpsuits were heavy. He'd lost his water bottle in a skirmish with a Tommy, sniping from the branch of a tree. He'd knocked him off with a bullet through the face. He felt no pity. It was either kill or be killed. He crawled his way out of danger, out of the close-range fire. He could hear a terrible racket going on some-where west. The sky was black with planes and men, but nothing was going to plan, and there was no welcoming party to greet them, as had been assured, only a hail of bullets. No road back indeed.

'This is the big one! The sky's black with the bastards!' yelled the Scottish orderly who was helping Penny move the stretcher cases further under cover. The guns had been screaming at the plague of black hornets discharging their load since first light. Wave upon wave came overhead. Orders were to get the walking wounded into slit trenches.

'Helmets on. Can't they see Red Crosses marked in the bloody sand?' Douglas Forsyth yelled. 'Nurse, get yourself out of the line of fire!'

Penny pretended she couldn't hear him as she guided some men from the tented marquee to the newly dug defensive trenches. It was slow work and the noise from above was terrifying.

She'd wandered round the exposed site only the night before, wondering where there was some decent cover. Whoever designated this site for the hospital ought, themselves, to be shot. All she could see were caves, and she'd suggested to the doctors they might be useful should things get worse.

Dr Ellis had dismissed her with a wave of his hand. 'Have you seen the state of those filthy holes? They're full of goat shit and worse. I wouldn't stall a horse in there.'

'But they're dark and cool. We could clean them up. At least we'd be out of range,' she had argued. In vain. Whoever listened to a nurse? 'There's four decent ones and they go back some way into the rock. We could store supplies in there. Better than being in flimsy tents open to the air.'

'Good Lord, look to the west. Is that what I think it is?' Ellis was pointing now to hundreds of yellow, red and green parachutes floating down, opening with what looked like dummies hanging on the end of them, which suddenly jerked into life.

'It's raining Jerry,' said Forsyth, pausing for a second before turning his attention back to his patient.

Penny watched the gliders hover over the sea, ditching and disappearing into the waves. The bombed buildings on the

shore were raging into a furnace and some of the enemy para-
chutists were sucked right down into them. Behind them came
a wave of other gliders jerking on the end of ropes like ghost
riders, discharging men into the sea and onto the rocks before
crashing, themselves, into splintered pieces on the distant shore.
It was a terrible haunting sight of certain death for those men
trapped as the Bofors guns blasted into them.

In response, the bullets from the low-flying planes tore into
the tent fabric and the hospital barracks. Everyone who had a
weapon was shooting the invaders but still they kept coming.

'What happens if they land here?' Penny asked, but no one
answered.

She watched burning planes crash and men struggling to
swim ashore. What if one of them were her own brother,
Zander? Helplessly she watched men drown, though one or
two scrambled exhausted onto the shore. They would soon be
prisoners. Then, to her horror, she saw armed figures darting
from the village, leaping out to kill the invaders as if they were
seals in a cull. She screamed for the guards to take them as prisoners, but no one was listening. Each of these boys was
someone's child, someone's husband, only doing their duty.
She had taken vows as a Red Cross nurse to help all wounded
soldiers, but now she was in battledress and British colours, and
under British orders. She felt torn between trying to help them,
and her duty to the wounded in the hospital crying out for help.
She had to look away, she couldn't bear to see the slaughter.

The number of wounded started to pile up on the beach, and
some of the paratroopers were carried in with the most appalling injuries, beaten senseless by village people angered at the
bombing and the invasion. Others were burned, blinded and
traumatized, young boys, frightened they would be executed
on the spot, wetting themselves in terror and crying out in pain.
Ellis and Forsyth were working flat out to save whoever they
could.

'Put them in the caves out of sight,' Ellis ordered, pointing to the rocks. 'This isn't going to end today, is it?'

The hospital was beginning to resemble an abbatoir, and confusion reigned.

Suddenly there was gunfire at close range and shouting in German in earshot as a group of paratroopers raced through the hospital grounds, demanding those who could should stand up and walk in front of them onto the road. Penny, breathless with fear, slipped away unnoticed and hid with the prisoners in the cave as the doctors were marched off in a makeshift shield. The German prisoners cried out to their own comrades that they were safe in the caves, and so Penny, hiding among them, was left undiscovered.

For several hours Penny worked on alone, terrified of what was happening outside, not daring to look out or even imagine how this might end. Stay at your post, look after the men no matter what. You can do no more than your best. *Courage mon brave*, she prayed for the strength to stay calm and face death if needs be. If this was to be the end then so be it

It was the longest afternoon of her life, swallowing back the fear and panic that rose in her throat like bile, but there were too many injured to nurse for the luxury of worrying about herself. *When I have time, then I will worry*, she mused. Then there was a roar of shooting, and, when the noise had faded, she saw the doctors walking back, accompanied by some New Zealanders, distinguished by their slouch hats. Penny felt such a relief at their appearance, wanting to fling her arms round them both but she held back, knowing a nurse must behave with dignity at all times.

'Thank God you're in one piece,' said Forsyth waving his stethoscope at her. 'We gave them a dose of their own medicine.'

Dr Ellis explained to her that the paratroopers had been ambushed from behind and the hospital was safe – for the moment. Immediately it was back to work as normal, though rumours were rife of fresh enemy landings in Maleme.

'It's all over,' said one of the orderlies, smiling, more in hope than truth.

'Not from where I'm standing.' Forsyth wiped his ashen face. 'Those men are well armed and mean business. What a bloody cock-up. Here we are, stuck in no man's land between the airport and Chania, right in their firing line, sitting ducks ready to be picked off.'

He turned to Penny with a shrug and a smile. 'I think those caves look like the Dorchester to me and, Nurse, you proved a point steering those prisoners in there. You must get yourself out of sight, young lady. You should not be here,' he said, lifting his hand as if to make her disappear. 'But I'm bloody glad you are.'

Under cover of darkness they examined each cave in turn, with surgical masks on their faces to weaken the force of the stench, which was unbearable.

'Any port in a storm, eh?' said Dr Forsyth. 'What do you think, Ellis?'

'Nurse George is right: it's out of the wind, sun and rain, and we can hide the entrance with sheeting. This one's for us and for the operating table, the others for patients, and the supplies had better stay here, what's left of them. We're running short of basics but how the hell do we make this sterile?'

'We can get the troops to help us scrape it out, wash it down with salt water, put duckboards on the floor?' Penny was thinking on her feet. 'We did something like this near Arta when the wind tore down all our tents.'

'Hell's bells, a hospital in caves! I've heard some outlandish schemes, but what's the alternative: move inland and start again? I'll get onto HQ,' said Forsyth.

'Let's just hope our lot hold them off, hold the airstrip and send them back to Athens,' said a young Scots orderly, his eyes were full of fear. 'Come on, Sister, time to round up anyone on crutches to shovel out as much muck as we can before Jerry comes for breakfast again.'

Penny rolled up her sleeves to join him, her back aching, her ears ringing with the sounds of bombs and gunfire. The sky was still black with planes not stars. They were trapped on the beach, exposed, outnumbered and in fear of their lives, but there was no time for regrets. There was a job to do, a filthy rotten job but it might just save her patients from certain death. She may be the only woman left on the beach but she could handle a shovel and muck out with the best of them. That was something she'd done since she was a child She smiled thinking of Hector, her pony, and the stables at Stokencourt. Little did she dream then how she would end up here. Suddenly her heart lifted. Nothing like sweat and purpose to keep you strong. They were all one team now, working against the odds and it felt good.

A girl in a thick cloak picked her way through the rubble, making slow progress through the smoke and broken glass, the scattered remnants of houses, searching for survivors, staring up every few seconds in fear of the raid resuming. She had to make it uphill to Halepa. She was already late for duty, as many others would be who had endured the bombs. She could hear the weeping of women as they searched through the stones, crying for their families. The body parts were already beginning to rot in the heat. The smell of the battlefield had come to Chania that morning. She must hurry – there would be so many wounds to treat – but who would treat the broken hearts, the grief, the fear of what was to come? To her relief this part of town had been spared and already there was a queue waiting outside the Red Cross clinic.

'Nurse, Nurse,' shouted an old woman, tugging at her arm. 'Come, find my husband, come and help me find my little birds.' The woman was half-crazed with grief.

'Nurse, you have to help my wife. She's in labour, she's bleeding . . .' A young man in a tattered shirt supported his fainting wife.

She helped the man gather up the girl and together they pushed with her through the crowd. 'Let her pass,' she ordered. It was fortunate that the clinic was nearby. The door opened and they fell into the vestibule.

'Thank God, you've made it, Nurse. We're so short of staff,' the doctor said wiping his blood-stained hands on his white coat. 'Who have we here?'

Yolanda gave the doctor details of the patient as they carried the girl forward to the treatment room and closed the door. But when they laid her out, she realized the poor girl was dead.

Yolanda wanted to cry out at the injustice of such a cruel fortune but there was no time. Even as they covered the young woman's face and escorted the weeping man to the door they heard the screech of bombers overhead. It was time to get the patients under deep cover again.

She sat crouching with her patients in the basement until the worst of the morning raid on Chania harbour was over. Her mind was not on her work, however, but on whether her parents were safe in the cave under Uncle Joseph's printing works. There'd been enough alarms now for many local families to flee to their family villages, or to find reliably safe shelter. Kondilaki Street, with its Jewish quarter, was only a few rows back from the ancient harbour, the Venetian *limani*, with its warehouses, and a large arsenal full of weapons and stores where Uncle Joseph's sons had gone in vain to beg for more rifles to defend themselves should an invasion come from the sea.

Since her unexpected arrival, Yolanda had hardly left the quarter. Her parents were so relieved to have her by their side, they insisted she be chaperoned and introduced to the other families of their Sephardic community. The printing works had been busy printing newspapers for the British troops. Papa was helping translate the *Crete News* from English to Greek so the compositors could lay down the text correctly.

Yolanda's uniform had hung useless on the hook behind her bedroom door since her arrival. Every time she went to wear it her mother would weep.

'You've done enough for Greece. We need you here, now we can be truly a family once more. I have such plans.'

How could she tell them she was here only by accident? Helping a wounded soldier onto the gangplank of the *Ulster Prince* from the ferry boat, he'd suddenly collapsed, clinging to her for dear life, and she'd had no option but to hold his hand and escort him right into the bowels of the hospital ship. She'd needed to pass on his notes and check details. It was only when she'd heard the engines roaring into life and felt the motion of the ship that she'd realized they were heading out of the harbour under cover of darkness. It had been too late to scramble up on deck and plead her case.

As the hours passed, her panic had turned into weary resignation. Nobody would turn back for one nurse, and besides, she was needed here. It had been a relief to learn that they were heading out to Crete. The decision whether or not to stay on in Athens had been taken out of her hands, though she worried about her nursing friends, especially Penny. What must she be thinking? Were they waiting for her to report for duty? What if Penny had boarded another ship? There'd been such danger on the crossing – was she still alive? Yolanda felt guilt as well as relief when she heard rumours that other ships had been sunk, and she had a sickening feeling she would never see her friend again. Already Athens was feeling a world away from her life now. She had no papers, only her Red Cross credentials and the knowledge that Momma and Papa were close by and would claim her.

Once her momma held her and wept, it was as if a soft warm blanket of love enveloped her, muffling all her good intentions to report for duty immediately. How quickly that blanket had turned into a smothering cocoon. Within this tight-knit community of 300 souls, she was welcomed, but she was also expected to return to being the cherished but dutiful daughter, in need of a matchmaker who would find her a suitable spouse.

When the raids on Chania began, some Orthodox Greeks left for the villages and hills, leaving their shops closed up, but the Jewish quarter stayed put and battened down their hatches when bombs set fires all around them. But there were no Jews or Gentiles when frightened families crawled out of the rubble, needing their wounds dressed and their dead buried quickly. Yolanda had donned her uniform, wrapped her cloak around her and rushed off to the clinic, refusing to hide away when she was sorely needed.

'How can you leave us again?' her mother cried.

'I have to go and help. Surely you want me to save lives?'

For that there was no answer, and instead, Solomon patted her arm and simply said, 'Be careful, come back soon.'

Now, as they sheltered in the clinic basement, listening to the whistles and thuds all around them, clutching terrified children, injured parents trying to smile through their pain, Yolanda knew she was doing the right thing. She had gone out briefly in a lull at the insistence of a man searching for his wife. She had stood shocked at the devastation around her: roofs ripped, mules and donkeys lying dead and bloated, and the terrible stench of death she now knew so well. It was a fruitless search, and she returned having gathered up injured stragglers wandering around in a daze of shock.

Then they got everyone tearing makeshift bandages – soldiers, civilians, anyone with hands that could function. With each new intake of wounded came more rumours: 'The Tommies have driven them back . . . No, the Tommies are defeated. The airport is landing fresh troops . . . they are coming from the sea. Tomorrow they will be in Chania.'

Yolanda was too weary to worry if any of this was true. She felt as if she'd been at battle stations for years, not months, and she knew everyone on the island was united in defiance of the assault coming from the sky.

'If they come into town, head into the hills with us,' said Andreas Androulakis, one of the young doctors who looked just like a storybook pirate with a black patch over one eye. 'If they think Cretans will open their doors and give them raki and biscuits, they are in for a big surprise. What will you do?' he asked grim-faced, full of concern. They'd worked together for three nights. He should have been on the mainland with the Cretan Division but for his being blind in one eye.

Yolanda shrugged. 'I have parents close to Kondilaki Street, living with my uncle. I'm not sure they'd want to move . . .'

'Get them out of there into one of the hill villages. Your community will be watched,' he insisted. 'I've heard bad things about round-ups.'

He didn't need to spell it out. 'I'll stay here with the Red Cross,' she said smiling.

'You're a good nurse but I urge you, change your name and get fresh papers. Better to be safe . . .'

Andreas meant well and she was flattered by his concern, but how could she abandon her family name? It would mean renouncing her religion and race. She could never do that. Or could she? Uncle Joseph had assured her parents that Crete was a good refuge for Jews. Their community was thousands of years old here. But no one had imagined this sudden attack. Whatever happened next, she could never abandon her parents, not now, and her skills and experience were needed. She was not going to desert her post just to save her own skin, but if her parents were in danger she might need to think again.

Galatas,
23 May 1941

Life in a cave was challenging. Penny was so tired she could hardly eat. The caves were cool and damp, and she was glad of the warmth of her faithful cloak as camouflage at night when she crept out into the darkness, stumbling from one cave to another.

'We've got to stop this bombing. The lines of stones marking out a cross in the sand have long been obliterated. Any ideas, Penny?' said Doug as he tried to lounge on the duckboard.

In the privacy of these caves all formality had broken down. She was now Penny and the two doctors were Doug and Pete. 'Have we got anything red? I think we should make ourselves a huge flag and advertise our position,' she suggested.

They purloined some white sheeting and found a bright tablecloth in Cretan stripes that Doug had bought as a souvenir for his fiancée, Madeleine. One of the villagers gave them a blood-red woven blanket and some needles and thread. They cut the fabrics into a cross shape and began to stitch up the flag by the light of the oil lamps. It gave the frightened and bored patients something to keep them occupied, and they knew a huge Red Cross flag would help protect them.

Penny peered out into the darkness with a heavy heart, seeing the sky lit up from the burning of Chania city. Only a day ago she'd been sitting by the harbour eating ice cream, admiring all the tall Venetian mansions with their carved lintels and the old Turkish wooden roof balconies. How many of them were reduced to ashes now?

When the flag was eventually finished they hauled it up onto the grassy promontory on top of the caves, weighing it down with rocks. No one could miss the emblem from the shore or sky. They stood admiring their handiwork. 'That should do the trick,' Pete said. Penny hoped he was right for they were in a desperate situation now. There was grim news that Maleme had been taken.

'It's just a blip,' Pete Ellis assured her in front of his patients. They had isolated the German prisoners for their own safety, and most of them were too ill to be any trouble. Some of them had even offered to help sew the flag, grateful to be safe in the caves. The Luftwaffe would respect the Red Cross badge, Penny was told in perfect English by one wounded officer.

Doug was guarding his ever-dwindling supplies and brought in some huge pithoi jars of *tsoukoudia*, raki spirit made from the juice of grape skins, fermented into a potent brew, to be used for disinfecting and swabs. 'If ever the dressings get overripe and you want to gag at the stench, I suggest two nips before you unwind them and tackle the rot. Oh, and two nips after,' he said with a stern face.

'On the wound?' Penny asked in all innocence.

'Down your bloody throat,' he roared. Then, seeing her flinch: 'And don't be so prissy. I heard you swearing in very fruity Greek . . . where did you learn to swear like that?'

'We learned a lot of new words on the Albanian border,' she smiled. 'And much more besides,' she added. You didn't live in the backstreets of Athens without learning how to shake off attentions, stop your bag from being stolen, or your place in the queue being usurped by pushy old women. Thank goodness her mother was not around to see how her skin and her language had coarsened. Her manners and English accent might sometimes remain those of an English debutante, but she thought nothing of tearing round the camp in shorts in her spare time, ignoring the wolf whistles. If they noticed her long legs then her patients were on the mend.

The next day they got no more strafing, which gave them time to make a burial party and gather anything useful from the wreckage of their hospital. Linen was sent out into the nearest villages for laundering and fresh oranges brought in. Everyone was trying to pretend all was normal but the roar of guns was never far off. A battle was raging for the airstrip and they must sit it out, come what may. Their wounded were in no condition to do much to save themselves if the camp was attacked again.

Penny felt such a sense of protection for her patients, like a tigress defending her cubs. Perhaps that was how her mother had felt for her girls – well, for Effy at least.

There were injured civilians creeping in, wanting help, bringing oranges, lemons and vegetables as payment for her services. Now there were hundreds of men to feed, and the store cupboard was almost bare.

'I wish we knew how the land really lies,' she whispered at the end of her shift, as she and Doug sat sipping fresh orange juice laced with raki, better than any champagne, under a starlit sky.

'We'll know soon enough if it's going badly. We'll be overrun in minutes but we'll put up no resistance. You get everyone under cover, no rifles or tin hats on view. We must stay neutral.'

One of the orderlies, overhearing them, shouted, 'We can't just take it lying down. There's some of us left who can take a few out with us.'

'You do that, Barnes, and I'll shoot you first. Give these poor sods a chance of life, even if it's in a Jerry prison camp. Shoot and we're all done for. They're not all barbarians. The Geneva Convention will protect us.'

Another voice piped up from the sand, 'Tell that to my friend Corky. They pulled him bleeding out of the ditch, and shot him.'

'We shot them out of the sky, they saw their mates axed as soon as they landed, I'm hearing, by old women with hatchets. War's a filthy business; fear makes you do cruel things. Come on, back into your cave.' Doug got up and saw them moved out of earshot.

'One hothead can cause trouble. Fear is like a virus infecting the whole jolly lot of them. I hear bad stuff happened on both sides. We just patch up whoever's brought in, friend or foe. If the planes come back, I have another idea up my sleeve, insurance, you might say, to protect us from more bombing.'

'What's that?' Penny asked curiously.

Doug disappeared and came back with a folded flag with a swastika in the middle. 'Just a trick I learned from my father in the Great War. If we put that up, they'll leave us alone and might even drop us a few supplies,' he winked. 'But keep this under wraps. I hope to God it doesn't come to this. If Jerry was to find out, we'd be in trouble.'

Penny stared up at the midnight sky studded with stars as far as the eye could see. The sound of ack-ack fire set her mind on a new track. Where was Bruce? Had he been evacuated with the Harrington party? How were Angela and her girls? Was the Harringtons' house or Villa Artemisa, Evadne and Walter's house in Athens, still standing, or were they all reduced to a pile of ashes and smoking rubble? Who was looking after the wounded civilian population in the burning city?

It felt as if she were living in some strange dream, bone-weary, the raki now having its effect, wondering what she was doing on this island. Why then was she feeling more alive than she had ever done before? What was going to happen next was way out of her control, but she felt excited knowing she was in the hands of destiny. All she could do was watch and wait and pray.

2001

'This gets more and more intriguing, Aunt Pen.' Lois was sitting by the pool, watching Alex jumping in and out of the water. 'I do recall Mummy once saying there was something in all the papers; something about a "Cave Nurse", they called her. There was a cutting in Granny's bureau. She said it almost made her grandmother forgive you for bolting all those years before. What happened to Doug and Peter, the doctors?'

I was about to continue when we heard a car braking in the drive and, shortly after, someone ringing the bell. Lois pulled on her towelling robe as a tall man with a clipboard peered round the door to the pool.

'Hi, sorry to disturb you,' he apologized. He was wearing smart cream chinos and open-neck shirt, and sandals showing bronzed feet. 'I'm Mack, from Island Retreats, your guide and rep. I'm just calling in to introduce myself and make sure you've settled in.'

In his late forties, he had one of those grizzled lived-in faces creased by sun, his fair hair sprinkled with grey, but he was still slim, athletic-looking, with a military bearing. He seemed a bit old for a holiday rep, but I liked the look of him and ushered him in to join us.

'Come and have a drink with us.' I can still be quite sociable when I'm in the mood.

'Mustn't stop too long,' he smiled, eyeing Lois with barely concealed interest.

She held out her hand. 'I'm Lois Pennington and this is my great aunt, Penelope George, and my son, Alex. Do sit down.'

I noticed he didn't protest as we moved the chairs further under the umbrella.

He checked we were satisfied with our accommodation, and handed us lists of emergency numbers and hospital data. 'We can easily arrange for you to be booked on any tours and excursions.'

I had wondered when the hard sell would come.

'We can also give you lists of tavernas but we can't single any out. Ask around and you will see the busy ones,' he smiled. 'If you want to walk round the old town of Chania, there's a Saturday morning tour. I have to admit, I did it once as a tourist and here I am now, working on the island. Funny how life turns out. You must visit the Palace of Knossos, and Samaria Gorge in the south, but only if you're fit.' He looked in my direction and I wanted to tell him I could've done the long downhill walk carrying a wounded soldier on my back if needed, a few years back, and many of my patients had to do it in the war, but I said nothing.

'You must go to a Cretan dance night, fun for everyone . . .'

'We're here for a special reason,' Lois interrupted him. 'We are attending the Battle of Crete commemoration.'

'You're interested in the island's history?' he asked.

'I am in its history,' I couldn't help myself replying. 'I was a nurse here.'

'Really? How interesting. Do the organizers know you're attending?' He peered at me as if I were some ancient specimen in a glass cabinet.

'No, this is a private visit. I have no wish to take part.' There was a silence and then he rose to leave, as if our request had unnerved him.

'Right then, well, I hope you have a marvellous holiday. If there's anything you need, here's my card and number. I shall see you around, no doubt. It's a small place. Must dash . . .'

Lois and Alex waved him off. 'I thought there was more to him than just trying to sell us trips,' she sighed, gathering up all the bumf. 'What a wonderful summer job if you're single. Let's make some lunch and then go to the beach. I'm sure Aunt Pen would like a siesta.'

'There is somewhere I'd rather like to visit later, another beach further west, if you don't mind?' I asked.

'No problem, especially if we can hear more about your Cave Nurse adventures.'

That nickname, given to me by the press in later years, always embarrassed me. It was only one tiny episode from my time here. No one ever realized how complicated my life became because of it. Never complain, never explain, they say, but if there's to be any peace in returning here I must relive those dangerous days before and after the fall of Crete. Besides, there are secrets from that time, I've never shared with anyone, secrets that have burdened me for years. Perhaps now will be the time to offload them once and for all?

Brecht stood in the village street looking up at the war memorial by Galatas church. Memories came flooding back as he walked up the steep hill, leaning on his stick. The wreckage of old houses was transformed, painted and pristine once more, the *kafenion* was exactly how he remembered it. How could this now peaceful hamlet have been the sight of a pitched battle of such ferocity?

These streets were taken and lost, over and over. Brave men on both sides died in those little alleyways, sacrificing their lives for a strategic hill post and guns. The tide of this epic struggle ebbed, flowed and finally crashed over the heads of soldiers and civilians alike, but he could claim nothing of the victory when it came. He was in another place by then. It was time to retrace that terrible journey one more time.

25 May 1941

For days after landing, what was left of his battalion patrolled outside the relative security of the thick walls of Agia Prison compound, making forays into the surrounding olive and citrus groves, gathering up remnants of shattered battalions still hiding, bringing in the wounded and burying the dead. Morale was low as they stuck helmets on grave markers. Devastation was all around them: flattened trees, dead animals, broken gliders, the detritus of a failed operation. Hardened men blanched at the carnage.

It was then that, for some, sorrow turned into anger. Rainer wasn't always there to stop some of the reprisals taken out on villagers who'd defied them and taken up arms. Whole villages were razed to the ground; men, women and children taken out and shot. No trials, no mercy. He didn't like such summary justice but he knew where it was coming from. The defiance had been brutal so the reprisal must be equally so.

This sullen avoidance, the snipers in the olive trees, the way they had sheltered British troops in their homes, tearing up leaflets warning them of the consequences, meant trouble. Then there was that look of utter contempt in the eyes of men facing eternity as they stood before the firing squad, singing their anthems of freedom and death. Rainer had never seen such bravery. It unnerved him to realize that the more they shot, the more others would take their places. He feared the consequences for his men should they lose.

Whoever had advised intelligence of a welcome here should be shot himself. There would be no flowers strewn before them as conquering heroes, only bullets, knives in their backs or stones. But orders were orders and must be obeyed. Freedom fighters would not be subject to the Geneva Convention. Instant reprisal sent a firm message that if a village resisted it would be destroyed.

Now there were fresh orders to secure the road from the airstrip to Chania city and the hillside village of Galatas. There was constant cover from the Dorniers flying above them and the first attack had gone well. They had secured houses, but then there had been an attempt to retake the village. Two brave tanks had appeared out of nowhere, but were soon blasted, stricken and useless, with wounded New Zealanders in shorts and tin helmets taking cover as best they could.

Now it was time to battle it out at the top of the hill. Rainer felt oddly calm, though he knew only the strongest would be alive at the end of the day. He felt as if he was entering into some strange tunnel of concentration. Kill or be killed, his only purpose was to fulfil his command orders.

He saw men rise and fall, rise and die, and still the enemy came up. He stood forward, watching for the unexpected, but the grenade that came flying took him by surprise. He felt no pain at first as a hand dragged him under cover, out of danger. He watched what was happening around him as if it were a film show in slow motion.

He saw the dark-skinned Maoris yelling in a strange tongue, a roar that sent his troops faltering and retreating, leaving him at the mercy of enemy troops. He felt his life sifting through his fingers like sand. There was no hope now and he felt oddly calm waiting for it to end . . .

He woke to find a water bottle at his lips and a tourniquet on his shattered leg. He was being jolted downhill on a board as a makeshift stretcher. Was he a prisoner or had his own medics pulled him clear? He was too dazed to care.

The hands that held the stretcher were tanned like leather. He felt no fear, only surprise that he'd not been finished off in the street. He'd seen enough soldiers being given the *coup de grâce*. Was he going to Maleme, to be flown out to Athens, or onto a hospital ship anchored in the bay? Surely his war couldn't be over when it had only just begun? The pain of his leg wound started racing through his body, and he kept passing in and out of consciousness. He heard himself crying, '*Wasser, Wasser,*' desperate to down the bottle in one go.

Where were his men? Was the battle still going on? Shutting his eyes he saw once more his own senior officer and others felled at a stroke, bodies hanging like grapes from a tree. It was a shambles, an utter shambles. They didn't deserve to die like rooks, all those hand-picked boys lost in the attempt to secure the island. *Operation Mercury* – what a cursed codename. He could do nothing now except bear the pain. He knew he was dreaming when a hand with slender fingers clutched his wrist, feeling for his pulse. He opened his eyes to see a young woman in khaki staring down at him. Her hair was bleached white by the sun yet she had the darkest eyes he'd ever seen.

He lay back with relief, knowing he could sleep for a hundred years to be woken by such a face.

This is impossible, thought Penny as she tried to mop Doug Forsyth's brow while he struggled to close up a complex amputation close to the thigh. They had pushed the operating table near to the cave entrance to gain as much light as they could. The conditions underfoot were appalling: slippery from body fluids and mud, with a stench of ether and infection that no swig of raki could ever stifle, and everywhere flies hovered over the wounded.

The orderlies were helping the stretcher cases to relieve themselves in tin cans, and others were dishing out tea sweetened with condensed milk from the last of their supplies.

'I think it may be time for plan B,' Penny whispered in Doug's ear as, later, they sipped the last of the tea ration. She felt filthy and sweaty in her battle shirt and baggy trousers, but they gave protection from the biting insects and the fierce sun beating down on their tattered camp, and also made her stand out less from the male nurses.

'I hoped it would never come to this,' Doug said, 'but we owe it to our patients to try anything.'

'I'll do it,' Penny offered, knowing how reluctant he was in taking this risk.

'No, it was my idea,' he snapped. His face ashen from tension and weariness.

Plan B was Doug's idea of flying the enemy's flag. It was a dangerous ploy, but there was a job to do and no time for reflection on what might happen next.

'We'll wait till dusk and do it together,' she suggested and he nodded. The two of them stretched out two captured Swastika flags next to the Red Cross one, which had so far kept some of the gun-toting raiders from the hospital. A few hours after dawn a Dornier obligingly dumped some crates of medical supplies and food that would save lives.

All the time, wounded from both sides were being off-loaded into the casualty tents. These patients had to wait their turn, lying in the sun, groaning and calling out. Those that were conscious looked up in surprise and relief to see a woman assessing their wounds. One young soldier, half delirious, was screaming out, '*Mutter, Mutter!*' holding his hand out to her as if she were indeed his mother come to nurse him.

Penny knelt down and clasped his hand, feeling for his pulse as it weakened, waiting, watching as it faded away to nothing. She covered him and stood in silence for a second while a voice from a German officer croaked in halting English, 'That was kindly done, Nurse.'

She examined the officer's gashed leg without speaking, nodded curtly and checked over his filthy dressing, replacing it with a fresh one, aware he could see that these were pads from German medical supplies, not British issue. He made no comment.

His eyes never left her face as if he were examining her motives in helping his men, wondering, no doubt, what a woman was doing only half a mile from a battle front.

For some reason she felt it important not to speak to him, so she asked an orderly to finish dealing with him, as slowly she went down the never-ending line to examine the fresh intake, searching out those most in need of treatment. The officer would be put with the other POWs in the far cave and guarded. Had he noticed the German flags? It was in everyone's interests to be free from strafing. He couldn't object to that, surely, but if he did and they were captured, they might all be shot. She pushed that fearful thought away.

That evening she watched one of those magnificent saffron sunsets, so soothing on the soul after such a bloody day. Penny was lying back, trying to gather up what was left of her flagging energy for more operations, when a staff vehicle drove into the compound. Penny looked up to see a familiar face staring at her as he strode over. His blazing look of fury said it all.

'I knew it must be you, but I had to see for myself who was the crazy woman they say swears like a Greek navvy. What the hell do you think you're playing at?' Bruce Jardine yelled.

'And it's very nice to see you, too,' she quipped, too tired to respond to him. 'Can't you see we're busy?' She made to storm off.

'Not so fast,' he yelled. 'What the hell are you doing here in a battlefield?'

'What I am trained to do. Just let me get on with it.'

'Orders are to shift this hospital, medics and instruments away from Chania, further inland to a place called Neo Chorio. The lorries will come to pick up wounded at eleven hundred hours under escort. I hope you have the sense to obey orders. Honestly, Penny, this is crazy . . . Have you no sense of the danger you're in?'

'What's happening out there?'

'Don't ask me, I only do what I'm told, but it's not looking too good. I want you out of here on the first truck.' Bruce stared round at the chaos. He called in the rest of the staff and repeated the news.

'We'll need time to move the worst cases,' said Doug. 'And we've got POWs.'

'They'll have to fend for themselves. From what I can gather, they won't have long to wait for their own doctors. Maleme airport has fallen and there are fresh troops landing every hour now. Our boys can't hold out much longer even though they're putting up a brave show. Sister here must be evacuated before that.'

'I'll take my chances,' Penny replied.

'You'll do as you're told. Don't let me have to pull rank on you,' Pete said as he flicked flies from his face.

'I'll finish my rounds. We still have a few hours. Why are we standing round like statues?' Penny snapped to the orderlies. 'We must decide who is fit to travel and who is not. Some of them will not survive a journey. I won't be responsible for unnecessary deaths.'

As the others shot off to spread the news, Bruce caught hold of her arm. 'Promise me you'll take the first transport. You've done your whack. You've been marvellous, a real morale boost. Your parents will be so proud, but not if you're dead. No more heroics.' Bruce pulled her towards him. 'It's dangerous out there now . . . please, Penny.'

She felt the full power of his eyes boring into hers and her resolve weakening. He cared, and the way he was looking at her made her heart thud. She nodded. 'I'll go when Dr Forsyth and Dr Ellis go, but I'm needed now.'

Suddenly the camp was a bustle of collecting up the walking wounded, patching up others who could stand, gathering up instruments, belongings and records. There was no time to think, only relief that they'd soon be out of this flea-ridden sandpit.

The trucks arrived on time with an escort, and the evacuation began in earnest. Only walking wounded,' ordered the officer in charge of the evacuation. 'We can't take stretchers. Let's have them up on the lorries. If they can hold a gun . . .'

'If they carry a gun or helmet, the convoy will be shot at. The red cross on the side will mean nothing then,' Barnes, the orderly, argued to a sergeant, who looked up at him with disdain.

'I suppose we must take some of your fairies with us too.'

Barnes made to punch him but Penny got between them. 'What about all our stretcher cases? Who's coming for them?'

'Another truck will be dispatched, at zero three hundred hours. Come on, Sister, up you come. Captain Jardine said there was a female . . .' He ogled her with interest.

'I'll be on the next delivery, must get the others ready,' she replied, ignoring him, then waving the men off.

The medical staff worked through the night, labelling up the patients. It worried Penny that some were barely conscious, still groggy from operations, while others had fevers and infections.

She was glad when the hour came and the expected transport convoy was late arriving, but when dawn broke and there was still no sign, she sensed all was not well.

'Do you think they've forgotten us?' she asked Doug, who was packing a box of operating instruments.

He shrugged. 'Who knows what's going on out there?'

Just as they'd given up hope a solitary truck arrived. Bruce jumped out of the cab, looking pleased with himself.

'We can take medics and some orderlies and Sister George, for evacuation down to the south coast.'

'But there are hundreds of men waiting here. Where's the convoy?' Penny asked.

Bruce was staring out at the camp, not looking at her. 'Sorry, but they'll be left behind. The Germans know the score. They'll be treated fairly. You're coming with me, now.'

At that moment everyone around them realized that all was lost. The army was in retreat, evacuating the island, leaving the wounded to become prisoners. For Penny there was the agonizing choice: *Do I go or do I stay and be captured?*

'I have to get my things,' she said, fleeing to her corner of the cave. She needed time to think – but there *was* no time. Bruce would keep her safe – he was her knight in shining armour come to rescue her – but did she even want that? Why was there no relief in such a thought? Why was something she'd been dreaming of for years suddenly not important? Why wasn't anything here going to plan? Suddenly her feelings for Bruce were all mixed up and this wasn't the time or place to examine them.

There was only one thing she could do. She pulled off her khakis and rooted in her bag for her whites, her cloak, her head-dress and her badges. Then she walked back out of the cave in full Red Cross uniform. The orderlies stood back, shocked at this transformation from battledress to the formal robes of her blood-stained uniform.

'I can't leave these men. I am with the Hellenic Red Cross, not the British Army. I take orders from its military wing so you are free to leave me behind,' she announced, standing tall.

'Like hell we are. You're coming with me . . .' Bruce made to grab her.

Doug stepped forward. 'You heard the nurse. She has made her choice. Sister Georgiou is a valuable member of staff, and if she chooses to remain as Red Cross we won't order her to leave. I think she knows the consequences.'

She could have kissed Doug there and then, but remembered her decorum and played the solemn nun for all she was worth.

Bruce shook his head in disgust. 'Someone else can take her place. Another medic?' There was a look of fury on his face as each doctor in turn stood back, pushing one of their orderlies forward for transport.

Bruce pulled Penny aside out of earshot. 'I'm disappointed in you, though not surprised. You always were a stubborn cow, but remember what I told you before. If you want to nurse the Germans, that's up to you, but there'll be other patients needing your help. *British* patients. Terrible things have happened to those resisting the invasion in the villages. I hope you know what you're doing.' He stormed away, jumped into the driving seat and drove off, not looking back.

She knew this was no way to end their friendship after all he'd done for her. He'd gone out on a limb to rescue her and she was refusing his help. What on earth was she doing? For one brief moment, she weakened. Part of her wanted to run after him and shout for him to stop, to take her away to safety, but her feet wouldn't move. This was her stand; too late for second thoughts. She must see this through to the end now. With this momentous decision came a strange calm. I must be going mad, she thought, but stay she must.

'You should've gone with him, you know,' Pete whispered.

'Don't you start . . .' she snapped, and marched off, knowing only too well her bridges had been burned by this impulsive action. Let no one say she didn't see a job through to the end. Bruce was right: she did have a stubborn streak that refused to give in to weakness. Would it cost her her freedom or even her life?

To have climbed on that lorry with him would have been giving in to her desire to be in his company again, to give love a chance to blossom.

Oh, why didn't you go? she cried to herself. Because it was

what Bruce expected I'd do. Evacuating was the easy option. Staying was duty, seeing my men were well treated was more important surely than a drive into the hills with someone who might not even love you back, she argued. There was always a niggle of doubt when it came to Bruce's real feelings and this was no time to be testing him out.

She sat hugging her knees, taking comfort only from the thought that, in war, duty must come before personal desires, no matter what the consequences might be.

Rainer lay in the filthy cave watching the other men staring up at the rocks and ceiling in silence. Another paratrooper had died in the night and they'd carried him out to join a pile of corpses waiting to be buried. Here in the hospital he watched the frailty of the human body, the slow struggle for breath, the sweats, the confessions. Funny how, in death, uniforms no longer mattered as they lay side by side, all now equal, just empty shells.

He couldn't fault their treatment. They ate the same basic rations as the Tommies, drank the same awful tea. He sensed by the wary look on the faces of the orderlies that it was only a matter of time before power would shift from the British to his own troops and they would be free. There had been movements in the night and some of the British wounded had been moved out. Only the serious cases remained.

His leg wound was not as bad as they'd first thought. Now the shrapnel had been removed and the wound cleansed, it was stiff and sore, but he was allowed out on makeshift crutches into the fresh salty air. He wanted to check on his own men.

His eyes searched for that nurse but there was only a woman in a stiff white uniform of the Red Cross. She was tall, upright, efficient and always silent. It was hard to read her as she walked along the stretchers, checking over them with care, nodding or shaking her head. She seemed pleased with his progress. He tried to converse with her but her dark eyes were inscrutable, and by then he was sure she was the girl he'd seen in army uniform.

He heard her shouting at some Greek soldiers fooling about in the sun. He decided she had a little English and no German and yet he saw her chatting in the distance with the English doctors as if they were all friends. And when she smiled he saw her face light up and he felt a flicker of envy that surprised him.

There was a flurry of planes overhead during the day. To reach each cave in safety the nurse had to flatten herself against the rocks to avoid stray bullets, despite the array of German flags he could see. He wished he knew her name. Someone said it was George, but that couldn't be true. How did one woman come to be alone with hundreds of men? She didn't look like a camp follower. He could see how even his own men respected her, not touching her skirt or whistling. There was something now of the nun about her dedication, a stern outward persona that discouraged intimacy. Yet there was also something vibrant about her that drew his eyes. He knew he was in danger of fantasizing he was falling in love with a beautiful nurse, a romantic foolish notion that made him feel ashamed. Yet there was something unreachable about her that intrigued him. That was the trouble with having too much time on his hands, lying about recovering.

Why should she notice him, the enemy, a prisoner of no consequence except to his own men? He was the unwelcome invader, a killer among killers. He cursed that he'd let his men down by being injured and now he had no idea where they were or how their campaign was progressing. No wonder she had no words for him. But he couldn't forget the way she had held the hand of that dying trooper. There had been compassion on her face, a warmth in her sadness as she had pulled the blanket over his face.

In another life they might have passed each other on an

Athens street, perfect strangers, but this was their life now, both of them living on the edge, staring into a precarious abyss of uncertainty. He just wanted to know her name . . .

There was no warning. The firing was getting closer, too close for comfort as she tried to concentrate, packing up equipment for their hasty retreat. Then a volley of shots and yelling heralded the attack and a scream of angry bullets ricocheted off the wall of the cave. No time to do anything but fling herself on the ground, face down as boots trampled past yelling '*Raus, raus . . .*' storming as only conquerors do.

She flattened herself, trying to hide her presence, hoping there were officers to control this pack of wolves as they yanked out the orderlies to line them up on the rocks.

Every second seemed more like an hour as she lay prostrate in the gloom, tasting the salty sand, the grit and the stench of dried blood on her lips, and her fear, trying not to shiver. She sensed it would be only minutes before discovery, so this was not the time to waver. Be British, be brave . . . Oh, be damned with all that guff, she thought. All she was feeling was a cold fury in her gut. How could she leave when there was still so much to be done? This was not how she hoped to end up.

Suddenly a pair of desert boots covered in mud stood at eye-level, a tanned hand jerked her upright. This was the test, the moment of truth and defiance. If she faced the enemy without fear, her bluff might just work . . .

They rounded up the medics, brandishing guns at their chests, and when someone came in waving the Swastika flags she knew there would be trouble.

Suddenly the polished boots covered in sand stood over her. 'God in Heaven! What have we here?' A strong hand pulled her up, examining her with surprise. She saw Doug and Pete straining in case she was harmed, but she calmly brushed down her uniform, wrapped her cloak tightly over her body and stood as tall as she could, looking the man straight in the eye. She rattled off her name and Red Cross details in rapid Greek, seeing the look of amazement on Doug's face. She warned them with a scowl, not to intervene.

The officer stood bemused, not understanding her, but then the wounded officer from the cave hobbled forward to interpret, questioning her in halting Greek. He said she had been left to look after the seriously wounded and that she had nursed their captured troops with great kindness.

He was looking at her with admiration and she found herself blushing. For a second she wondered if he recognized her as the nurse in British uniform, but he seemed to be accepting her as a Greek national. The other officer ignored her and turned to Doug.

'What is the meaning of using this flag?' he ranted, waving the German flag in their faces.

Again Penny stepped forward, turning to the tall paratrooper to translate for her, and explaining in Greek that it had been her idea.

'We were running short of supplies and your bombs were hampering us nursing all the patients of all nationalities, including your own. It is important to save lives, don't you think?' She stared up at him, uncertain if he would translate this accurately. 'I have taken vows to nurse all sick, no matter what their nation or religion,' she added.

The wounded officer stumbled out a translation, his eyes turning back to her for confirmation. The other officer clicked his heels and saluted her.

'The captain says they were fortunate to have such a brave example of womanhood. She must be repatriated with the wounded prisoners to serve in another hospital.' His English was good enough for her friends to look relieved.

'You are a nun in a nursing order?' the captain asked,

surprised. She did not reply. 'Have no fear, your uniform will protect you. The Red Cross is honoured where its symbols are not misused as camouflage.' He turned back to the men and they opened a path for her to walk through.

Only when she was out of earshot did Penny feel her legs wobble. Thank God she had stayed silent and they thought her Greek, not English. Her war would be over once she was evacuated to the mainland. The uniform had saved her – that and her grasp of the language.

Her relief turned to concern for all those brave New Zealand and Aussie soldiers now at the mercy of their enemy. What would become of them?

'You've got them fooled, Penny. Good on you!' Doug leaned over to speak quietly.

'Not all of them. The wounded captain from Galatas, he saw me in khakis though I never spoke to him.'

'Well, he didn't say anything. He sang your praises to his superior for helping his dying men. He said you saved his life. I know enough German to get their drift,' said Doug.

'I didn't save him. He was never in danger. He exaggerates . . .'

'They'll be flying you out to Athens with the stretcher cases and you can nurse back there.'

'I'll go when you all go and not before. I'll see them on that plane first,' Penny insisted, as she found herself picking up things that had been scattered by the troops.

She needed time to think this all over. What had she done? Made it easy for herself? She recalled that look of fury on Bruce's face when he'd driven off. There were other alternatives. 'Head for the hills,' he'd suggested only a week ago. How had things changed so quickly? Were there really freedom fighters willing to continue the battle if the Brits were retreating? If she could pass for Greek, escape out of here, where would she go? She had seen the torn leaflets threatening instant death to citizens who resisted. That would be her fate if she took the path into the mountains and took up arms.

Why had the wounded officer spoken up for her? Had he not recognized her disguise? She thought he had, and she didn't want to be beholden to the enemy, even in defeat. The fight must go on, but how?

I have three choices: to stay and be evacuated; to escape and find Bruce, join the retreat into the hills; or to fight on somehow here. Oh Lord, what do I do next?

Chania,
28 May 1941

Yolanda Markos sheltered in the basement of the Red Cross clinic through days of non-stop bombardment. District by district, Chania was being reduced to rubble. The nurses lived in a subterranean world lit by oil lamps and candles, trying to calm terrified civilians who were cramped together with soldiers from both sides, too sick to complain of the conditions.

Then, at last, came a morning when the skies were mercifully silent. Hardly daring to hope they had been spared another air raid, the medical staff cautiously opened the basement door. Was anything in their world left standing?

All Yolanda wanted was to head back into the city and find her parents in the Jewish quarter. All through the air raids she had prayed they were still alive.

Dr Androulakis went upstairs to view the damage which, to everyone's astonishment, was minor: just broken windows, dust, glass and a queue already forming of blackened-faced patients who'd crept out of cellars and caves with their injured. Halepa district still remained almost intact.

Yolanda stepped into the daylight behind the doctor, almost blinded by the sunlight.

'No more steel birds,' cried a woman, crossing herself, tears rolling down her cheeks. 'But they have murdered our holy churches and our houses. God will revenge Himself on them!'

she shouted to anyone who would listen, but most people stood stunned with shock, looking up to the empty sky with relief. Halepa might have been spared but there were more tongues of flame coiling up in the distance, and the choking smoke of destruction inside the city walls.

'I have to find my parents,' Yolanda said to Andreas Androu-lakis. 'They'll think me dead.'

He smiled and nodded. 'You must go, but take care. We'll need you back.' He himself had been working all night.

Over the last four days something stronger than work and respect had pulled them closer. Amid all the darkness, danger and destruction, working alongside him Yolanda felt herself drawn to him in a way she'd never felt for a man before. There was a look of tenderness in his face when he talked to his patients, a quiet confidence in his manner that inspired hope.

'Remember, you'll be needed more than ever,' he told her now. 'You don't flinch at the terrible injuries or when the bombs drop. The young nurses look up to you when they're afraid and overwhelmed. You give them confidence by staying so calm.'

Yolanda felt a glow of pride in his praise. 'I shall check Momma and Papa are safe, then return,' she said, covering her head with a scarf as she picked her way down the cobbled street. The closer to the old city wall, to the Kastelli district, the worse the devastation. Barrels of wine spilled over the street, rats were gorging in daylight, broken pots of burning olive oil fouled the air and everywhere unburied corpses festered in the heat. Children wandered among the rubble searching, calling for pets, while woman keened at the devastation around them. Where once stood elegant Venetian town houses there was only smouldering beams and rubble.

Yolanda hurried on, not wanting to stop. It was a beautiful morning. The sea glistened in the bay, a deep sapphire-blue merging into emerald and pearl. How could there be such devastation on such a beautiful day?

*   *   *

No one quite knew what to do with Penelope Georgiou. Now it appeared she was a Greek citizen, not a British Army nurse, having trained in Athens, with a bona fide address there. She kept up this pretence, claiming all her papers had been lost at sea, and so far it was working. Only a true Greek would pick holes in her accent. She explained she'd been educated privately with an English governess, which explained her good grasp of English. She told them she was estranged from her wealthy family when she took up nursing. No one queried all these half-truths. The doctors in the camp confirmed she had arrived late, sent by the Red Cross to train up local women.

It was the wounded captain who translated on her behalf, who accompanied her around the camp as she tried to find orderlies to help the prisoners. When she expressed interest in Cretan history, he told her he had, himself, been keen on archaeology, and he seemed glad of common ground. Off guard she told him about the lectures at the BSA, open lectures, she added, and he asked her if she had read about the palace at Knossos. He recommended books she might like to read about Schliemann's dig in Mycenae but she refused to be drawn further into intimacy.

The notoriety of her status as a single female in the caves, nursing men from both sides, caused curiosity, not least among senior officials. They wanted her interviewed, with an idea to further publicity: as an example of co-operation between Greece and the Third Reich. But attention was the last thing she needed now if her cover was not to be blown. They'd offered her a flight back to Athens with the wounded troops and her doctor friends, with the promise of a newspaper article about her experiences and a chance to continue nursing in the city. It was tempting, but her heart was in Crete and she had decided on staying on the island. In the brief moments she was alone with Pete and Doug before their departure, she begged them not to reveal her whereabouts or her English roots to anyone.

There was always the chance that Bruce was still on Crete, and she could find useful work in the local hospital. Perhaps, though, he had been whisked away already with important officers, as the rumours from the bush telegraph were hinting. Thousands of escaping British troops reached Sphakia in the south and were taken off the island by the Royal Navy, but not all of them, as the arrival of fresh prisoners here every day indicated. They were made to crawl back over the high mountains, barefoot, starving and demoralized, only to be caged back in the hospital now a prison camp

Then came the inevitable invitation to Penny to go to HQ to meet some of the senior staff, medical officers who would decide her fate, and she had no choice but to accept graciously. She was in no position to refuse. To her horror they sent a staff car for her and the captain offered to escort her into the city. She felt him watching her as if he was unsure of her motives. He had seen her working as an army nurse – why had he not called her bluff, or did he believe all the lies she had told them? Surely he had recognized her as the nurse in khaki, but he said nothing. It was unnerving.

There had been one terrible moment when one of her patients returned to the camp. Sick with bites and sunstroke, he waved, recognizing her. 'I knew she'd still be here. Hello, Nursey, am I glad to see your pretty English face.'

'There is nothing English about my face,' she snapped in broken English. 'Many of us Greek girls are blonde,' she added, walking away, not wanting to see his surprise, but worried that her German escort had heard their exchange.

As they drove through the smouldering city on that sunny morning, she wanted to avert her eyes to all around her: the sad-eyed children, the broken doorways and arches, the women in black searching the rubble for their pots and pans. She sat stiffly in her freshly starched uniform, no longer caked in blood and dirt. How was she going to convince the Germans to let her stay on in some useful capacity?

The officer kept glancing at her and she tensed. He was always asking questions, trying to pry into her personal life.

'You are brave to stay alone in such conditions. I'm surprised the medical authorities allowed it,' he said.

'They had no choice. I was sent. We were busy. My ship was sunk,' she replied in slow Greek.

'What did your parents think of your career? It is not the chosen work for a daughter of quality, not in my country.'

'It is the highest calling for any woman to help the sick,' she snapped, turning her face from him. 'Even the queen herself supported our hospital in Athens.' She wanted to scream, shut up, let me out of here, leave me alone, but instinct said she must keep on the right side of him. He might be the key to her escape.

Stay polite but not too warm. Give him hope that she found him sympathetic, but not too much, and every now and then drop the hint that she had taken vows of devotion to her profession, that all thoughts of a normal family life or romance were no longer an option for her.

She found herself back in the Halepa district, not far from her stay in Stella Vista and the diplomatic quarter. She passed the French convent school, largely untouched by the bombing, and she prayed all the little girls she had seen before the invasion, darting around the grounds like butterflies, were unharmed.

It was a shock to see the German flag flying above the Venezelos Palace. The British HQ was now in other hands. Her heart thumped as they entered the gracious building, the formal hall where the German adjutants were busy shifting furniture around and adorning the walls with posters proclaiming the virtues of the Third Reich.

She was shown into an office. A senior doctor stood stiffly to attention.

'Miss Georgiou. We have heard all about your exploits. You are a credit to your calling. Please sit down.'

They passed pleasantries and, with the help of the captain, Penny explained how she thought herself suited to work among the Cretan Red Cross staff.

'You don't wish to return to Athens?' He looked surprised. 'A woman of your calibre will find nothing here but rough peasants and brigands.'

'I had thought to return until I made this journey, but as I was passing that school down the road, St Joseph's, I think it is called, it reminded me that I have knowledge to impart. The Red Cross needs young girls to train since many of its older women will return to their families now the hostilities have ceased.' She looked to her chaperone, who was translating. 'I would like to work with my own people.'

'But you are not Cretan,' said the doctor, spitting out the word as if it was distasteful.

'Crete has been part of the Greek nation for many years,' Penny smiled, looking from one of them to the other. 'But I confess I do have another more selfish motive, having some interest in Minoan archaeology. I might be given permission some day to visit the famous sites, under escort, of course.' She was laying it on thick for her interpreter's benefit.

The doctor seemed impressed. 'You are certainly a woman of many parts, but where would we house you?'

'I have thought of that, Sir. There is a hostel attached to the convent. I am, after all, Red Cross, and a convent would be a suitable residence for someone dedicated to nursing.'

'A sensible solution. You would be cloistered under their roof, chaperoned and out of harm's way if there were any disturbances. We can make this happen but on one condition: that you do not do anything to support any British or local resistance to our governance here. We expect your loyalty at all times.'

'The Red Cross is always neutral,' she replied, not exactly answering the question, but it seemed to satisfy him.

The captain hovered when she left the office. 'Shall I drop you off at the school? When things are settled and safer in Heraklion, let me take you out for the day to Knossos. You cannot come to Crete and not see this wonder of the world.'

'I'm sure it is a wonder, but first I must return for my things and hope that your commanding officer is true to his word.'

So far it was all going her way and Penny could hardly believe her ruse had worked. But she had to be realistic – how long would it be before her luck ran out?

They drove back towards the city in silence until they found themselves behind a troop of marching soldiers waving German flags. 'It's von der Heydte's men. They're making for the square . . . Driver, follow them!'

The last thing Penny wanted was to be travelling with a German officer through streets lined with silent onlookers. Everywhere the red, black and white flag was flying high. And now they were following the parade as if they were part of it.

She wanted to shrink back into the seat, cover her face, make herself invisible, but all she could do was pull down her head-dress as far over her forehead as she could. How she wished for her beloved cloak to hide her.

The sound of marching feet grew louder as Yolanda reached the city square. Here, a crowd of wounded soldiers in green-grey uniforms lounged against café walls, filling the street with their cheering. It was impossible for her to cross the square without drawing attention to herself, and she found their numbers, their arrogance, everything they stood for, threatening. Everywhere the German flag fluttered in the breeze: from building windows and even the top of the minaret of the old mosque.

She flattened herself against the wall of a ruined shop, edging round the gathering groups of curious bystanders. Then into the square marched a battalion of the scruffiest paratroopers, in that confident stride that only victors make. At their head was a tall man in shorts with a handkerchief round his head as a makeshift cap, his legs sunburned to toast-brown. He looked like a gypsy vagabond rather than their leader.

Local officials in suits were stepping forward in some sort of surrender, but they looked puzzled by the commander who stood before them. If ever an insulting message was given, it was here, as the officer clicked his heels. He couldn't be bothered to smarten up for the occasion. The city had fallen, and even the priests trying to make a ceremony of the defeat could not redeem this humiliation. Yolanda could not bear to watch as a parade of British prisoners marched slowly into view, their eyes dead with exhaustion and defeat. Behind them, trucks of wounded were followed by other German officers in open-topped cars in some victory cavalcade through the ruined wreckage of a once-proud city.

Her eye caught one of the cars with a woman in familiar nurse's uniform, staring ahead. It was the white headdress that stood out from all the camouflage and olive-grey uniforms. For a second the woman turned her head, staring at her. Yolanda almost stepped out into the road to get a closer look. No, surely not . . . it couldn't be? She raced to keep up with the car just to be sure. She felt the sky spinning above her as she craned her neck, hoping against hope that she was seeing things. That woman with the Nazi in the car couldn't be Penelope, her friend Penny, not after all they'd seen on the mainland? It was a mistake, she must have a double. But then she saw the nurse turn her head again. They locked eyes in one terrible glance of recognition.

Slowly the staff car edged through the streets. Faces were staring at them coldly and Penny wished she could jump out, run away and hide. This was not how it was meant to be. Ashamed, she averted her eyes for a second and saw a face, an oh so familiar face among the crowd. A face she would've recognized anywhere; those pinched cheeks, that strong nose, black hair covered by a floral headscarf. Their eyes locked for a few seconds. It was without doubt Yolanda. Yolanda was alive, here in Chania, looking right into her eyes as if she had seen a ghost, but with a look not of joy of recognition but of utter disbelief and contempt. Penny went cold at the thought of what her once-dear friend might be thinking and there was nothing she could do. She must not blow her cover.

Yolanda tried to keep pace with the car to make sure what she'd witnessed was real. There must be some mistake. No English nurse would fraternize with a German officer in such a public display of unity. It must be the heat and confusion of this awful day that was making her imagine things. But in her heart she knew immediately this was no mistake. It was Penelope, her friend. After all they'd been through together, how could she forget a friend's face? Had her friend become the enemy too?

Penny caught that second of instant recognition and amazement, and she had to tear her eyes away in case she shouted out and drew attention to them both. She forced herself to look forward and show no emotion. Unsmiling, trying not to shake, she struggled not to look back. Her mind was racing. Now it made sense. Yolanda's parents had come to Crete to relatives. Why shouldn't their only child follow them? And now, instead of a joyful reunion, Yolanda had looked at her as if she was a turncoat. What a mess, what a bloody mess!

Yolanda fled from the noise and confusion through the back alleys that led to the Jewish quarter under the old city wall, avoiding the smouldering gaps and fallen debris at the top of Kondilaki Street, praying that the houses round Portou would be still standing. But to her horror Biet Shalom, the synagogue, and all around it had taken a direct hit.

Smoke and dust blinded her path but she had to go on, to learn the worst. At first she could see no one. Then she saw faces looking out through cracked windows. The cobbled street was deserted, just dogs sniffing around for scraps. She gasped aloud in relief and joy to see Uncle Joseph's house still standing, pockmarked by shrapnel, battered but upright. She rapped on the door and faces peered through the grill.

'Yolanda, blessed be, she's alive!'

She was gathered into the house full of relatives and children, all hugging her as if to make sure she was real, all staring at her as if they couldn't believe their eyes. Momma was crying and laughing with joy at the same time. 'You came back to us. My child is spared.'

Then the questions started. 'Is it true, are the enemy at the door?'

'They're down in the square with the mayor. I heard he's surrendered to save us from more bombs,' she said, seeing the look of concern on their faces.

'You came without an escort? God preserve us, four nights with no chaperone,' said Aunt Miriam, bustling in to see who had arrived. 'Who will marry her now? I will bring food, she looks so thin.'

'I'm fine,' Yolanda said, but no one was listening. 'You must save your supplies; half the shops are burned to the ground. Everywhere is the same.'

Momma clung to her and Yolanda felt again that stifling concern for her every whim. Her clothes were laundered despite there being so little water. Over the next few hours, visitors came to see for themselves the miraculous return of the Markoses' daughter.

Five days later she sat at the Shabbat table, aware that she had been unable to step out of the door in all that time in case her mother collapsed again into weeping fits.

Always at the back of her mind was the image of Penny in

the German officer's car. It *was* Penny. Had she been here for weeks and never made contact? But how would she know I was here? she reasoned. Unless she thinks I deserted my post, took the chance of a ship to Crete and escaped to be with my parents?

That's why she ignored me. Over and over she saw that strange look. Was Penny ashamed to know her, thinking her a deserter, as she was ashamed to recognize Penny as a traitor? How could she think such things of a friend? But then what was she doing in a German staff car? If there was to be any relief from this torment she just had to know the truth. She must find out more. If only they would let her leave the house alone . . .

Six days after the surrender of the city, Yolanda received a visitor. Dr Androulakis stood in the street, having searched out where she was lodging. Miriam kept him outside, unsure of his intentions, but Yolanda rushed out to greet him with relief and brought him inside, where everyone stared at his eye patch.

'When you didn't return I thought the worst had happened,' he explained, clutching his battered Panama hat.

'As you can see, I am quite well. The family has been lucky but my mother has needed me. Mother, this is Dr Androulakis, one of our medical officers in the clinic. It was he who gave me permission to return home, but I have overstayed my leave.' She silently gave him a pleading look to which he responded nobly.

'We're short-staffed and Nurse Markos is our most experienced attendant. I don't know how we would have coped without her. She is a constant example to the younger volunteers, who have much enthusiasm but little training—'

It was Papa who stepped in to interrupt him, eyeing him with suspicion. 'Yolanda is needed here.'

'But, Papa, I am still under orders. I can't just walk out.'

'You have done your duty. Your place is in the home within this community.'

Yolanda felt herself flushing with embarrassment. How could she argue with her father before a stranger, a Gentile? Andreas saw her distress and came to her aid.

'I understand, sir, how important it is for you to have your daughter close to hand in such terrible times, but there are battles still raging outside the city. The British are holding a line close to Souda while their army is escaping over the mountains to the south coast. There are many wounded left behind who need our help.'

'You have other nurses,' Papa argued.

'If they go, who will look after our people here? The General Hospital is flooded with injured. We need every nurse we can get. Miss Markos will train others to take their place.'

'I have to go back, Papa, please.'

When her father shook his head Andreas butted in: 'Once the roads are clear and order is brought back, there will be no more bombing raids over our heads, sir. Your daughter will be free to return here.'

Solomon raised his hands in protest. 'But it's important we all stay together. The rabbi fears we will all be registered as Hebrews and our addresses made known to the Germans. Who knows what will happen then? I thought Crete would be a safe haven but now we are prisoners twice over, once as Jews and then as islanders.'

'Don't worry,' said Miriam. 'We have good Christian neighbours who will look after us.'

Yolanda could read the fear and concern on their faces. Poor Papa had thought he was bringing them to safety. How cruel it had turned out.

'I'm sure it won't come to that, sir,' Andreas tried to reassure everyone. 'The Cretans have always lived side by side with people of all nations. Your community is one of the oldest on

the island, far older than even the Turks. At least now there will
be law and order, however draconian. Nurse Markos will be
safe, I will guarantee that personally.'

'You mean well, young man, but you know nothing of how
it can be for us. We have lived in Salonika and Athens. My
daughter must stay among her community for her own safety
and respect.'

'Papa!' Yolanda was furious. Her father was treating her like
a child. 'We will discuss this later and I will see Dr Androulakis
to the door.' She was shaking with disappointment. What must
Andreas think of them? Papa was being blunt and discourteous.
He had not even offered him a drink. She was ashamed.

'I'm sorry, Andreas,' she said as she led him to the door, 'they
are frightened for my reputation. My uncle is very traditional.
He doesn't like to see an unmarried woman working out of the
home.'

'I understand, but we do need you. I need you,' he whispered, and she shivered with a flood of love for his honesty. 'I
have plans of my own. I hoped I could rely on you to achieve
them.'

'You're leaving us?' Her heart began to race at this unwelcome news.

'Not exactly, but from time to time I may have to disappear
up into the hills. There's news of bands of stragglers prepared to
hide out. Many have walked sixty miles over rocks with no
shoes, others have died en route. They've been shot at, parched
of water and starved of food, hidden in olive groves, flushed
out. A fleeing army will not be a pretty sight. Hundreds of men
didn't make the beaches and were left to fend for themselves.
They need our help.'

'It sounds dangerous,' Yolanda whispered, for she sensed her
mother hovering in the passageway.

'I can relax if I know you are back in the clinic supervising
the volunteers. I may need to disappear at short notice with

instruments. I won't say any more. You, of all people, mustn't be compromised.'

'Yolanda! Has the doctor gone?' Mother was shouting now.

'Just one moment, Momma,' Yolanda yelled back. Then to Andreas: 'Give me a few more days to win them over.'

Andreas gripped her hand with both of his and smiled. There was no need for words. Something precious passed between them in that lingering farewell. She shut the door behind him and sighed. Nothing and no one was going to stop her going back now.

Galatas Beach, 2001

It was a glorious sunset on Galatas beach, the sun sliding down into the sea like a ball of flame. We parked on the busy main road from Chania, walking down steps past a little taverna and onto the sand. I'd forgotten where the turning was into the old hospital barracks, but there was now a campsite in the trees, and far in the distance a small white chapel. Perhaps it had always been there and I had forgotten. The caves were exactly as I recalled them and just as uninviting.

Lois wanted Alex to take photos, but I was reluctant to be a tourist here. How could I explain that you don't take snap-shots in a cemetery. I wanted to remember it as it once was. Now it was just a sandy beach like many other suntraps. The view to Theodori island was unchanged and there were no reminders left now of how this place had once been, only the landscape.

I'd been dreading this return and wanted to get it over with so we could enjoy the rest of the holiday without sombre reminders. It was throwing up images and flashbacks of scenes I'd tried to keep buried all of my life.

It was a vision of hell in those final days. That terrible unex-pected encounter in the street . . . I could feel my pulse racing.

'I need a stiff drink,' I announced, but Lois ignored my plea, taking my hand.

'Just come over here and see the carpet of flowers clinging to the rocks, all the colours of the rainbow. You'll know their names; I'm hopeless.'

There were flowers and poppies of every hue, white mallows, silver stachys, yellow euphorbias, purple sea holly and tiny rock roses. How strange that so many of my own herbaceous perennials from the garden at Stokencourt were growing wild, unfettered, on this very spot, and I'd never known they were here. Who had time to notice such things in an air raid?

The sea was the colour of expensive jade, the mountains still snow-capped, even at the end of May.

'Just give me a minute,' I said, walking away from them for privacy.

Alex was bored. There was nothing for him on this deserted beach. He couldn't see what I was seeing: those German troops laying posts and fixing wire, turning my hospital into one vast cage for the captured soldiers brought in after the surrender in Chania. There were guard towers just like the ones you see in war films. It was a camp with few facilities left standing, a few tattered tents and marquees, poor latrines and slit trenches, battered chairs and utensils scattered on the sand. How many wounded soldiers lost the will to live corralled into this bug-ridden space already full of dirt and disease?

Deserting my patients was one of the bleakest moments of my life. Other, far worse, things happened later but never did I feel so alone. Now I was reliving the anguish of having to relinquish my post, leaving the weakened men to the tender mercies of an indifferent army bent on revenge for their own losses. I had my own problems. There were decisions to make about my own future and pressure was coming from an unlikely source.

I thought again of the officer, my German patient, my rescuer – how that time haunts my mind like old wartime music. It was here I thought to give him the slip, but he had other ideas.

Chania Harbour, 2001

The Limani Ouzeria was a good spot for watching the world go by. It was early Friday night and families were out, enjoying a stroll round the harbour. One by one the lights flickered on in the cafés and restaurants, and the touts were out with their menus, trying to attract tourists inside with their smooth patter.

This place suited Rainer well, overlooking the old Firkas Turkish fortress, now the Naval Museum. A place he had no desire to revisit.

Most of the old harbour houses had been rebuilt over the years. There were bars and gift shops. One or two were still crumbling ruins in need of repair, like bad teeth in need of filling, but that somehow added to the charm and character. He'd just browsed in the harbour bookshop, which had a good selection of novels and maps in English, German and French, and bought a detailed map of northwest Crete to refresh his memory and plan his next trip out into the mountains. His memory for place names often failed him these days, but there were one or two here that were etched into his brain: Kondomari, Kandanos, Alikianos. Who could ever forget what had gone on there?

He sipped his ouzo, watching the water clouding into the spirit, tasting a plate of *meze:* squid*, tiropita,* sausage, cheese balls.

Chania was now a bustling tourist destination, a vibrant city full of life. The local families walking past him were well dressed, pushing prams, old *yiayias* clustered round tables in their widow's weeds, hair dyed all hues, laughing and shouting as only the Greeks can.

He had chosen this place for old times' sake, and as he turned to look into the dark recesses of the tavern, ancient men were busy playing backgammon, smoking, arguing, entirely unaware of him. How many of these old men had fought and suffered in the old days? How many would shake his hand now if they knew?

The swift-filled sky was noisy with their screeching as darkness descended and the young of all nations came out in their finery: African students, lean-limbed, selling fake CDs; Asian girls with trays of trinkets; Roma children pushing roses onto the unwary; American military from the NATO base, out on the town in baggy shorts and baseball caps. There were Scandinavian girls of such beauty, white-haired and leggy in sundresses, and his fellow countrymen with cameras and portly wives. How different it all was from the last time he was here, this pulsating mass of humanity smelling of aftersun, all mixed together.

None of these revellers would be reminiscing about such dark days of the past. He was sober and silent, solitary and in need of company, but there was no one of his age or nationality sitting close by. The memories kept flooding into his mind of the first time he had sat in almost this very spot, and all he could feel was the pain of being young and overwhelmed by responsibility. Why must duty always clash with personal desire in a war?

June 1941

'You didn't waste much time, Rainer,' sniggered Helmut Krause, gulping down his beer. 'Picked yourself a classy plum of a nurse before we could get a look at the fruit bowl. Quite the little heroine too . . .'

'Shut it.' Rainer felt his cheeks burning from too much *krassi*.

'Don't worry, she's not my type, too skinny-arsed, bit of a cold fish, don't you think? I like my fruit well ripened in the sun.'

Rainer wanted to kick his teeth into his throat at such insults but they were both so drunk it wasn't worth a fight.

They'd taken over a taverna close to the cathedral square, spilling out onto the pavement, singing, shouting, eyeing up the women strolling past, whose eyes were averted in a brave attempt to pretend the evening harbour stroll wasn't ruined by their noisy presence. The Germans were not welcome though their drachmas would be.

They'd spent the day making sure all their scattered dead were buried with full military honours, all information collated. It was a miserable job; no wonder everyone wanted to blot out the memory of their comrades' remains, rotting in the fierce heat. Rainer was in no mood for ribbing about his personal life, not even from his friends.

He looked around at what was left of his men, once so cocky and confident. They had about them now a familiar world-weariness, their eyes blank with exhaustion, the same look he'd seen on the faces of British prisoners in the camp on their arrival in their old hospital.

Soldiers were all the same under the skin. He thought of all those wooden crates of personal effects being sent back to Germany, and the families who would not understand what a hellhole this place had turned out to be.

As for Nurse Georgiou, she was a mystery. So formal and on guard in his presence, with no intention of responding to his overtures. Yet the more she ignored his obvious interest the keener he became. She was becoming a challenge, a distraction from the weariness of mopping up the last of local resistance. He was running out of excuses to visit her, now she was housed in the French Catholic school, but being Catholic himself he hoped he'd catch sight of her in the local church.

He sensed she was relieved to be out of his company, though she was ever polite. 'Thank you,' she said, gathering her carpet-bag, nodding curtly to his driver, when he dropped her off.

'What about that trip to Knossos, I mentioned?' he offered, leaning forward.

She stepped back, holding up her hand. 'I'm sorry. Thank you. I shall be working here from now on,' she replied, not looking at him, and then retreated into the convent hostel with-out a backward glance.

There was talk of the paratroopers being deployed to the North African desert, but until he was fully fit Rainer was ordered to remain here to quell any trouble and to flush out the remaining British in the hills.

He had hated his first duty: the destruction of two villages whose men had put up resistance to the parachute descent alongside a remnant of Greek soldiers. If this was what he was reduced to doing, he wanted none of it, but orders were orders, straight from Berlin. Punishment must be meted out with no trials or juries, just executions and villages on fire. Ten to forty Cretans for every paratrooper killed and no mercy.

How could he explain to ignorant peasants that they were collectively responsible for any act of resistance in their village, and that this would extend to whole families, children included? He also read out the demands for labourers of both sexes to make repairs to roads and airstrips without delay, detailing young men and old for backbreaking work so they could relieve their own soldiers in the heat.

He couldn't sleep for seeing the bewildered looks on children's faces as the soldiers lined up their fathers and shot them under the olive trees, forbidding anyone to return for their bodies for days afterwards. There were soldiers who were hardened and furious, who took pleasure in carrying out these orders, who counted heads, who joked and ransacked houses looking for arms, setting fire to beds and linen for the sheer hell of it, tearing up crops out of the ground and cutting down olive trees just because they could.

His head knew this had to be done to stamp their authority over the island, but in his heart this cruelty lay heavy. He had not pulled a trigger on women and children but he gave the order nonetheless. He had not slept properly since.

There was no point meeting with the Cretan officials. He didn't trust them. They drank too much raki, always giving him assurances that there'd be no further trouble, but their sullen compliance and sly looks made him uneasy.

Meanwhile, here they were, stuck on the island; a key Mediterranean gateway to the Middle East, a strategic supply point for North Africa and Rommel's army.

The revenge they had wreaked in the villages was already being avenged in sneak attacks, ambushes and the disappearance of soldiers on guard duty. The prison camp on the beach was a shambles until the Hitler Youth Brigade took over and began a reign of terror, but those fit enough escaped under cover of darkness and some even in broad daylight. There was no respect for their authority, even when they imposed harsh punishments and cut rations.

Rainer had been given some useful ideas on how to flush evading enemy soldiers out of the hills but he had sympathy for their plight. If roles had been reversed wouldn't he have done the same thing?

They were taking on new interpreters and agents, local men who could sniff out collaborators, but even these employees were under careful scrutiny. What if they were secret informers? Who could they honestly trust but their own men?

So why was he wasting time drooling over some foreign nurse? Was it her graceful figure, those long legs, sun-bleached hair and chocolate eyes, or something more potent to his senses? She was like no other woman he'd ever met, his equal in every way, but there was something unreachable within her that fascinated him. It was almost as if she was the victor and he the vanquished: a ridiculous fantasy. There could be no serious fraternizing, no romancing. If they needed relief, all the troops of any rank were free to make use of brothels, behind the harbour for the rank and file, and a more discreet house and club for the officers. It was ever thus.

Yet nothing could curb his admiration for the nurse. She'd saved lives and endured much hardship. Perhaps it was difficult for her to let go of her own fear and distrust after what she had witnessed. God! If I were Cretan, I wouldn't like us much, he thought, knowing these thoughts amounted to treason. How could he doubt the policies that claimed they had the right to rule the world for a thousand years?

So far it had brought only death and suffering for his men here, but he must believe their leaders knew what they were doing, that their presence was of strategic importance and their sacrifices were for the ultimate goal.

Rainer swallowed his drink and staggered out across the

square to the harbour, staring out towards the ancient Venetian lighthouse. He knew it was time to get over his infatuation before he made a fool of himself. He must stiffen the sinews, cool this childish ardour and flush out all resistance to the Nazi rule. There was no place in his life for romantic foolishness. Nurse Georgiou was the enemy.

Chania, 2001

'We've just had such a brilliant tour of the city, Aunt Pen. I never knew it had such history,' Lois announced as she came strolling down the street to meet me, wearing a new straw sunhat and dark glasses, her shoulders already bronzing in her pretty sundress. 'We met Mr Fennimore at the "Hand" monument and he walked us up through the street where El Greco was born and past the hand-weaver's studio. We met Michaelis there. You just have to see some of his work . . . Oh, and then we wandered in the back-streets viewing the Venetian palazzos and architecture. We even caught a glimpse of the little synagogue, the last one left on Crete. It's Saturday so it was closed for services, I expect. There was so much to take in, and Alex enjoyed it, didn't you?'

Alex was too busy staring into a window full of knives to reply.

'He walked us through Leather Alley and up to the Market Hall. Guess who we bumped into there? Mack, our rep, was shopping and told us about the open-air market. He says there's a taverna at the end of the street that sells delicious *souvlaki*. Shall we join him there?'

What could I do but smile and go along with them as if I had never wandered these streets before? Soon we were staggering under bags of oranges, tomatoes and ripe cherries. Alex had to carry the thyme honey, mysethra cheese and early melons.

Mack was waiting, looking relaxed in long shorts and T-shirt, offering to find us shade, ordering cool bottles of golden Mythos, and barbecued pork *souvlaki* for Alex as if we were all one big happy family on holiday. He was eyeing Lois with interest once again, and she was starting to look relaxed at last.

I had made my way up from the harbour, up Halidon Street to a bookshop I could've sworn was there sixty years ago. I had already found shade behind the cathedral. I'm fine if I take things at my own pace, and I wandered through the huge agora, savouring the familiar smells of grilled fish and chicken, tobacco smoke and strong cheese.

It was noon and the outdoor market would soon be closing for siesta. The heat and the heaviness was making me feel nostalgic. What stories these streets could tell – tales of despair and courage, cunning and defiance. Every Mediterranean town has its market, the very heart of its community.

I was entranced to see all the colours and smells, the variety and abundance on offer. There were stalls full of nothing but greens: great bunches of fresh parsley, mint, mountain herbs, spinach, artichokes. Chickens and rabbits were caged, ready for the pot, netted bags of snails, stalls of silvery fish lying on melting ice, tomatoes like billiard balls, vats of all the local cheeses, jars of honey and bottles full of raki.

Farmers' wives and *yiayias* were sitting under umbrellas, watching as their sons yelled to the crowds. Down the streets came the busy matrons pushing trolley bags, widows bent double, slowly edging their way, bowing to long-haired priests pushing their children in buggies, and flame-haired beauties swaggering down the alley, catching the eyes of the farm boys.

It warmed my heart to see life restored. Suddenly I was back in the same cobbled street all those years ago, glimpsing my young self reflected in the shop window in a drab grey dress and overall like a nun. How could I have been so fearless and determined in the middle of such danger? How could I have done what I did?

July 1941

Penny found herself settling into the life of St Joseph's with relief at being away from the turmoil of those last desperate days in Galatas, the sight of the POWs and her constant wariness of the German captain. It was a relief, too, to be in female company and have the distraction of caring for orphaned children in the makeshift nursery.

There was a stillness within these walls. When the gates were closed, the world outside could be forgotten for a few hours. She had not realized how exhausted she felt; she could sleep for hours, but for the discipline of the religious life.

They knew her situation. She had confessed to Mother Superior that she was asking for sanctuary as a Protestant, an alien, without proper papers, and fleeing from the attentions of a German officer, which was an exaggeration but helped her cause.

If Mother Veronique was dismayed by the responsibility of taking on a fugitive, she didn't show or disclose it to anyone. She patiently listened to Penny's story and, when she had finished, she sat back smiling. 'You were sent here for a reason, my child. I can find you useful employment. We sent some of our staff to the hospital in Heraklion, but I fear they can't return so you are a timely addition to our staff. We have a maternity wing here for mothers in difficulties. Since the bombing we have seen such sad cases, many stillbirths and miscarriages.'

'I'm not a midwife,' Penny replied with dismay, thinking of Effy and all she had gone through. She had never even delivered a baby.

'Watch and learn, my dear. Nature usually takes its course but sometimes there are complications and fevers. I'm sure you are well rehearsed in dealing with such emergencies.'

Once again Penny recalled those terrible hours when Effy miscarried in Athens. Had she managed to achieve her dream yet? Was a nanny now in residence in Stokencourt? Had they all retreated into the country, away from the terrible bombings in London that some of German soldiers bragged about in the cafés for all to hear?

Thrown into the deep end, her learning was swift. How far away was Stokencourt Place and England and her family. It was as if she was a complete stranger to that way of life now. Would she herself ever go through such an undignified process as giving birth?

They gave her a long plain grey dress to wear, a serviceable apron and a headdress like a novice, treating her with kindness as she struggled with her halting French. She was not one of them nor ever could be. Much as she respected their life of religious observance and devotion, none of their ceremonies touched her heart. In services she found her mind wandering to the world outside the walls. Where were Bruce and Zander, and had that really been Yolanda she had seen in the crowd? She no longer trusted what she had thought. All she hoped was that the captain had moved on from Chania and that she was forgotten by the authorities now.

The favourite part of her day was when she was allowed to play with the orphans brought into the day nursery. They sat like docile pets, wide-eyed, silent, too quiet for children. She wanted to take them to the beach to play but the shoreline was forbidden to all without permits. Even fishing now was difficult unless a guard was on board.

The convent had grounds and the vegetable garden was their storehouse. As supplies grew scarcer, Veronique asked a group to go in search of fresh fruit at the market. Penny was to accompany Sister Clothilde and another novice on the trip. It was her first outing for weeks and she felt like a girl let out of school. They rose early and made for the city, to arrive as the market opened. They walked in single file.

Clothilde was not one of Penny's favourite sisters. She had a pinched, pale-faced ageless look, small eyes behind metal-rimmed glasses that missed nothing. She habitually eyed Penny with suspicion, appalled that she never received Mass and curious as to why. She corrected every wrong inflection in her accent, envious of her acumen as a nurse who commanded respect among the other sisters.

The market was disappointing, only a few stalls. 'Where's the fresh fish?' demanded Clothilde. The fish had gone to the occupying army, they were told.

'Where's the fruit?' she demanded, storming up to the empty tables. All gone, trees smashed by planes and fire, crops stolen in the night or dug up in reprisal for villages that had resisted the invasion. Many farmers were too scared to come into the city and many were dead.

'I think it's disgraceful that so few have made the effort to supply us,' Clothilde sneered to one stallholder.

'Yes, ma'am, and it'll only get worse. Everyone is hoarding and hiding what they can before winter comes. We have some snails in a bucket?' He offered them up.

'They don't smell fresh to me,' she sniffed.

Embarrassed, Penny walked away to see if there were other stalls around the corner but there were just a few tables of second-hand clothes. People were rummaging over them as if it was a precious sale.

A girl turned away and almost bumped into her. '*Signóme*' she said. She looked up briefly and glanced again as if she couldn't believe who she was seeing. They both jumped back in recognition of each other. Penny's stomach did a somersault and she stepped forward, shaking with emotion at such an unexpected meeting.

'Yolanda? Oh thank God, it is you! You're alive . . .' Penny called out, but Yolanda backed off, stumbling into a crate in her anxiety to flee from her. Penny ran forward to help her up. 'Come back, I'm not a ghost . . . Please, we must talk.'

Yolanda picked herself up, scowling. 'I have *nothing* to say to you.' She turned to walk away but Penny was quick to dart in front and block her path as shoppers stopped to stare at them, hoping for a fight.

'Well, I have something to ask you. Where have you been all this time? I searched for you? Why did you abandon us without so much as a word, desert your post, leave us in the lurch?' she yelled into Yolanda's face.

'How could you think that?' Yolanda replied, her eyes flashing in anger. 'I might ask what a British nurse is doing in a German staff car. I saw you . . . you didn't waste your time,' Yolanda spat back.

Penny felt indignation flaring up. 'How dare you suggest such a thing? I was being escorted back to the prison camp, which was our military hospital before it was overrun. I had no choice in the matter, none at all.'

'And I was too busy nursing on a hospital ship to notice it had set sail. Lucky for me it came to Crete. I sent you all a postcard to explain.' She paused, then her voice softened. 'You never got it? I'm here with the Red Cross.' She stood with her arms folded, waiting for Penny's explanation. They both stood staring at each other.

Penny shook her head. 'I left Athens in a caïque. It was blown out of the water and we were stranded on an island. This is where I ended up too . . . It seems we both had no choice in the matter.' The crowd, hoping for a fight to begin, melted away.

Suddenly they locked eyes and their lips quivered with emotion. Penny threw her arms into the air in disbelief. 'Oh hell . . . All this time here on Crete, both working ourselves into the ground . . . Yolanda, I'm so sorry,' Penny smiled, and they fell into each other's arms in a hug of relief and joy, crying with excitement.

'Here's me thinking *you'd* deserted us or were dead, and you, thinking I'd gone over to the other side. How could you ever think that after what we've both been through?' Penny laughed. 'Oh, it's so good to see you and know you're safe.'

'So where are you now?' Yolanda asked, tears of joy rolling down her face. 'It's been so long.'

'In a convent. Can't you tell, in my smart uniform?' Penny whispered.

'You've taken vows?' Yolanda looked astonished.

'Do I look the type?' They both burst out laughing and it was only when they recovered that they noticed Sister Clothilde was standing only a foot away, eyeing them both with suspicion, her arms folded in disapproval at such displays of emotion in public.

'Nurse, it's time to leave. This has been a useless outing; let's not waste any more time here.' Sister Clothilde turned and made her way to where the novice nun was waiting for her, holding the empty shopping baskets.

'If you want vegetables, I know someone who can find you a supply, but under cover of darkness,' Yolanda whispered.

'Black market?'

'Not exactly. He relieves the Germans of their surplus, shall we say, supplies they stole from us. Let's just call it reclamation . . .'

'Oh, do be careful. If you're caught . . .'

'Not me, I'm too busy training up orderlies. Come and join us. I'm so glad to see you. Momma and Papa will be so happy to know you are safe. Come and have supper with us on

Friday . . . Sabbath supper. We have rooms in Portou Street. It has a dark-green door, the street under the wall behind Kondi-laki. It's all a bit of a mess down there but our house still has a roof.'

Penny held onto her arm. 'I can't believe this. I thought you . . .' she hesitated to repeat what she'd really thought. 'I thought you were dead. I've so much to tell you.'

'And so have I.' Yolanda waved her farewell, her gold neck-lace glinting in the sunshine as she raced passed Clothilde and the novice down the street.

'Did I see the Star of David round that girl's neck?' Clothilde snapped.

'I never noticed,' Penny replied. 'She's my friend from Athens, a Red Cross nurse. Oh, I am so glad she made it here. There were so many nurses drowned . . .'

'Nurse or not, she's a Jewess. We do not consort with such people.'

Gladly I do, thought Penny with defiance, but said nothing, taking her place in line for the walk back. She would love to see the Markos family again but first she must ask permission to leave the convent. For the first time in weeks she felt the constraints of her chosen refuge. Every choice had its price, she sighed.

On Friday morning, Mother Veronique sent for her in the playground where she was teaching the girls to play 'In and out the Scottish bluebells'. They were dancing in and out of each other's raised arms and Penny was beating time to the tune on an empty oil drum, everyone trying to sing in English, French and Greek, and making lots of happy noise. She was asked to go to the study where Mother Superior told her the visit to the Markos family would be allowed, under escort as far as the Jewish quarter, with strict instructions to be back before dark. Penny tried to explain that Sabbath would begin at sunset and this would not leave much time for her meal.

'I fear you are taking advantage of our hospitality here,'

Veronique chided her. 'Perhaps you should go and lodge with your friend.'

'I'm sorry for causing inconvenience to you all since you've been more than generous to me. I've been used to my own freedoms, I fear.' Penny reflected that nothing in her upbringing, or since, could have paved the way for a convent life.

Veronique nodded. 'You are an unsettling influence on some of the younger girls. Sister Clothilde . . .'

Penny didn't hear the rest. Poor plain petulant Clothilde was jealous, suspicious and bigoted. It was time Penny left the convent and joined Yolanda at her clinic or the hospital.

St Joseph's had sheltered her when she had no address that would satisfy her captors. It had given her refuge when exhausted and confused, fed her and given her back confidence in her skills, as well as adding a few more. What was one nun's spitefulness amongst such loving kindness?

She dropped on her knees for a blessing. 'Mother, you've given me back my strength, my courage and dignity. Your convent was a rock to cling to and I'll never forget such love, but you're right. It's time for me to go back out there and use my talents, not hide them away. I do know my Bible.' Penny smiled. 'I hope you'll accept my deepest gratitude and forgive my impulsive ways.'

Veronique patted her head. 'Get up, young lady. You've been a breath of fresh air wafting amongst us, scurrying about, teaching short cuts, dancing with the children. One day you will make a good mother. You have a big heart, Penelope. There's much for you to do in this world. Go and see your friend and I will pray that the way forward for you will become clear. Stay with us until you see where that path takes you.'

With such a blessing ringing in her ears, Penny had a spring in her step as she made her way down the hill towards the ruined city with Sister Irini, who was taking some food to an old Algerian couple confined by sickness to their rooms.

On street corners, spilling out of the tavernas still standing were the troops in their distinctive olive-green-grey uniforms, cluttering the streets, three abreast, shoving locals into the road, loud, bragging, enjoying the sunshine and eyeing the girls.

Penny was glad to be invisible in her plain habit and head-scarf, even if she was a head taller than her escort. No one would bother looking at her, and this sowed the seed of an idea as to how she might travel unmolested with the right papers. There was no doubt in her mind that the hills were calling. She had looked on them every morning with longing. They reminded her of Scotland and the freedom of stalking in the mountains. What must the view be from them?

She'd not forgotten Bruce's challenge to her to go native and disappear. It was important that she could justify why she'd defied him and stayed on. It was in one of those moments in the bustle of the streets that she looked up and saw the snow tips of the White Mountains, even in the heat of summer, and sensed they were her next destination. How or when, she had no idea, only this flutter of certainty in her gut. It was time to move on.

It was a crush around the supper table, the sun had just set and Yolanda's uncle's house was full of lodgers who'd lost their homes in the bombing. The synagogue had lost its top floor but enough remained for a gathering for prayers. Now, as the candles were lit and the prayers around the table began, Penny sat in silence, the honoured guest at the humble feast. The chicken had had to be killed according to custom in secret because it was now illegal for animals to be slaughtered in the kosher way. There'd been an order to hand in all ritual knives, all knives from the Jewish residents, but, as ever, someone managed to hide or 'lose' theirs, and in a city famous for its knife making, there were always replacements ready to be cleansed and blessed for the purpose.

How different this was from their dinners together in Kifissia.

Sara looked pinched and tired, her face drained of emotion. Solomon had aged, his hair now entirely white, and he had grown a long beard. Penny tried to follow what Yolanda was doing and listened to the Classical Hebrew coming from the lips of even small children.

There was talk of the new instructions, read out by their rabbi, that soon all their shopkeepers must place a large sign in their windows announcing: 'This is a Jewish Business . . . Germans prohibited from entering.'

'They will beggar us, for who else has drachmas but the soldiers?' said Aunt Miriam, her eyes wary, looking round the table for support. People shrugged. 'What can we do but obey?' said another. 'We heard the rabbi has to give a list of all the Jews of Chania with their addresses and ages to the Town Hall. What does it mean?'

'It means we're registered, that's all, so calm yourself, Mother. A sign on the window, a name on a list means nothing. If it was anything more, Giorgos would nod me the wink,' Joseph interrupted. 'We keep our heads down and do nothing to alert attention. The children are in school, they have good friends, as long as we stick together . . .'

'You are wrong, Joe. We should be heading for the hills, away from places where we're known, find a ship and leave,' said a young man with thick glasses. 'Don't forget the old saying: "Drop by drop the water wears away the marble . . . One by one their laws will destroy us."'

'That's defeatist talk, Mordechai, I'll have none of that here. The Almighty One has spared us, we have life and we must live it as He ordains. The Jews have lived here in peace for over a thousand years. He will not allow His congregation to be destroyed.'

When the formalities of dinner were over and Mordechai made to talk to Yolanda, she grabbed Penny's arm and made for the door. 'Let's get out of here so we can talk. I don't want

Mordo to get the wrong idea. I've seen how his mother and my mother are making plans.'

'He looks a nice young man,' Penny whispered.

'Precisely, nice but with no spark,' Yolanda smiled, and nudged her. 'You know what I mean. Nothing happens when I look at Mordo.' She patted her groin. 'Nothing down there.'

'Yolanda Markos, what's got into you? You weren't like this in Athens.' Penny nudged her back and they giggled.

'I hadn't met Andreas Androulakis then,' she whispered.

Then Yolanda told Penny all about her doctor friend, who was working for the freedom forces, she was sure, taking supplies to hidden soldiers who had escaped from the camps. There was such tenderness in her eyes as she talked of him.

'Last week he came on shift late. He said he'd been to see a sick patient. I don't know where he went but when he comes back his boots are filthy and he's covered in blood stains. They say he's gone into the hills to treat wounded escapees . . . When he does his shift his eyelids are drooping with exhaustion. He's such a brave man. I wish he'd take me with him.'

'What do your parents make of your young man?' Penny asked.

'They must know nothing about him. Father is treating me like a child. He's changed since he came here. He has gone back to his faith and is far stricter. He's afraid I will leave them. If he thought I was seeing a Gentile . . . They don't understand.'

'You are all they have, they need you,' Penny replied, though she knew it wasn't what Yolanda wanted to hear.

'I know, but times are so strange now. I have to lead my own life. Who knows what will happen?'

Penny envied the passion she could see flaming out of those dark eyes, dangerous though it might be. When she thought of Bruce, she felt only frustration, anxiety, no longer any excitement or passion. That part of her life was over. She had no energy left for romance. She told Yolanda about her time coming to an end in the convent, how she missed the danger of the field hospital, even in those terrible conditions. 'I must be mad to miss the caves, and all those hospital trains, but action gets in your blood. Now I feel numb and useless.' She explained about the convent and the German captain's interest in her.

'I think he guesses I am not Greek but he's said nothing. I hope he's left Crete by now.'

'Was he the man in the staff car? He looked terrifying – all Nazis do,' Yolanda whispered.

'He scares me, too . . . I don't want to think about him. I'm so glad we're friends together again. Knowing you're safe and with your family is all that matters now. But it's time for me to go.'

'You can stay with me here; don't go yet,' said Yolanda.

'I have to. My escort, Sister Irini, is waiting in the square. I think they fear I'll be converted overnight,' Penny laughed. 'I must go inside to thank your family for their hospitality.'

She made her farewells and Yolanda walked her down the rubble-filled street.

'You've set me thinking. I promised Bruce I'd go native, go into the mountains. It sounds as if I could be useful there but I need a guise, identity papers and somewhere to take me in. A stranger in a village is soon news. I haven't even got a map,' Penny confessed.

'Let me ask Andreas when he returns. He'll know what to do,' Yolanda replied.

'Bruce told me to dye my hair. How can I do that?'

'Leave that to me, we'll do it one night.'

They paused at the harbour end and hugged. 'I envy you, Penny. You have the riches of freedom and choices, I have only this,' she sighed, pointing to the broken buildings.

Penny shook her head and waved as she left. 'You have a loving family, deep roots, a vocation and a lover in your heart. From where I'm standing, you are the wealthier one of us by far.'

2001

The market was emptying. Dogs scavenged for scraps among the litter. The smell of the pork *souvlaki* was tempting as I sat daydreaming of dear Yolanda and that last supper in Chania with them all. Finding her again kept me sane during that first hot summer. War had a habit of separating people, dividing families and friends, tearing lovers from each other's arms.

Those who could, fled into the hills, took refuge in caves and stone huts like animals seeking shelter from the heat or the snow. Others, like the Markos family, huddled in basements undercover. There was safety in numbers – or so they thought . . .

'Aren't you glad you came back?' Lois interrupted my thoughts. 'Was that school you pointed out the one where you stayed in Halepa?'

I nodded. 'It's a college now. I'm glad it survived.'

'Were you really a nun?' Alex was looking at me intently.

'Yolanda asked me that,' I mused, still stuck in past thoughts.

'Will we meet her too?' the boy asked.

'No.'

'Why not?' Alex could be so insistent.

I shook my head. 'Let's not talk about all that on such a lovely day,' I said. 'Take me home.'

Part 3

RESISTANCE

All the good things of the world are written in ink
But Freedom asks for a script written in blood from our own heart.

A Cretan mantinada from *The Leaden-Sky Years of World
War II,* Kimon Farantakis, translated by P. David Seaman

2001

The taxi drove Rainer east along the old road to Heraklion and Rethymno, turning into the hills at Vrisses, climbing up into the mountain passes and onto the Askifou Plain along narrow winding metalled tracks gouged out of the rocky landscape. It was all so different from the mule tracks, dusty riverbeds and gorges that this old veteran had once struggled along. 'You have to see the *Kriegsmuseum* in the hills,' he was told in the hotel. 'Georgos makes everyone welcome and there's nothing like it in the whole of Crete.'

As they turned down the narrow lane from the village of Kares, he wondered just what he was coming to. It was indeed a unique war museum, judging by the rusting machinery cluttering up the entrance of the old house. A man in a black shirt and jodhpurs introduced himself as Georgos Hatzidakis, owner of a motley collection of weaponry and armaments.

He found himself in a small living space taken over with exhibits: posters and field equipment such as he hadn't seen for sixty years, radio sets, medical instruments, binoculars, helmets of all nationalities, caps, guns; a collection that Georgos and his family had put together since 1941 when the Battle for Crete passed his door as a boy of ten.

They had watched the British retreat, the German pursuit and the capture of the remnants as they stumbled back over the mountains as prisoners of war.

'Me see everything,' he explained in broken English to a visiting English couple.

They all browsed among the memorabilia, stunned at the comprehensiveness of this collection: motorbikes, iron crosses, even a set of dental instruments, all sorts of hardware had found its way here. 'This is my family and no favourites,' the curator smiled as he gave them all thimble glasses filled with raki, and biscuits. 'And you, my friend, were here?' he asked.

The veteran nodded. 'Not during the evacuation. No, I was wounded,' he said, slapping his hip as if to excuse himself from anything the man might relate of that time. 'But later, yes. There were no roads then, just tracks down to the port of Sphakia and the south coast.'

'It used to take two days for us to travel from there to Chania, now it's just an hour. The island has shrunk, but memories are still long,' Georgos said.

'Many bad things happened,' he replied: better to say this first.

Georgos shrugged in that Greek way. 'Here we take no sides. These are just witnesses and I am a living bit of the history.' He pulled back his *sariki* to show a big scar. 'Shrapnel from a bomb. It killed my uncle and my brother . . . Boom, boom, out of the sky. Come, my friend, another raki and another biscuit. '*Siga, siga* . . . go slowly in the heat. Many soldiers come here to remember.' He walked away, leaving the visitors to read the testaments on the walls, the newspapers and photographs, the tragic human detritus of such a hasty scramble for freedom. There was too much to take in at one sitting.

He felt the raki taking its effect and needed to sit down in the shade. His driver would be in the *kafenion* waiting for the return journey. As he sat on a bench overlooking the plain and the hills, memories flooded back again.

Kares looked so peaceful: fields of crops, neatly painted houses, gardens full of geraniums and roses. He must have passed by this spot in those early months, tense, uncertain, still shocked by their struggle to hold the island. It was an unsettling time; so many bad memories to settle. He looked across at the pile of rusting weapons, once gleaming with menace. *Why does it always come to this?*

1941

The late summer campaign into the hills was to flush out the stragglers, knowing many were being sheltered in the villages higher up in the White Mountains. How shocked Rainer was to discover the primitive conditions in which these proud Cretans lived: often in one room with an earth floor, cooking over an open fire, drawing water from deep stone wells underground. His men assumed they were ignorant peasants and treated them with contempt.

Yet these people were handsome, strong and hardworking, with rich traditions and deep superstitions. The gangs of men and women they rounded up for road work bent their backs without complaint in the arid heat of the day, at least to their faces. They had a proud stare, often singing at their work, strange rhymes and folk songs; mantinades that defeated his basic Greek, words that changed from day to day. Judging by the looks and laughs in their direction, his men were the butt of their words, though he couldn't prove anything.

The further into the hills they pushed, the less he felt secure among the overhanging rocks and narrow gullies, slipping on gravel sharp as razors. The threat of an ambush was ever present, making sun-soaked men tetchy, ready to shoot anything that moved.

Spotter planes swept over the mountains and plains, while

armed patrols scoured the bridleways, searching for fugitives. They had secured the services of dubious local men who knew the best hiding places and the tricks of secreting stores against the order not to hoard goods. But there must be places known only to goatherds and shepherds that defied anyone discovering. Rainer didn't trust the turncoats, willing to sell their fellow neighbours for a few drachmas, but in war you took help where you could.

It was on the Askifou plain that they scented out a trail leading up impossible scree. Dogs and troops scrambling up gave a warning and a flurry of men in rough costume began to run for cover. The grim fight that followed left two of Rainer's men dead, and wounded some ragged soldiers. Schiller, one of his patrol leaders, wiry and short-tempered at the best of times, was incensed by the resistance and took his men up into the caves, flushing out at gun point some pathetic remnants of the British Army, dressed in rags, half starved, with wounds and on crutches. They surrendered without any fight left in them.

At the back was a bearded soldier covered in mosquito bites, dragging a wounded leg. Rainer examined them. Some had made pathetic attempts to pass themselves off as locals. This lot would be better off in a camp. The food they had left was little more than water bottles and a bag of snails. They wouldn't survive much longer in this condition. How could you not feel sorry for proud soldiers who had come to this sorry state?

The Cretan sun showed no mercy on any of them as they slid their way down to the track, to march them on to base for further questioning.

It was going to be a long trek and the prisoners begged for time to rest. Schiller was not happy; he wanted them to push on in front in case there were any snipers hiding in the olives or pines. He wanted to torment them and punish them for the death of his friends. But Rainer knew that soldiers under pressure explode, so he insisted everyone be rested under the shade of the olives where even the sheep were nestling under a cloud of flies. The prisoners were given water.

Rainer strolled away to relieve himself, smoke a cigarette and wonder what the hell he was doing halfway up a mountain when his skills were needed in Egypt or on the eastern front. This was all part of his rehabilitation to stretch his weakened muscles, get his fighting strength back for long marches.

As he stood up to return he heard a gunshot. He hurried back to the olive trees where the prisoners stood around the body of a man, shot in the head. There was bruising where he'd been kicked around in the earth.

'Who did this?' Rainer stormed.

'Sir, he wouldn't get up. It was time to go. He refused,' said Schiller with a look of utter contempt in his eyes.

'He was sick, you bastard,' shouted one of the British, actually an Australian by the sound of him. 'He was sick!'

Rainer looked closely, realizing it was the poor bugger from the cave, ginger-haired, covered in bites and wounded. Uncontrollable anger rose within him at such an act of cruel vengeance reaped on a defenceless man. Schiller had been waiting for a chance to beat the daylights out of his enemy. The look of triumph on his face turned to a smirk and then surprise as Rainer pulled him aside.

'What are you thinking of? The man was unarmed,' he spat.

'These pigs shot my comrade.'

'Not this man, as well you know.'

'They are all pigs!' Schiller ranted.

'Speak when you are spoken to, Corporal!' Rainer ordered, but Schiller was unhearing.

'We should shoot the lot of them, murdering bastards.' Schiller pulled out his gun.

'And you, Corporal, kill a man in cold blood, sick and unarmed. I will not have this behaviour under my command.'

In one smooth movement he pulled out his Luger and shot Schiller in the temple. His body hit the ground like a felled tree and then there was a stunned silence.

'That goes for any of you,' Rainer shouted, looking slowly round at his men, seeing the shock on their faces. 'We are German soldiers, not a rabble. Bury these men now,' he ordered.

It was only when they had marked the spot with stones and helmets, and the patrol was marching back to base in silence alongside shuffling prisoners, that Rainer realized what he had done in killing one of his own men. But it was too late for regrets. Was it fear, frustration and the fury of knowing he would have to explain his actions that had made him mete out such a punishment?

There had to be standards of behaviour in a conquering army; decency, humanity. Hadn't a British medic rescued him in the heat of battle, given him a chance of life on that street in Galatas? At least now he had repaid that mercy. He would make a full report, knowing his behaviour would not go down well. Strange as it was, he had no regrets.

2001

Mack was becoming a regular visitor to our villa, escorting Alex and Lois on jaunts to the beach and suggesting we make a day trip up into the hills to the ancient Roman village of Lappa, finishing with lunch at the waterfalls at Argyroupolis. We were getting used to the heat and wanted to make the most of our remaining time here, but I was nervous of making my way back into the hills, even as a tourist.

I was beginning to like Mack, but anxious that his obvious attention to Lois might be his habitual ploy with single women. Was he on the make? I hoped not because Alex was warming to his presence. Mack was divorced, with children in the UK; that much I had gleaned from his eagerness to show me his children's pictures. He mentioned his father had served in the Royal Navy on submarines in the Med during the war. He was the youngest of four boys and had hardly known his father, who had died many years ago. It had left him with a fascination to trace his father's journey and Crete was the perfect harbour to make his base.

When he offered to drive us up to Lappa village on his day off, I took this as a sign of his genuine interest in Lois, who'd been through enough last year to make her wary of any man's attentions. Perhaps a little holiday romance would do wonders for her confidence.

The villas in the cobbled streets of Lappa were a revelation. It was like stepping back in time. I kept wondering how they fared during the occupation. The buildings had been untouched by bombs and burnings. How many jackboots had strolled along these streets as we were doing, admiring the columns, the architecture and the view to the coast from the ramparts? Whoever was stationed here among the fruit groves must have felt very secure, I mused.

As we drove though the winding roads banked with flowers and gorse, climbing ever higher to another of the nearby villages, the landscape became even more familiar. I thought of that first journey made there in the winter of 1941, that fateful foray out of the city in disguise.

November 1941

As winter approached, the nuns of St Joseph's and the Orthodox convents in the districts prepared to stock up supplies, sending Penny and other helpers out into surrounding villages to scrounge vegetables, fruit, and grains to help feed their growing school of orphans who needed clothing and shelter. They were also searching for kin to take these children into the relative safety of the nearby villages. Who was to guess that this was part of a ruse, and that this innocent-looking young woman had other motives? The convent had continued to be her home. It made a useful part of the front she now presented to the world.

Riding their trusty mule, Penny was learning the bridle paths and tracks, river beds and bridge crossings, resting under olive groves, finding the *kafenions* to avoid and the hospitality of courageous priests. They became familiar sights in the foothills of the Apokoronas, regular visitors at checkpoints, showing their identity papers to guards and policemen, passing through unnoticed. Who was to know that Penny's cloak was lined with medical supplies or that she carried vital letters strapped to her chest? There was even a parcel of dental instruments that Andreas requested to be left near Vafes for future use.

She alone took the risk, hiding loaves, cigarettes, anything portable in her stocking tops and shoes, for use by the growing number of British escapees and freedom fighters.

Yolanda had asked her to help her lover, and once Penny had met the spirited young doctor she promised that he could count on her to make deliveries to designated drops, which were changed regularly to stop poaching from other groups.

She soon discovered that the special Cretan bush telegraph was more efficient than any GPO. Why was it that on delivery day there was always a friendly police chief patrolling the checkpoint, waving her through unsearched, or a door was left unlocked and barking dogs were silent in the shepherd's hut?

One night, Yolanda had crept through her window with a bottle of walnut juice, which she painted onto Penny's hair with a comb to darken it, tying it in a headscarf until it had dried. That fancy English rollover style was replaced by a severe plait. They darkened her eyebrows and she marvelled at herself in the mirror; she really did look convincing. With her heavy scarf hiding her features, stooping in black overalls and thick stockings, she was unrecognizable as the tall blonde nurse. It was a good disguise.

The winds were chilly now and she spent many evenings learning to spin wool and knit stockings, mittens and scarves with her pupils. The nuns laughed at her clumsy fingers and frequent mistakes, and teased that she had no home-making skills. Penny wondered what her own mother would make of her appearance now, her coarse hands and leathery skin. England seemed a lifetime ago, another world, not that she had any regrets for choosing to stay.

The more she travelled round the countryside, the more she loved the people. They accepted she was an Athenian nurse, unmarried and religious. She was introduced to mothers, *yiayias*, young girls who brought their ailments into their conversations, discussing them over mountain teas and *glyka*, little spoonsful of jam, forced on her from their precious and dwindling stores. Everyone wanted news of relatives in Chania. What was in the shops and market? How were the soldiers treating them? Who had died or been shot, and when were the British coming back to free them?

What could she say but that she lived in a cloister and knew nothing much. It was the perfect cover for her secret activities. Everywhere there were complaints about shortages, looting, sabotage and reprisals. Every village had heroes, villains, traitors, gossips. Some were on the make and take, but at the heart were men like Father Gregorio whose passive resistance to oppression gave his parishioners the courage to defy the ban on sheltering the evading troops.

Often the distances were too far for one journey and Penny, alongside Sister Martine, an older nun who had become a good friend, would stay the night with the local teacher, doctor or priest and his family. She knew their every movement was watched when they entered a village. Could she be a spy or a German agent? Dr Androulakis's reputation went before him, and the secret grapevine let it be known the Athenian nurse could be trusted. Her papers called her 'Athina Papadopouli'. She knew never to ask family names. The less you knew, the less you could give away, should the worst happen.

Just before Christmas 1941, they made one last trek into hills, which were already covered in snow. There had been a trawl through the White Mountains by German alpine troops searching for escaped soldiers. The conical stone shepherds' refuges were full of escapees, some in need of medical treatment, and the local doctor had run out of supplies.

Andreas had been spotted too many times for him to risk delivering more, and there was news of British officers hiding in the hills with instructions to set up a wireless link with Cairo. Penny and Sister Martine volunteered to make one last trip.

Laden with panniers of supplies, the old mule stumbled up the rugged track and Penny walked behind, glad of her nurse's cloak and patched-up boots. The medical supplies were strapped like a corset under her shift, making her body plumper and weighing her down. Poor Sister Martine had no head for heights and felt sick, but together they forged a path through falling snow towards the first of the villages, which seemed to be carved out of the very rock. It was good to be out in the mountain air, striding out as she had done in Scotland all those years ago, her lungs bursting with exertion, but her companion was no mountain goat and stumbled on the uneven ground. They had to find shelter, and soon. The icy flakes stung her cheeks as the storm grew. Thank the Lord, the old mule knew its path and got them safely to the edge of the village, where they took shelter under the olive trees before one last hike to the square and the café close to the church. There, Kyria Tassoula ushered them in and proceeded to sit them down and wash their frozen feet, massaging them in oil, making Penny want to cry with gratitude at such an act of welcome.

'*Po . . . po. . . po.*' It is too dangerous to send you so far but you are God's angels of mercy,' Tassoula cried, shoving cups of warmed goat's milk into their hands.

Sister Martine coughed and sneezed, her cheeks reddened from exertion and a hint of fever, Penny suspected. 'I must say my daily prayers,' she croaked, then stood and promptly fainted on to the earthen floor.

Tassoula helped carry her to the family bed where she began to moan, tossing and turning. 'This is no cold, Sister,' she sighed, and Penny knew they would not be making the return journey when Martine was so sick and the weather was closing in.

Tassi's two young daughters, Maria and Eleni, were helping in the kitchen preparing the food for the evening *glendi*.

'You will meet all our guests later,' Tassi smiled, revealing only three front teeth left. 'They'll come when the night covers them, come for something warm. You will see.'

While Martine fought her fever, Penny worked with the girls to prepare the meagre dinner of roots and dried beans. All the cooking was done on the fire while the smell of the very last of their roasted coffee beans scented the air.

Tassi's husband, Yiannis, sat watching them, silent, flicking his amber beads. Men in the mountains, or in the town for that matter, did no food preparation, no laundry, dairy or house-work or child rearing. That was women's work, as was tending the vegetable plot, spinning and weaving, sewing, praying. Penny had observed this over the past months on her travels. Women ripened early in the sun and aged quickly with the toughness of their daily lives. It seemed so unfair.

Tassi was an energetic and loving spirit. 'You are a guest, you do nothing,' she insisted, pointing to a stool, but Penny was ready with a firm reply.

'When the night comes and the snow traps us, we will be your lodgers and a lodger must pay. I have no money so there-fore I must work. It is my orders from the convent. You do not want me to get into trouble; Sister Martine will say I am lazy.'

'*Po, po, po* . . .' Tassi threw her hands up in despair. First round to Penny.

Later, when the beans were bubbling in the pot, men sidled into the café one by one, unshaven, stinking to high heaven, old uniforms disguised as country rags, feet wrapped in cloths or wooden-soled sandals. A few were clearly fair-haired Brits and Antipodeans trying to pass themselves off as locals.

Penny eyed them from the corner of the room. No one must recognize this dowdy, dark-headed spinster in black as Nurse Penelope George. No one must know she was here in the hills on a mission, that she too was a British escapee.

The girls brought out the stew and hunks of bread. The men tried not to wolf down their portions, savouring every last drop. How pinched and tired they all looked, these weary remnants of a once-proud army, dependent on the charity of these moun-tain folk for some warmth and succour on such a cold, snowy night.

As the local *krassi,* tasting of liquorice, flowed, so tongues loosened and then the songs of home began: 'Roll out the Barrel', 'Waltzing Matilda', 'Good King Wenceslas', and Penny felt a wave of nostalgia washing over her for Stokencourt, for Evadne, for childhood memories of Christmas Eve when the church choir sang carols in the hall under their tall Christmas tree. She wanted to weep for these poor men, stranded. Here they were far from home, in a foreign country, at the mercy of strangers, though for tonight all was well.

The café filled up and there were rumours of ships waiting to take them off the island to Egypt, if only they could dodge enemy patrols and reach the south coast.

Penny wanted to warn them to shut their mouths in case there were quislings. Andreas had warned that not every Cretan welcomed this raggle-taggle invasion of soldiers on the scrounge, especially those who had seen their houses blown up, villages burned and relatives shot in reprisal for sheltering Allied soldiers.

As in all Cretan parties, someone had a lute, and music was struck. The old men danced the *syrtos* dances, round and round in circles, pulling the boys into the ring, and a young shepherd boy jumped and turned in the air like a gazelle. Everyone was clapping and whistling as the music grew faster and wilder.

Maria and Eleni sat in the shadows under their mother's watchful eye. Then the outer door opened and a flurry of snow and chill cooled the air. For a second everyone froze as the snowman shook the flakes off his shepherd's *kapota.*

'Panayotis! Come, sit down, warm yourself, my friend. How is it out there?' shouted Yiannis, giving him a bear hug.

'Like the Arctic,' the man said in perfect English before replying in Greek. There was something familiar about the accent, a hint of a New Zealand twang. Penny watched the tall man in Cretan costume unravel his scarf to reveal his beard. She felt herself go cold and shrank back into the dark recess to compose herself. Oh good heavens, it was Bruce Jardine, in shepherd's clothes! She couldn't believe that he was still here on the island after all this time. What a shock, and what a relief that he was still free. She felt a surge of joy that he was safe, mixed with exasperation that he kept turning up at the most inconvenient moments.

Unaware of her presence, he sat down to warm himself, winking at the two girls in the corner. 'Maria, Eleni, my beautiful maids of the mountains.' They rushed to find him food and wine and he tucked into it with relish. He glanced round the room, clocking faces, smiling and acknowledging each of them before he turned his attention to Penny, eyeing her with interest while two old men stood and sang a defiant mantinada about how they would take their guns and go into town to kill the enemy. It was a sad, mournful tune and the mood was sombre, but then, as if to lighten the gloom, Bruce was on his feet, urging any of them with Scots ancestry to show them some Highland dances.

They took two shepherds crooks, placed them in a cross on the floor as one man found his mouth organ and started up a bright tune and Bruce attempted a Highland fling. There were cheers and chatter, more wine and raki as the *glendi* got into full swing.

It would go on all night, for the evaders must hide out during daylight, return to their caves and huts, and hole up well out of the sight of villages. Any journeys must be made by moonlight with shepherd guides who were as sure-footed as the goats on the scree.

No one would be going anywhere tonight in this blizzard. They were trapped. Snow left tracks to hiding places, snow brought frostbite, hardship, hunger, danger and boredom, but it mercifully kept the Germans in their barracks too.

All Penny could think of was escaping before her cover was blown. She crept up the wooden ladder to where Martine was sleeping. Her fever had worsened and she would not be fit to leave any time soon. Their cover story was that they were searching for the relatives of orphan Elefteria Mataki, thought to be in the area. The chances of finding her relatives were slim now the weather had closed in. Soon their own travel papers would expire and questions would be asked why they were still here.

'Who is this Panayotis?' she asked Tassi, curious to know what the locals knew about Bruce.

'A British officer returned from Cairo with arms and explosives, they tell us. He travels from village to village, counting the English. It is dangerous work for a man with no uniform . . . A handsome man for a foreigner, don't you think?' Tassi cackled. 'He will make good sons.'

Penny blushed, shaking her head. 'Be careful, if you know all this so will others. There will be talk,' she warned.

'No one will talk tonight. They'll sleep by the fire on woven blankets and sheep skins. By the time they have drained all the raki, they'll be fit for nothing and forget what they've heard here. It is Christmas, time to dance and sing. No Germania will stop our festive day.'

It was hard to be so close to Bruce, to go unrecognized, to have to remain undercover from all these English-speaking boys. Penny tossed and turned as Martine snored. He was alive, safe and still on the island. She recalled their lunch in Chania when he'd suggested she could be useful in the hills. She couldn't forget their last angry exchange on the beach. Would he be proud to know she was doing her bit? His good opinion still mattered to her but it would be better to keep a low profile and not draw attention to herself or her secret mission. She didn't want another lecture.

Bruce was a link with home and with her old life in Athens. Seeing him brought such a yearning for those days when life was uncomplicated. She was so torn between wanting to know how he was and yet . . .

Martine stirred, needing more mountain-herb tea to cool her fever. Penny crept down from the bed shelf to see if there was water left to boil on the embers of the fire. The floor was littered with snoring bodies creating an animal fug of sweat, tobacco, wine and garlic.

She was making for the ladder to return when a voice whispered, '*Despinis, pos sas lene?*' What is your name, miss?'

'Athina,' she whispered back without turning round, aware now of Bruce sitting in the shadows.

'Why have we not seen you here before?' he continued.

She shook her head, wishing she'd put her scarf over her dyed hair. 'A family friend, visiting,' she replied, wishing he'd go away.

'At this time of year, and dressed like a nun?' She could hear suspicion in his voice. 'You are not local.'

'I'm from Chania, from the French school, here to find the relatives of an orphan with Sister Martine, who is sick. I must go to her.'

'Not so fast.' She could feel Bruce standing close now, his breath on her neck.

'Nuns don't travel so far from their convents and I've never come across French ones here before.'

'They go where they are sent to find homes for children,' she replied, turning her back on him. The cup shaking in her hand.

He rattled something off in rapid French to which she could make no reply.

'So, you are not even French or you'd have kicked me hard for what I just said about your mother's ancestry . . . Who are you and why are you here among these men?' His voice hardened. 'Who sent you to spy on us?' He grabbed her arm, sending the cup crashing to the ground.

'Now look what you've done! Don't touch me!' she snapped as he pulled her arm roughly behind her back, making her face him.

'Look at me, dammit.'

She had no choice but to face him full on and he examined

her features with a wry smile. 'So it *is* you,' he whispered. 'I knew there was something suspicious about you from the moment I came in and you cowered in the corner. Good Lord, Penny. Thank God you are safe. We had heard you were captured and sent to Athens but I knew you'd disobey orders and escape somehow.'

'Shush, I'm Athina now, a Greek nurse. I speak only Greek.' She spat the words, flashing him a look of desperation.

He grabbed her arm. 'How are you?'

Then Tassoula bustled in. 'Heavens, you didn't waste time.' She looked shocked at them both.

'No,' Penny jumped back, 'I recognized Panayotis. I was a nurse in the Red Cross clinic. He was one of our patients.'

Bruce nodded. 'She was very strict with us but a good nurse, and you are still in the clinic, Athina?'

'In the convent with Sister Martine, nursing mothers and orphans, finding them homes,' she said, not looking at him.

'I would never believe Nurse Athina would be a nun, but they'll take anyone these days,' he laughed.

Penny scurried up to the loft where Martine was half awake.

'Are you feeling better? We must leave,' she ordered. 'It is too crowded here and dangerous.'

Martine fell back on the rug. 'I'm too sick to move.'

'And it's Christmas, Athina,' said Tassi, following behind her. 'There's much to prepare and few ingredients to cook with, but we'll manage. You must go to church, meet Father Gregorio, and no more making sheep's eyes at Panayotis. Shame on you, a holy woman!' Tassi chided, smacking her on the bottom. 'He is for one of my daughters.'

2001

'And that's how I came to spend my first Christmas here, or close to here,' I said, staring round at the square and the white painted church. 'It was the beginning of quite a story. Anyway, what shall we order . . . ?'

Lois and Mack were staring at me as if seeing me for the first time.

'This Panayotis, you never mentioned him before.'

'Oh, I have but you weren't listening. He was really my friend Bruce Jardine . . . Walter and Effy's friend: the one who called me a mountain goat all those years ago in Scotland. Everyone had cover names to protect them.'

'Was he your lover?' Lois smirked. 'Heavens, Aunt Pen, you are a dark horse.'

'Don't be so rude.' I smiled to indicate I was teasing. 'A lady doesn't ask such things and expect a truthful answer. I didn't always have a face like a wrinkled prune. I had my moments,' I replied, not sure how much of this part of my story I was willing to share.

'Oh, do carry on, this is fascinating.' Lois leaned forward.

'Your aunt may not want strangers listening in,' said Mack.

'That's very thoughtful, Mack.' He'd risen in my estimations over the last couple of days, 'But it's time for lunch and mine's a chilled rosé. You've had the start of my story, the main course will come later when I am ready and not before.'

Later, away from the heat of the day, we sat by the cool waterfalls at Argyroupolis, the sun sparkling on the spray like diamonds, water tumbling down onto the rocks in the shade of the cool pines like the thoughts rushing through my mind.

There are times in life too beautiful, too poignant to share, some too painful to recount to others. Yet some memories are sources of peace and you feed on them in those dark nights of the soul when sleep is elusive.

I had such experiences here, some happy and some so tragic that I'd boxed them away all my life. Those first months of freedom and peace in the convent came to an end when I went into the mountains on that mission. Suddenly everything changed.

December 1941

Martine was well enough to come to the village church on Christmas Eve, where the fugitives stood crushed alongside villagers who stared at them with interest as they chatted amongst themselves until the priest told them all to shut up. For those few festive days the memory of occupation seemed to fade, food was pulled out of hiding, and chairs pushed back for dancing and singing. The wine flowed. It was as if everyone was making the most of a party, as if life was normal. The Anzac stragglers ventured in each night to join in the festival and keep warm.

After that brief conversation with Bruce, Penny hoped there would be a time to talk more freely but Tassi kept eyeing her with concern, suspicious now for her virtue. Penny smiled wryly as she served the hungry men. If only she could trust them enough to explain the *real* purpose of her mission, but their tongues were loosened by wine and she'd learned that most Cretans found it hard to keep any news to themselves.

Eventually the weather eased enough for Penny and Sister Martine to return to the convent and explain such a lengthy absence. There was no reason to stay on and the secret supplies were collected from their hiding place under cover of darkness.

How could she get word to tell Bruce that they were leaving, escorted as they were by a bevy of matrons heading to Chania and its market on the rickety old service bus that ploughed its way back and forth on the one metalled track that passed for a highway? It was hard to leave without saying goodbye but Martine was restless to be back, anxious to explain to Mother Veronique their delay.

Penny boarded the bus with a heavy heart. So near and yet so far. Their identity passes were checked over, the precious cargo of nuts and olives safely packed in pannier baskets. Tassi shoved the last of the Christmas biscuits and rusks for the journey in Penny's pocket, relieved to see them on their way. What risks the brave couple ran in harbouring fugitives.

As the old motor coughed and spluttered on its climb over the pass, Penny's eyes kept closing with the rocking and rumbling of the engine. Suddenly she was jerked awake by the bus's violent and abrupt braking, which threw everyone forward, sending cages, baskets and crates hurtling down from the overhead racks.

A shepherd was flagging them down with his crook, his head covered in his heavy cloak. 'What the hell . . . ?' shouted the driver, spitting out oaths.

'Bandits!' a passenger screamed, crossing herself in fury. 'We'll all be murdered . . .'

Penny exhaled, relieved it wasn't a German patrol demanding to search the bus, snatching all the produce on board. Not everyone here was Cretan. Like herself, one of the escapees was in disguise, dressed as a simpleton sitting with an old *yiayia*, carrying false papers. He would be easy enough to detect once the questioning started.

The shepherd leaped into the front of the bus. 'We need the nurse, the Athens nurse. There's been an accident.' He pointed to the rocks. 'The nurse from Chania, she is here?'

Penny immediately stood up. 'Yes? What is it?'

'A man has fallen. He needs a doctor, but you will have to do,' explained the rough voice.

'Where is he now?'

'In the cave, come quickly, *Kyria*.'

There was no time to think. She quickly made her way down the bus aisle but Martine pulled her back. 'I will come with you.'

'No, just the nurse,' insisted the shepherd.

'But you can't go without a chaperone, you'll be alone with men.' Martine clung onto her. 'Please, Athina, think. It's not right. What will I tell Mother Veronique?'

'Don't worry. It'll be fine. I will be protected. I have to go.'

'But it won't be fine with Mother Veronique if I say I left you alone in the hills.' Martine was crying now. 'And it's my fault we were delayed.'

'It was the Will of the Good Lord to bring us here,' Penny argued, pushing her way out. 'Now he's found me another job to do in these mountains, who are we to question or ignore His command? He will protect me and I can return on the next bus.'

'But that isn't for another week, and if the weather is bad . . .'

Penny didn't listen to Martine's tearful protests as she alighted, waved to the startled women staring out of the bus in horror, before turning to the shepherd with a smile. 'Your accent does you credit, young man.'

He grinned sheepishly. 'Sorry, Miss, orders to get you off the bus.' She'd instantly recognized one of the Aussie escapees, his fair hair covered by his shepherd's cloak.

'It will soon be all round Chania that I've been abducted by bandits. What the hell's going on?' she blurted out in English, much to his surprise and hers. He, like all the others, assumed she was Greek.

'There's one of our blokes in the cave in a bad way. He needs help.'

'I see,' she replied slowly, recovered now, as if English was her second language.

'Sorry, Miss. Orders is still orders up here. We try to keep the gang together. Not easy, and when one of us is crook . . .'

Orders? Whose orders was he obeying in pulling her off a bus in broad daylight? Penny fell silent as he strode out in front of her, up a steep bank and down into a gully full of goat muck and melting snow. The track petered out into a gorse bush and rough scree, behind which was the entrance to a small cave, a hole in the hill covered with a makeshift screen of branches.

Penny stumbled into the cave, her eyes trying to adjust to the darkness. There was a small group of men waiting there, staring up at her in silence. An oil lamp flickered dimly by a straw palliasse on which lay a soldier she hadn't seen before. He looked up at her in surprise.

'This is my mate, Bluey, he's crook, can't keep anything down. We want to head south and find a boat. There's talk of subs sending boats out. We just want off this godforsaken island. What's wrong with him?' said the Aussie shepherd with concern.

'I'm not a doctor; he needs a doctor,' Penny said, kneeling down to examine him.

'The local doctor here's being watched and Bluey can't walk to him.'

'I need more light,' she said. 'How long have his eyes been yellow?'

Two others carried him into the daylight and he cried out in pain.

Penny felt his liver and looked at his skin. 'I think he has severe jaundice, his liver is swollen. What has he been eating?'

'Just snails and mountain greens, like the rest of us. We bring him back stuff from the taverna but he can't keep it down.'

'Give him clean water until he recovers. He's very sick. I can give you some mountain-herb tea, too. The locals swear by it. There's nothing else I can do. He'll need time to heal. How did you know I was on that bus?'

A deep voice from the recess of the cave laughed. 'Nothing

happens that isn't whistled across these hills faster than an eagle in full flight.' Bruce Jardine stepped out of the shadows. For a moment Penny was surprised. Then she was determinedly unimpressed.

'I wish you'd stop jumping out like this. You're not the Red Shadow,' she snapped, thinking of the hero from *The Desert Song*. 'I can't do anything for Bluey, as well you know.'

'Sure, but he's not the only one needing your expert eye. The doctor from Chania is far too conspicuous. Besides, I didn't want you disappearing back to the town when you'd be far safer up here. We need to talk out of earshot.' He pointed to the cave entrance.

'This man needs a hospital. He'd be better off in a prison camp,' Penny added, keeping up the pretence that she was Greek. The less these men knew about her the better.

'Evidently the nurse hasn't seen the state of the camps,' Bruce replied. 'He'd not last a week. At least here he's got fresh mountain air and clean water.'

'Perhaps it's the water that's foul. It must be boiled for all of you. I can give him nothing but herb teas and local remedies; one of the village mothers can do as much. I ought to go back to the village right now.'

'Not so fast, Penny!' Bruce whispered as he came closer.

'Athina, my name's Athina . . .' she hissed.

'Don't disappear. Your presence will give the men heart, knowing they're not forgotten, and it gives me heart to know you are safe up here for a while. You and I have so much to catch up on . . .' Bruce was giving her one of his wolfish grins. 'I was one of her patients,' he explained to the curious onlookers. Her bark is worse than her bite.' He shrugged to the waiting men and ushered her out of the cave.

Penny sighed. It was the field hospital all over again, one woman among many desperate men. Perhaps this was for the best. Bruce had come for her, sought her out, given her a role among this hidden army of evading troops. Part of her was feeling flattered, surprised and relieved to see him again.

'You know I can't stay alone, it will be talked about,' she said as they left the men in the cave and walked out of sight of the others, sitting on a bank of thyme where the snow had melted, gazing down to the valley below.

'Not if we tog you out like all the others, in trousers,' Bruce suggested as he moved close to her. She could feel his breath in her ear.

'No, not that old trick again. It was bad enough in the hospital in battledress,' she replied, wondering when she would ever get to wear decent clothes again. She suddenly had a yearning for her blue silk dress and pretty sandals.

'You're tall, you've lost weight – you look quite boyish now – and if we cut your hair—'

'My hair stays where it is. Everything I wear is drab and dark. No one notices me,' she insisted. 'This is my uniform now. These clothes suit my mission, plenty of pockets and layers,' she replied, not looking at him.

He grabbed her arm. 'This isn't a game of charades, Penny. There are still hundreds of poor stragglers stuck out here. It's going to be a hellish winter. If you can keep a check on their health, get them accommodation if they become worse, gather news, as well as run errands for the doctor, you'll be doing sterling work for us. You're my mountain goat, fearless afoot . . .' he laughed, his sunburned face crinkling like worn leather.

'All the more reason why I must look like any downtrodden peasant. But I'm not a bloody goat, I'm a woman, not that you ever notice,' she blurted, unable to hold back her frustration a moment longer. 'I'm not your dogsbody!'

'Don't I know it, the bravest, toughest woman I know? Who else would hang on in a cave, nursing, refusing to leave until Jerry had to turf you out? Everyone knows what you did. I was so proud of you. They held back a ship in case you escaped to down to Sphakia but I knew you wouldn't make it, not my

Penny. When this lot's over the whole world will know just what you did for your patients.'

'I was only doing my duty, and you must call me Athina. Penny George doesn't exist.'

'She does to me,' Bruce smiled, pulling her into his arms. 'She has to stay safe. I promised Evadne, and I couldn't bear to see you cooped up in a prison camp, not my beautiful gazelle.'

He kissed her forehead tenderly and she turned up her face, staring at him in surprise at such tenderness, parting her lips as they fell back onto the thyme, kissing slowly, languorously as if they had a lifetime of love ahead of them. Penny sank into his body as if it was the most natural thing in the world to be making love on the side of a mountain with the wind whipping round them, the call of the black eagle soaring above them and the wondrous infusion of crushed herbs scenting the chill air. How long had she waited for such a moment . . . ?

But Bruce jumped back. 'I'm sorry, Penny, forgive me, most unprofessional. I didn't mean to . . .'

'But I wanted it too,' she gasped, surprised by this sudden caution 'We're only human, we have feelings and desires . . .'

'Not in war, not here and now. I have a job to do. I'm in no position to offer you anything . . .' Bruce stood up. 'I'm sorry.'

Penny stared up at him, shocked. 'Why? War or tempest, fire or flood can't stop such feelings when they erupt.'

'Love in war is a distraction. It stops us taking risks if we attach ourselves, holds us back from danger. Oh damn, perhaps I shouldn't have sent for you . . .'

'That's enough.' Penny jumped up angrily. 'I've got the message loud and clear, but I don't understand you, Bruce, I never have. You blow hot and cold. What's so wrong with find-ing comfort with each other at such a time as this? Who knows what the future holds? Better to have memories than nothing at all.' Penny shook her head. 'But don't worry, I am professional too. Show me the next patient on your list.' She twisted round, brushing the soil from her skirt, not looking at him in case he would see the tears in her eyes. 'But don't expect me to take orders from you now. Just find me somewhere to stay.'

'There's a network of houses in the hills. And I'll be out of your hair soon enough; I will be returning to HQ shortly. Come on, we'd better go back; the others will be curious. Our work mustn't be compromised. I have my reasons to stay sensible.'

'Sensible' – what a stupid word, thought Penny, feeling sick and confused as she scrambled down from their trysting place. What did Bruce mean by 'compromised'? Why was he afraid to express his feelings? She'd given him every encouragement over the years. His body had stirred just as much as hers when they were kissing. Why was he afraid when she had more to lose than he did?

She felt the irritation and anger mounting, choking her like acid in her throat as they made their way down the stony path. How dare he play with her feelings like this, encourage her one minute and then distance himself? It was natural for them to want to be physical. Who knew when or if they would ever meet again?

It had been her dream for years for such a thing to unfold, and now this rejection, this abandonment. What was so wrong with her for him to react so?

Now she was stranded high in the White Mountains at the mercy of the weather, the terrain and the unpredictable hospitality of strangers. She had never felt so confused or so alone. If only Yolanda were here to share all this with her, she felt she could face it better.

Now there were only the wild winds of Crete swirling around her like all the frustrations tearing through her heart. Penny paused to draw in the chill air to steady her nerve.

You chose this rough path when you stayed in the cave among the men. Now a new and dangerous journey has begun and who knows where it will lead?

Spring 1942

Yolanda had heard nothing from Penny for weeks. Perhaps the weather had trapped her in the hills above the snow line separating mountains from shore. Andreas told her only that there were rumours in the clinic that she'd been abducted by bandits from a bus en route for Chania, but he guessed her friend was now helping to nurse the Allied stragglers. He was worried that spies were pulling them in, tricking them into surrendering.

The harshness of their first winter of occupation was easing. There had been no more restrictive measures against the little Jewish community other than strict trading laws imposed. No Jew could sell to the occupying force, only to locals, who had little money. The winter had brought starvation even to the shore. There was not much trade for soaps, jewellery, books, but everyone knew where the black market supplies could be found hidden in the backstreets. How could they not go hungry when the enemy stole the first pickings of crops and meat? But as ever their community thrived on its resourcefulness.

The cobbler bartered for services, food in lieu of repairs or information. The rabbi and his wife went in and out of homes begging food for the starving children on the harbour front. The rich merchants began to sell their artwork and jewellery, aware that one by one they were being evicted out of their gracious houses to make way for German officers. Now they must find humbler properties or move in with relatives. The Jewish quarter was becoming even more crowded.

There was, however, another more pressing and delicate matter hovering over Yolanda's future. She sensed her parents were plotting to find her a suitable young husband from within the Sephardim.

'We're not getting any younger. We must see you settled and hold our grandchildren before . . . Solomon Markos sighed in a rare moment of shared contemplation, brought on by a headache from a party he had attended the night before.

Abram Carlos had ordered his own hand-woven silk burial shroud and, according to custom, spent the evening with friends demonstrating its quality with the aid of enough raki and sweetmeats to make his future wake entirely unnecessary.

Yolanda thought the sight of an old man dancing with a shroud over his head morbid but it was an honoured custom among the Haniote Jews. It may have been a jolly evening but it left her father with a residue of gloom. 'Who knows when we will be free to leave and make our way to Palestine?' was his latest lament. 'Now you are old enough to make your own household, and there are many young men looking in your direction, if only you'd give them a second glance. It will bring joy to Momma's heart to start sewing for your wedding trousseau, to line your skirts with golden coins.' he smiled.

She knew he was trying to soften her resolve to stay single, to make her feel guilty.

They were all locked in the past. No one here had money for dowries or wedding feasts. Those days were long gone. The few recent nuptials had been quiet modest affairs. It was hard for businessmen to see their incomes fall, their houses commandeered for soldiers, property looted. Most in her community were scratching a living sewing, serving at tables, begging for menial jobs and selling their best jewellery for peanuts. This was no time to be marrying and, besides, no one would ever stir her heart like Andreas Androulakis.

'Dear Papa, this is no time for taking vows. Our world is falling apart, can't you see how it is? Marriage can wait . . .' Yolanda argued. Her parents meant well, wanting her happiness in these dark times. Women were working hard, were more independent, demanding education and choice as to who they would marry. But there were positives too, she thought guiltily.

If only Penny were here to bolster her resolve. How could she tell them she couldn't marry a man she didn't love? If only they would accept Andreas as a son-in-law, but she knew it was impossible.

She must stay resolute. It would not be easy. Uncle Joe and Aunt Miriam were behind this scheming too.

Yolanda was worried that she was living on borrowed time. A tiger doesn't go willingly into the cage when it has known the freedom of the jungle, she thought. Better not to marry at all than spend a lifetime chained to a man she didn't respect or love. But for her to disobey, to refuse point-blank would bring such shame to her parents. How could she hurt them? She was all they had now, their only hope for the future. Oh, why had this war come and destroyed everything?

The worry was affecting her work at the clinic, distracting her. The morning after Papa's little talk she spilled precious disinfectant, tripped and banged her knee, bursting into tears at the slightest mistake, so that the other nurses complained that Nurse Markos was sickening for something.

Andreas found her weeping in the storeroom. 'What on earth's got into you?' he shouted. 'My best nurse weeping like a junior on her first day in the mortuary?'

Out it all poured – all her fears, her consternation and frustration: how she missed Penny and worried about her fate, how she dreaded going home in case she found Mordo and his parents waiting to greet her.

'Who's this Mordo? Do you want to marry this man?' Andreas said, lighting his pipe and deliberately not looking at her.

'No. He's a good man, but no. He is not for me. I have no wedding plans,' Yolanda replied, wiping her eyes and feeling foolish for crying at work.

'That's a relief. I don't want to lose one of my best nurses. Though should you change your plans I'd rather fancy eloping with you myself one day. Cretan style, of course, in the middle of the night, out of the window,' he said with a very straight face.

Yolanda looked up at him in shock, hardly believing what she was hearing. 'Really?'

He made no move towards her but busied himself with packing some instruments into a box 'Perhaps it's time you spread your wings a little, now I can't rely on Athina. I've got an idea. If you take her place, pedalling a few supplies here and there round the district . . .'

'My parents will never agree to me travelling unchaperoned away from home,' she argued.

'It's either one or the other, my precious, freedom or the cage.'

'You make it sound so simple.'

'It's dangerous work being a courier, but women make the best ones. They get stopped much less than men. We'll start with a few little forays, let the street guards see you going on rounds in the daytime, returning home. Your parents will soon get used to you being absent for longer. It's vital work. You'll find a way.'

Yolanda blew her nose. 'I'll try. I suppose I could present things in a way that seems just an extension of my work in the clinic.'

'There, you see, you can do it. I'll join you when I can but not yet. I meant what I said, Yolanda. 'I'm serious. You are the one for me.' Andreas pulled her into his arms and kissed her hand. 'So no more tears. You can't marry Mr Mordo if you're already spoken for, yes?'

'Oh, yes, please,' she laughed, stopping his smile with a kiss.

Maleme, 2001

Rainer Brecht caught his breath back, sitting on a bench in the German War Cemetery close to the old airstrip at Maleme. He sat staring out from the slopes onto the bay. This visit had been put off ever since his arrival from Athens, although he always knew that one morning he would have to brave the terraced garden to walk along the lines of flat headstones as a mark of respect.

It was a silent peaceful place now, but once it has been the scene of a frantic battle for survival known only as Hill 107. Now it was tended and guarded by none other than George Psychoundakis, one of the great Cretan heroes of the conflict, who had chosen to end his working life making peace with his enemies by tending the garden and the grave markers.

As the veteran patrolled along the aisles with their flat grave markers, so many familiar names and dates reminded him of those early days of combat, parachute drops, skirmishes in the hills, executions. He paused to wipe away the tears. All those lost boys who never got to live out their lives in peace as he had done.

There was a torrent of feelings pent up inside him for so many years, buried under the busyness of his academic career, bringing up his family, watching his sons flourish in a way he had not. Sometimes it felt as if none of this slaughter had ever happened, but here was the brutal reality. How could he be the same man who had once sat panting under the Cretan sun, willing his wounds to heal so he could escape Crete, cross the Libyan Sea and fight on? This island had kept both its victors and vanquished captive.

Summer 1942

At HQ in Chania there was an interpreter who came to his notice. He was from the outer district, from a village close to Vrisses, an area known for trouble. He was the smartest of all the quisling agents, sharp-eyed, cunning, charming and utterly ruthless. There were many of these agents who promised much and delivered little of value, willing to sell their friends and relations for privileges, cash, or the chance to revenge some feud, but this one was befriending a known suspect, feeding him snippets, gaining his trust. It was only a matter of time before they made significant arrests.

Most agents were weak men, vain, and Rainer despised them as he despised himself for not being able to get a transfer back to active service. He was needed in Rommel's push across the desert into Egypt. Once the British succumbed to the onslaught, their own foothold in the Middle East would be secure. Crete was proving a valuable staging post for troop carriers, fuel and supplies. The oil tanks were guarded day and night against attack, and he was in charge of the troops stationed close by.

His leg wound had stiffened his thigh muscles and no amount of sea bathing and treatments eased the pain of his restricted movement. Rainer was beginning to feel he would be crippled for the rest of his life, stuck in a second-class desk job. His future was looking grim and now he was pinning his hopes on some doctor in Chania. It was worth a try since his own medics had not offered anything but standard treatments, but he had no high expectations of a cure.

The premises were not promising, just a room with a manipulation bed close to the Red Cross hospital. The first visit consisted of little more than questions from a one-eyed clinician of his own age and an examination of his wound, how he stood and bent, and his musculature.

'The wound is healed but the whole of your side has contracted and the limp twists you to the other side, putting strain on your balance. Have you heard of osteopathic manipulation?' asked the young doctor.

Rainer shrugged. He'd had no need of such treatments before.

'We should make progress in about four sessions, if you can spare the time from your unit.'

Rainer gave brief details of his present work, careful not to give anything away to this stranger.

'Sitting at a desk won't help you. You need to correct the damage, so exercises, walking, swimming too.'

'But the pain?'

'Ah, pain . . . If we sort out your frame and your balance, the pain will ease. Pain in muscles is often a state of mind caused by tensions and the stresses of duty.'

Dr Androulakis dismissed his troubles as if they were nothing, but Rainer was curious enough to give him one or two sessions. To his surprise the sessions were brief, repositioning his spine, his stance, showing him exercises to do every day and even suggesting a change of footwear to rebalance the length of his bad leg.

Getting an appointment with the busy doctor wasn't always easy, for he worked in the Red Cross clinic and he travelled round the district with a special pass. He had picked up his osteopathic knowledge in Athens. Rainer was impressed with his efficient approach. He would run a tight ship in the hospital and Rainer wondered if the doctor had the cave nurse working in his clinics. He often thought of her but he'd not heard anything of her since she entered the convent months ago. When he passed the convent he found himself slowing down outside the gates just in case she was in sight, but the walls were high and there was no sign of her out shopping or escorting lines of orphan children in the streets.

'There was a blonde Athenian nurse called Penelope, very tall. Does she work with your clinic?' he asked as his lower back was pummelled hard.

'No,' Andreas smiled. 'I think I'd notice a tall blonde amongst my local girls. How does that feel?'

'Much better these past few days,' Rainer replied.

'Why the hurry to get yourself out of the desk job? I should think it's pleasant at HQ?' Was the doctor fishing for information? But Rainer was so relaxed he felt like sharing a little of his desire to leave the island and join a fighting unit.

'You don't like our beautiful island? Many call it lotus-eaters' land,' the doctor offered, and Rainer didn't know if he was being serious or not. It was a leading question when he was lying in such a vulnerable position.

'You lost your eye, I see. In battle?' Rainer asked, changing the subject.

'It was a stupid injury with a loaded gun when I was young. Besides, I prefer patching people up to blowing them to pieces.' There was a silence as both of them drew back from this remark. 'Still, keep up the good work and you will be collecting your kitbag before long, but don't rush it. It's taken months to recover, a few more won't matter. I still need to work on your leg.'

Rainer soon began to enjoy these sessions, to relax and learn how the tension of the past year had caused such a violent reaction to his body. He felt his joint loosening, strengthening, and the pain was easing.

In that second year of victory many changes were happening: the arrival of Gestapo officers, who were cold, clinical and efficient as they sifted through information brought by the agent known only as 'K'. He knew that a wireless was operating in the White Mountains, relaying details of ship movements in Souda Bay. Several supply convoys had been attacked on strategic routes, the dates and times too accurate to be guesswork. Agent K had the full confidence of a local Resistance leader and the plans for a surprise raid on the Resistance group were well in hand.

The other irritant to his men was evidence that some 300 evaders were still roaming free, sheltered and supplied by rebel villages and guided to the south coast by shepherds and British officers from Cairo. Flushing them out was not proving as easy as they had first thought.

The slightest attempt to fool them with their own volunteers who had English relatives or could pass for South Africans pretending to be evaders themselves had failed and resulted in grisly executions. They betrayed themselves by the silliest slip-ups: using old-fashioned slang, not knowing which football players were in which team, not knowing how to make tea, or the words of certain romantic songs. Now they decided that it was better to send in Greek bogus officials and policemen to trick villagers in the hills.

Despite these minor setbacks morale was high. Rommel was racing across North Africa and here resistance was proving weak. And one thing was in their favour on the island: no one could get Cretan warrior bandits into one united army. There were too many feuding factions and egos amongst those ruffian mountain men, brave and foolhardy as they were.

It was time to enjoy summer fruits and sun, watch the labour force building roads and fortifications. As Rainer built up his stamina, he felt his spirits lifting. Soon he'd be off the island for good. He was only marking time.

One evening he was strolling down to the harbour, staring out across the water with hope in his heart. There were a few tavernas in operation close to the bombed-out Venetian Arsenal and he caught sight of his Cretan doctor sitting under the shade of an awning with two women. One was short and dark; the other was tall, wearing black. and she rose at the sight of his approach and disappeared into an alleyway. There was something about her silhouet tethat was familiar. He would know that figure anywhere. Why had Androulakis said he didn't know the cave nurse? There was only one way to find out the truth.

Strolling up to the couple, he clicked his heels. 'Herr Doktor, you see I am taking my exercise. I am pleased to see you are enjoying yours.'

The doctor stood up, flushed. 'Please sit down, Captain Brecht. We were taking our break. This is my fiancée.'

Rainer saw the girl flush and touch his arm. 'Andreas, please . . . it's not public yet.' The girl in the Red Cross uniform had that well-defined sharp profile of a beautiful Jewess. He saw she was uncomfortable in his presence but she was not his concern.

He peered down the alley. 'And the other young lady who rushed away . . . Did I scare her away?'

'Athina? Ah, she's already late for duty. I'm afraid she'll be in trouble.'

'What a pity. She reminded me of someone I once knew here. Penelope, the nurse I was telling you about the other day, but I must be mistaken.' He saw the girl flinch at the name and then quickly recover, standing up.

'Excuse me. I have some shopping to do before the shops shut . . .'

'What a striking girl. She lives locally?' Rainer leaned forward, smiling, looking after Yolanda with interest.

'From Athens, her parents are strict . . . I shouldn't have called her my fiancée. It is a secret for a while,' said Andreas, looking at his watch.

I bet it is, if the race laws imposed over Europe were upheld here. It was forbidden for German soldiers to intermarry with Jewish or alien women but this evidently didn't hold among the Greek population. 'Your secret is safe with me, Doctor.'

He rose and walked on. How interesting, the doctor and his lover . . . and if that was Penelope, why was she working under the name Athina? How intriguing. What other little secrets lay uncovered here?

Penny fled blindly down the ruined alley towards Splanzia Square, edging as far as she could from the harbour, over rubble and rocks, tripping in desperation to flee from the German. Had he recognized her, even in her widow's weeds? She couldn't risk exposure, not now when she was so involved in the network of escapees. Why had she been tempted to come back to Chania? It was stupid to think she could go unrecognized in public. She had dropped off a letter of apology to Mother Veronique for deserting her post and she had come to see Yolanda and collect letters from Andreas. It had been a touch of normality to sit with them in a café, catching up on news and taking instructions, but one look at the man crossing the street, smiling in their direction, and she had to get away.

She'd been restless for company, for the bustle of town, but now she'd put all of them in danger. Why was that captain still here? She'd assumed he was long gone. There was always something in his commanding presence that disturbed her. If she had recognized him even from a distance, surely he must have guessed who she was.

Now she must leave on the first bus, any bus going south, even if she had to walk miles out of her way to reach her village.

Bruce had placed her with a merchant, Ike, and his wife, Katrina, as a servant nursemaid to their two children, Olivia and Taki. Ike had returned from America, from Chicago, before the occupation, and his English was useful with the escapees. His

large villa was a haven for sick stragglers who hid in the basement. Katrina came from a long line of Cretan warriors and
could wield a knife and a gun as well as any man. No one used
their family names, just in case. The less you knew, the better,
but one thing was shared and that was the knowledge of an
ancient burial chamber hidden in an olive grove behind the
house, a place of refuge if all else failed.

Once she was living at Ike's, Penny regularly walked the
distance back to Bluey's cave to check on him. He'd stay there
until she felt he was strong enough to be brought down to the
underground hiding place among the olives. He needed fresh
greens and the warmth of the stones in the sun, and his friends
would visit to keep his spirits up. She was the girl from the villa,
seen regularly under the shade of the olive trees playing with
little Taki. No one knew she brought food and water down to
her sick patient hiding in the Minoan tomb chamber. It was a
perfect ruse.

Lately his mates brought wine, which she'd forbidden. Trying
to stop Aussies celebrating was hopeless. Their raucous songs
echoed across the valley in the small hours until Bruce threatened to chuck them out if they drew any more attention to
their position. She had met him many times under the olive
trees, but never alone, and there was never a repeat of that first
passionate encounter by the cave. Much as she longed for it.

Now Penny trudged back to the villa, savouring her brief
reunion with Yolanda. It had been good to see her friend so
obviously in love. There was no chance to talk privately with
her and confess her own despair since that passionate encounter
with Bruce. She knew he was forming a Resistance group with
some local men to protect the wireless operator working close
by in a farmhouse. Everyone knew the risks this family was
taking in broadcasting so close to the coastal strip. God help
them if they were caught.

Katrina kept their own household busy preparing preserves

with their meagre sugar ration, gathering in vegetables and herbs for salting and drying. Most food supplies were hidden deep underground in case of a raid. They buried a stash of oil and beans in a hole under the olive grove. There would be no warning if German troops were to arrive demanding everything out of the store cupboards, and looting and smashing anything that took their fancy.

One day a German patrol did arrive. The officer watched as one of his men snatched an ancient icon of the Virgin Mary, which had been handed down through the generations in Katrina's family. She had to watch him remove it from the wall without muttering a word of complaint, but her black eyes blazed with hatred. When they had left she lit a candle, pricked her arm, mixed the blood into the wax and pressed her crucifix into the mould, uttering an incantation. 'He and his kind will rue the day he took that from my wall,' she spat.

What worried the village most was that so many of them were forced to work on the roads and quarries so that there was no time to tend their olives and crops, water their vegetables or feed their animals. It was left to the children to work in the fields as best they could. Many schools had been bombed and closed, teachers forced into labour gangs, but some of the Anzacs risked exposure, dressing as local boys, hoeing and watering, helping with milking goats and making cheese in the shepherds' stone huts. They scarpered into holes if soldiers appeared on the horizon.

The Cretan's own secret wireless service, carried over the air by runners and children, was accurate in giving warnings of patrols on the move. Only the previous week, three German officers had called in at Ike's house for a drink while Bluey's mates were still in the house. Penny served the officers, staying calm and composed, while Katrina smiled and played the perfect hostess, dressed in her American cotton dress that enhanced her magnificent bosom, neither of them giving any inkling that above their heads, three Aussies were hardly daring to breathe.

In the height of summer, men gathered in groups high up, planning daring raids and ambushes when they had enough arms to make a decent attack. Once autumn came and winter drew in, there would be fewer opportunities for raids. There was no sign of an Allied counter-invasion of the island. They were far too busy trying to hold back Rommel in North Africa. The wireless had brought grim news of the fall of Tobruk.

Bruce had explained how important it was for the Resistance to detail all troop movements and convoys. The enemy was depending on supplies from Crete, and there was great elation at news of an air raid on the oil tanks outside Chania when thousands of gallons of precious fuel for tanks were destroyed. The sky was black with smoke for days. It was a victory for which many hostages lost their lives.

As Penny sat on the bus rattling back eastward on the road to Heraklion, past ruined houses, scattered flocks and burned olive groves where the wrecks of British planes lay rusting, she wondered if she would ever have a normal life again, that well-ordered life she had led in Athens. Her country childhood home at Stokencourt seemed so far away, she could no longer even think of herself as English.

To think, once, all she had to worry about was resisting her mother's plans to give her a debutante season in London. Now she felt a hundred years old, battered and bruised, but proud to be still battling here. There were so many far worse off than she; destitute, bereaved, homeless. She had a roof over her head, a good billet. She had been fortunate so far. But seeing Captain Brecht had shaken her complacency.

To the onlooker she was just another worn-out peasant woman with coarse hands and sunburned face, but underneath, her heart was racing. From now on she would take no risks of being recognized as a British escapee, especially if found in a village house. There was one German officer in Chania who was suspicious. What if he came searching for her? She would never forgive herself if she put her Greek comrades in danger.

When Yolanda finished her shift, she walked wearily home. She'd been tending to some poor kids who'd set off an unexploded bomb, killing three outright and leaving two almost limbless. Their bodies were mutilated and showing them to weeping mothers had been unbearable. Her heart was heavy with the frustration that there was so little they could do when these undetected bombs were lying around, hidden and lethal where children were playing.

When she came through the door there was a posse of women gathered round the table staring at her with such glares, she wondered what new restrictions had been placed on them now.

'Sit down,' Aunt Miriam ordered, pointing to a chair.

'What's happened?' Yolanda asked, flopping down, hot and exhausted. All she wanted to do was close the door of her room and shut her eyes from the horrors of the day.

'That I should have to tell my own child . . . What's happened? You were seen,' Momma said, not looking at her.

'Seen where? What's all this about?'

'Seen in broad daylight sitting in a public place with two men, one a German and both goyim.'

There was silence as the women glared, waiting for her reply.

'Oh, you mean Dr Androulakis. You've met him before; he's my medical officer,' she smiled, relieved. 'We were taking a rest. It's been a terrible morning. You heard about the bomb in the Kastelli district, three little children—'

'I don't want excuses, I want an explanation. You were with a man, sitting alone, and then a German officer came and sat next to you.'

'I'm sorry, it was an awful morning and I met Penny . . . We had coffee or what passes for it now,' she tried to joke. This was not going well and she wondered if she could win them over. 'Dr Androulakis joined us and then one of his patients turned up just as Penny was leaving. I had to be polite.'

'You were seen laughing together. It will not do, this shaming yourself in public, flaunting yourself when you are about to be betrothed. What will Mordo think?' said Aunt Miriam.

Yolanda jumped up. 'Who said anything about marriage? I have no intention of being betrothed to anyone, not while we are occupied and under surveillance.'

'You spend time alone with this doctor in the clinic. It has to stop.'

'Andreas is an excellent doctor and a brave man,' she argued, her arms folded in defiance.

'You are not the daughter we brought up. He is not one of us.'

'In these dangerous times, is that so important? And who's been spying on me?' she demanded angrily.

'So you are attached to him? I feared as much,' Momma sighed. 'How can you do this to your own family?'

'I've not done anything. Yes, he and I have become close through our work. He's a good man. Surely you would want me to be happy with a good man?'

'Only with a good Jewish man – that is what is expected if we are to survive. You carry the seed of your race. There must be no mixing of race or religion. It never works.'

'In Athens there were friends who married Greeks. You always told me a heart must be free to choose its mate. Penny is a Gentile and she saved Papa's life, or have you forgotten that?'

'That was then, this is now,' Momma said simply.

'That's no argument.'

'Don't cheek your mother in my house, ungrateful girl,' said Miriam. 'Remember the Commandment, thou shalt honour thy mother and father . . .'

'How can I honour what is bigoted and unfair?' Yolanda cried.

'Yolanda, you have said enough. Don't make it any worse than it is. You must leave the clinic at once and come home and learn obedience to our Law.' Momma had changed so much since she came here, defending the stricter rules of their religion where once she was happy to ignore them. 'It will kill your father to hear such disobedience and ingratitude. Spare me the task of telling him all this.'

'Why are you making me choose? Please don't ask me to give up my work. If you could only see the injuries of those children and the faces of those poor mothers, it would break your heart. God hears the prayers of both Jews and Gentiles in their distress. He makes no distinctions. How can I sit here cooking and sewing when lives need mending? You can't ask this of me now,' she cried, fleeing the room of angry and judgemental women. This horrid day had suddenly got even worse. If she made her choice she would, she knew, break all their hearts.

2001

There comes a time midway in a holiday when you've done enough sightseeing, especially at my age. Trips to the beach, people-watching from the shade of a sun lounger, and gadding from one museum, church or taverna to another, were exhausting in the heat. What I needed was a good book and my own company. And no more questions about my wartime experience. This visit was bringing memories flooding back into my dreams, making me feel ancient and weary and more than a little anxious for what might I might discover next.

Lois kept fussing, imagining me falling into the pool or dying of sunstroke while she and Alex went off on a mountain excursion accompanied by Mack, who was becoming her permanent companion.

It would be bliss to hide among the olives and do nothing. I'd found an old tree, gnarled and nobbly with a beer belly of a trunk, hundreds of years old but still standing proud with sculpted branches and its blossoms promising a good yield of olives. It reminded me of one I knew all those years ago with its kindly face. I can never look at an ancient tree without seeing the living creature within. They are so majestic.

Everything here had changed beyond recognition. I could no longer find my way through the hills that I had once scampered over so easily, nor scent the crushed thyme in my fingers, nor hear that screech of cicadas that deafens all conversations. But some things remained: those vibrant colours of Crete; the crimson bougainvillaea arching over the walls, the ripening apricots, the turquoise sea, the sandy ochres of the monastery towers, the cerulean sky. The girl under the olive tree is now a *yiayia* sitting in the shade, trying to recall why she had stayed away from such a beautiful place for so long. You never think old age will come to you but it does . . .

I felt myself dozing off, a good way to escape the memories of what happened next.

On the opposite side of Chania, Rainer took a taxi to the beach at Georgioupoli, a little town halfway between Chania and Rethymno on the north coast. He fancied a break from his pilgrimage, a day by the sea on the golden expanse of coastline he'd once known so well. He found a deserted spot where the river met the shoreline, somewhere to sit in the shade with his book and be a tourist. Time to do nothing, think nothing. He'd bought a German translation of *The Winds of Crete* by David MacNeil Doren and he fancied tracing the steps of the author who had lived here in the 1960s with his Danish wife.

What had once been a quiet fishing village was now a lively resort, popular with German and Scandinavian tourists, famous for its lines of giant eucalyptus trees and its royal connections. It suited his mood and he knew there were good fish tavernas to sample later.

The National Road linking the north coast towns had changed the pace of everything. He recalled a slow trip in the back of a truck to this very spot with friends on embarkation leave, lying naked in the sand, diving into the sea, getting very drunk as they prepared to sail to North Africa. How he'd envied them leaving before him.

He woke from his daydream, putting down his book and making for the sea. It was no good getting steamed up about the past. Time to wash all these maudlin thoughts out of his system.

November 1942

The early morning chores were over, chickens let out, children fed and watered. It was a bright November day. The sound of whistling suddenly pierced Penny's ears. It was the warning alert.

'What's happening?' she yelled.

'Troops, hundreds of them. Just carry on, take no notice. The men know to hide in the hills,' yelled Katrina through the window.

Suddenly they were overwhelmed, pushed aside as the men rushed into the villa, bashing doors open, their dogs let loose to snarl and bite anyone who moved.

Penny's first thought was for the men hiding in the burial chamber. Please God they'd heard the noise and pulled down the stone slab. Were they far enough away for the dogs not to scent? Penny picked up her laundry basket and made to move.

'*Kalimera*,' she smiled to a soldier with her lips but not her eyes.

'Where are you going with that?' He eyed her with suspicion.

'Taking clothes to the old lady.' She pointed to a stone hovel where the widow Calliope lived. He snatched the basket and threw the clean things onto the ground. 'Get inside!' There was nothing to do but retrace her steps back into the villa, hoping Ike had got away from the back, but when she returned they were all there, standing at gunpoint.

'What is the meaning of this intrusion?' Ike stood firm.

'Papers!' came the order, and Ike produced a leather wallet full of documents.

'You are Ilias Papadakis?'

'I am.'

'You come.'

Ike shot an anxious glance at his wife. 'What is this about? Our papers are in order?'

'No questions. Come. Your wife?' The soldier was looking at each woman in turn 'Or have you two?'

'I am Katrina Papadaki,'

'And this one?' The soldier stared at Penny.

'The servant, Athina.'

He seemed satisfied and shoved Ike at gunpoint out the door. Ike turned to his wife in farewell.

'Make sure the mules are watered, Katrina. Don't worry. This is all a mistake. I'll be home soon.'

He joined a line of village men, who were marched down the hill, sandwiched between a line of armed soldiers, and loaded onto a waiting truck. This was no ordinary raid. Katrina let out a howl of anguish as she saw the dust of the vehicle disappearing out of view. 'What will become of them? Who has betrayed us?'

Penny shot out of the villa, running down through the field to the olive grove where the three evaders were entombed in the chamber with only a crack of air to breathe. They had heard the echo of the warning and barking dogs, and retreated to their hole. She brought fresh water and food, warning them not to move until they knew more.

It was midnight before a runner crept down the hillside with news of arrests all over the district. The leader of the Resistance group, Andreas Polentas, had been arrested, and the wireless operator working from a house in the village of Vafes was caught trying to escape. 'Forty good men are arrested and in the hands of the Gestapo by now, but not the wireless,' said the runner, flushed with anger.

'How was that possible?'

'For that we must thank the quick thinking of the operator's sister, Elpida. She knew the code papers were in his pocket and when he left she made him change into a better jacket, snatching the papers and hiding them. She knew where the radio was hidden and she carried it on her back and is guarding it in a cave with a gun. No one knows where she is now so no one will be able to tell the enemy . . . God protect them from those evil murderers. We were betrayed! Every one of Polentas's contacts is taken.' He crossed himself before heading back into the hills.

No one slept that night. The children kept crying out for their papa, Penny and Katrina taking it in turns to comfort them.

They heard later that their mayor and his assistant had gone down to Chania to protest and plead the cause of the village men but they didn't return and were arrested themselves.

'What did Ike mean about the mules? We haven't any mules now?' Penny asked.

'It's a code between us. I must get word to my father and brothers. This must be avenged and the man they say betrayed his friends will die . . .' Katrina was crying, distraught about her husband's fate. 'Ike has done nothing but attend meetings.'

Penny said nothing. No use reminding her that they had British escapees on their land. There were guns hidden, buried, and a hoard of food, which was also forbidden. Thank God the Anzac boys had not been in the house scrounging breakfast. They must leave at once in case there was a more thorough search. The enemy was meticulous in such matters.

'I'm taking the boys down the line,' she announced.

Katrina looked up in alarm. 'You can't go alone, there are checkpoints.'

'I'll have my soldier escorts and we'll go in darkness. Panayotis has told me a little of the route south on his last visit. It's not safe for us to be here now.'

'But this is your home. Panayotis insisted we keep you safe. It will be noticed if you disappear, and winter is coming.'

'I will return. I'd not leave you on your own. When Ike returns, then we will think again. You have been so kind to all of us. If anything were to happen to you, how could I live?'

'You think they will come back to us from the white-walled prison where death has taken up his residence?' Katrina was staring at her new icon of the *Panagia*. 'She will help us in our hour of need.'

Penny sighed, fearing something terrible was happening in Agia Prison. She walked down to the chamber to tell the boys to prepare to move. Then she sat under her favourite olive tree until it was dark. It had a face that reminded her of uncle Clarence, with his whiskers, and leathery but kindly face.

Funny how she had taken to this old tree, with a hiding place close by under its low branches where she could think undisturbed, praying Bruce was safe. Here she could sift through all their recent encounters, one by one. She was sure he loved her but couldn't commit to any future while they were living in such danger. Now she had seen how right he was to stay alert, sacrificing their own desires for the good of others when danger was so close.

Was she up to the job of leading men out into the stony rocky trail she hardly knew? She thought of the stalking expeditions in that other life. If anyone could do it she could. Perhaps she *was* a mountain goat, sure of foot, but the Allied soldiers weren't. Bluey was recovering but hardly fit to walk two miles, let alone ten. If all else failed, Frank and Reg would carry him on their backs, such was their courage and loyalty to each other.

The journey was treacherous, the path stony and the men's shoes were just makeshift rubber-tyre soles tied on with leather straps. They were cold and ill-clad but in good spirits. The night was clear and the moon bright enough to follow the path. It was the hill-climbing that soon had Bluey in trouble. They took it in turns to make a sling with their arms to carry him over the rough paths. The shadows loomed over them and the night sounds echoed around the rocks.

'You must keep up with me,' she ordered.

'Slave driver!' cursed Frank under his breath in English, but picked up his pace. Penny smiled, knowing the shepherd's hut was just above the snowline and praying that the old man and his son would be wrapped in their cloaks with a firebox for warmth.

It was dawn before they found they'd been going round in circles and had missed the hut by only yards. Bluey was exhausted and fit to go no further.

Somehow, word had got to Manolis and Giorgos that the strangers were heading out, and they welcomed them into the sweaty fug of their milking hut, plying them with warm sheep's milk to revive their flagging spirits. Penny left the ragged soldiers in their care, making an emotional farewell; all the boys promising to name their first girls Athina after her, if they got back home safe.

She borrowed a few sheep to take down the mountain as if she was just a peasant girl bringing a flock off the hills in case of bad weather. No one would stop her journey in daylight. The sheep were as cussed as *she* could be, and were not keen to be separated from the flock, but with her crook she pushed them into some order until it was safe to let them loose.

She returned to a house of gloom and the news that all the men were in Agia Prison, as Katrina feared. Soldiers had returned in force to search for the wireless set in Vafes, tearing the house apart in their search, destroying furniture, smashing crockery in an orgy of destruction. Elpida had kept quiet about the cave, though.

Then, two weeks later, just when they had given up hope, Ike returned, thin, bruised and silent. No evidence had been brought against him but he had endured days without food. Three men had been tortured, broken by every cruel method until, unable to walk, they were tied together and executed in the yard. This was learned later from others. Ike hardly spoke a word of any of it. He clenched his fists and spat, showing broken teeth. The name of the traitor was on everyone's lips but never uttered.

'They will be avenged,' Ike said. 'And the traitor will know the point of our knives one night. Let him live a while longer with the uncertainty of knowing when or where his blood will be spilled. Let him spend his pieces of silver on wine and whores, they will bring him closer to his destiny.' He sank back on the couch, shaking his head in despair.

Katrina brought a wash bowl and kneeled to sponge his feet. 'Come, sleep, rest. We have you back.' She looked to the corner where once the icon had been. The waxen image of the crucifix stood as a reminder. Tonight another curse would be laid on the traitor.

Penny slipped away, up into her loft to leave the couple to their reunion.

It was a sad Christmas and Epiphany. The loss of good men meant no dancing or rowdy celebrations. Food was scarce and no one had the will to stand, but they all sat singing their traditional songs of freedom, knowing life would be even harder in 1943.

Rainer Brecht was promoted to major. His expeditions brought arrests but no radios. He was told that torture had broken the key leaders, but no wireless was located. Winter kept the garrison close to base and the barracks were tense after news of the defeat at El Alamein.

So many of his bronzed comrades were lost in the desert. Others were brought back to Maleme, blinded by the sun, with septic wounds, paralysed throats, their hopes of further victories as tattered as their uniforms.

Their Christmas party was a drunken affair, a few carols and a feast for the men; boredom was making drunks of them all. There was no further talk of being transferred. Rainer could volunteer for service on the Russian front but only a madman would swap the warmth for those icy steppes and certain death.

He amused himself playing cards and drinking with Kurt Anhalt, not one of his close friends but someone who had time on his hands. There was a group of card sharps betting on anything they had to hand. It was from them he learned how much looting was going on.

'The peasants have nothing worth taking but their daughter's virginity. I leave them to my men, but now and then they pick up trifles in the better homes and churches, ancient pots, cruci-fixes. You're our expert – what do you think of this little thing?'

Kurt pulled out an exquisite clay bull, a perfect piece of Minoan pottery.

'Where did you get this?' Rainer asked, knowing it was thousands of years old.

'Can't recall. Some shelf, or maybe it blew out of the ground,' he winked. 'It's old?'

'How much do you want for it?' Rainer fingered it with care.

'Nothing you could afford but I've got something more up your street.'

Kurt brought out a wrapped piece of wood, which opened out into a beautiful icon of St Katerina. It must be from the Cretan school of iconography, a fine example. He touched it reverently, knowing it was sacred. 'You don't like it?'

Kurt shrugged. 'Her eyes follow me round the room. Gives me the creeps. I don't go in for religious stuff. If we win the next game, she's yours. There's plenty more where she came from. They hang on every wall of any half-decent house. These people are so superstitious. Didn't she end up doing cartwheels? See, I haven't forgotten all the priest told me.' Kurt laughed. 'Oh, take it. It's worth nothing. I can see you fancy her.'

'I have a sister called Katerina, she might like it. I'll package it up and send it to her for her birthday.'

Rainer thought no more about the icon until it was posted back to Germany, but a week after the card game, Kurt was dead, ambushed in some alleyway and knifed. Twenty-five hostages were shot for his murder. The post from Germany was getting less reliable but a welcome letter from his mother arrived, thanking him for the lace tablecloths and Father's cigarettes he had sent at Christmas. There was news that poor Katerina had been knocked off her bicycle in the blackout after a bombing raid. She was in hospital with a head wound and it was causing fits, but she had loved the sacred picture of her namesake.

The things not said in the letter worried him. All was not well at home. The news of heavy bombing was a surprise. The soldiers on Crete had been told that the RAF was feeble and the Americans had suffered heavy losses, and now his little sister was injured. He'd been so long out here, he was beginning to forget his homeland. He wondered if he'd ever see his own family again. It had been two years since he left them and suddenly he felt anxious and trapped.

Who could you trust here but your own men? Certainly not the locals, anxious to serve them? He'd heard rumours that the Red Cross doctor from Chania who'd healed his limp was not all he claimed to be, that he was part of a network of resisters passing information down an invisible line they couldn't penetrate. Tradesmen smiled, delivered promptly, made the right noises, but who knew what was going on behind those swarthy faces?

The recent reprisals had done nothing but inflame the population into further acts of violence. Any fool could see that this race was not bred for intimidation. God help the garrison if it were to be overrun and they were left to the Cretan hot-bloods to finish off. He'd seen enough now to know what his fate would be.

Yolanda was tiptoeing round her family, torn between trying to be an obedient and dutiful daughter and a desire to persuade them that she would have no man but Andreas. His name was unspoken but his presence wafted above them like incense. Momma would sigh and look soulful as she went about her chores.

The Mordo betrothal plan had fizzled out and was replaced by news of his and Rivka Katz's wedding. She was a young seamstress who would make him a much more suitable wife than Yolanda would ever have done. Why couldn't Momma and Papa see this?

The pool of suitable grooms was shrinking. There were prettier, younger girls looking for husbands now. Those boys who could bribe their way out of the city had gone and others were working in labour camps. She thought this fact might be in her favour, wearing down her family's opposition like water on the limestone rock.

At least she'd been allowed to stay on at the clinic as a nurse. The rabbi had intervened, saying it was good for Jews to be seen abroad doing works essential to the wider community.

Yolanda began to travel out of town with other helpers, armed with food parcels and clothing to the starving and sick families stricken by the harsh winter and poverty. The clinic had only a small store of vitamin syrups to spare but they asked the local priests to intervene and beg supplies from doctors in the garrison hospital, who donated what they could from their supplies. The staff no longer cared where the precious medicines were sourced. Saving children from starvation was all that mattered now.

There'd been a poor crop of olives and oil, and much of that taken by the billeted troops. Without oil few could survive the rigours of winter. Wood was scarce, trees were chopped down and even furniture was broken up for fuel. Women exhausted themselves in an endless search for driftwood, snails and mountain greens. Goats and sheep were killed. Yolanda wept to see little children holding their hands out to German soldiers begging for food. To their credit, many gave them pieces of chocolate and hunks of bread to share out. Who could look into the face of a starving hungry child and not feel pity?

But for every good one among them there was the other sort, the pestering drunk, the foul-mouthed abuser, the greedy glutton and the arrogant, pushing Cretans out of the way and into the traffic in their rush to find amusement in the town.

The nurses dealt with girls from the brothels, beaten and degraded, with injuries Yolande could never explain to her parents.

They thought they were sheltering her honour but she, in turn, was protecting them from knowledge of the real price paid for occupation. Their world was changing beyond recognition, leaving them confused and clinging on to old ways. She knew this in her heart but it didn't make her own life any easier.

Andreas' private clinic helped supplement their meagre medical supplies, while his treating officers brought scraps of information, useful in finding out who was deployed and where. Extracting these facts was not without risk, however.

Andreas had known nothing about the big raid near Vrisses, but there were brave girls risking death in the German HQ offices, passing down crucial details of the arrests and who had been executed, risking exposure even when they knew a traitor agent was in their midst posing as an interpreter. This Agent K was moved for his own safety to a villa close to Venizelou Street but the address was known now to the Resistance and his days were numbered.

One night Andreas met Yolanda at their secret rendezvous, flushed and out of breath. 'I'm being followed. I had to give someone the slip. I think some young hostage talked in the prison under torture. Now his mother is mad with grief, deranged and calling through the streets to anyone who'll hear that her son was innocent and it should be others who should be shot, men who should know better. She's been pointing out our clinic. I daren't put any of my staff at risk. I'll leave.

'There are others to take my place. I'll carry on my work up there, *sta vouna*,' he said, pointing towards the shadowy mountain range. 'You must come with me too. There's no future for us here. If they capture me, they'll take you and your parents, any excuse to harry Jews. There have been new intelligence officers flown in to toughen things up. I heard one of my patients complaining only the other day. Your community has been lucky so far but on the mainland it's another story.'

'I can't leave them if they are in danger,' Yolanda wept.

'If you stay you will compromise them. Everyone in the clinic knows about us, tongues wag and there are paid spies, gaolbirds without an ounce of loyalty who wouldn't care who they denounce if it brings booze, cigarettes and whores. There's no time to delay. I hope to God it will all be over soon, but until then we have to survive. But I won't go if you don't . . .'

'Please, go. I'll follow when I can, but how will I do it?'

'No, we'll go together. Carry on as normal, as I will, but one afternoon when I give the signal we'll just walk out. There are secret routes out of town avoiding checkpoints. We'll look as if we're going for a lovers' stroll, no walking boots or luggage,' he said, smiling down at their feet. 'As if we have a half-decent pair of leather shoes between us. You wear your uniform. Leave a letter and bring only your purse and papers.'

Yolanda sat down, winded by such a plan. 'How can I desert my parents? You have family up there,' she sighed, waving her hand up to hills. 'What'll become of me as a Jew among Christians?'

'You will be Kyria Androulaki, no one need know anything other. It doesn't matter as long as you're safe.' He kissed her and they clung to each other as if the whole world were coming to an end. It felt like it was. 'Be brave, my lion-heart, but we have to go soon.'

Yolanda lay awake all that night, Andreas' warnings echoing around her head. If she stayed and she was denounced by some traitor in the Resistance, they would arrest all her family. If she left with Andreas, and the soldiers came for her, her parents would know only that she'd eloped with a Christian and disgraced her family. She would be dead to the community, her name never to be uttered again. It would be a scandal and the talk of the streets in hours, but her parents would be blameless and pitied. Would this ruse work?

The clinic would continue. There were other, older doctors who would step in. She and Andreas could continue their work together, man and wife. She loved him so much that the thought of living without him, spending the rest of her life sitting with the women upstairs in the synagogue trying to pray, was unbearable. If he stayed because of her and was arrested, she would be overwhelmed by guilt.

Somewhere up there in the White Mountains she knew Penny was working and hiding out. There was the chance they might meet up again and work together with the Resistance groups. She'd not be alone with her two dearest friends.

She felt her decision was made, and as dawn broke, the cock crowed and the first dogs were barking, her mind was set. She found an old notebook, tore off a page and began to write.

*   *   *

When would this wretched winter ever end, Penny sighed. Nothing would grow until the snows receded. They had been cut off for a week, their food and fuel almost exhausted and there was talk of cutting down the precious olive grove.

How could she be getting sentimental about a tree? But the need to lop down Uncle Clarence was getting ever closer. Pruning was one thing, but a wholesale hatchet job was unthinkable. Olive trees were the lifeblood of the island, but people had to eat and live. The decision was not hers to make, but Clarence had been the scene of a wonderful and unexpected reunion when Panayotis and his men made a detour for the Easter celebrations before making one final round-up of stragglers hiding out with families.

It was always a shock and relief when they turned up, as if out of the mists, strolling down the mountainside, guns across their shoulders like yokes in Cretan style, peeling off right and left into village houses for the night.

She knew not to ask any details of their escape route or who took them off the island and where. One day, she imagined, they would all sit down over glasses of wine and all questions would be answered. It was enough to see Bruce looking so lean and craggy in his mountain breeches and black shirt, sporting a moustache, with the traditional black-lace bandana wound around his head. How could she ever tire of those craggy features?

They met as usual under Clarence's watchful eye, close to the ancient burial chamber that had sheltered passing soldiers on the run. Now it was proving a useful storage space for the last of their oil and grain, out of reach of looters.

Bruce was concerned about infighting between different factions of the *andartes* groups. 'Politics is rearing its ugly head,' he moaned. 'The communists won't sit down with the royalists. You'd think we'd enough to do keeping the enemy from over-running the whole terrain, but no, every gathering is like the clash of the Titans. It's driving us demented and my bosses in Cairo are getting impatient.'

It was the first Penny had heard of such divisions. She only saw resisters with aches and pains and wounds, who were as docile as lambs in the hands of a strange woman. She assumed everyone was up in arms for the same reason: to rid their land of the enemy. Why was she surprised that human beings fought for their own ideals first?

'It's making our job harder and harder. You need the wisdom of Solomon and the patience of Job to deal with that lot. I'm glad I'll be out of it.'

Penny had not seen Bruce so dejected before. He looked tired, thin and in need of a break, so they walked through the mountain slopes into fields where, to her delight, she saw the first hints of green shoots. Soon the field would be a riot of poppies, chamomile, daises, vetch; a rainbow of colours in a field full of bees and with the promise of honey to come.

Easter week progressed as it had for centuries: the ritual household cleaning, fasting days, everyone in black mourning, the procession of the body of Christ, carried on a bier surrounded by flowers, round the village streets. The total darkness of the church on Easter Eve before the lighting of the Resurrection candle and the small candles, lit to the shout of 'Christos Anesti' . . . Christ is risen, risen indeed.

To a flood of flickering lights came the torching of the Judas bonfire and the sharing out of the blood eggs, boiled in dye, just a few for the children's treat as many of their hens had been butchered for the feast. No one went hungry, with the slaughter of a sheep and a basket of Easter biscuits, though it was a meagre feast.

Penny was just pleased that Panayotis, as she had learned to call Bruce, was here sharing it with her.

Katrina missed nothing. 'He is your man, I can see, and you

are his woman. You should marry,' she laughed. 'Life is short, the priest can do it now that Lent is passed.'

Penny smiled and shook her head. 'All in good time.'

'No, take your chance when it comes to you or it will disappear. You walk to it. It won't walk to you.'

How she wished Bruce was around to hear Katrina's advice, but he had left the day after Easter, parting from her with only a kiss on her cheek. 'I'll be back. I know where you are, and Clarence will keep you safe.'

She'd smiled, trying not to cry. So even hardened Resistance organizers could be sentimental. Suddenly her spirits plummeted. Once these men were gone south, her role as nurse and guide would be over. She was surplus, another mouth to feed. All she could do was tend the fields, help in the house. She had no money, dependent on the charity of these kind people, and utterly alone.

It was with a sad heart she returned to her hideaway from seeing Bruce off, only to hear Katrina's news. 'We're going to a wedding. There'll be a feast and dancing . . .'

'Whose wedding is this?' Penny asked, since there were no telltale signs in the village of such a big event. No one had money for anything lavish.

'It's a family near Vrisses, in the hills. Ike has done business with them. We are all invited. Come on, don't look so glum. It will be your turn one day.'

'But I've nothing to wear,' Penny sighed, looking at the drab skirt and shirt she had on.

'Don't worry, I have a case of American dresses I brought back. You will wear one of them. I am sick of seeing you in widow's weeds.'

'But I am supposed to be in mourning for my aunt in Athens.' This was now her cover story for why she had sought asylum on Crete with distant relatives.

'Even the bereaved brighten themselves up for a wedding,

and if you wear a pretty headscarf, no one will see the state of your hair.'

Since staying hidden Penny had not retouched her hair dye and now her blond roots were six inches long. 'It's such a mess,' she sighed.

'I have some root powder to colour it again. It may turn everything reddish but Crete is famous for its flame-haired beauties.'

What could she do but go along with preparations; a shivering shower under the cascade of a spring waterfall, a change of clothes into a pretty checked-cotton frock that came down only to her knees. She brushed out her newly orange-tinted hair and wound it into a plait, covering it with a pretty lace-edged headscarf.

Spring had burst out at last and, with the shoots and blossoms, up came mountain greens and salads, herbs and snails. The olive grove was spared, the prunings hidden away for precious firewood before they could be stolen.

The family would travel to the wedding in the cart together. It lifted Penny's heart to know there would be something cheerful to watch, instead of following behind funeral processions, as she had these last few months, as older villagers and babies had succumbed one by one to the rigours of this hard winter. There were so many rituals to follow when this happened: days of fasting, special memorial services, special food. Every aspect of life had its superstitions and rituals, so different from the simpler English way of doing things. How plain the English ceremonies seemed compared with the processions, chanting, candle-lighting and icon-kissing she now observed. She wondered what would St Mark's vicar have made of it all. That set her thinking of Stokencourt – would she ever see her own family again?

Always at the back of her mind was danger. Penny must not draw attention to herself at this wedding. She was an alien in disguise; her very presence put Katrina and Ike in jeopardy. She must remain invisible in the crowd, but she wished the lucky couple, whoever they were, all the luck in the world. She envied them their courage to look to the future in such treacherous times.

If only it could be me, she sighed, looking down the valley. If only she had a clear understanding with Bruce about their future together but there was nothing for them on the horizon. How could there be with danger lurking round every corner? It was enough to know he was still alive in the world. That must suffice for now.

The smell of the fresh unleavened bread floated down the backstreets from the ovens and Yolanda sniffed the aroma with sadness. I may never do this again, she thought as she prepared the table, while Momma polished the Pesach pots and pans for the Seder supper.

Everything was prepared for the supper when they could relive how their ancestors made a hurried exodus out of the slavery in Egypt to freedom. Each ritual dish was eaten in memory of this event: roasted eggs, the shank bone of a lamb and a dish of bitter herbs in salt, reciting the Haggadah, a story so familiar to every Jewish family. Then followed a real feast of roasts and cheese pies, honeyed pastries, just a few reminders that there were eight days of festival, but finding treats to put on the table this year had been such an effort. Precious spices and delicacies to be squirrelled away for just such an occasion were few and far between, but that didn't stop the excitement in the homes along the Jewish quarter.

Yolanda had made her decision and now she sat trying not to cry with guilt at her devious plans, knowing no one here would understand. Yet she felt strangely calm. There was nothing to pack from her life here, just her precious toothbrush, identity papers and her gold chain and Star of David. The chain alone would fetch a good price.

Now she looked along the table to her parents with longing and love. If only they had managed to get to Palestine and not been stuck on Crete. How good it would have been to know they were safe. But at least fate had brought them back together for these past two years, and for that she would be forever grateful.

Perhaps one day, if she brought them a grandson to hold . . . She sighed, knowing it would be a far-off dream. She must make the most of every moment with them. She felt tears welling up at the thought of deserting them. Perhaps her tears were being seen now as devotion. Just seven days left before she changed her life forever.

On the morning of her intended departure, she took the letter she'd hidden, explaining her elopement.

I know you will be angry and withhold your blessing, which will be to my eternal shame, but I do not do this lightly. I want to carry on working alongside the man I love. I go of my own free will. I never meant to hurt or shame you but I know I will have, and I have no right to beg your forgiveness. What I do, I do for love. It is the only way for us to be together.

She put the letter on her pillow, slipping out as usual for an early shift, making her way through the backstreets as they came to life in the dawn light: housewives busy beating rugs, children whimpering from the upstairs windows, the bustle as the baker lit his oven. She paused to look one last time at the scene she knew so well. Under her uniform cloak she wore all her underwear and in a small *sakouli* she carried her best shoes and a crumpled frock and the only portrait of her parents she had from their days in Athens. Her purse was almost empty; she had left her wages for them with the letter. She could picture the scene when they found the note; Papa's face crumpling with grief, Momma's lips pursed in fury and despair. They were better off without a disobedient and thankless child, Aunty Miriam would chide.

Andreas was waiting at the clinic. 'Everything must be as normal. You do your rounds with the junior nurses.' He could see the agony on her face. 'Be brave, my violet flower, in a few hours we'll be free. I have arranged everything and by tomorrow we'll be married. I promise. I have no intention of shaming you. Here's the package of supplies to be delivered. You walk out to meet Giorgio's cart with it as normal and wait for me. I will be following behind.'

Yolanda worked like an automaton, only stopping to breathe when she wondered if her mother would tidy her room and see the letter. Even now they could be rushing to get her . . . Her thoughts were racing as fast as her heart. Of course they wouldn't come. They were proud and she had shamed them before the community. They would be dignified, counselled by the rabbi and his wife. Everyone would pity them, and Papa would hate that.

It was this thought that almost made her turn back and retrace her steps, tear up her letter, but her feet wouldn't budge. Her stubborn heart was fixed and there was no going back.

True to his word, Andreas left his clinic, locked the shutters and doors as normal, and was waiting for her as arranged. They walked out of the town for miles and then picked up a mule cart and drove through the dusk, walking through a gorge and up a sheep track to a village cut out of the rock. Here a group of rough-looking men with guns were waiting. They patted Andreas on the back as if he were a hero. Then they banged on the priest's door with rifle butts. The old man came to door in his shirt, puzzled and half asleep. He recognized Andreas.

'We want to be married,' Andreas said.

'This is no time to wake a respectable holy man. It's barely daybreak. Go home and see me in the church like everyone else.' The priest made to close the door but the men stuck their boots in the way.

'He will be married now,' they ordered.

Yolanda slunk into the shadows, horrified.

'No, you will not, Doctor.'

'Who says?' said his friend, built like a tree trunk, waving his gun in the priest's face. The old man got the message, put on his robes. They were married in minutes as he conducted his office at full speed and heard their vows.

'Now you are married. May I never see your faces again.'

Yolanda didn't feel a bit married but Andreas crossed himself, satisfied. 'Now to the mayor's house to make it legal.'

The mayor was knocked awake in the same fashion, told of the ceremony just performed and persuaded at gunpoint to give them a certificate of marriage, which they duly signed on the dot in the light of the rising sun. Everyone cheered '*Chronia Polla*', many years. Even the mayor got caught up in the romance of it all and gave them a pitcher of wine.

'Welcome, Kyria Androulaki.' Andreas kissed her deeply, and his friends melted away as he kissed the silver twisted ring he'd put on her finger and they sipped the wine. 'Not much of a wedding breakfast, but that can come later.'

It was barely light but the night was warm. Their escorts walked ahead, leaving them alone in the narrow ravine before the track climbed steeply into the hills. Andreas paused to tether the mule and brought out a woven wool blanket of red, gold and black stripes from its saddle and put it down on the grass under the nearest olive tree. They sat, kissed again lying down until the moon dipped away and the sun began to rise. It was as sacred a wedding night as anyone could wish for, Yolanda thought as she lay back, expectant of what would happen next.

Now they were truly alone with no guards to quench the burning desire she'd felt inside for so many long months; all those sleepless nights, tossing under the sheets dreaming of such bliss, were over. Now she was locked in her lover's arms, sinking down into an embrace that would change her for ever. He was tender and loving, but there was no shame in the passion they expressed with their bodies, the kisses they exchanged as their bodies melded into one. She lay back in his arms, hardly believing so much could happen in the course of one day. Yolanda Androulaki – how lovely it sounded. She was truly a married woman now.

Next day they made their way to his family's farm high in the hills, walking through fields of yellow daisies and poppies, and over tracks high up so they had a wonderful view of the coast below. As they drew nearer Yolanda began to fear how his parents would react to his news. He had broken all their traditions marrying out of his faith, bringing a town girl into the family without asking approval. She had no dowry of beautiful embroidery to offer, no olive trees or livestock. Nothing but the clothes she stood up in. Even she knew this was not how most Cretans went about their marriages. What if they turned her away in disgust?

She need not have feared. She was treated only with kindness, if a little surprise. When Adonis, Andreas' father, heard about the midnight nuptials, he roared with laughter. 'Heavens above, and the poor girl not even a Christian!'

It was the only time they referred to her religion. Andreas swore them to secrecy. From now on she was to be treated as any bride. All the talk now was of a feast and singing and a proper celebration in the village, which made Yolanda shudder. Her own parents would be in deep mourning for her elopement. For her husband's sake, she would learn the Christian traditions. What was done was done and she had no regrets.

Now the heat of summer was coming, all talk was of the wedding feast, a sheep or two to be slaughtered, pies to be made, flour to be found. Everyone in Chania was starving, but this was the country and they had ways of eking out their supplies from hidden stores.

Besides, farmers knew a thing or two about making a little go a long way. No one would come to the feast empty-handed, and they would invite everyone so no one would go hungry.

Kyria Dimitra, Andreas' mother, smiled. 'It's like the story of the loaves and fishes; much comes from little. It is a miracle how we always have enough to go round.'

Yolanda smiled and kept kneading the bread. She had nothing to offer but her gold chain, which they refused even to look at.

The night before the wedding feast, Andreas' mother produced a simple white dress with lace at the sleeves and hem. It smelled of camphor balls. 'You will wear my wedding dress. It will suit your slim figure. You town girls are like sparrows.'

Only then was Yolanda presented to the crowd of curious faces, her hair braided with blossom, her dress freshened with lavender water, a country bride, a stranger among strangers, but in wartime no one was surprised that customs had been ignored. His family towered over her, and to her it felt like living in a dream where music was playing, and she was expected to dance with all the handsome men and receive little gifts of money in a special purse. She felt like a ghost floating among them, half expecting to wake up in her little boxroom listening to Momma and Miriam arguing from the stairs.

Round and round she swirled, dizzy with dancing, drunk with wine, until her eyes alighted on the face of a woman standing by the wall and she stopped. Could it be . . . ? Surely not, here . . . And the red hair . . . ? What a wonderful surprise. Should she draw attention to her in public? No one would know their connection here, why shouldn't they recognize each other. And yet . . . oh, why not?

'Penny!' she screamed. 'My friend Penny is here.'

The girl in the cotton dress and headscarf rushed towards her with open arms, startled. Hugging her, she whispered in her ear, 'Athina, please, not Penny . . .'

'Why do I get everyone's names wrong?' Yolanda shouted to cover her mistake. 'Of course, it's Athina, one of my nurses.'

The mayor, who'd been snapping the party with a tiny box camera, drew close. 'Smile,' he commanded, but they were too busy grinning with delight at this unexpected reunion to notice the click of the shutter.

2001

And so for a few precious months, a brief spell of brightness flickered in a tunnel of darkness. We danced and sang as if the world was not going to fall in on our heads, as if there were no enemies lurking on the fringes; even at these celebrations, loose tongues wagging that the doctor from Chania had brought a Jewish bride back to the farm. Yolanda looked so beautiful that night and I envied her. Oh, how I envied her for having a lover who would bang down doors to make her his bride.

But war or no war, I must wait for Bruce to return and do things the English way. I was furious that he wouldn't even make love to me when he had had the chance. Was he not man enough to take the opportunity offered to him? It still rankled that his mission came before personal desires, though I despised myself for such terrible selfish thoughts.

All these frustrations I poured out to my silent audience, Clarence. If a tree is a living being, he was the nearest thing I ever had to a father confessor. I wondered if he was still there, grown fatter and more pock-marked in the last sixty years. I would love to find him again. Perhaps with a detailed map we could locate Katrina's village, if only I could recall its name. I think it began with a K . . .

I wrote to them after the war but my letters were returned. Little did I realize that after the war far worse things happened between neighbours in the name of politics than ever happened in the conflict.

Memories of my time with Yolanda were so precious now. Our paths crossed many times after that. Being in her company was like an oasis in the desert of my life before the bad times returned . . .

Now I could feel the warmth of the sun easing my bones, its brightness lifting my spirits, my senses touched by familiar sounds and scents. Siesta time over, I felt refreshed, ready to carry on my pilgrimage as if those cheerful memories had given me the courage to face the darkness to come.

Part 4

BETRAYAL

When will the skies grow clear?
When will the spring come round?
So I can take my gun again
My beautiful patroness
And go down to Omalos
And the path of the Mousouri . . .

Extract from 'When will the skies grow clear'
A traditional Cretan folk song

Knossos, 2001

The Minoan Palace of Knossos outside Heraklion city had changed out of all recognition. Coaches disgorged thousands of tourists in the heat of the May morning. There were entrance gates, tickets to buy, garish stalls selling souvenirs, all the usual trappings of a world-famous site. Rainer found himself ushered towards a guide and told to join the queue, which was not his intention. He would much prefer to wander through the excavations at his own pace. He wanted to consider whether he liked what had been reconstructed since the last earthquake, to revisit Sir Arthur Evans's layout with a fresher eye.

Now there were roped-off areas, duckboards, guides with umbrellas waving their flocks from one section to another. He'd chosen a busy day in the height of summer and his coach party were more interested in finding benches in the shade and taking snapshots than taking a detailed tour of the buildings. They didn't realize that the huge blocks of crystallized stone glinting in the sun, the timber-framed stonework, the sophisticated drainage systems and storage areas full of pots, hid an even older civilization underneath. This had been a sacred grove since the cradle of man. Who had lived here – a king, a priest, a dynastic family – no one was sure, but everyone seemed to have an opinion.

He filtered away from the group to look at the wall frescoes. He never tired of those ancient figures, men in pleated skirts, their jewelled ankles and wrists, and on the fabric were detailed patterns with symbols long lost to modern man: blue monkeys or birds, animals, figures. This place had been the centre of the archaeological universe when he was a student, but all their certainties were blown apart now by new theories. There were so many layers: Neolithic, Minoan, Mycenaen, Greco-Roman, and earthquakes shunting layers into each other making more puzzles. His own interest in Minoan history was fuelled by visits here before the war. The heat was too much for an old man, and as he sat watching the other tourists he thought how empires came and went. This had been a real centre of power once, but now all that was left were dust, stones and theories. Enough was enough; he needed a beer. These crowds were too much for him.

He found a taverna on the main road, cooled his hands on the chilled lager and took stock. He must be close to the Villa Ariadne, the HQ of the most senior German officers on Crete, the most famous being Commander General Kreipe, kidnapped towards the end of the war. The event was later made into a film. What a fiasco, and the consequences . . . But that was not his story to tell.

If he recalled correctly, if he walked up the side lane he would find a back entrance somewhere into the grounds of the villa now owned by the Greek Government, not the British School of Archaeology in Athens. He'd like to see it again.

It was a steep climb and he paused to turn and view the expanse of still-green valley where there were hectares of unexplored ruins waiting to be unearthed. He wondered if the gate was locked and if the tennis court was still there at the side of the main building, built in the style of an English country house by Sir Arthur Evans when he began his excavations.

He pushed open the door in the wall and followed a rough path towards the outbuildings. He was trespassing but no one was around to challenge him. There was an old taverna lodge still used by students as a field study centre somewhere towards the proper entrance. He'd stayed there once so he just wanted a peek at the villa for old times' sake.

It was exactly as he recalled, surrounded by palms and a riot of plumbago, with morning glory tumbling over the walls, scattered pillars and plinths dotted around the grounds, a headless Hadrian at the foot of the stairs. The veranda remained to the side where he had watched generals dining alfresco all those years ago.

This place had seen many occupants, as a garrison mess, a hospital clinic, a refuge, a seat of learning. It was the signing place of their final surrender in 1945. The house had ensured its survival and Knossos remained untouched, in so far as any site could be undisturbed when there were bombs and battles, earthquakes and civil war. It would have been a pity to have lost such heritage. He was glad work was still going on, finds being recorded and students pursuing their dreams.

Why was it important to see all this again, he mused. He'd not been stationed here. He stood in the overgrown court and shook his head. How full of plans he'd been in his youth, none of them achieved. The war had done that to him. This was a place of shadows. He must find another beer and get out of this empty place. It meant nothing to him now.

July 1943

That first journey into Heraklion was not without incident. They fought off an ambush on the road somewhere close to Rethymno, a band of partisans, wild men with beards and rifles shooting at the convoy, thankfully with armed guards giving them as good as they got. These bands of rebels leaped out of nowhere with an uncanny knowledge of where and when they were coming, a worrying trend, which meant spies close to HQ. There was now a co-ordinated push into the badlands of the White Mountains to find the caches of arms and supplies being dropped from the air, ambushing the bandits in the act of retrieving them. They'd had some successes but the groups were being trained up by British agents into fighting platoons to make smash-and-grab raids, for which the villages supporting them must be rendered useless.

Recently there'd been a campaign of chalked messages scrawled in German on walls around the town, propaganda, with news of Italian capitulations and warnings that they feared were coming from their own men. There were disgruntled elements based on the island, a spate of suicides and desertions that had to be stamped out quickly, but an uneasy standoff with locals produced some informers.

The plan was to capture some of these enemy agents in the act of sabotage, squeeze out names and contacts, and Rainer hoped to meet a young man able to assist them in this. He was to give him the once-over and check he wasn't a double agent.

He met him on site at Knossos, exploring the ruins with interest. To the casual eye they were two archaeologists on an outing, just talking over their interests. But there was another agenda.

At first Rainer didn't know what to make of Agent Stavros. He was a strange mixture of English good looks and fiery Greek temperament: fair-haired, blue-eyed, full of zeal to follow the Führer and his creed, an ardent National Socialist, friend of Oswald Mosley, anti-communist to the point of fanaticism, and he could play a mean game of tennis, too. He thrashed Rainer six games to one. Rainer's leg was healed by now so there were no excuses. The boy was too good for him, placing the ball just out of his reach, his face a picture of determined steeliness. When Rainer admitted defeat, Stavros replied in perfect English, 'You can thank my public school for a killer forehand. I perfected it on the bottoms of my fags.'

Stavros was a student in Athens and keen to join the excavations out west, but he'd been told he must earn his keep. He was recruited after the fall of Athens and there was no doubting his loyalties. Converts always made the most fervent soldiers. Tested out in the hills in the Italian sector, he picked out a few British boys on the run and made sure they were executed before they could doubt his cover, as a spy.

He was the genuine article. There would be no silly gaffes with this man, the perfect English gentleman with the accent of the officer class. They were working up a new legend for him as his first attempt had backfired. He'd moved further towards the coast and filtered into the hills as an escapee, sheltering in a village for the night, where he was promptly beaten up and returned to the local gendarmerie as a prisoner of war.

This was either a rare case of Cretan loyalty to the occupying forces in yielding up evaders, or a clever ruse to play them at their own game. Either way, he had to be moved on with a better cover story. It would be hard to explain his presence on the island when most of the evaders were gone long ago. He must claim injury and that he had been staying on to help the natives in their struggle, but was now desperately trying to head south for a boat. Now he was happy to join the Resistance fighters and meet the agents. Stavros had added his own flourish, playing the absent-minded professor, keen on all things Minoan. This would explain his wandering around in search of findings, behaving like a total British eccentric in accent and looks. He would be perfect for reporting back any news from the White Mountains closer to Chania. Here he had a better chance of being picked up by a sympathetic village passing him down the line. If he got to Cairo he'd be implanted in the British Army. It was a daring scheme but this boy was unstoppable.

'You're a brave one,' Rainer commented.

'It has to be done. From what I've heard they're all a bunch of thieves and bandits feuding amongst themselves. Divide and rule – long may it continue, I say.'

'If you're caught, there's nothing we can do to save you,' Rainer warned. 'You are on your own, I'm afraid. We'd claim no knowledge of you.'

Stavros clicked his heels and gave the salute. '*Heil Hitler!* It's my honour to die for him.'

How confident, how committed and how naïve this boy was to think the Führer cared a hoot about him, dead or alive, but Rainer had to admire such loyalty. It made his own uncertainty and lazy compliance seem so hesitant. He'd seen too much now to be certain of anything but that innate desire to survive long enough to see his family again. His sister, Katerina, would be sixteen, a young lady. How was she growing up in the midst of such turmoil?

'You have papers under your false identity. Is there anyone I should inform should . . .' He hesitated to continue.

'I have no family I wish to contact.'

They spent a pleasant evening in Heraklion, walking round the harbour and dining in the square. To have such an agent working in the Chania area was just the fillip needed. They were not going to rush; one false move and his cover would be blown. '*Siga, siga*,' slowly, slowly, as the Greeks say. Stavros might be a bit of a cold fish but he was a brave one and needed the best support they could offer. Rainer wondered what whales or minnows he'd trawl into his net.

Yolanda was finding country living daunting: the pungent smells, the routine chores, all the physical work expected of a woman. She was a city girl at heart, but that part of her life was over. She was learning fast to understand the thick accent, the gestures, the rules she must live by here if she was to be accepted. The close-knit community watched her with interest and kept its distance.

There were no books to read, no music to listen to on a gramophone, no piano to play, no services that held any meaning for her, but she kept her head down, trying not to worry about her parents. How she longed to write to them and receive their blessing. She begged paper and poured out her heart, telling them she was safe, that Andreas was kind and she still helped him in his work.

She told them about all the village superstitions and remedies, some good, some harmful. She sent the letter down to Chania on the bus, praying for a reply, but there was none. Then there was a skirmish and shooting, and she was needed to hide a wounded man in case the enemy did a search, tending him hidden in the caves until he was fit to walk again.

Adonis and Dimitra treated her well but she recalled the old saying: 'The groom cannot become a son nor the bride a daughter.'

The times when she could meet Penny were so precious, a link with her old life. Sometimes they could meet halfway on the hills, gathering sticks for fuel. Penny was working in another district, and she looked so thin and worn-out. Who would recognize them as those lively nurses in Athens? Her friend lived for news of 'Panayotis', but there'd been no word of him for months.

Yolanda had never met the man or his group. It was dangerous to know anything of other bands, even false names. The British agents and runners went by nicknames, Greek versions of their own names: Michaelis, Ianni, Manolis, Vasilios. Who they really were, no one knew.

Andreas said little about his mysterious disappearances in the night. He would unhook his sack from the door as it grew dark, grab his knife and what little food they had to spare. No one spoke, they knew not to ask any details. Yolanda followed him to the yard, fearful of the dangers ahead. She wanted to cling to him and beg him to stay, but stood clenching her fists watching him until he was just a speck in the darkness.

It was such a relief when he returned, bloodied, exhausted and famished. He still risked excursions into Chania, disguising his blind eye with ill-fitting glasses and bandages, wearing filthy peasant clothes. There were safe houses where he picked up medical supplies, new intelligence from the girls at HQ, news of ruthless SS men, and agents to pass down the line, lists of wanted men on which, to his amusement, was his own name.

Yolanda could hardly breathe until he returned to her arms each time. He'd brought news that Mussolini had been deposed, that Italy was on the brink of changing sides, that there were anti-German slogans chalked on the walls, posted for all to see.

'There'll be an invasion soon. We must be prepared. Then we'll be free again. I hear the words, but the enemy looks strong to me,' he warned.

One night he came in with a stranger covered in blood. He'd slipped on the rocks and fallen badly, gashing his leg. His name was Stavros, and he was tall, bronzed, with sun-bleached hair.

Stavros was apologetic, hesitant, and Yolanda recognized his accent. He'd been trapped for months, trying to escape and join the British army. He said his mother was English but he had the look of a German deserter to her. It was good to talk Greek without straining to understand the dialect, to hear familiar vowels . . . such a charming, handsome young man. Her heart warmed to him.

She dressed his wounds, asking how he'd managed to stay free for so long.

He smiled. 'I was a taken in by a farmer in Lassithi district close to where the famous scholar-soldier John Pendlebury had his dig before the war. The farmer took one look at my arms and kept me digging in his fields. They fed me like a son but when the farmer left the house his wife had other ideas and made to seduce me . . . It became difficult. She was a pest, making eyes at me across the table. I had to get away before he killed me. One night I left. I've been wandering for weeks, moving west, but everywhere they say our soldiers are gone.'

'You must be tired then,' she replied, noticing how firm and brown his legs were, as if he had been living in shorts.

'What brings an Athenian so far into the hills?' he said, sipping her tea with relish.

'It was my husband's wish to return to his family. I came with him, of course.'

'You are his nurse?'

'Yes, in the Red Cross clinic.' Yolanda stopped, fearing she was saying too much and changed the subject. 'The wound is only superficial, looks worse than it is, no real damage. Keep it clean and fresh air will do the rest.'

'Yolanda is a lovely name. It means violet flower,' he offered. 'Unusual . . .'

She nodded. 'It was my father's choice. He loved the colour, I think.'

'A very discerning man. Is he still in Athens?'

'No, he died,' she lied. What am I saying? Yolanda shivered. This boy asked too many questions.

Later, when he'd gone back to sleep in the sheep hut, she lay with Andreas but couldn't sleep. 'Where did you find Stavros?' she asked.

'He was lying injured on a rock, dehydrated, in shock. Another poor soldier who'd missed the boat, I fear. Why do you ask?'

'He told me he was running away from a farmer's wife. I suppose that explains why he is so well fed and sunburned. He's been on the run for two years, surely that's a long time?' she added. 'He has no sores or lice. He clearly hasn't been living rough. He would be filthy and bitten raw.'

'He's an archaeology student from Athens, a little touched by the sun,' Andreas laughed.

'Perhaps Penny might know him? She studied there before she was a nurse,' Yolanda whispered.

'Of course . . . but we must be careful, no names, no risks. He looks as if he can hold a gun. We'll be glad of another sniper.'

They gave Stavros no more thought as they drew closer. The pleasure of making love had lost none of its delight in the past months, despite the hardships.

Yolanda kept Stavros close to the farm, watching him closely to check if he knew how to milk sheep and make cheese. He was quite an expert, and so handy with a spade. His strong arms were useful on the farm in Andreas' absences, and Dimitra thought him a Greek god from Olympus.

There were no evaders left for him to join so he began to go out with Andreas on his round of meetings, joining his runner to pick up news, but his stamina was weak on long marches and scrambles. For all his fitness, he was soon out of breath.

'I think his lungs are weakened,' said Andreas' runner. 'He's always last and can't keep up. He's led a soft life, too many cheese pies and *krassi*. We need to help him find his mountain legs if he's to be any use in a raid. He's just a city boy and half English. They aren't built for the mountains. Give him time. Take him to Chania. His Greek is perfect, no one will challenge him.'

Stavros was keen to stretch his legs downhill too. 'I've been to Heraklion but never Chania. Are there still any Venetian palaces standing or a museum? Will we pass any frescoes on our journey? I have read that Crete holds so many treasures.'

'You're not going as a tourist,' Andreas snapped. 'There's nothing left there to see, and anything of value has found its way overseas. There are Germans everywhere so be careful, don't draw any attention to yourself.'

Yolanda watched them leave, glad that Andreas had company, but there was something about Stavros that puzzled her. There was just a chance she might find Penny out on the slopes, picking berries for preserves. There was so much to check out about their new recruit and Penny was just the one to ask.

No one noticed a tall young shepherd striding down through the alleyways towards the old western gate in the ruined Kastelli district. It was market day and many countrymen brought panniers of vegetables to barter for paraffin and salt. He paused by a well to scoop water over his face. No one saw him pull out a loose stone from the wall and shove in a letter – no one, that is, except a skinny boy with stick limbs who waited for the man to turn away. He would retrieve the drop under cover of darkness.

HQ were pleased with Stavros's first missive. He was embedded on a farm under the safekeeping of the osteopath and surgeon Dr Androulakis and his bride from the Jewish quarter. He wrote that most escapees were off the island apart from some too sick to move from their lairs, but their spy network was active, receiving fresh guns and supplies from airdrops, just as they expected. Stavros would stay close to the centre of operations and to make sure no units picked up the spies until he was sure of their plans.

Was it true, he asked, that Italy had capitulated in September and was now an ally of Greece? He had heard from secret wireless broadcasts that Americans were in Sicily. He trusted these were propaganda rumours and lies being spread just to dishearten morale. Crete must be held; it was the Führer's wish.

Rainer smiled at the note. Poor Stavros was in for a big disappointment if he thought they could hold off the inevitable collapse now the battle for Africa was lost. Rumours that new weapons would be brought here to smash the armies across the Libyan Sea were just that. Rumours.

As for active enemy agents, they knew most of their code names: Leigh Fermor, Dunbabin, Fielding, Woodhouse, Reade; clever brave men toughened by years of outdoor bivouacking. They'd not be easy to flush out, no matter what this young hothead thought.

Penny spent another long winter cut off from civilization. A heavy fall of snow blocking the tracks made a visit to Yolanda impossible. She stood looking out over the whiteness and grey mist in despair. The routes they used were made by following the shepherd's guide marks, stones piled on branches of trees. One false step off the trail could mean a drop into a ravine and certain death. Every slow journey was prodded out with a crook to find solid earth. She worried about the gangs roaming in the hills, living rough at the mercy of the elements and the 'wind men', bandit sheep rustlers whose allegiances were often only to their clan but who could be called upon to defend their territory should the enemy intrude.

This was the time when all the backbreaking work, cutting the olive sticks and collecting the kindling brushwood in the dry months, kept the cooking pot on the boil. It was the time for huddling together as the village women worked their needles and looms, spun wool, weaving cloth for cloaks and blankets and rugs, which kept the families from freezing. It was a time for stories of the old days when the Turks ruled over them and their own grandfathers fled into the hills to make a bid for freedom. They sang the songs of liberation and battles, sad haunting tunes in rich voices.

Too many were in mourning for relatives burned, shot and driven from a village raided further up the mountain. The younger women and children fled up the rocky mountainside to hide in caves, but the old were sometimes too frail to move and were left to burn in the raids on their homes. It was a terrible time. Christmas came and went with little celebration. Now they were waiting for the men of the Resistance to return for fresh food and supplies. It was a dangerous business appearing in villages where Germans were billeted, but it still went on.

News flew over the mountains that the Italians in the east were allies, though many were prisoners of war or deserters. Now there was talk of serious squabbling and feuds between those nationalist villagers who fought for the king and those who were communist sympathizers and wanted only to fight alongside their comrades. Secret meetings with the British agents were ending in disagreements and suspicion.

Ike would not speak either way. Since his arrest he had not been so eager to take sides with anyone. He drank heavily and snapped at Katrina. The atmosphere had changed in the villa. Everyone was tired, fearful of the future and sick of winter. Penny worried for her friends and for 'Cyclops', whose reputation was spreading. No one could halt Cretans from praising their heroes and gossiping. The one-eyed doctor was well known and she prayed their early-warning whistles would keep him safe.

Sometimes she shut her eyes and tried to imagine her old home: Nanny and Zander and Effy playing cards by the flickering flames of the nursery fire, toasting muffins on the brass fork with the horse handle, the tincture of Mummy's perfume as she came in to say good night, how the sequins on her ball gown glistened in the lamplight. How safe and cosy those childhood winter nights had been. Where were they all now in the world? Did they ever think about her?

Penny tried to make up for being a mouth to feed by amusing the children, making cards out of anything to hand, telling them her own childhood fairy stories, 'Cinderella', 'Hansel and Gretel' and 'Snow White'. She learned to spin fleece with a distaff over her shoulder. It was lumpy at first but with practice she got it smoother and fine. The lanolin in the oil soothed her rough hands and her hair grew out into its natural colour. When she coiled it up she could almost catch a fleeting glimpse of the smart young woman who had idled away her time in Athens. She sighed and turned away from the cracked mirror.

It was as if her whole life was on hold, as if she was waiting. There was no word from Bruce. No one could move in such snow storms. Her hopes dwindled of ever seeing him again. For the first time in months she began to wonder if it was time to head back into Chania, give herself up, even. How she longed for the safe routines of the hospital wards again, and the calm of St Joseph's Convent. Then she recalled how eager she'd been to escape the restrictions.

How could she even think of giving herself up, compromising her friends? She knew too many faces and locations. This was hunger, worry and boredom talking. Soon it would be 1944, a new start; surely this occupation couldn't go on much longer?

She was sick of the same old village gossip; who had set their cap at whom, who would not see out the year, how widow X was hoarding. I will go mad with this, she sighed. The only good thing was that the snow kept the Nazis from the door, the patrols preferring to stay in their barracks and get drunk on looted wine and raki, plying kids with handouts and scraps, and keeping their heads down.

These troops distributed leaflets, claiming a new amnesty with the population on condition the villagers took no part in the criminal acts of bandits; asking them to report movements for which, in return, they would be left in peace, but any resistance would be dealt with harshly. It was the same old ploy. Be good children and you won't be punished. Still the paper came in handy for kindling.

Then one morning towards the end of January, Penny woke to feel the warmth coming in through the shutter, the drip-dripping of snow and the chatter of birdsong. Spring had won its annual battle. Soon there'd be almond blossoms and fresh greens to pick. Hope lifted her spirits.

A few days later a runner came down saying a group was resting above them and needed fresh food and supplies. He took back what he could and Penny offered to take up the rest.

'There are twenty of us and we have another Englishman to feed now. Come soon,' he shouted.

She set off with a pannier strapped to her back, taking with her Ike's daughter, Olivia, who was twelve. She was so excited and proud to be a courier, providing cover for Penny.

'Remember, we are gathering food, we zigzag across the hills in case binoculars are plotting our path. Don't draw attention to yourself. The mountains have a thousand eyes,' Penny warned the wide-eyed child. 'You are my special helper but don't say your name or where you live to anyone. Loose tongues cost a whole village its men and its homes because somebody was boasting . . .' She had to warn the child, scare her from blabbing out information. Penny knew by now that isolated gangs of men, trapped for weeks in caves and hiding holes, were desperate for fresh news to chew over. It was only natural, and the little girl might say too much in her eagerness to please.

They made the trek up the side of the ridge through cypress woods and pine trees dripping with snow melt. Penny felt it was so good to stretch out her limbs after being indoors. She was like a colt let loose into a meadow, wanting to leap over rocks, but she was aware her little helper was struggling under her load so she pulled a few almonds and raisins out of her pocket to spur her upwards in the climb.

Then they heard a familiar whistle: the approach was being watched from lookouts hidden in the trees. One by one, faces appeared, smiling and waving, and out of the mountain cave emerged men like trolls, unshaven, long-haired, with smoke-black faces, all in rough clothes that blended so well into the earth and rocks. Then a young man stepped out into the sunshine, took off his cap and shook out his blond hair. His beard was flaked with glints of gold.

Penny stared up in amazement at the face she'd seen all those years ago in Athenian bars, the very guy who made a nuisance of himself until she gave him the hard word. It was Steven Leonidis. What was he doing here? She remembered some of the dubious attitudes he'd held before the war and she felt a flicker of unease. Luckily he hadn't yet seen her. Pushing Olivia forward she whispered, 'You go and take the basket, I've got something in my shoe.' She bent over to adjust her scarf right up to her chin and over her forehead like a widow would do. Her heart was thumping. Why was Steven here? Should she go and greet him?

One of the *andartes* rushed to lift off her pannier and take it into the cave. 'Come and meet our new man, Stavros. He's from Athens, Athina . . . Come and talk to him.'

'No, no, we must head back and collect sticks.' She made her excuses, sorry that Olivia must rush away from her first important mission. They were happy to see a child, patting her cheek. What if she told them Athina was a nurse from Athens? She must stop her talking and drag her away.

Then there was a shout. 'Athina! Come and look at these sores,' cried a young man. 'They won't heal.'

Steven was looking at her but to her relief he turned away. She shuffled and bent herself to look older, examining the lad. 'Boils again, always boils,' she croaked in her roughest accent. With the lack of fresh food, the dampness and dirt, no wonder their arms and necks were covered in festering boils. She turned to find the pot of poultice ointment, smearing it onto a clean rag and bandaging it onto the young man's arm, all the time trying not to look where Steven was. He mustn't recognize her.

She'd never rushed away so fast, but she was propelled down that hillside by a sudden irrational fear that seeing her student boyfriend had brought on. Something wasn't right.

Why had he suddenly appeared here out of nowhere? All her antennae were on alert as she and Olivia hurtled through the pines, picking sticks to fill their empty panniers. Olivia was upset. She thought she'd done something wrong.

Penny recalled all those political arguments they'd had, drinking together; his distaste for his Greek heritage and his delight in being so fair and blue-eyed. If anyone was a Fascist sympathizer, he was. Now he was a British escapee on the run when most of the men had long gone. He was fluent in Greek, he could have escaped so easily unless . . . unless. Oh God, could he be a plant? Was he passing himself off as English for the enemy?

Perhaps seeing all the atrocities committed on the island, he had had a change of heart. People did change. That was it, surely? How long had he been here, and how did he come to be so close to Ike and Katrina's village? How could she be sure he was genuine? The seeds of doubt niggled all that night. One word to Ike and his group, and Steven Leonidis would be dead. How could she live with the possibility of killing an innocent man, especially one she could defend in many ways? But if she identified him, he would identify her as being English too. She must warn Andreas, and find Bruce, flag up a warning that the Athenian might be a spy. It was the only answer she could hear in her heart.

Sometimes you have to make a snap decision, one that changes everything, she thought, waking from a nightmare, reliving those moments when she sensed her friends were in danger. She had so few facts to go on, just an instinct. If she was wrong, Steven would be executed; if she was right, others far more precious might meet the same fate.

Next morning she sought out Ike to make her excuses. 'Your kindness is too much. I am a burden on your family. I'm going back to Chania and to the convent life I left. Please give my good wishes to everyone, but I am a town girl at heart. If there is danger here, I will only make things much worse for you all.'

She saw the look of disappointment on his face. 'Please be careful who crosses your threshold,' she warned. 'Keep the *andartes* out of the village. If anyone asks for Athina, show them the door, unless it is Panayotis, of course. Tell him I am back in town.'

'What are you trying to tell me, my friend?' Ike asked. 'We have no secrets.'

'Oh, yes, we have, more than most. I wish I knew why, but I feel danger coming, I must check things out.'

'We shall miss you,' Ike said.

'When all this is over, I will return,' Penny said, feeling the tears filling her eyes.

'Bring your children to see us and we will be happy. You've been like a daughter to us, dear Athina. May the Blessed Saints guide your path in safety. *Kalo taxidi* . . . safe journey.'

It was hard to sneak off so ungraciously. Katrina came rushing out to hug her. Penny pressed into her hand a letter scribbled between the lines of an old pamphlet. It was the only paper to hand. She'd written it to Yolanda in formal Greek, warning her best friend that there may be a spy in their midst. She wrapped it in that precious little hanky kept safe all these years, which Yolanda would know came only from her.

'Give this to Yolanda or her family. It explains a little. Tell everyone to be on the watch for smiling strangers.' Penny kissed them all, tears now coursing down her face. She turned away down the track towards the village and the main road. She prayed there was a bus to Chania that day.

Andreas brought his augmented group down to the isolated farm for fresh milk and bread. There had been no troop patrols for weeks and the *andartes* were beginning to hope the worst was over.

The new man in their group, Stavros, was a useful pair of hands on the farm, and Adonis thought him a champion for an Athenian. One night they sat outside and Dimitra proudly brought out all her family snapshots of Andreas and Yolanda's wedding feast, taken by their mayor. 'We didn't always live like beggars. See, we even had a photographer. We fed 100 people that special night,' she boasted proudly. Out they all came for the men to look at and pass around: bride and groom with the village children, all the family, the dancing – and one of Penny and Yolanda laughing together.

'Good Lord, I know that face!' Stavros exclaimed, peering closely at the two of them.

Before Yolanda could stop her mother-in-law, Dimitra smiled, 'Yes, the nurse is from Athens too . . . Athina . . . like Yolanda, from the town.'

'Oh, we don't know that,' Yolanda was quick to butt in.

'But you said she was a nurse in Chania?'

'Did I? I don't recall.' Yolanda stared at the older woman, willing her to shut up.

'Where is she now, this Athina?' Stavros's eyes were focused on the image of Penny.

'Not sure.'

'But she came with the Greek-American and his wife to your wedding feast. You have met her many times . . .'

Oh, please shut up, Yolanda prayed.

Andreas picked up on her anxiety. 'Come on Stavros, back to work.'

Yolanda couldn't settle after that. He'd recognized her friend and that meant he knew her real name. She must warn Penny. There was something about the stranger she couldn't work out. He was helpful, polite though distant, he seemed to pull his weight. He was a crack shot but hadn't seen action yet.

Andreas always said you couldn't judge a man until he was under fire. If he was captured and tortured, he could give away the farms, the caves, the nicknames and the families feeding them. She knew he spoke good English and Greek, but he was different, not like the other escapees and she felt uneasy.

'I'm going to visit Athina,' she announced. 'It's far too long since we met together.'

'But it's a day's walk in your condition,' said Dimitra, looking at her stomach.

Yolanda smiled at her concern. Her monthlies had stopped for two cycles now but she still wasn't sure if she was really pregnant. Hunger stopped many a girl's courses, she'd noticed, and it might be a false alarm. Mountain women worked hard right through to the birth. She would have to do just the same if this joyous event was really happening for her.

'I'll be fine if you can spare me. I must speak with my friend. There are things she must know.'

They gave her the old mule to ride side-saddle down the paths to Ike's village. Spring was bursting into green, the smell of fresh leaves and flowers was overpowering, above her wheeled the buzzards mewing, and she saw a flash of the mysterious *kri-kri* goats, darting as they got wind of her, long before she crossed their path. She sat in the shade, excited to be seeing

Penny. How surprised she would be. What good news she had if there was a baby on her way.

Her arrival caused consternation. Katrina was busy at her chores and there was no sign of her friend.

'We thought she'd come to see you at first, but poof . . . she rushed away. You got her letter . . . ?' Katrina paused. 'Holy Mother, I forgot . . . in the rush. It's somewhere on the shelf. I'm sorry.' She rifled through the plates and jugs and holy picture cards. 'I think she's gone to find her young man, Panayotis. She must have taken the bus to Chania. I don't understand young women now. In my day our father would not let us out of the house in daylight in case we were dishonoured, but this war is changing everything. Girls come and go as they please,' she sighed. 'There are no men left to check them. Now, where is that note she left . . . ? Here it is.'

Yolanda took the package. She recognized the hanky and shoved it in her apron pocket for safekeeping. She sat down with them to drink mountain tea and biscuits, then rested for a while, reading the note, which didn't make much sense and was barely legible as it was stained with red wine and the paper faded.

With a weary sigh she set off back uphill, troubled, even more uneasy now. Why had Penny gone? Panayotis could be anywhere on the island. The British officers came and went, kept their couriers close and trusted only their runners and guides. She would never find him. It was a crazy scheme, full of danger. What was she thinking of, leaving her best friend without a word. What was she trying to tell her? Could it be she was sensing danger too?

The next letter from Stavros found its way from a drop at the crossroads, hidden at the back of a holy shrine. From there it was given to a friendly policeman and taken down to German HQ. Stavros warned it was time to trawl in the catch. He knew their key operating area, the friendly farms and outposts. This was the usual information, useful for sending a silent patrol in a first-light operation, catching them by surprise. Meanwhile Stavros would escape to find the next group. It was the last bit of his letter that intrigued Rainer.

> The wife of the doctor is a Jew from Chania. She has a friend I recognize from a photo, living in the hills, a nurse called Athina, but I knew her as Penelope George, a fellow student from the British School in Athens. She is passing herself off as a Greek national and helping the Resistance. She should have useful information.

So Penelope had slipped out of town and it *was* her he'd seen with the doctor. All these years hiding in the hills. He'd often wondered what had happened to her. She'd fooled them all with her Greek accent.

Why had she not come clean and been interned with all the other Brits? What hold had this island on her to make her risk her life for it?

Now it would be only a matter of time before she was brought in for questioning. He'd not like to see her subjected to the methods of those SS sadists who had their own particular ways to make women talk. Stupid, stubborn woman. Why hadn't she left?

Rainer looked out of the window onto the bay and recalled the image of Penny in the caves; calm, strong, unflappable, determined to stay by her patients. If anyone deserved a medal she did. He would hate to see such a beautiful woman destroyed by that gang of thugs and rapists bent on terror, but there was nothing he could do to save her now.

2001

'Wake up, Aunt Pen. Are you OK? Shall I fetch the doctor?' Lois was hovering over me with concern. 'You've been asleep for hours. We're going out for dinner soon. Mack knows a special place in Chania, but if you're too tired . . .'

'I'm fine, don't fuss, but you should go on your own. Alex can stay with me,' I offered, not wanting to be a gooseberry. I knew what it was to have my heart broken and I was determined that Lois should have the chance to mend hers.

'No, this is my treat. We've been neglecting you, going out all day, leaving you here with only a book for company.'

'Books are the greatest companions, and this one is a gem: *The Winds of Crete*, you must read it. Besides, I've had time to put all my memories in some order.'

'Don't forget the ceremony on Saturday. Mack says we must go early. Are you looking forward to it?'

What a silly question. Only the young could think such a thing. Remembrances are often so painful. 'It's what we're here for.' I replied, stretching my stiffening limbs. 'I'll go and make myself decent.'

'Don't forget you've promised to tell Alex what it was like living rough in the hills,' she shouted as I made for the door.

'Perhaps . . . but tonight is not for my old stories. This Mack seems very attentive all of a sudden.' I couldn't resist making her blush.

'I know, and he's being brilliant with Alex, but he's good with all his clients, I'm sure. He's going to the ceremony. Do you remember, he said his father was on submarines around here in the war?'

As I brought out my blue silk dress and pashmina shawl, pulled my hair back into shape and slapped on the mozzie cream, I smiled: it was time to leave wartime behind for a while and the memory of those fearful days trying to find news of Bruce among the ruins of Chania, seeing its citizens sheltering in shacks and caves, destitute and starved of hope as well as food. It had been a mistake to go back there but I was desperate by then.

Mack led us through the busy streets to a restaurant in a building with no roof, open to the night sky. It was packed, musicians playing Cretan songs in the corner, waiters dashing around with trays held high, a noisy vibrant tavern in the heart of the old city. For a moment I was taken aback by the coincidence: it was in the very quarter where Yolanda's parents had lived. The ruin had once been a soap factory close to their synagogue, bombed later. How strange to see laughing and singing by candlelight in the very place where once I'd made such a painful visit in the spring of 1944.

March 1944

Penny found the only *kafenion* she recognized by the ancient walls where she knew there would be friends of the Resistance. She hovered outside, hoping for work but looking so rough and downtrodden, she feared she'd be turned away as a vagrant. She'd not eaten properly for days and now she was feeling faint and nauseous. She grabbed hold of a chair to steady herself. A woman came out and she asked for water.

The woman paused. 'Sit down, *Kyria,* you look ill. Have you travelled far?'

'From the Apokoronas,' Penny nodded. '"When will the skies grow clear?"' she whispered, knowing the first line of this freedom song might help her cause.

'Do you know the bone doctor then?' the woman was clearly fishing.

'Cyclops, the hero with healing hands, his wife is my friend,' Penny replied.

The woman smiled. 'I thought I recognized you. You came here once with them. I never forget a face.'

Penny felt herself relaxing. 'I'm Athina. I'm looking for work and I have to find someone. It's important.'

'You won't find any work. Come inside . . . Athina, come and meet Nikos. Help me in the kitchen and at the tables and you can eat and sleep here.'

Stella and Nikos found her soup and dry rusks, a bowl of

water to wash herself, and she pulled put on her one decent dress, which made her feel human again.

'We still have a few regulars from the offices, priests and teachers, and soldiers, of course, the better sort.' She paused. 'There's no money; even the soldiers count their drachmas. They come to play backgammon, to gossip, anything to forget this war. We hear things and we pass it round those we can trust. You have news?'

Penny explained her dilemma and the fear that there was an agent planted in their group who could betray everyone. 'I need to find Panayotis or Michalis.'

Stella laughed. 'They swagger around like natives, more Cretan than we are. Michalis is a terror. He drinks with German soldiers. They have no idea who they are talking to. First you must renew your papers. There are spot checks. You must go to the town hall, register again. It's the safest way. They are on the lookout for "suspicious visitors". Always check with us first before you speak to anyone. They got that agent who betrayed his village and made martyrs of so many last year. A death squad came into his house in September and stabbed him. Now the Polentas family is avenged. Trust no one, Athina, especially those asking questions. Your accent is good but gives you away among the locals.'

Thus warned and fortified, Penny felt ready to search out news of Bruce, but her hopes were dashed when she realized he was back in the hills on a mission and there were plans for big raids in the offing.

One afternoon during siesta, she took herself down to the *limani*, to the old harbour, past the shuttered shops, up to Kondi-laki street and the ruined houses round the corner into Portou, the street of the gate into the old Venetian wall. It was a visit long overdue, one she was making for Yolanda's sake.

No one recognized her at first. Yolanda's parents stared at her with suspicion as if she were some official. 'It's Pene-lope . . . remember, from Athens? I came to see how you are.'

Solomon's lips broke into a half-smile. 'Ah, yes, we remember you, don't we, Sara?'

Sara Markos's face looked blank. She had aged so much in the last year, Penny thought with a pang.

'Momma has been ill. She doesn't remember things so well now. She may repeat herself to you. How are you? Come in.' Solomon ushered her over the threshold, guiding Sara with her two sticks. 'You are still with the school in Halepa?'

Penny shook her head. 'That was a long time ago, sir. Much has changed since then. I have been nursing in the mountains. Now I'm back in town. I wanted you to know I have met Yolanda only recently and she is well . . .'

'Please don't continue. It will upset Momma.'

'We have no daughter, she died,' Sara added, turning her face from Penny.

'But she doesn't know I am here. I just wanted to check that you are safe and well so I can tell her. She worries about you so . . .'

'The girl should've thought about that before she ran away and broke our hearts. I see from your eyes you do not understand this.' Solomon shook his head and gave a long sigh. 'There's no joy in life for us now she is gone but she made her choice. If you belong to a faith community you abide by their laws. There is no picking and choosing what you believe in or not.'

Sara became increasingly agitated at his words. 'Why does she talk about the girl? She died. We don't talk of her, do we, Papa?' Sara was tugging at his sleeve in distress.

'You see how Momma is, her mind wanders, strained by worry and pain. It is not easy for us here.'

'I am sorry,' Penny said, feeling the weight of the old man's sadness. 'What shall I tell Yolanda if I meet her again?'

'Tell her what you like. There is nothing we can say. She wrote us letters. They were burned. You do not receive letters from the dead, no matter how much you want to read them. It is not our way.' Solomon saw Penny's face fall. 'Oh, tell her we are well and making our lives without her, if you must. How long we remain so is in the Good Lord's hands. Our men are always the first to be taken hostage if there is trouble.'

Penny left them with reluctance, longing to argue on Yolanda's behalf. It was as she feared, but she didn't understand how a faith could disown its daughter for loving the wrong man. Surely in times like this everyone should be glad of finding happiness, no matter what the differences were? What would she say to Yolanda now, she sighed. Better to say nothing at all.

The *glendi* was going to go on all night but Yolanda was too exhausted to join in now.

The men were celebrating a successful drop, which brought them fresh uniforms, guns and boots, and they were like children dancing round in new riding breeches, slouch hats and berets. They'd killed a sheep; brought out the better wine in the oak cask that kicked like a mule. Everyone was relaxed.

The only shadow was the death of a brave Kiwi, *Vasilis*, killed in an ambush in February. He was mourned as a great leader of men, brave to the point of foolhardiness. The legends were already spreading of his deeds. His lavish funeral had united some of the warring groups for a few hours in mourning.

Only two days ago, strangers arrived with another British agent for a meeting in the beehive field where plans were discussed and argued over. It was here Yolanda had come face to face with Panayotis.

She could see why Penny was so smitten with him. He had that *levendia*; charm, high spirits, a devil-may-care bravura, a zest for life and living dangerously. Here he was, trying to dance the ring of fire. Everyone was clapping, waiting for him to leap or burn his pants. Andreas was taunting him, shouting and joining in. He was wearing himself out trying to keep the peace among warring factions but tonight he was drunk and like a boy again. Yolanda's only wish was that Penny was here to share in the fun.

Stavros was sitting by the fire, drinking with the others. Her worries about him had proved unfounded for he'd fought bravely when a patrol came in sight, held his fire and proved he was on their side.

Now she wanted to single out Panayotis from the group without drawing attention to herself. Pregnant women didn't speak to single men, so she sat in the shadows watching them dancing, peeling off their jackets, and this gave her an idea how to let him know that Penny had left the district.

She pulled out the wedding snapshots from the drawer and found the one with herself and Penny together. She was sad to be parting with it but she slipped it carefully into the British soldier's jackets pocket after she'd written on the back 'Your friend is in Chania.'

Next morning at first light they were all gone. It was better not to know where.

Penny had been working in the kitchen of the taverna for over a month and feeling herself growing stronger on Stella's meals. She'd gone to the offices to queue for fresh papers but felt her height made her conspicuous and the wait was too long to endure. Her confidence in public places was gone. She felt perpetually uneasy.

One night, as darkness fell and the streets were patrolled by soldiers, she sensed people watching from doorways, the flash of a lit cigarette. She rushed into the back, warning Nikos they were being watched.

He laughed. 'I think not. We have visitors tonight.'

But as Penny cleared away the debris from the wooden tables on the pavement, she became aware she wasn't alone. She paused and spun round. There was no one was in sight, but she just knew she was being watched. She felt her hands shaking as she picked up the last of the wine jugs. She took a deep breath. 'Come out whoever you are . . .' she shouted, trying not to quake.

The outline of a tall figure in Cretan dress, a black shirt and bandana emerged out of the shadows and came swaggering across the cobbles. 'Athina? So it is you?'

She'd recognize Bruce anywhere. 'Thank God, you're here . . .' she said in English as she ran towards him.

He put his hands to his lips. 'I'm not alone.'

One by one, dark figures emerged out of the walls, smiling sheepishly. 'This is the beautiful mistress who warms Panayotis's heart,' they sang.

Suddenly six of them hurried through into the back room and Penny felt a tinge of disappointment that this was a secret meeting from which she would be excluded.

'How did you find me?' she whispered as she gave them plates of *meze* and *tsoukoudia* glasses.

'Now there's a strange thing, I found a picture in my pocket of you and my lovely hostess, Yolanda. It told me where to look.' He smiled up at her and her frustration melted.

'Chania is a big city.'

'Not really when you know where to look. There're not many Greek blondes who can swear like a trooper and kick a wandering hand into touch.' Trust Bruce to make a joke of everything. 'Still as disobedient as ever. I told you to stay in the hills. You didn't even tell your friends.'

'I had my reasons. There's a guy from Athens, Stavros, they call him . . . He knew me from Athens. We were students . . .'

'Yes, with Andreas' gang. Good chap. I met him last week.'

'I don't trust him. He was a Fascist sympathizer as a student . . . we were close for a while. I think he's a spy.'

'You're wrong, old girl. He's out there fighting, he's half Greek. People think he's a German deserter so we can use him to trick other German prisoners into thinking he's one of them.'

'But when we were in Athens—' she began out of the corner of her mouth.

Bruce was impatient. 'What did he say when he saw you?'

'He didn't. I recognized him first. I really think you should check him out.'

'We have already. Do you think he would last five minutes if we thought him an agent? The traitors are local men with grudges, criminals let out of gaol with families to feed. Yes, there were quislings from the mainland but they were flushed out long ago. Besides, he's quite an expert on Minoan pottery. He wants to come back after the war and excavate some sites he'd found, so no more worrying. You were safe up in the hills. Go back to your friends. I think Yolanda is in the family way, judging by how Andreas is strutting like a barn cock.'

'Are they coming here?' Penny asked, seeing so many *andartes* under one roof.

'They are about their own business and so must we be now, so scoot. I don't want you knowing anything of our affairs. There's a big push coming, we've heard on the wireless. We need to be ready.' He gently pushed her from him.

She could have cried. Bruce was being the old Bruce, treating her like a child.

'Athina, pee-pee,' said Viki, Stella's little girl. 'Come with me . . .' Stella and Nikos were busy, the children were awake and needed her. To be so close and yet so far from Bruce was agony, but there were matters far more important than her now. Perhaps, she hoped, at the end of the meeting there would be time to be alone.

The men talked and argued all night, drank and sang and ignored the women until first light when, scoffing down fruit and bread, they all made for the door. Bruce stopped to thank

his host and took Penny by the arm, just as he had all those years
ago in the caves.

'Promise me you'll go back to Yolanda. I'll contact you
there.' He pecked her on the cheek and then she watched him
disappear. It was Athens all over again.

Rainer read Stavros's instructions, passed down from a soldier
on patrol who'd stopped him and searched him and let him go.
There was a map showing where the wireless was hidden deep
into a cave. There was news of the British agent Panayotis
working round the Apokoronas area and his girlfriend, the
nurse Athina, had left the area for Chania. *Wasn't it time she was
brought in for questioning?*

Rainer didn't like being told what to do. He had nothing
to do with Gestapo tactics. His role was to tighten up the
co-ordination of mass raids in the mountains and make sure the
local police didn't take liberties. There had been too many
escapes from capture, accidental arrests of the wrong men.
Discipline was either slack or deliberately loose. You could not
trust one of these smiling Cretans, who promised plenty and
delivered little. Some of their chief officers had fled into the
hills themselves to avoid arrest.

So Penelope was here in Chania again. But she wasn't attending the Catholic church services. He always looked for her
there. How sensible to come to the coast. Where better to hide
than in a crowd?

Yolanda sensed the tension. Everyone was in makeshift uniform,
with bandoliers of bullets around their chests. Father Pavlo
came to sprinkle holy water and bless them. Andreas had his
medical sack at the ready. Please God, he'd not have to use it
much. She waved them off, not knowing when they would
return. She felt restless to join them as she knew other girls were
arming themselves and following their men, but the family
would not hear of her risking her baby.

They were joining another group on the road to Sphakia somewhere before Askifou. She looked up into the sky on that April morning. There was nowhere as beautiful as the White Mountains in spring, the colours so brilliant; fresh leaves, the sunny gorse bushes, scarlet poppies, yellow daisies, the whiteness of dry rocks and the emerald greens. There would be fresh herbs to pick and lambs fed on spring thyme.

Easter had come and gone and she thought of the Passover Seder happening without her. Her heart ached. How she longed to tell her parents her good news. Perhaps she would bear them a grandson. Surely they wouldn't turn their backs on her then?

Later in the morning, a shepherd's wife came running up from the village. 'Have you not heard? The general has been captured. He is in the mountains . . .'

'What general?' Yolanda asked. 'We know nothing.'

'The big one, from Heraklion . . . General Kreipe. They are searching for him everywhere. The British and our men stole the chief of the island from under their noses.' She spat on the ground.

Yolanda felt no elation, only terrible fear. Was this anything to do with Andreas' group? How could it be? They'd only left before dawn. Heraklion was a hundred miles away. It was nothing to do with them and yet . . . There would be searches and reprisals. She felt sick. To capture the commandant of Fortress Crete was a great coup for morale, but at what cost?

How could she settle to her spinning after this news? Better not to worry Andreas' parents with it. Everyone was making the most of the good weather, digging, planting, preparing the fruit trees and olives. This knowledge weighed heavy on her. What if their company didn't know about this drama and ran into patrols bent on revenge, angry, vicious and determined to release the captive by any means? They'd put a ring of steel over the mountains, block all paths south. That was what she would do. Were her men heading into a wall of guns?

There was just a chance she might warn them before they went too far. Yolanda covered her head with a scarf, took her *sakouli* with a flask of water and cheese, heading out in the direction they must have gone. No time to waste, she thought, walking and then running as if her life depended on it. She knew a short cut towards Omalos, a tough trail but it halved the time if she battled through the heat of the day.

The whole of HQ was in turmoil at the news of Kreipe's abduction by British agents. No one believed they would get off the island and so all the garrisons were mobilized to surround the mountain ranges from Mount Psiloritis to the White Mountains, and the coastline tightly patrolled to prevent evacuation. Reconnaissance planes scoured the ranges for sightings but there was no visible evidence to put them in this district yet. Rumours abounded that they'd already left by ship from the north. The general's car was left by the coast road. Inside was a British Army cap and a message in perfect German saying no Cretans were involved in the snatch so there must be no reprisals. Rainer smiled, sensing it was just a ruse to distract them and put them off the real scent.

He could think like an agent too. The car was left north so they could zigzag south, travelling by night. There were dogs with Kreipe's scent to follow. He must be found alive and that meant a thorough, systematic trawling through the gullies and gorges and caves they already knew. There would be a big prize for the general's rescue, and many takers, but to be sure of success and their loyalty, Rainer was determined to be part of the search himself.

Yolanda was tiring. She'd hardly rested, and too much sun made her dizzy, but she soaked her head in a stream and filled her water flask again. It was good to know she was tracking in the right direction. A shepherd pointed the way. He offered to come with her but she preferred to go alone. The *andartes* would be holed up in the heat, out of sight, with no idea they were heading into danger unless the bush telegraph had reached them, but as they were on the move without a wireless it could take days for such tremendous news to reach them.

Her legs were shaking with tiredness and just when she thought she could go no further, she saw, quite by chance, a glint of movement behind some rocks. Binoculars would be trained on her as she walked up, pulling a piece of red cloth in her hand, red for danger, waving it until her arm ached. Then she saw them spilling out of the cleft in the rock to meet her.

Andreas scrambled down. 'What are you thinking of? Sit down at once. What has got into you, woman?'

She told him her news, that the island was covered with search parties. He didn't look surprised.

'But that's what we're here for, to disturb their progress.'

'You *knew*?'

'We were told to prepare for something. What a victory if they pull it off. Come inside into the cool. You must rest. You were foolish to come.'

Yolanda felt deflated. They didn't seem to be troubled by the news and now she lay exhausted by her effort. Andreas was not pleased with her at all.

'You shouldn't have left Mama and Papa, and in your condition. Did you not think we are warriors enough to take precautions?' he accused her.

'Is this all the thanks I get for chasing after you?' she snapped back, tired and frustrated. 'You should have told me.'

'You know the rules: we say nothing, but it was good of you to be concerned,' he replied, turning his back on her.

Yolanda felt fury bursting over her. '*Concerned?* You're my husband, the father of my child. Who will look after us if you are gone for ever?'

'Don't talk like that in front of my men.'

Yolanda charged at him like a bull, yelling in Ladino, the old Jewish Spanish dialect, like her parents did when they argued. Out spilled all the frustrations of the past months. 'Do you know what I gave up to follow you? Do you know I am now *dead* to my parents because of you? Now you call me *stupid* to come and warn you?'

Andreas argued back. 'I didn't say that, but this is men's work.' His men slunk away trying to be invisible. 'Be quiet woman. This is what happens when women put their noses in matters that don't involve them.'

This was a side to her husband she'd never seen before. They flung insults at each other until Yolanda was crying and screaming. Then Andreas threw his hands in the air, walking away. 'Don't be hysterical! The baby will not like it.'

'To hell with you!' She stormed off in fury. They'd never rowed in public before, or with such venom in private, and Yolanda was heartbroken. Why was he exerting his control before his men like this?

Now it was growing dark and she was stuck with them for the night. She was cold, tearful and sulking. Andreas kept to the other side of the cave, ignoring her. She kept her distance as well, too ashamed to move into the light.

At first light she rose and gathered her sack, tiptoed over the sleeping men and left, scrambling down the ridge, down towards the track as the sun rose like a golden globe. She'd not gone far when, to her horror, she saw a line of soldiers, hundreds of them, spread out with dogs, walking up the track far below. They were making a dawn raid. She was by now far too far away to give any warning and could only duck behind a boulder and wait to see what happened. As the line of soldiers moved forward, there was nothing she could do but pray.

It was good to be out in the cool dawn air, stretching his legs on a mountain hike. This was a patrol Rainer was leading himself. Now the whole island was on alert. His instinct was that the

British Agents would be hiding somewhere up on the ridges. The patrol knew the Androulakis gang was lying up somewhere ahead, dozing off the night's drinking. Stavros would take himself out to relieve himself and signal the exact position in Morse. There must be no warning and they'd net them all this time. In the battle, or after he was 'captured', Stavros would make a quick escape. No one would be any the wiser. Everything depended on silence and surprise. With luck they would retrieve the wireless set and the operator's codes. This was war and the honour of the island garrison was at stake.

Rainer hadn't realized how far south the trucks had brought them before they set off on foot. They had marched through the night and the men were thirsty and weary and needed regrouping. Every platoon leader had orders to rein in noise and muzzle the dogs. Rainer felt the old battle adrenaline kicking in, the excitement mounting. Action gave a thrill like no other; all his senses were heightened, tension taut as piano wire.

This was too well planned to go wrong. Right was on their side. Resistance was futile. He looked up towards the rocks. For many up there, it would be their last sleep in this life.

Yolanda crouched, her back aching, looking up and down, helpless. If only she had a gun to draw their fire and give warning. All she had were rocks to throw. Better to watch and wait. She prayed from the psalms for mercy for her husband. She closed her eyes and then opened them and noticed a pinprick of light, flickering, flashing on and off. She'd seen this on the Albanian front. The mirror was positioned to catch the light of the rising sun, on and off in a code. Someone was signalling from Andreas' cave, sending a message to the soldiers down below, bringing the enemy to their lair. Who was betraying them?

In an instance she guessed there would be only one man, one stranger capable of doing this to them. Stavros, the man who had asked so much about Penny.

'Your guts never lie to you,' she heard her father say. 'You were wary of him from the start . . .' Her heart was thumping with fear for Andreas falling into a deadly trap. She tried to scream but her voice was carried away in the wind. She felt bitter hatred well up like acid in her stomach. 'You will be sorry you ever saw my face,' she cursed into the wind. 'I will find you if it's the last thing I do.'

The German soldiers were about two hundred yards from the cliff when they were spotted. Rainer glimpsed figures darting and fleeing in all directions, opening fire and scattering his men into cover. This was not going to be as easy as he'd envisaged, and by now the escapees would have made for other, deeper caves where the wireless was supposedly hidden. But grenades soon flushed the remaining *andartes* out from their original hiding place. The living were dragged out and tied together, the dead and dying left to their fate, but there was no sign of the doctor or Stavros.

Instructions were to make sure their agent was captured, but with enough loose rope so he could fake an escape. He would be the hero of the hour among the villages. To Rainer's surprise there weren't as many here as he had hoped. Stavros had signalled there would be two groups, and there was no British agent among the dead. Something wasn't right. Rainer's instinct kicked in. What if this was a trap?

It had been too easy, too quick, too predictable. Even as Rainer thought this there came a sudden burst of gunfire from the far side of the opposite ridge, pinning them down. The rebels had the advantage of height and now they must slug it out.

So. Stavros was a double agent and had drawn him into an ambush. 'I'll kill him with my bare hands,' Rainer muttered.

A runner was sent for reinforcements, bringing back the men chasing the escapees. How could you find mountain men in their own mountains?

Rainer's old training kicked in as he crawled from cover to cover, encouraging every trooper to make every bullet count. He saw three snipers felled but they were evenly matched now and he noticed the rebels' guns and uniforms. This was no raggle-taggle band of freedom fighters but an army with berets and bandoliers, confident on their own terrain. The outcome was not looking good, Rainer decided, so he ordered his men to make an orderly retreat, rock by rock, dragging their wounded and dead with them.

The prisoners they had would have to suffice. This fierce arid moonscape was like a second enemy to defeat. There was no point trying to gain the advantage here. It had been lost before they began.

Rainer pulled his men back, chastened by the humiliation, wondering how many more bandit armies were lying in wait to ambush them. Defeat wearies legs and spirits. Now he would have to explain how so many troopers were lost and wounded, and why Stavros had made fools of them all.

Yolanda listened to the rattle of gunfire echoing around the valley: rapid fire, breaks and then more fire. But then the explosions and screams, sporadic firing and a blaze of guns puzzled her. Who was battling from the other side? She sat shivering, hugging her body in a ball to protect her unborn child. Andreas must be dead or captured. Yet she saw the German patrol gathering their wounded and retreating with only a handful of prisoners. She counted no more than ten out of the group, and so far away she couldn't make who they were. In the silence that followed she knew she must make her way back up and see who was left, her heart in her mouth fearing the sights she must surely find there.

In the cave the grenades and flames had done their worst. She had seen charred bodies before in Arta, but here she knew each one by name: the shepherd's son, Manolis, and the baker's boy,

Lefteris, and the widow's grandson, Giorgos, but there was no sign of Andreas. He must be one of the prisoners. She heard a figure approaching and, terrified, she hid.

'*Kyria, Kyria*, come we have injured men, please quickly . . .'

She followed the boy, scrambling up the other side to a group of uniformed men, strangers who had been waiting for instructions to join Andreas' group when they had seen, as she had, that signalling to the patrols approaching. So they had held their fire and stayed to ambush them.

Andreas was not among them and, seeing the state of their wounded, Yolanda thought there was just a chance that in flight he'd left his medical bag behind in the cave. She called a boy to run back, describing the leather satchel and watching with relief when he had returned with it.

'I'm the doctor's wife. I can help you. I was a nurse on the Albanian front . . . Have no fear, I have seen worse things,' she said, seeing the concern on their faces. She went from one wounded man to another, giving orders to tourniquet, to press pads onto open wounds.

Then a man was tugging her sleeve. 'You must come, back here, one of our leaders, he needs your help.'

The men were standing round a prostrate figure struggling to breathe, his chest open, his shirt blackened. He looked up, his eyes glazed. 'Kyria Yolanda,' he whispered, trying to smile. 'Stopped a bullet in my chest . . . Did the others get away?' he gasped.

She nodded, recognizing at once the British agent.

Bending down to examine his wounds, holding his wrist to take his pulse, Yolanda tried not to cry.

Chania Harbour, 2001

The dishes kept coming: a plate of warm melted cream cheese called *staka,* a rich beef *stifado* in luscious sauce, thick crusty bread, wine, chicken in lemony sauce, followed by *tsoukoudia* with syrupy semolina cake. But I could only pick my way slowly through the feast. I haven't got the appetite now of my youth and my stomach was knotted with tension by the location of this restaurant. How could I sit here under the stars and not recall all that had happened in these streets? But, for the others this was a night for music and dancing by flickering lamps. I must enjoy the view, all around me fresh faces, well fed, relaxed, all nations chattering under one roof, no curfews or uniforms to restrict our fun. Mack and Lois were laughing, Alex was stuffing his face as only boys with hollow legs can, listening to the lute and the accordion group singing lyrical ballads and jaunty upbeat folk songs, some of which I could just about understand. I was glad I'd returned to see the city repaired, prospering. It helped banish such sad pictures in my mind.

The old Jewish businesses on this street had been replaced by boutiques and stores selling the usual tourist gifts, a few craft outlets with fine jewellery and stones, and tavernas touting for business night and day. I wanted to buy something for Lois as a thank-you, something Cretan as a keepsake of our visit. I would make an excuse and wander down to have a recce. I said I'd meet them back by the car on the harbour.

'Don't get lost,' Lois warned, not trusting me to put one foot in front of the other.

'I'm coming with you,' said Alex. 'I'll look after her.'

I wanted to snap that I'm not in my dotage yet, but I bit my tongue and smiled a gracious thank-you.

When we were outside, I explained my mission and we strolled down the busy street examining necklaces, earrings and bracelets, scarves, olive oil bowls. It was then I noticed the sign on the wall to the synagogue: 'Etz Hayyim'. 'Let's have a look down here,' I suggested, marching down the alley into the enclosed yard where the walls of the synagogue were standing but the wooden gates were shut for the evening. I stood looking at the notice board. Here were posters of services and times of opening.

I must pay my respects before I leave, for Yolanda's sake, I decided. How could I not remember my dear friend?

'Why are you staring at the wall, Aunt Pen?'

'I had a friend who lived near here, a special friend,' I replied, jumping out of my reverie.

'Where is she now?'

'She died in the war like so many of my friends did,' I replied, not wanting to explain to the boy what I knew of her terrible fate. 'This is one of her churches but it's called a synagogue.' It had been restored from a ruin, that I did know, but the other one that the Markos family attended had disappeared.

'Does she have a shrine with a candle in it?' Alex was still fascinated by the little roadside memorials and kept photographing ones that interested him.

'I don't think so,' I smiled. 'Come on, let's find something pretty for your mother.'

'She likes chunky beads,' Alex offered. 'I'll show you where she was looking.'

I turned from the wall, knowing I must return. It was a relief to fix my attention to the job in hand, to stay in the present with Alex's company, rather than dwelling on a past I could never change. Yet I couldn't help noticing my surroundings, changed as they now were, the past was all around me, dredging up so many memories. It was here in this very street that my stay on Crete began to unravel. The more I saw, the deeper I went into my memory, facing things I had never told anyone. How could such a lively bright street have once been a street of death and despair?

May 1944

After the kidnap of General Kreipe and his evacuation to Egypt, something civilians were not supposed to know about, the atmosphere changed in the city. There was a stirring of pride among the agitators, a flicker of hope. Perhaps the occupiers were not so safe after all, perhaps it was possible to attack and defeat them.

The soldiers on the streets were wary, quick to lash out, checking papers as if everyone was under suspicion. Penny hardly left the *kafenion*. Stella was stricken down with fever and Penny was needed night and day to help run the household and look after the children. She shopped for ever-dwindling supplies, knew who had secret stores under the counter for favoured customers. Babies she had helped deliver were now toddlers running around, and their mothers would greet her, shoving gifts they could ill afford into her hand. She knew better than to insult them by refusing. It was in the streets that she heard there had been heavy raids in the hills and men were captured and brought back into the city. Andreas' raid had been repelled but nothing more was known.

Penny felt guilty about not being up there to help the rebels. She had not seen Yolanda for months, nor had she written about her visit to the Jewish quarter. This was not something to put on paper. It must be spoken, face to face.

The *kafenion* was quiet, no more midnight meetings for

andartes groups behind closed doors. So she was able to hurry down to Kondilaki Street where there was a little cobbler who did good repairs out of his house. His stitching was the best and most reliable, but materials were scarce. If she was to go back into the country, she must have decent soles on her feet. But on arrival she found a crowd jostling at some commotion. A soldier was pulling an old man into the street, beating him hard.

'What's he done?' demanded Penny.

'Jew,' yelled the soldier. 'You cheating bastard!'

The man covered his head, protesting, 'I have done nothing to you.'

More soldiers were kicking him down the street. At last a man yelled down after them, 'Pigs! You take a little man because you can't find Kreipe!'

The soldiers stopped and the object of their ire shot off to freedom, swallowed up by the crowd.

'Who said that?' No one spoke. He pointed his gun at the crowd. 'Line up . . . papers.'

Penny joined the queue, searching for her identity papers, somewhere in the bottom of her apron pocket, along with her badge pinned to the inside of it.

'Hurry up . . .' The soldier's voice was cold and threatening.

'I am doing my best,' she snapped in exasperation, pulling them out. He grabbed her papers and looked down at them, then at her. 'These papers are out of date . . . Name!' He pushed her to one side.

With a sickening heart, Penny realized she'd completely forgotten to go back and join the long queues in the documentation offices all those months ago. Not only were these false papers, they were out of date. God help her now.

'I'm sorry, I was busy . . .'

'Come with me.'

'But I have to shop. My mistress is ill,' she pleaded. 'I will get them renewed.'

He pointed his gun. 'Come now.'

There was nothing she could do but walk in front of him, people staring with pity. This was her own doing, her own stupid fault, and there was nothing she could do to warn Nikos of her arrest. She wanted to cry with frustration and fear.

Yolanda followed the sad procession of men carrying the wounded and dead on mules down through the gully by moonlight, a slow, tortuous journey back to the nearest village where the priest came out, nervous at first, to give them the funeral rites.

'My poor boys,' he sighed, looking into the faces of each of the bodies. 'We will not forget them.'

She had done her best to nurse them on the hillside but their injuries were just too severe. If only Andreas had been with her, she felt sure their leader might have been saved. The sorrow weighed so heavy when the villagers came to collect the bodies of their sons. They were all buried side by side and the spot marked by crosses. There would be more painted black crosses on doors all over the district by the end of the day to indicate each family's sacrifice.

Yolanda felt so weary and sick with worry about Andreas. No one had heard anything from the group for days and she was sure they must now be prisoners. She watched the village women keening over the dead boys. When she returned to Dimitra and Andonis with no news, they were distraught.

'You must go into the far tops, out of sight, to grieve; take the flocks with you to stop thieves stealing them,' Yolanda advised. She helped them pack up and load the mule for the journey. She still ached from the climbing and the terrors of the past days and her back was stiff and tight. She couldn't go with them, not when Andreas was missing.

Where was he, in the prison under torture? She dare not think of what he was going through. Who would speak for these heroes or defend them? It would be the execution post for them, but not until the Gestapo had burned out every last drop of information from their broken limbs.

It was her duty, she decided, to get more information, to follow the captured men and find someone to help their cause down in Chania. This would be no easy task and fraught with danger but she was not going to sit here doing nothing. Leaving the hills was not easy. Perhaps she should wait for Andreas. She was so torn by the need to know what was happening down there and there must be travel papers to find. She had been away so long, she'd forgotten when a bus would pass through the village going north. The mayor would give her a travel pass on some pretext of market trading. Perhaps she would find Penny there and they would draw strength from each other in this bleak time. The mayor promised if Andreas appeared Yolanda would be sent a message to return.

Penny stood before the civil servant in the rimless glasses, waiting for her interview. She had been standing for hours trying not to shake. 'Papadopouli?'

She was pushed forward, her hands were sweating.

'Why are your papers out of date?' he snapped. 'Do you not know the order and the punishment?'

'My mistress is ill. She keeps me very busy. I did come and queue but I was going to be late . . .'

'She must've been ill for a long time. These are years out of date.'

'I was in the country.'

'Were you now?' he said sternly. 'Miss Papadopouli.'

'I came to help my aunt and uncle Nikos.'

'Nikos who?'

'Kyrie Mandolakis in his *kafenion* . . . His wife is sick.' There was a pause as the man examined her documents. Had she brought Stella and Nikos into danger now? 'They warned me to update my papers but I forgot.'

'But these papers say you worked at the convent, what were you doing there?'

'I wanted to train as a nurse but it didn't work out. I was needed in the café.' She sensed his suspicion growing.

'You are quite a mystery, Miss Papadopouli, but I see no mark against your name.' He stamped on the documents. 'But I will have to check. This is most irregular. Wait over there.' He pointed to a chair. 'See she doesn't move.'

A clerk stood eyeing her with deep suspicion. It was hard to sit calmly, her left leg desperate to keep tapping the tiles. She swallowed back the fear and tried to make conversation with him.

'You must be very busy in this office,' she offered, but he ignored her. What man wouldn't ignore such a rough peasant woman in a shabby overall, her face darkened by sun and exposure. Her own sister would walk past her and not recognize her now.

Had she come to the end of her journey in this little office? Her mind was racing with doubt and fear.

Then the little civil servant bustled in and waved his hand in her direction.

'She can go and queue for the rest of the stamps. Dismissed.' He let the clerk leave, then he marched up close to her.

'Miss Athina, be careful. You have been lucky this time,' he said quietly, then showed her the door. 'Don't go wandering in the Jew quarter again. It's not advisable in these troubled times . . .'

Later, Penny stood on the court house steps gulping in deep breaths of relief. Of all the officials in there she had found one who was sympathetic to the cause. Was it by chance or design? He knew Nikos' *kafenion*; perhaps he'd eaten there and knew the secret set-up. She'd had a lucky escape, but she wondered what he meant about the Jewish quarter. It seemed to be some kind of warning.

*   *   *

Yolanda arrived in the city after a bumpy tiring journey, not knowing where to go to find help. After the quiet of their mountain life, she was unnerved by the bustle, the noise, the squalor all around her. First she had to set up a table in the market and sell the cheeses, eggs and greens that validated her journey.

It was a beautiful May morning and her spirits rose for a second until she remembered Andreas, possibly imprisoned in chains, perhaps already mutilated or dead. Someone here would know of his fate. No news was good news, she prayed. In her widow's black she looked no different from hundreds of other women keeping to the shadows of the walls. Somewhere here, Penny was hiding out. She must find her, but first she must visit her parents, even if they shut the door in her face. She wanted them to know she was pregnant so they knew their family would go on, no matter what.

When the market began to pack up, and it was getting too hot to be outdoors, she wanted to find somewhere to rest her swollen feet.

There was one place, not far to walk, where she would be sure of a welcome. Why hadn't she thought of it before? Yolanda made her way uphill to the Red Cross clinic, a place where she had found both purpose and love. It would be good to see who remained there, and maybe the doctors would help her find Andreas. She wanted to be among friends if there was terrible news to bear.

Nikos threw his hands in the air in horror when Penny confessed her mistake. 'Are you crazy, girl? Do you want us all arrested? Lucky you were given one of our men to interview you, one of our regulars who keeps us up to date with anything we should know.'

'I'm sorry but it was terrible to see those bullies in the street.'

'It will get worse before it gets better,' Nikos replied, flicking his beads and throwing his head back in agitation. 'They have to blame someone now Kreipe is gone. Jews are always the first to be taken hostage and there are rumours they are clearing them out of cities on the mainland in thousands, taking them up north to work in camps. It's only a matter of time.'

'We ought to warn them,' Penny said, thinking of Yolanda's parents.

'What did our friend tell you? Keep your nose out of what you can't control. If they take you, we can't protect you from torture. When Stella is better you must head back into the mountains, though that'll need a travel permit and they are not so easy to forge. Keep your head down and be careful who you speak to. Things are quiet just now, too quiet, but it's better just to carry on and sit it out.'

Penny felt uneasy after what she'd witnessed. Nikos was right to be cautious. She didn't even know who she was any more: one minute a student, then nurse, farm hand, waitress, like a chameleon changing colours, from a British deb with a Greek name now passing herself off as a Cretan. It was all so unreal, living in this nightmare world where one false move could cost the lives of so many.

That night she had a nightmare: trying to jump into deep water, figures chasing after her, pushing her where she didn't want to go. She woke sweating. Chania was no longer a safe hiding place; it was time to climb out of danger. She felt a strange foreboding of danger, a feeling in her gut that all was not well.

Rainer returned from the abortive mission to find Kreipe with only a few prisoners in tow. Androulakis had escaped. Stavros had been taken because Rainer was not so sure of his loyalty now, but the Greek protested his innocence vehemently when interrogated.

'How was I to know you were spotted and the second group held back to make the ambush. The British agent is a cunning devil and his men have the advantage of knowing every bloody nook and cranny in these godforsaken mountains.' He was nervous when they dragged him out of the cell for questioning. They knocked him around so when he returned with bruises his story about being one of the *andartes* would be reinforced.

Rainer's commanding officer was unimpressed with the whole outcome of Rainer's mission. 'No excuses. This time you will oversee something that will not go wrong, executed with the utmost surprise and secrecy. We have orders to deport all the Jews here to Athens.'

'There has been no trouble from that quarter,' Rainer replied. 'What's the rush?'

'Orders, Major Brecht. The final solution to the problems they have caused worldwide must be completed. It is already in hand. We have a list updated by the rabbi himself, and every one of them must be accounted for . . . babies, children.'

Rainer stared out of the window shaking his head.

'Every newborn of their race is our enemy. The evils of Europe are to be laid at their door. You will see every exit and entrance is cordoned off, that transport is waiting, so the exercise will be swift and efficient and done before dawn.'

'Where are they to be taken?'

'To Agia, of course, to be sealed off in the prison until arrangements are made and so we can bring in any outlying Jews.'

Rainer took a deep breath. From the heights of commanding those brave paratroopers, to this: pushing women and children onto trucks, shoving them in that filthy hellhole. Is this what his army career had come to, obeying such orders? In his heart he realized this was a step too far. Every decent humane reason urged him to refuse to obey. What the hell should he do now?

*   *   *

It was like old times, sleeping in the basement of the clinic as Yolanda had done in the bombing raids in 1941, lying on a mattress among familiar hospital shelves with the scents of Lysol and ether. She'd been welcomed in, fed a hot stew, checked over. Now she was resting with her feet up. No one had news of Andreas but someone who knew someone in the police assured her that he was not being held prisoner. The doctor was too well known and respected not to have been sprung from gaol by sympathetic police officers. Now Yolanda felt the ache in her back loosen and she hugged her stomach with relief. Perhaps he would live to see his baby born after all. When she was rested she would go back to the Jewish quarter to make peace with her parents. She must make the first move . . . But the next morning she felt so exhausted and achy, no one would let her move from her mattress so she sank back and slept while she had the chance.

Penny was woken by the roar of trucks grinding through the streets. There was a racket outside as if troops had landed in the harbour, and a flicker of arc lights through the open window had them all on their feet. It was still the middle of the night.

'What's happening?' Penny muttered, fearing a raid on them. She flung on her dress and peered out of the window to see a line of trucks backing up.

'Don't go out!' Nikos shouted. 'Don't move.'

Penny nodded, but across the square, faces peered out at the noise and shutters were hurriedly closed. She crept through the *kafenion* to the stairs up to the balcony that gave a better view and, opening the door, peered out. She watched as a battalion of soldiers raced round through the streets with loudspeakers. 'Out! Out! Jews out!' She could hear screams of alarm, doors bashed, dogs barking. 'Ten minutes with food and one bag, one bag only . . . Out! Out!'

'They're in the Jewish quarter, taking them out of their houses onto the street,' she cried.

'Close the shutters and stay indoors. This is none of our business,' snapped Nikos. Penny could see a straggle of men and women with sleepy children, half dressed, whole families forming queues while soldiers barked orders at them as if they were criminals. She stood silent, watching them being pushed onto trucks. No one had had time to gather much to take with them on their backs. Children were clutching toys and bits of bread while their neighbours, roused by the noise, stood by silent at first, then waving and shouting to their friends as if they were going on a journey,

'We ought to be doing something,' Penny muttered, but Stella shook her head.

'There're too many of those black sheep with guns. We'll save our bullets for where we can harm them most.'

'But I know some of them . . . my friends . . . oh my God, Solomon and Sara! I must go . . .'

'Athina! Don't be a fool . . .'

Penny was out of the door, racing down the street, pushing through the crowds. 'Where are they taking them?' she asked a woman standing watching.

She shrugged. 'To prison, where all prisoners go, and good riddance.'

Penny ran on, trying to catch glimpses of Yolanda's family, but it was hard to see who was who in the half-light. It was then that she looked up and saw Captain Brecht, standing tall, his arms folded, watching his animals behaving like bully boys as if this was some victory parade to be proud of.

There was a confusion of children crying, some separated from their parents, girls crying to friends. 'Take my books . . . tell Maria I will write when we are settled . . .' Many voices lost in the flowing river of faces.

The stragglers limped slowly at the back, one of them a woman hobbling on two sticks with as much dignity as she could muster. The soldiers grew impatient, dragging her off her feet. 'You will have to wait,' she said.

An old couple found it hard to walk and she saw a soldier kick them as if they were mules. Penny couldn't help herself: fury propelled her forward. 'I will help you,' she whispered. 'Take my arm.' It wasn't Sara and Solomon – that was too much to hope for – but they held onto her arms. 'We will do this together,' she smiled. 'I am Red Cross. We will see you treated well,' she added, giving the soldier a look of utter contempt. 'We Greeks know how to treat our old people even if you don't. Shame on you, show some respect!'

For one second he was taken aback by this rebuke but, not wanting to lose face, he shoved his rifle in her chest. 'If you love Jews so much, get up there yourself.'

It all happened so fast. One minute she was escorting the old couple to the trucks and then she was shoved on, herself, with no time to protest. All she could think of was how the old lady would get up, she was so crippled, but they threw her up like garbage. Penny was stunned but she held her head up high and stared hard at the officer. She fingered her Red Cross badge pinned on the inside of her pocket. So, Captain, this is all your doing. Someone must be witness to what is happening here, she thought. It looks as if it's going to have to be me . . .

Rainer supervised the arrests of the civilians like an automaton. The pathetic sight of women and children shoved through the narrow alleys in a funnel to collecting points was sickening. It was their usual efficient, ruthless oppression, no different from other villages where people were roused from their beds, lined up, executed, and their homes destroyed. Why was this act, just one among many, any different? Surely it destroyed the last crumbling hope of any future rapprochement with the Cretan population?

He felt ashamed, all his previous efforts to be merciful thrown into question as he stood by and watched these families going to certain death.

No one protested because the Nazis had perfected a regime of fear and obedience. These people were now too hungry and demoralized to make any fuss, though one girl had stood out.

He watched her helping the stricken couple and for her trouble she was arrested with them. He was too far away to step in and plead her cause. It was only when she stood up in the truck, defiant, that he recognized her face.

The cave nurse looked across at him. She recognized him and saw him for what he was now: contaminated, polluted by this cowardly act of hate and cruelty. He felt sick to his stomach. That stare of contempt would live with him for the rest of his life, a stare that stripped him bare of hope and dignity.

Yolanda awoke after her long sleep, refreshed, but the atmosphere among the nurses had changed overnight as they tiptoed round, not looking her. Everyone was smiling with their lips but not their eyes and kept telling her to stay put. What on earth was going on? Had they heard bad news of Andreas?

'Why's everyone not looking at me? It's Andreas . . .'

'No, Yolanda, calm yourself, it's not that.' The doctor paused. 'It's just that we heard there'd been a raid in the night, well, more of a round-up.'

'So?' She rose, knowing it was time to leave this safe haven.

'In the Jewish quarter. They've taken away all the Jews they could find.'

'I don't understand,' she cried, making for the door.

'Your parents still live there?' he asked as he wiped his glasses.

'Yes, yes, and Uncle Joseph and Aunt Miriam.'

'I'm afraid all the streets have been cleared.'

Yolanda could hardly take in what he was saying. It seemed too big, too terrible an act, even for their enemies here. 'No, no, this can't be true. Not all of them? I must go and see for myself.'

'That wouldn't be wise. There's a list and you will be on it. It may not be safe yet.'

'Where have they taken them?' she cried.

'I don't know yet, we can't ask these things. You know how dependent we are on the garrison hospital for relief supplies.'

'But we are Red Cross. They can't let such a thing happen. I must find out if my family are safe,' she said, ignoring his warning.

'Yolanda, calm down. You need to rest those ankles. I'm sure the Red Cross officials will be monitoring the deportation.'

'How can you be sure? I have to go and see for myself. This can't be true. Why didn't their neighbours stop them?' She flung on her cloak.

He knew there was no stopping her. 'Oh, do be careful. If you must go, wear this uniform and no one will challenge you. I wish I hadn't told you so soon. There's nothing you can do.'

'I have a right to find out what's happened.'

'Please, Yolanda, if you protest and they find out who you are, you'll be deported too.'

Once dressed in a nurse's uniform, she made for the harbour as fast as her swollen legs would carry her, hoping that, by some miracle, this was all a false rumour.

She saw others rushing uphill carrying rugs and pots and furniture on their backs, and with a sickened heart she realized these things were looted. When she arrived the sight made her weep. Every house was stripped to the floorboards, stuff chucked out of balcony windows, women fighting over bedding and even feather pillows. Strangers were rifling through homes like vultures picking over bones. The streets were littered with torn photographs, pretzels and biscuits scattered on the cobbles, trampled into crumbs, picture frames smashed to release any silver. Such desecration stunned her to the point of numbness. There was nothing she could do to stop it, and in the distance soldiers merely stood around observing, laughing and joking.

How could human beings do this to each other? How could neighbours stand by and let this happen? Had they no decency?

Yolanda froze, the scream of protest rising up in her throat quashed by the sights before her. The whole community was gone! The saintly friends, the nosy neighbours, the rabbi and his family, and her beloved parents, all gone, and she knew she would never see them again in this life. She crumpled to the ground in agony.

A young woman rushed to her aid, lifting her up, leading her to her door. 'I know you, you're one of the Markos family, the nurse.'

Yolanda shivered at this recognition but the girl smiled. 'Don't worry, I'll say nothing. I'm so ashamed for us all. They were our friends and neighbours. My daughter is weeping for her school friends. Your family were good people. Come inside, you should not be seeing such things. The soldiers were in the houses the minute the people were removed, rough types searching for treasure. They looted down to the very door nails,' she said, making Yolanda sit on a chair. She brought her a glass of water from a jug. 'Drink, you are so pale. When they had their fill they let in the scum of Chania to take what is left, and still they search everywhere, tearing down walls in case jewels and gold are hidden. I tell you, who would live here in this rabbit warren if they had gold to sell? Beg pardon, I don't mean to offend, but it's a day that brings shame on all of Chania. It will not be forgotten. Now you must go. If I have recognized you, others will too, and I cannot vouch for their loyalty. Shame doesn't bring out the best in us. Don't ever come back while the enemy is here.'

But Yolanda wasn't listening. She doubled up again in agony as a wave of pain surged from her back into her groin.

'What is happening here? It's too soon. Please help me . . .' she appealed to the young woman. Then she knew no more.

June 1944

Rainer Brecht stood to attention before the commandant, erect, smartly turned out. 'I would like to volunteer for transfer onto mainland Europe, sir,' he said, looking straight ahead. His superior looked up from his desk in surprise.

'Think again, Major Brecht. Why now? Have we not promoted you enough? Are you tiring of sunshine and warm sea?'

'I feel it's my duty to serve my country where I am needed most,' he offered, still looking ahead. He could give no rational explanation for this decision, only that he must redeem his honour, challenge himself in a proper theatre of war.

'What's brought this on? Not the Jew deportation? I heard you found it distasteful. It's not wise to air such sentiments in public, young man. You have a good and varied service record here, and are held in respect by your men. You set a good example. You are needed here.'

'Sir, I know there may be heavy losses to be replaced. I would like to fight wherever I can be useful in an active capacity. I feel I have had my turn in the sun. I just want to serve.'

'Plug the gaps, you mean? Do you really want the eastern front or France? However, I can see you've made up your mind and I admire your courage. It will be a hard slog now to defend all we've gained. Who knows where it will end? Take some leave in Athens. We can fly you out . . .'

'Could I request to sail, sir? I flew onto the island, I'd like to return by water, as part of my leave, of course.'

'The Sea of Crete is not as safe as it once was. British and Italian submarines are on the prowl, but as you wish. I shall be sorry to lose you.'

'Thank you, sir.' Rainer saluted, suddenly feeling lighter. He was running away, perhaps to certain death, but he wouldn't stay on this cursed island a moment longer.

May 2001

'Do you mean to tell us, where we had supper last night was where all of it happened?' Lois gripped my hand. 'I'd no idea. Granny never told us.'

'My sister, Effy, didn't know. I've never told anyone this before. It's a terrible story and no one talked of such things after the war was over. We all wanted to forget and get on with our lives. Evadne and Walter were posted abroad when your mother was born. Zander made it home, almost in one piece. We shoved all such unpleasantness under the carpet. The only person I would've shared any of it with was my father, and he had died. My mother was not speaking to me. That's how it was, but I'm not sure ignoring terrible events in your life is the best way. Looking back now, I don't know how I survived.'

'Your friend, did she survive the roundup?'

'No. She disappeared, as did so many Jews. Things were chaotic for years afterwards. Greece was torn apart so many of the Resistance fighters took sides in the civil war and were executed by their own people. I wrote to people who might know what happened to Yolanda, of course, but nothing came of it. But now I am here, I will ask around. I'd like to pay my respects.

'We can help you do the leg work,' Mack offered. 'My father wouldn't speak of his wartime exploits either. He just came home and got on with his life, but his marriage failed and he remarried much later. I was the baby of his old age . . .'

'What happened to you afterwards? Did you go to the prison camp with the old couple?' Lois asked.

'I think that's enough for tonight,' I said, keen not to let unhappy thoughts intrude on our lovely evening. Tomorrow's the memorial service so let's do something different, relaxing and cheerful. Let's just be tourists for the day. Any suggestions, Mack?'

'I know just the place for you all,' he smiled, bringing out a map. 'What about a trip to Rethymnon? Lots of shops and restaurants. What do you think?'

I nodded, not wanting to spoil their enthusiasm. I had my own memories of the pretty town from the back of a cargo truck, but enough of all that. This was a holiday as well as a pilgrimage, but there was no forgetting the darkness of those hot June nights or the terror of my last days on the island. No one who survived them would ever forget the horrors we witnessed. Is it right to burden young ones with such terrible accounts? There would be no peaceful slumbers for me that night, only the nightmare that haunted my fevered dreams.

Agia Prison,
June 1944

The fact that Penny's name was not on the list caused confusion, as did her claim to be a Red Cross nurse. The prison guard eyed her with deep suspicion.

'So what are you doing on this truck?'

'I was helping these elderly people. I was made to get on with them as a result,' she said as she eyed her surroundings with dismay. All the rumours of this walled prison camp were true: the walls were high and forbidding and cast dark shadows over the prisoners.

'So you were arrested?'

'For helping old people? No, of course not. I am Red Cross. We must be present for the sick and weak.' Staring into his face had no effect.

'You are a Jew then?'

'No, I am Athina Papadopouli. As you see, my papers are in order. I am Red Cross.'

'You are not in uniform.'

'Look, here is my badge. There was no time for uniform in the rush,' Penny protested, seeing the guard even more confused now. He pulled her to one side.

She could only watch as the civilians were off-loaded, herded out into a courtyard inside the prison, crushed in a tight space and guarded over by soldiers with guns and dogs. Her papers were taken to a superior, and the soldiers kept looking at her, over and over again. Penny sensed danger and found herself escorted away from the others and pushed into a stinking cell where about twenty women were sitting, crushed together. The door was slammed behind her.

The women eyed her with interest. 'Another lamb for the slaughter,' said a girl in a torn dress held together with strands of rope. 'Welcome to hell,' she added.

Penny was bombarded with questions. 'Where are you from? Do you know what happened to . . . ? When will we be leaving?'

She couldn't help them much. She was in the company of other *andartissas*, partisan Resistance fighters, captured for bringing food to their groups, betrayed by villagers and now sentenced to deportation to labour camps. They looked as if they had been beaten, stripped, abused or worse, and now lay exhausted on the filthy straw.

She told them what she had seen in Chania and how the Jews were separated, how she feared for the babies and children in the heat and dust of the compound. How she wanted to be a witness to their treatment but now she was unable to do anything.

'Better get yourself released so you can warn the Red Cross what is going on here,' one woman recommended. 'We hear terrible noises in the night. It is no place for children.'

Penny lost count of the days she stayed cooped up in the crowded cell. No one came to release her, no one knew she was here in the heat and flea-bitten straw, allowed out only briefly for exercise in the yard. It was a filthy hovel, unnerving with the screams in the night, the footsteps down the stone, the sound of gun shots. She felt sick with fear. How had she got into this place? What was happening to Solomon and Sara? Had they picked up Yolanda too in the raids in the outlying districts?

Days without proper food and foul water played havoc with them all – how would the old couple survive such treatment?

There wasn't enough room for them all to lie down except in turns. Maria, Rosa, Angeliki – all had tales to tell of their exploits, of their menfolk, each taking courage from each other. She, in turn, told them about nursing on the Albanian front and the hospital trains, and the bravery of the Cretan 5th Division. A camaraderie of suffering grew quickly between them, forced together by the intimacy of sharing a bucket as a convenience. The fleas bit and the sores scratched. Maria began to bleed and they had nothing but straw to soak up her flow. Soon they would all be ill in these conditions, but they were far better off than those poor people outside. Nothing had prepared Penny for this captivity and the boredom of being cooped up in the heat of the day and the chill of the night. How could they work if they were so weakened?

Then came the day when they were roused, given a bucket to wash in and told to prepare to leave, lined up, one after the other like children.

Penny demanded to see an officer in charge. 'I came of my own free will to help old people. I demand to be allowed back to Chania.'

'*Demand?*' the guard laughed. 'No one demands here. Get in line!'

'But this is outrageous. I've not been on trial. You have nothing against me. Why am I being kept?'

The guard hit her with his rifle butt. 'Shut up, whore, Jew lover . . .' Penny staggered back, blinded by the force on her cheek. 'Out, out now, move!' the guard yelled as Maria helped her stumble her way. Penny knew she was lumped with these women for deportation. There was no escaping this fate. She was no different from them in what she had done for the Resistance, a strange sort of justice indeed.

There was a line of cargo trucks waiting for them in procession, and through her bruised eyes she tried to see what was happening further up: more herding and shouting, but the crowd of frightened civilians were quiet. Now they were curtained off, none of them able to see out as the convoy rattled through Chania and out eastward towards Heraklion, a slow, winding, bumpy ride, guarded by soldiers at the entrance, sullen men staring out at the road behind them, unable to look anyone in the eye.

Sometimes, in the pauses and over the sound of the engine, they heard singing, freedom songs, which lifted the spirits with courage and defiance, irritating the guards until they fired shots in the air. The first night was spent camped in a Turkish fortress close to Rethymnon, high up, and cool at first lying on the stone floor. They were woken early and back onto the trucks again next morning. It was a painful, exhausting journey and they were still young. God help those poor souls who were frail. How many of them were dumped by the wayside, thrown out of the trucks as they died?

Penny scoured her brain to think of ways to make sense of this forced ride. Perhaps she should try to explain again her mission, but without uniform or proof, even her British name wouldn't help. She'd kept up the pretence for so long, who would remember Penelope George or even care? She had no passport, lost long ago, nothing now to verify even her British status.

She watched the faces of her new-found friends staring out for the last time at their beloved island. There would be only Bruce and Yolanda to mourn her going. Even Bruce seemed like a ghost to her now. It had been months since that last embrace but she trusted he was out there giving the enemy hell. That was the hope to cling onto in all this. You step out of line and end up here, she mused, feeling a strange defiant pride.

I tried to do what I was trained to do and I will go on doing it, no matter what. It will give me the courage to stick this out, give me purpose, some dignity in these terrible times. I am Red Cross, and if I get out of this alive, I will dedicate the rest of my life to making sure no one else suffers like this again.

❊   ❊   ❊

Rainer took leave of his fellow officers and men with a sense of urgency now that the second front was underway in France. They had known it was coming. With the might of American troops behind the Allies, France would fall. No one spoke much about the news, but there was a look of resignation on faces. He was ordered to deliver documents to HQ at the Villa Ariadne, and take the first ship out from Heraklion to Piraeus.

Now he was leaving he tried to find some regret in his decision but found none. He would be needed more than ever now. His resignation was no coward's way out. In his eyes it would be cowardly to stay here in comfort and sit out to the end.

Yet in the midst of all this he thought about the cave nurse. He knew the convoys had left from the gaol. He wanted nothing more to do with that business, and yet there was a saying that for evil to happen, good men stood back and did nothing. How sad it was to know how hardened and uncaring he'd become out here. Civilians didn't count, only the safety of his men, and now he was deserting them.

There were hints of creating a ring of steel round Chania, retreating behind it and ruling from there, should the worst happen. No, he was glad to be leaving, no matter what the cost.

He was driven under escort of armed guards. It was no longer safe to drive alone. Better to have sailed from Souda Bay but there'd been a spate of ships sunk in the outer bay by submarines. The journey east was without incident. He was given a bed and lodgings in the taverna close to the villa, spent a night of hard drinking with officers who told him of courts martial and demotions after the capture of Kreipe. The politics at HQ no longer interested him, he just wanted that special brotherhood of combat soldiers intent on doing their duty. The ship he'd been booked on had not made it through the straits, due to Allied attacks, so he was to be put on a steam ship called the *Tanais*, an overnight crossing to reduce risk of being spotted, escorted by an armed sailing ship.

'There's a special cargo on board, all hush-hush,' said his drinking companion.

Rainer looked up, wondering what looted items he'd be escorting.

'Jews, thousands of them, heading for Auschwitz,' he sneered.

'There's barely a few hundred on the island,' Rainer replied, his heart sinking at the news.

'One's too many,' laughed the man slurping into his beer.

Rainer didn't reply. There was no point. Fate had caught up with him. He was not going to be let off the island lightly. Why did he fear the fate of these Jews was somehow caught up with his own?

May 2001

Rainer sat in the square on a bench close to the cathedral opposite the museum. He'd walked around the archaeological displays, wondering at such magnificent pottery and statues, trying to forget the memories of those final days on Crete. This was the future now, where all nations could marvel at these ancient civilizations, learn from their designs and techniques. He watched a party of school children, earnestly wanting to draw and touch everything for themselves. They looked so well-dressed, plump and enthusiastic to be let out of school for the day, so different from the cheeky urchins who begged around them with their hands open, young old faces shrunk with hunger. Those children got little schooling.

The flags were flying high on the harbour for the Battle of Crete week and the ceremony on Saturday evening in the war cemetery by Souda Bay. It would be good to see this; old men now, like himself. Old age is not for cowards but it comes to everyone nonetheless, he smiled. He was curious. Someone there might know what became of his cave nurse.

Heraklion,
June 1944

Another night, another prison cell floor, crushed together in conditions no rat would endure. The stench of unwashed bodies, the sweat of fear – Penny felt all her resolve weakening as each day dragged out, confined, starving, and with snarling dogs waiting to pounce on anyone falling out of line. The old Turkish fortress had even more prisoners waiting to be deported, prisoners of war, more partisans. It was going to need a big ship to transport them all.

The guards were efficient, separating them off into groups away from the Jewish crowd. She caught only brief glimpses of the Jews, helpless to do anything now. Her brief stand had been for nothing, only a bashed eye. Then down the lines of the waiting captives came a whisper of a rumour, a trickle that grew into a flood. The Allies had landed in France, the liberation of Europe was beginning, and there was something in the telling from secret wireless reports that rang true. Could it possibly be that the end of the war was in sight?

Then came the trucks again, and by the afternoon they were jostling in a slow convoy down to the port, to be greeted by the sight of a huge expanse of sea filled with ships. The smell of water filled Penny's nostrils with hope until she saw the ship waiting for them. It was small, too small for all these people, a rust bucket of a vessel, moored up, belching smoke from its one funnel. Around the harbour were signs of recent bombing, the charred remains of buildings, wrecked ships and burning fuel.

There was no time to take stock of these bearings as they were pulled out in line, counted again, and the gangplank was down. Queues of men, women and children were being pushed into the ship's hold, names ticked off, constant counting out. It was like no embarkation she had ever been on before and it didn't bode well. She looked up to see soldiers peering down at them from the top deck. '*Courage, mon brave,*' she muttered. Just one more night and by tomorrow morning she would see Athens again. But where after that?

Rainer stood on the deck of the *Tanais*. He was not impressed with the size or state of the old vessel. It sat low in the water with a single funnel rising up mid-ship. It was a battered troop carrier, with a couple of boiler engines, a crew of about ten and only a couple of armed sailing ships for escort. It was a miracle this was still afloat after the heavy bombing overnight, but it had survived, stinking of oil and fumes. Just two lifeboats were on view, which didn't inspire confidence should the worst happen, but it would get him to Athens in the morning.

As he stood on deck watching the procession of men, women and children boarding, he noticed they'd added Italian POWs and civilians in ragged groups, a sorry bunch being put down into the hold. It would be hell for those three or four hundred prisoners, crushed in those cargo spaces. It was no place for children. There was a group of women going up the gangplank together. One looked up and, to his horror, he recognized his cave nurse: unmistakable, taller than the rest, with fair hair in a plait like a thick rope down her back. He could not turn away.

These unwilling passengers were just numbers to him, name-less, until he saw her. Here was the proud English nurse who had fooled him: Penelope Georgiou. He'd seen her act of kindness in the square and her condemnation. Why on earth was she embarking with prisoners?

Keep calm, Penny prayed, it will only be for a few more hours. They were crushed together, hardly able to move, and she pitied the others even more confined. Her heart went out to the Markos family, wherever they were holed up, and those small children clinging to parents, not understanding why they were squeezed in a dark place with no air, no conveniences. It was unforgivable to treat human beings in this way, she raged. Soldiers would cope with confinement, but not babies and their mothers trying to protect them.

Maria was finding it hard not to panic. Angeliki held her up, trying to edge towards the door. The heat was overpowering. It was going to be a long night standing upright as the ship chugged its way out of the harbour.

How dare they be treated like cattle and animals? Penny tried to calm her rising fear by pretending she was back at Ike's villa under her favourite olive tree, seeing the majestic rise of the snow-capped mountains, hearing the buzz of the honeybees in the meadows. She thought of Blair Atholl and her first crack shots on target, the smell of heather and gorse, the freedom to roam high like a stag. If she could cling onto these images, she might escape this hell.

Suddenly someone was screaming with panic, 'I need air, give me air.'

Penny banged on the heavy door. 'For the love of Mercy, let us breathe in here. I am a Red Cross nurse, I will report this in Athens. This is a disgrace. You can't treat people like animals.' Her fists were banging on the door in fury, a futile gesture, but then to her amazement the door opened, a chink of light and a waft of air.

'Penelope Georgiou . . . Red Cross nurse?' a soldier yelled. 'Come to the door.' A mutter went round the crush of prisoners, jostling to breathe in the air, pushing her forward out of the door.

'I am Nurse Georgiou,' Penny said, pushing her way to the front. Turning to her friends, she shouted, 'I will be back. I'll make them see . . .'

'Come!' she was ordered, and she heard the groan as the door was shut behind her. Up the iron stairs, she was shoved with a gun in her back. What was going on? How did they know her real name? She clutched her false papers stuck down the front of her garments and fingered her badge, fearing the worst.

Then she found herself among the guards, who parted to make room in the crowded space. A man was groaning on the floor, bleeding, his arm at an angle with bone sticking out of his shirt.

'You've given him morphia?' she asked, but their Greek was poor.' She mimed the action and they nodded.

There was no ship's doctor on such a little ship but there would be a first-aid kit somewhere. She ordered one of the crew to find it. The man needed splints and a bandage. She set to the task in hand, knowing exactly what must be done. The man was drunk and thrashing about, which didn't help.

'Hold him!' she snapped.

He'd fallen in his stupor, hit iron and cracked his arm badly. She felt nothing for him but for the job in hand and a chance to breathe in the cool air. She wondered how they had known she was on board. She sealed his wound, cleansed it carefully, strapped him up as best she could. Unfortunately he would live to fight another day.

'Thank you,' a voice said in English. 'I know you will do a good repair.'

Penny turned round and saw Rainer Brecht standing smoking in the doorway. 'Why are you on this ship?' he asked. 'It should not be so.'

'No one down below should be on this ship,' she replied, trying not to shake at being so closely observed by him. He looked thinner, drawn in the face, his hair bleached by the sun and greying at the temples. Why was *he* on this ship? She was just about to ask when there was a sudden and ear-splitting explosion from below deck. Immediately bells and alarms sounded, but then all power was lost, the engines died and the lights failed. Black smoke caused a roar of panic and confusion among the crew still standing. Penny was thrown backwards in the darkness, banging herself against the wall. They'd been hit mid-ship.

'Up on deck!' Brecht yelled.' Life jackets!' There was no time to search. Penny pulled the drunken guard to his feet, half dragging him, stunned by the noise.

The rest was a confusion of scrambling for jackets, gasping for air as men were trying to loosen the lifeboats before the ship went down.

'Let them out, for God's sake, let them out down below!' Penny heard herself crying, not wanting to be pulled out of danger, but the ship was already listing. Then there was a terrible whirring noise as the ship exploded from another hit. 'I must go and help!'

An arm grabbed hers. 'No, Miss George, you stay on deck. You can do nothing now but get yourself killed.'

'Let me go. We can't leave them to drown,' she spat at Rainer.

'There is nothing we can do . . . come.' His grip tightened on her arm.

Then came such a loud bang, right underneath them, throwing Penny into the cold black water as the ship was torn apart, dense black clouds of smoke and pieces of metal hurling into the water too. Arcs of burning fuel spurting out, people were screaming, men abandoning the ship as it broke up, sliding rapidly down into the deep.

Penny woke, stunned by the cold water over her body as the instinct to survive took over, her lungs bursting with the effort to stay afloat. Brecht was swimming close to her, urging her forward. They were swimming for their lives through a fog of smoke, swimming in the dark rippling Sea of Crete.

Penny felt nothing. She was strangely calm as if this were a dream she knew so very well. There had been no time to think anything but water and waves, the fear of being sucked under by the swell. A life raft bobbed out of reach, taunting her to catch it, pulling her further from the ship, from Maria and Angeliki, and Sara and Solomon Markos. She swam away from the burning oil and the debris of broken bodies blocking her way towards the escort ship, *Hera*, already rushing to the rescue.

She felt herself weakening, the panic rising that she was not going to make it, but when she sank, an arm was locking hold of her arm, guiding her until she was lifted up out of the murky waters where the *Tanais* had sunk down to the sea bed, pulled up the ladder onto deck alongside wounded, dying, burned men, survivors shivering, blackened faces, shocked beyond reach, who needed reviving.

They were mostly German guards, crew with clothes burned off in the blast, a few others sitting with blankets round their faces, weeping. She searched every face for one she recognized but she knew in her heart that none of the captives in the hold had a chance to escape the watery grave. She did what she could for the rescued crew but many were too far gone.

Opposite, sat Brecht, smoking a cigarette, trying not to shake. For a second a flicker of compassion sparked inside her for the man who had kept her afloat, but she doused it quickly with knowledge of all that she'd seen of his kind.

Penny couldn't cry or feel anything. It was as if her whole body had shut down, pared back to the most basic instincts: to sleep, to drink, to stay alive and do her job. They found her a blanket and trousers and a battle shirt of sorts. No one questioned her presence when they docked briefly on the island of Santorini to report the incident. The *Hera* carried on to Piraeus port with the limping, stricken, silent passengers who'd been to hell and back.

Part 5

THE REUNION

A lady in black is sitting
At Maleme and crying
Holding in her arms
A lifeless body
Washing it with her tears and
Dressing it with rose petals
In lamentations she speaks
And utters a thousand curses.
Hitler, Never be born again.

'Olympia's Lament', Olympia Kokotsaki-Mantonanaki,
translated by Susana Kokotsaki

May 2001

I woke seeing the sun burning through the slats in the shutters. The nightmare that never left me was very real tonight. I sipped the taste of salt water on my lips, saw the faces of the dead staring up at me accusingly from the deep. Why had I been rescued? Why me above all others? For years afterwards not a word was mentioned of that sinking or what happened to all the Jews of Crete; an ancient community wiped out in an instant.

Some will say a quick death by drowning was better than what was in store for them: cattle trucks from Athens in the heat of summer to the death camps in the north. I think not. Drowning, trapped in a hold, doesn't bear thinking about, but it happened and should be remembered. Who sunk the ship? Who knows? Most probably a British submarine on a routine patrol. But deliberately? There are theories but I don't know the truth of any of it. No one came forward to explain. It was just one more act of war among many.

How much of this should I tell them? How could I explain why I was favoured without telling the rest of it? I didn't know but I'd have a damned good try. Keeping secrets had become a habit I wasn't sure I could break, even now.

Don't think about all that stuff on your day off. Just stay in the present, enjoy the holiday, forget all those nightmares. This is your holiday too. You'll have plenty of time for tears later at the memorial service.

*   *   *

I was glad it was Mack parking up a narrow side lane leading to the Commonwealth War Cemetery, struggling to squeeze past coaches and police patrols on bikes to find a spot. It was a beautiful afternoon and the sun was hanging high over Souda Bay, still the largest inland harbour in Europe.

We had dressed for the occasion. Even Alex looked smart in his shirt and cargo shorts. Mack was in a blazer and chinos, and Lois all in white, which suited her dark looks. I had brought a black linen jacket and silk scarf, glad of dark glasses against the sun. We could hear a military band tuning up on the grass, that special sound made only by British soldiers in scarlet and gold.

There were veterans in berets and blazers, with medals jangling, holding poppy wreaths, calling out to each other. Cretan veterans took my eye in their black shirts and *breeches*, white knee boots, standing at the entrance alongside officials of every nationality and uniform: dress whites, air-force blues and army khakis and greys. The lump already in my throat swelled up, seeing so many people assembled. I suppose I hadn't known what to expect.

I kept imagining this peaceful commercial port full of battleships and wrecks, belching smoke and fumes. Now there were warships trimmed up ready for a gun salute. Where were the craters from the screaming Stukas diving down onto the port? The hills were now covered in smart villas and buildings.

We made our way slowly down towards the central cross, to get a closer view, collecting a service sheet on the way. Lois and Alex followed behind among the throng of tourists and locals, and the ceremony eventually began. I smiled, knowing this was a British-organized event with a royal visitor, so it would run like clockwork.

A lone piper played a haunting lament as he led a parade of old veterans with their wreaths slowly down to the white cross and the clergymen waiting to greet them. I felt my eyes filling up behind my glasses.

The wreath-laying ceremony went on for ages. I was glad when I was offered a chair. There were hymns and blessings. We sang the national anthem in croaking voices. The gun salute from the warship was impressive. Who could not be moved?

I was glad to be anonymous, free to patrol down the aisles of pristine white gravestones, marvelling at the precision and neatness of the green grass, the borders of red roses and the names of so many men and women cut down before they had really lived.

A war cemetery has a strange quietude; it humbles even the most effervescent of youth as they stare at the ages on those stones, grateful not to have been tried and tested in such a way. It is a place of sadness and regret, guilt and reminiscence, so many emotions filling my heart. Why had I left it so long?

I paused at the gravestone of Captain John Pendlebury, who I'd met briefly before the war. His was a mythical martyrdom, another one-eyed hero, athlete, academic, curator of the British School at Knossos, vice consul at the embassy and soldier extraordinaire, who was executed while injured in the first days of occupation. He was still a legend for his bravery and his love of this island.

I moved away from the others quickly, wanting to make this a private viewing, a reunion and a moment to come to terms with long-forgotten memories of some of these names whose faces I had known.

Slowly down the rows I walked, reading each name until I came to one that took my breath away, the name that had meant the most to me in those years: Bruce Jardine.

I had not expected him to be here, but buried somewhere on a hillside in New Zealand. I had found out he was dead, only when I returned home. Evadne broke the news to me one morning in the garden at Stokencourt when they felt I was strong enough to take it in. I've always hated that rose walk ever since for reminding me of the utter desolation and futility I felt at the news. It was like a punch in the stomach, taking my breath away in its intensity. I walked away from her to the lake, shaking my head in despair. I think she thought I was going to jump into the water as she ran after me. How little they knew of me to think I'd take an easy way out of life. Better to live out my span in honour of all those who couldn't.

I had waited so long for news that never came, but by then I was another person. So much had happened and I knew my feelings for him had altered irrevocably, but not to know he'd been lost to me even before I left the island . . . Like everything else, it was shoved in the suitcase in the attic of my mind, not to be disturbed.

Now, as I was touching the stone, bowing my head, I noticed, lying half-hidden on the manicured brown earth, a posy of mountain flowers and herbs wrapped in a black, red, gold ribbon: the colours of the Cretan flag. The inscription was in Cyrillic script from a poem: 'Your blood spilled on our soil was not in vain. Thank you.' That was all.

I stepped back, shocked to see Bruce honoured, looking round to see if there was anyone hovering, but there was no one else down the row. I wished I had something of my own to put there, suddenly ashamed at this careless oversight. We'd not brought even a rose or a poppy for remembrance. I was still trembling with the shock of seeing his name.

Who else was here who knew him? A wave of frustration and confusion flooded over me that all in my generation were so old and altered by time, unrecognizable to each other without labels. The veterans who marched so slowly, and some in wheelchairs, were mere shadows of the cocky bronzed men I'd the privilege of nursing. Who would recognize me now?

The posy was dry. Whoever had come to pay their respects preferred not to attend today for some reason . . . Curiouser and curiouser. A posy was a women's touch, delicate, unlike the flamboyant foreign wreaths covered in national ribbon and palm fronds, piled high now on the cross steps where veterans posed for their photographs.

Yes, it was comforting to know he wasn't forgotten or neglected, but unsettling. Someone who was still alive might have also been part of my life too, but I knew the special ones were long dead.

How could a little bunch of flowers suddenly throw all we'd done in the past weeks up in the air? Why hadn't they put on their name? I had to know just who it was.

I stood looking out to sea, feeling foolish. All this time Bruce was here and you never bothered to find out, I sighed. Didn't you care? All these friends and relatives travelling halfway across the world to attend today and you couldn't be bothered to come back once in all this time to remember him?

Everything is heightened on Crete: light and shade, black and white, human passions in the heat. In such a place where big things happen the emotions lie in wait, dormant, never forgotten, waiting only to be reawoken. There was no more escaping from the past, and I knew why I hadn't returned.

In the beauty of the sun-drenched evening, I was retreading those stormy days. I knew the reasons why I couldn't face this island, hadn't mourned Bruce as he deserved. I wasn't worthy to be linked with his name. At least he never knew of my shame . . . The tears were dripping slowly. I gulped to gain control. I could not stay here among these worthy people. *If they only knew the truth about me . . .*

'There you are, Aunt Pen. We thought we'd lost you.' Lois linked my arm. 'This must be a sad place for you. Shall we go now?'

I swallowed my tears as we walked away from the grave I was not ready to share with them, grateful that her simple gesture of love had brought me to this sacred place. This pilgrimage had taken a new turn and I was not going to leave until I knew just where it was leading me.

*   *   *

Rainer stood on the fringes of the crowd, leaning on his walk-ing stick, surveying the proceedings with interest, his eyes hidden behind tinted glasses. He was unsure of his welcome here. The absence of his own national flag was no surprise. Who wanted reminding of their occupation?

It was enough to recognize some of his old enemy agents, those daring officers who'd played havoc with his men in the mountains and stolen General Kreipe. He'd read their memoirs with interest, spotting Nicholas Hammond; Monty Wood-house; the hero of Galatas, Sandy Thomas; Patrick Leigh Fermor, the brashest of them all. He would like to shake their hands. Soldiers are the same under the skin, only the uniform marks them as different, he mused.

It would be good to meet them on equal terms and see what they had made of their lives. Some were statesmen, politicians, authors and adventurers even in old age. Others he knew lay here, as did so many of his comrades in Maleme.

The contrast of their two resting places was marked: one on land gifted by the Cretan peoples in gratitude on a shoreline overlooking the bay, the other a darker, shadier spot but just as poignant. That's where he belonged but he wasn't in a hurry to join them yet.

He stood back, not wanting to introduce himself now. This was their moment of victory. There were always two sides to a story and it could have so easily been himself interred under the Cretan sun. It was touch and go, who had been the victor in May '41. So much had changed since their defeat. Didn't they say history is written by the victors?

He was proud that there'd been many acts of reparation by his countrymen after the war: rebuilding village houses, repair-ing wells and water supplies, scholarships for students.

He stood under the olive trees watching the crowds dispers-ing slowly. His eye caught an older woman in a black jacket and white slacks, bending over a grave in a private moment of grief.

But there was something about her that flashed an image into his mind. She had that upright English posture of a certain class of woman, a military air, and the sight of her tugged at his memory.

He was still curious when her granddaughter, the grand-daughter's husband and son came to lead her away. He would like to have seen who she was visiting but somehow it felt discourteous and intrusive to follow. He watched them striding away and there was definitely something familiar in her gait and composure.

I've seen you before, he smiled with relief, realizing that they'd been on the same night ferry from Piraeus. He'd seen her standing alone on the deck as the ship moored into Souda Port at dawn: another pilgrim perhaps?

It was fanciful to think she had any other claim on his memory, but there was something ageless in her presence that reminded him of another time and another shore.

June 1944

As the outline of Piraeus harbour came slowly into view, Rainer stared down from the crowded deck of the *Hera* at the sorry state of the survivors. About thirty ragged burned soldiers, slouching in shock, some crew men staring blankly at their feet, also shocked, like himself, to have survived the attack on the ship.

He watched Penelope working down the lines of prostrate men, handing out cigarettes and drinks, never stopping, as if her whole concentration was just on the job in hand. Not once did she look up or talk to him. He'd saved her life but she was not going to give him the satisfaction of a thank-you. Her face was grey as granite, hawkish features, lips tightly drawn, the baggy trousers hanging off her skeletal frame.

By rights she must be handed over as a prisoner of war, a British Resistance worker, to be shipped north to some camp, perhaps to nurse under fire.

If she was not on the deposition list or if she was under her false name of Athina then she would be listed as missing with all the others. Once they landed she would have to be given papers, statements taken, identity proven and he knew he held that power over her. It made him uneasy. Was she too proud, too angry and shocked to care what happened to her any more?

He felt such a relief to be free of the island, free to go north away from the heat and dust, free to be an active soldier again, but Penelope wouldn't be free to return to England to see her family. Who *were* her family? Who were the people who had reared such an iron-willed warrior? He was curious to know more about her before he let her go.

She had nothing but the sorry outfit they'd cobbled up for her from the crew. She looked good in trousers, reminding him of that first time he'd seen her walking along the line of stretchers at Galatas with that look of grim endurance on her face. Now she needed kitting out with uniform. Her oil-sodden hair was coiled up, her complexion leathered by squinting into sun and wind. Yet she'd never looked as awesome, in his eyes, as she did now. How he wished he could dress her in silk, with a corsage of orchids on her shoulder, and whisk her off to a fine restaurant to fill out those gaunt cheeks. He flushed at his ridiculous fantasy.

The ship shuddered, throwing him onto the deck railings, nearly somersaulting him into the murky black water beneath. Rainer scrambled to retain some dignity as Penelope watched, and for a second their eyes locked, and the corner of her lips twitched with amusement. It was in that brief softening, like sun blotting out the shadows, that he knew he was lost for ever.

The survivors of the *Tanais* shuffled off the ship, lining up to state their name and numbers and transit plans. There were no prisoners evident.

When it was Penelope's turn, Rainer stepped forward in front of her. 'You'll not find her name on the list. She was a last-minute addition, drafted under the Red Cross, not an official passenger, and I would like to commend Nurse Georgiou for her bravery. Without her prompt attention some of these survivors would not have made it here. She has treated them despite injury to herself. As she is Red Cross, she must be billeted back in hospital as soon as possible.'

'And you are?' the official looked up.

'Major Brecht. First Paratroop Division, late intelligence in Chania. En route for the front after two weeks' leave.' He saluted, clicking his heels even though he was barefoot.

'*Kyria*, is this correct?'

'Apparently, the major knows my history better than I do,' Penny said, staring at Brecht in surprise. 'I can tell my own story, thank you. I want to report that hundreds of prisoners were locked in the ship's hold, unable to be released when we were torpedoed. It must be reported to the highest level . . .'

'Yes, yes, leave that to further enquiries. I take it you have no identification now? You must be registered at once. Next!'

Penelope stepped aside, uncertain where to go next, but she paused. 'Don't think I'm ungrateful that you helped me stay afloat or that your sending me on deck when you did saved my life, Major, but I can take care of myself now.'

'Really? You have no papers, no money, no clothes, not even a pair of shoes. Please let me assist you. After all, you did that for me once,' he said in halting English.

'I did my duty, no more, no less,' she snapped.

'Then please allow me to take you for something to eat. You have eaten nothing for days, I suspect.'

'Whose fault is that?'

'I am not to blame for decisions my superiors made to put you in that truck or arrest you. Not all of us are animals.'

'You stood by and did nothing. You let it happen. I saw you there.'

'I am not standing by to watch you starve now, or be worked to death in some slave camp. That's something I can do for you. Don't be too proud to refuse help when it is offered sincerely.'

'I know what officers expect from starving girls; I've treated enough of them,' she said, but he was not willing to back off now. This was a battle of wills.

'Why do you throw everything back in my face?'

'Because of what you are wearing and all that I have seen done in its name,' she spat, staring at his tattered uniform with contempt.

'So if I were in civilian clothes, would you treat me any better?'

'I don't know,' she answered after a pause, not looking at him. He could see she was hesitating, almost faint with exhaustion and hunger. He pressed home his advantage.

'Then we go into the city and buy one dress for you and one shirt for me. Don't look a horse's gift in the mouth.'

The sun lit up her face as she smiled. 'It is "Don't look a gift horse in the mouth." Am I really free to go?' she asked, her dark eyes burning into his.

'As far as I know you are a Greek Red Cross nurse from Athens. That is all that is necessary to know, but you must have papers.'

She brushed her hands into the air. 'Papers, papers, why can't we exist without wretched papers and numbers?'

'Bureaucracy, I'm afraid, a good Greek word.'

'Democracy is a better one,' she argued as they limped slowly along the rubbled street, trying not to wince. Rainer felt a spring in his step for the first time in years.

Souda, 2001

After the memorial ceremony was over, Rainer found the fish restaurant, recommended by the hotel receptionist, close to the port in Souda. It was filling up with veterans and their families, but he was given a table on the roadside. The selection on display for him to view in the kitchen was mouth-watering. He waited, sipping his Mythos, glad of a seat. His old wound was aching again.

The English widow had reminded him of Penelope. Why were all his memories of this island suffused with glimpses of that nurse? Was he still searching for her after all these years, still pretending he'd meant anything to her? Had she used him, humoured him, deceived him? And yet . . .

He was old now, no longer so aroused by romantic feelings. Only the music of Bach, Mozart, Chopin and Schubert touched the soul of him. He lived a quiet life of the mind, reading, fishing. His hunting days were long over. When his wife, Marianne, died, he'd learned to live alone, cook for himself and not be a nuisance to his children.

It was with his two grandchildren that he was recapturing his youthful spirit, watching their football and tennis matches with pride. It was good to see them grow up with freedoms he'd never known.

They didn't carry the same burden of guilt he'd noticed in his own boys for all that was done by his generation. He had never shared his wartime experience with them because they'd never asked about it. He was longing to see Joachim and Irmelie again. He must take them some presents now his thoughts were turning to home; perhaps a good sign. It would soon be time to leave for Athens but not before he made his own private reparations. There was something in his suitcase that must be returned, but quite where it would find a resting place he wasn't sure. He had kept it far too long. Time to let go of the past and find some peace for himself.

2001

I spent a sleepless night listening to the owl whooping in the olive grove, the dogs barking in the village, waiting for the cock to crow. My mind was racing with the knowledge that someone alive remembered Bruce.

I tried to recall the names of all the Cretan friends who'd sheltered us. Ike and Nikos, Tassi and Stella; Yolanda's husband, Andreas, but for the life of me I couldn't recall his second name. Had he remarried and had children? Where would I start with so little time left before we flew home?

That posy was a woman's touch. Had Bruce found a woman in the hills to comfort him? He'd not be the first to go native. There was so much I didn't know but I wasn't leaving Chania until I found out who had placed the flowers on his gravestone. There would be enough people still alive from that time who knew the truth.

As dawn broke I was making lists in my head of ideas to follow up. The island was full of visiting veterans, evaders, escapees. Why not catch them before they left for home? I'd need to know where they were billeted, but Mack would have his ear to the ground about that. There would be Crete veterans' associations who might help in the search. Lois would help me drive around tomorrow and find out more.

More than that was the shame I felt in neglecting Bruce's memory. I wanted to thank whoever it was for tending his memory far more than I had done. Perhaps it was time to leave a legacy here in his name, a scholarship fund. I wondered why I had left it so late in the day. I hoped I'd not left it too late.

Lois drove me to the resort village of Platanias, close to the beach where the tent hospital had been erected and the battle for Galatas village. The olive groves had shrunk away from the sea; villas and hotels were springing up, taking advantage of the view over the bay. Many of the veterans might already have left so the chance of making contact with someone who knew Bruce was slim.

Over breakfast I'd tried to explain to Lois what happened and how I needed to find out more about the person who had left the flowers. As I thought, the veteran party had left, not for the airport, but a day trip to Lake Kournas, and were not expected back until late.

Victoria, the resort receptionist, was concerned that my visit was proving fruitless. I told her a little of my mission and its urgency. She smiled, offering her own idea. 'If your friend was in the Resistance, you should contact the Cretan Resistance Association. They will have tales to tell you. My grandfather was a partisan – if you like, I can contact him.' She asked the name.

'Bruce Jardine,' I replied. 'But no, they would only know him as Panayotis, his cover name.'

'That's easy to remember, it's my boyfriend's name,' she smiled, taking down contact details, promising to get back to me if there was anything useful.

We drove back and I must have looked as exhausted as I felt.

'Siesta, now,' Lois ordered. 'You need to rest.'

I had no energy left to protest when we got back to the villa.

Alex was excited at the latest mission. 'Are we going to find Aunt Pen's boyfriend?' Lois shooed him outside to the pool.

'Bruce was always your special one,' Lois said. 'I thought Adam was mine but things change.'

'They do indeed,' I sighed. 'At least you lived with him, found out what he was really like. We never had that luxury. Our love affair was never earthed in the physical way. It was fuelled by danger and separation but we never actually . . .' I paused, flushing. 'I never really knew what he thought of me.'

'But you never looked at another man? We often wondered . . .' It was Lois's turn to hesitate.

'Oh, I wouldn't say that. Things were complicated then but I had my moments.'

'Tell me more,' Lois said.

'Certainly not! Bruce was my first love and you know the saying, first love leaves the longest scar. I had no idea he was buried here. Isn't that awful? Once I knew he was gone, I just shut the pain of it out of my life. Now I feel ashamed. I saw all those widows and orphans, read what they put on their crosses yesterday. I was so cold and cut off, just like my mother when Papa died.'

'But you went on to do sterling work, devoting your life to caring for others, all that teaching work in Africa. You should be proud.'

I leaned back in my chair, uncomfortable with compliments I didn't deserve. 'Don't think I wouldn't have given up some of it gladly to have a family, children and a home of my own.'

'But you have family, children and grandchildren; we are your family. You're the nearest thing I've had to a proper granny, but we never think of our parents and grandparents having lovers and dreams and disappointments like our own.'

I reached out for Lois's hand. 'You've had a rough two years but I think you're coming out of that dark tunnel?'

She blushed. 'Actually, Mack's asked me if I'd like to return later before the season ends for a bit of a break. He's coming back to England then, planning a travel book: *Crete by Car,*

Cycle or Foot.' She smiled. 'I have to admit this holiday's gone rather better than I thought.'

'I like Mack. He strikes me as genuine. You do right to seize the moments that spring out of nowhere. I'd like to see you settled again.'

'Oh, not yet. I don't want Alex involved.'

'Come on, he's got his own life to lead, school. Blink, and he'll be off to college. Follow your heart in this, Lois. Don't shut yourself off like I've done.'

'I'll try. It's good to share all this but it feels like beginning all over again.' She paused for a deep breath. 'I know you're not telling me everything, but I hope coming back has helped you.'

'It will when I find out what I'm looking for. I feel it's just out of reach, round the corner, very close, waiting for me. Oh, listen to this romantic tosh! Everything we've done here's prepared me for this moment. I'm getting excited, and at my age it's good to have something to look forward to.'

I wasn't lying. I could feel a bubbling up of hope. The odds might be stacked against finding someone who didn't want to be found, but it was a small island and people talk and remember. Tomorrow I was going on another private pilgrimage, something I'd been dreading but must be done, and it would be a private visit. Now I had seen Bruce's resting place, I needed to find Yolanda's.

Mid-morning, the door to Etz Hayyim synagogue was open. The bustling of Kondilaki Street hadn't begun yet but it was already hot and I was glad to come into the enclosed courtyard, with its palm trees and pergola of shade, just to sit for a while.

Truth be told, I'd never been in a synagogue before. I don't do churches any more, but the moment I stepped into the little oasis of green and calm, I felt the quiet and the peace of a house of worship restored from rubble and ruin, brought back into the life of the Chania community.

I felt a link back to those old days when the houses around teamed with noise and bustle, preparations for the Sabbath, the smell of the bread ovens. I recalled sitting at supper with the Markos family and their relations, sensing the tension in poor Yolanda in being expected to marry within her faith, her secret love for Andreas, that wedding party in the hills and that last visit I made to her parents. It all came flooding back.

I knew their fate only too well. I was there, I saw them drown, locked in the hold. I will never forget that sight for the rest of my life. I bore witness to a Red Cross official but never heard anything more about an inquiry. If there was one, I was never called. I was on no one's list; as far as the world was concerned I was never there.

A surge of sadness washed over me.

A young man came to welcome me from the office. '*Shalom*, do feel free to look around.' I felt curiously reluctant to go inside, but I wandered through the porch and saw how it was now a simple house of prayer. The young American guided me through its history, from a Venetian church given to the Jews by the Turks during their occupation. I sat down. 'I just want to remember my friends who lived here before . . .'

'You knew people before the war? Please, come when you're ready, I'll make us coffee. We want to know anything we can about those times. There are so few left, and of course none of them returned. Who was your friend?'

'We nursed together in Athens and here for a while. She was my dear friend.' It was hard to speak about her without crying and usually I am not one to break down in front of strangers. 'I have come to pay my respects to her family.'

'We do have a list of all those taken that night, and others,' he offered, but I was not sure I wanted to face the enormity of a long list. Yet I knew it was my duty to the lost community to face who they all were in life.

'The rabbi had to register all the names of the Jewish residents, their place of birth, ages, occupation and dependants.' My guide brought out a booklet in which were pages and pages of names.

I scrolled down, marvelling at the detail, putting faces to some of them: Alegra, Soultana, Iosif, Miriam . . . My hands were trembling, my finger shaking as I came to the ones I dreaded most. It was then I noticed Yolanda's name separate from the others.

'Why is she not with her family?' I asked.

'Because she wasn't there on the night of the roundup,' he replied. 'She married a Christian and they hid her. The Nazis never found her . . .'

I did not hear the rest as one glorious thought overwhelmed me. She was never on the ship . . . Yolanda lived.

'Yes, but wait . . .' he called after me as I fled. 'Your name would be so useful to us.'

I sped out into the little alleyway and down the busy street. Yolanda survived. Was she still here on the island after all this time?

June 1944

Yolanda woke, back on the mattress in the hospital basement. The dream had been so real: all those figures looting the houses, carrying away pots and chairs in their handcarts, shouting and laughing to each other, ransacking what had already been ransacked. The pain in her back had turned to agony, there was a rumble of wheels of a cart and the touch of a stranger holding her hand. It was a nightmare she didn't want to recall, but then she felt the cotton shift of a hospital gown, the mattress was upended with books so her feet were raised, and she felt raw and sore inside. Her tongue was rough and there was a stench of ether on her pillow. Only then, as she came to her full senses, did she realize the nightmare was real.

Slowly she slid her hands down her stomach, feeling for the quickening of life. There was nothing but an emptiness, an aching void and wadding between her legs.

'Lie back, Yolanda, rest,' a voice said and she saw old Dr Frankakis peering down at her. 'It all came away. We had to stop infection. I'm sorry.'

'My baby, where is my baby?' she mouthed without hope.

'He was too small to live, it was too soon, the shock brought on the miscarriage.'

She turned her face from him. 'I thought it was just a dream. How did I get here? I was down looking for my . . .'

'We know, and you were lucky not to be denounced. Thank God some people still have the decency to protect their neighbours. You were hidden until dark and brought up here hidden in a cart. They saved your life.'

Yolanda tried to rise up. 'I have to find my parents.'

'They're all gone, along with the captured partisans. We've heard to Heraklion and by ship. You've lost a lot of blood and we've not got a match for you so you must rest here and build up your strength.'

'Is there news of Andreas?'

Frankakis shook his head. 'Sadly no, but that is good news. Bad travels faster than the wind. Now rest. It is the best cure.'

How could she rest when everyone she loved was lost to her: Andreas, the baby, her parents and their heritage? What was the point of being alive when there was no future?

She felt the tingle of breast milk spilling across her bandaged chest. They were taking away the baby's food, stopping the flow to ease her pains, but nothing would ease the ache in her heart. How could she recover from such a body blow?

Even as she cried she felt a spark of rage blazing into the life. *You will pay for this, all of you will pay for my loss. I will be avenged, even if it takes the rest of my life. I will have justice and I will defy you by living. I defy you in the name of all that is holy, someone will pay.*

It was the fire of revenge that made her eat, though she had no taste or appetite; made her build the strength in her legs and arms; made her snap and snarl as she went on light hospital duties until she felt strong enough to return to the farm on the old bus. It had taken almost two months to recover and now, in the heat of August, she saw the landscape dry, scorched and brown.

Then as she approached up the track she saw an army of partisans encamped around the farmhouse in the olive groves, men in uniforms round a campfire ringed by stones. She wondered why they were here. Could it possibly be . . . Then, in the doorway of the farmhouse she saw their *kapetan*, Andreas. *Andreas!* He was talking to a woman but on seeing her running to him, he stepped back as if he'd seen a ghost and crossed himself.

'Andreas!' she shouted. 'It's me. Oh, you're safe!'

'They told me you were arrested, picked up in the raid. What were you doing in Chania? No one told us you were still alive.' He seemed genuinely shocked at her arrival. 'Look what they did to the place when they came to find you . . . ransacked it.'

'But I'm here now.' She fell into his arms, crying with rage. 'Why didn't you come for me?'

Andreas pulled her into the house, embarrassed at her making a scene. 'Come out of the sun. I was told you went to see your parents and you were picked up and taken with them. You were on the list and they came here looking for you first and did this . . .' He was pointing to the burned shed, the broken furniture, smashed pictures piled up outside the farmhouse, the smell of burned carcasses in the air. She couldn't take it all in.

'What list? Who told you that?'

'Stavros. He escaped from prison. He saw the Jews in Agia Prison and there was a nurse taken from the Red Cross. I thought it might be you. They took Manolis and Taki. I didn't come because I thought you were dead.'

'I went to find you at the caves to warn you about Stavros. I saw him signalling to the enemy on the path, the morning you were nearly caught. I saw them take prisoners and I thought one of them was you at first.'

'Nonsense, he was signalling to the other group to stay back, the band on the other side. We sensed they were coming,' he replied. 'Why do you always blame him?'

'I don't trust him. He's not one of you,' she snapped.

'You're not one of us,' he argued, looking at her as if she was a stranger. 'You're from the mainland too.'

'What do you mean? How can you say that when you know my parents and all my family have disappeared? Aren't you glad to see me?' She felt such a panic. This was not her Andreas, her husband.

'I'm sorry but we have important orders. The Allies are freeing Europe from north and south. We expect an invasion from Egypt. We are grouping to flush the enemy out of each district now we have regular supplies.'

'Panayotis died. I was there,' she said, hoping he would comfort her.

'Yes, and many other brave *palliakaris* like him. We mustn't rely on the British any more. We have our own national army, other allies now. Come, no more talking. Anna will find you something to eat.'

A black-haired girl in army uniform stepped out of the shadows. She had overheard everything. 'This is Anna, who comes with us on missions. She can decode messages faster than anyone I know.' He beamed at the girl and Yolanda felt sick.

'There's something else I must tell you,' she whispered.

Her husband turned impatient. 'Well?'

'In private, please,' she pleaded. Anna had the decency to saunter outside into the sunlight.

'I lost our baby. They say it was the shock of seeing those looters, on top of thinking you might be dead . . .'

'I thought there was something different about you. You look so thin and pale. I'm sorry, of course, but I think it was for the best. This is no time to bring a child into a battlefield, not when we have so much unfinished business.'

Yolanda was too stunned by these words to reply. What had happened to them? Who was this man who looked on her and their baby as distractions? What had happened to that warm beloved doctor, where had he gone? In his place was a stranger, a hardened warrior, armed to the teeth, full of plans that didn't include her. He was too busy being a hero to come and find out about the fate of his wife.

Why was it Stavros who brought the news? What did he
know about lists of Jews? How could he claim to have seen her
when she wasn't there? Why had he, of all people, managed to
escape from the prison? Suddenly she felt an overwhelming
sense of dread. Her home was turned over to an army camp, the
farm was in ruins almost, land untended and his parents no
longer there to support it. Now there was an attractive young
woman swaggering around the leader. Had Anna been quick to
take her place?

In the past months Yolanda's whole world had crumbled to
dust and she was left dangling in a strange empty space, stuck
between the living and the dead with no place to call her own.
She stared out at the neglect around her.

No, that was not strictly true. Here was her abiding place. If
she was surplus to Andreas's life now, she was certainly needed
here on the farm. Once he rushed off with his band she would
be alone, and the land that had fed them and nurtured them
would return to jungle and brush. That was not going to happen.

There were livestock roaming round; they must be counted
and brought back. With milking came cheese to sell. The land
needed her, ham-fisted though she was. This was all there was
left to her now and she'd not shirk from the task of restoring it.

There was honour in such hard labour and the pain of it
would keep the madness of grief from her door and the memories of happier times from overwhelming her.

June 2001

'She's alive, Lois. Yolanda survived. Can you believe it? We have to find her.' I could hardly contain myself, seeing Alex and Lois lounging in the Limani Ouzeria by the harbour, sipping glasses of freshly squeezed orange juice.

'Calm down, Aunt Pen, you'll have a turn, sit down. You need a cold drink. Tell me what happened.' She turned to the waiter for another juice.

I rattled through the visit to Etz Hayyim, the book of names and Yolanda not being there, or that she was but only as a survivor. 'I thought she was dead and she was safe all along. I can't believe this. We have to find her.'

'What did the guide actually say to you?' Lois leaned forward. I had to admit my mind had gone blank. 'I just fled. Oh, how rude. I didn't even ask his name.'

'Look at me, Pen. Did he say she was still here or if she . . .' Lois paused, '. . . if she was still living?'

'Oh, no, surely not, I didn't ask.' I got up to leave but her hand pulled me back down.

'Sit down, calm down. There's no rush. Let's do this systematically. What was her married name?'

'It began with an A, I think, no, her husband was Andreas, Dr Andreas something, but he had a cover name, Cyclops. All their surnames seem to end in "akis".'

'How many one-eyed partisans who were once doctors with

the Red Cross are there on Crete?' Lois laughed. 'Victoria at
that hotel said she'd help up link up with their Resistance veterans. We'll go back to the synagogue together. They probably
know the answer, but be careful. It was a long time ago and
there was civil war, earthquakes and a dictatorship. Please don't
get your hopes too high.'

Lois meant well but I wasn't ready to hear her reality. 'But
those flowers on the grave, they must be her doing. Now it
makes sense.' My thoughts were racing so fast I could hardly
breathe.

Rainer Brecht was sitting by the harbour enjoying the last few
days of his holiday. All the Battle of Crete ceremonies were
over. There'd been a reunion of German veterans, which he'd
attended out of politeness: lots of back-slapping, talking over
old comrades, a ceremony at Maleme, low-key but moving
nonetheless. He was shocked at how old they all looked, and he
soon tired of endless toasts and old battle songs. No one could
sing 'Red shines the sun' without tears in their eyes for all those
for whom there was 'no way back'.

He would be flying into Athens soon and staying a night at
the Hotel Grande Bretagne for old times' sake. He had strolled
through the narrow Leather Alley to find belts for the boys with
studs, a wallet to replace his tattered one, and a fine pair of fur-
lined gloves for his granddaughter, Irmelie.

In his travel bag he carried the package nursed so carefully in
his luggage. His first stop was the Museum of Byzantine Art in
the old street where El Greco was born, but it was closed so he
sauntered slowly to the old monastery church in Halidon Street,
which now housed the Archaeological Museum.

The sight of the building reminded him of that terrible night
of looting when officers and men sifted through all the sacred
objects and texts from the synagogue, scattering ancient books
and scripts onto the pyre in a spree of destruction.

He had turned away from the burning of all that knowledge and scholarship, sickened by the ignorance of men who knew nothing of a dedicated lifetime's study for truth. He had seen the cave nurse staring at him with contempt, her eyes searching into his soul, stripping him of any pretence of honour in what had been perpetrated that night. He had reached the depths of his shame, facing the worst of their excesses and knew then he must leave the island.

Now he felt the coolness of the old building a relief from the hot pavements. He sat on a bench fingering the once-looted icon of St Katerina, which had brought nothing but bad luck to his family, first to his sister, who had lived a diminished life of fits and pain after her accident. He recalled his mother's dying rebuke. 'You sent her this gift but I've never liked it. She looks down on us with such accusing eyes. I'm sure it is valuable but take it away. We are good Catholics, we have our own saints. I fear she has a bad history. Return her to Greece. Don't keep it, it will blight your life, and don't tell me how you came by it, Son.'

He'd been too rational a man to be superstitious but he did recall the fate of the officer who threw it at him. He'd sent it in good faith, not understanding how precious these devotional pieces of art were to those who owned them, venerated, handed down from generation to generation.

He'd read up about the Cretan school of icons and how the painting of them was an act of worship. This belonged in the house from where it was looted, a house where it would have meant so much. He had stared into those dark pools, those almond eyes, and knew he must take St Katerina home to Crete. It was this little object that had challenged him to make this pilgrimage in penitence for all the vandalism. Only then, perhaps, would he be cleansed of the past memories that haunted his dreams.

Now he was here, he felt nervous, awkward. How could he explain its soiled heritage?

There was no one on the information desk, no bell to ring. He planned just to leave the wrapped package there but that was too easy, too anonymous. It needed some explanation. He found a garden courtyard full of statues and remnants, outside in the very yard where the fire had burned. He found a shady spot to write a note, but what could he say?

> Please accept the return of this icon. It was stolen by a soldier of the occupying forces in 1942 but I have no idea from whom. Please give it to a church to be rededicated to the praise and glory of God and forgive those who separated it from its rightful owner: A well-wisher.

He walked back through the cases of antiquities and saw with relief a young woman busy at the desk. He paused.

'Will you take this for me?' he said, sliding the loose package across the counter. She smiled, opening the paper, but he had already made for the entrance.

'Wait!' she cried. 'Where did you find this?'

He fled down the busy tourist street before she could chase him. That was the last of his 'must dos'. If only it were so easy to wipe away the memories of those far-off days.

Now, as he caught his breath in the harbour café, he felt safe enough to smile. He wondered what they were making of the mystery package he'd left. He hoped they didn't think it was a bomb scare. Would it find its rightful owner or end up in a church dedicated to St Katerina? He hoped the former.

Funny, how ready he was for home now. There was nothing holding him here but this last important task.

He sat watching the glass-bottomed boats chugging out of the ancient harbour with its stone wall reaching like an arm into the sea. There were ponies clip-clopping on the front, holiday-makers slurping ice-cream sundaes under the shady awnings. We didn't destroy it all, he thought, just ourselves for a while.

These are tough people who threw off layers of invasions from Minoans, Romans, Turks, Venetians.

The garrison held out to the bitter end in Chania, cordoning itself off by a ring of scorched earth and fire, retreating from the rest of the island back to a single fortress until the surrender in May 1945, when they were escorted off by the British to POW camps, but not before they were strip-searched for loot.

He knew how they feared the revenge of the Cretans for all the misery heaped onto them during occupation. Eventually they all went home from prison camps to devastation, to a country divided into sectors, to starving families, broken homes, tribunals, executions. They had sown the wind and reaped the whirlwind. He had heard the bitterness in the voices of ex-soldiers at the reunion, excuses for being misled by leaders. There were no excuses, and in the end you fought for the comrade next to you, as he fought for you.

Perhaps the world had learned a bit of sense but there were always fanatics who believed only they had the truth, who wanted to stamp their politics or religion on everyone else. He was glad he'd not be around to see another catastrophe should it come.

His eyes were following the family across the table, the same family on the ferry and at the memorial. The old lady looked so animated, so alive, the daughter reaching out to calm her down, the young boy already bored, playing on his Nintendo game.

He wondered what their pilgrimage had been. Were they now coming to the end of their holiday, suntanned, relaxed with carrier bags full of souvenirs?

We north Europeans like our sun, he thought, smiling, to make up for long dreary winters. He was curious about the English family as they chattered. The grandmother sat upright, alert. She caught his eye for a second and he smiled and she smiled, then turned back to her family.

He'd always had an eye for a handsome woman, and even in old age this one had that fine bone structure that never aged. He'd love to know the history etched on her face. It was a face that had seen much. He'd like to have captured her features. That was one of the few perks of the prisoner of war camp in Canada where he had time to learn to draw with a competence to capture the essence of a face with a few lines, just as the artists on the harbour pavement were copying photos or sketching children for their parents and a fee.

Stop being fanciful, he thought. The one face he'd wanted to capture, he never had, though he'd tried many times afterwards to hold onto the memory of Penelope.

He smiled, thinking of those precious days in Athens when the barriers between them relaxed enough for him to catch a glimpse of the woman behind the mask she presented to the world. It would be in Athens that he would feel her presence most.

June 1944

Rainer was shocked at the devastation of the ancient city. It was a jungle of warring tribes, factions loyal to communists, nationalists slugging it out like outlaws in the Wild West. The centre of the city was recognizable but the rest was a litter of ruins, shanties where gun battles between police and partisans made every corner of these streets dangerous. He was glad he was only passing through.

True to his word he'd escorted Penelope into the shopping quarter. Hermes Street was still open for business. She bought some sandals and a cotton dress and underwear. He bought a shirt and plain slacks. It was strange to be out of uniform, if not illegal for an officer, but being on leave and not known, it was worth the risk.

They made awkward shoppers. He didn't want to let her out of his sight. She didn't want to be seen with him in case they assumed she was his whore. She was silent, still clinging to her scruffy rescue ensemble, embarrassed at his presence, but there was a truce of sorts.

He was stepping out of line in not reporting her. Nothing was said about the explosion or the contents of the ship. It was as if no one wanted to know any details. The nurse was never registered. She'd continue to pass herself as Greek, fooling them as she'd fooled him for long enough, but he could see she was still in shock. Was she fit to return to nursing? Would they accept her back? She didn't seem even to notice her change of city. It was as if she were sleepwalking.

They made for the open green spaces of the National Garden but sporadic gunfire sent them heading back for safety to a quiet street where they found a taverna. He watched her eat without tasting any of it, darting glances at him as if she wasn't sure who he was or why she was here.

'What will you do now?' he asked, breaking the silence between them.

She shrugged. 'What I am trained to do.' There was no enthusiasm in her voice.

'But what would you like to do? You once told me you were an archaeology student here.'

'Did I? I forget so . . . but I'd like to see the School of Archaeology again, if it's still standing.'

'I'll take you there.'

'I know where it is,' she snapped.

It was like trying to smash through a bell jar to reach her. Why was he doing this? He could be enjoying his leave with nightclubs and willing girls.

'I haven't seen it. They say it's a famous landmark. There's so much of Athens to see.'

'Not now, not since you lot came to conquer.'

'We're not in uniform now.'

'If you say so,' she sighed. Her face registered no reaction.

This was hopeless but he wasn't going to give up on her. He couldn't let her wander the streets in this state. She'd not last the night.

Why did he feel such an overwhelming instinct to protect her? She'd lost that brittle shell of competence and he feared for her sanity. Penelope had seen and suffered too much. He'd seen that look on the stunned faces of his stricken paratroopers on that first descent. It was the face of war.

June 2001

I sat in the back of the car trying to breathe. My heart was thumping with anticipation. Would she be there? Would she remember me? What if they were out? I'd tried to rationalize all the scenarios and obstacles.

Finding Yolanda was easy, once I returned to Etz Hayyim and apologized for my rudeness. Yolanda had never come back into Chania, not since the roundup. She lived in a village in the Apokoronas district on her son's farm. Yes, she was still alive. That was all the guide could glean.

'I think she gave an interview, many years ago, but I've never seen it. You could ask our director here, Nikos Stavroulakis, but he is on holiday.'

Then Victoria from the hotel rang, true to her word, with information about Cyclops and his wife. Her uncle knew the village. No one can disappear in northwest Crete, everyone knows someone who knows, and cities are made up of little villages too.

I dressed with care, knowing how traditional Cretan families like formality on big occasions, smart in my best silk dress and sunhat. We set off mid-morning and as we snaked over the newly cut roads I marvelled how I'd roamed these hills, lean, tough-limbed, thinking nothing of a steep climb. I had indeed been a mountain goat.

The mountains were strangers to me now and I wondered if I had passed anywhere close to where Bruce had fought or died? Now they all looked the same, browning in the dry heat, just a few of the higher peaks covered in snow. This was my home for so many years – how could I have forgotten the majesty of these high peaks?

Lois and Alex were in charge of the map. Alex had his camera at the ready on the lookout for more shrines and crosses for me to translate. I only hoped Yolanda would be able to understand my now faltering Greek.

What if she was forgetful and losing her marbles? No more forgetful than you, I chided myself for such an ungracious thought, but I was nervous, nervous. Was it right to be intruding on her life after all this time? What if she didn't want reminding of the past?

I'd been content to put it all behind me. It was only Lois's pushing that got me back here and now I didn't want to leave. I wanted to soak in all the beauty and majesty as if for the first time. We were so busy keeping our heads down, there wasn't time for much star-gazing during the occupation.

'This is the village.' Alex pointed to the sign. 'We have to look for a track to the left. Stop! Up there . . .'

I could see in the distance a familiar outline of a white-washed cube house with a flat roof, but by its side was a tall three-storey modern villa, painted a golden ochre hue. The drive up to it was rough and we crunched and bumped our way to a cacophony of barking dogs heralding our arrival. I could hardly move for excitement and nerves. 'Oh, please God, she's at home.'

Yolanda was bending over the last of her globe artichokes in the vegetable patch she'd carved out of a side field on the farm. It was protected from marauding sheep and goats by a stone wall and wire fencing. There were roses planted round the borders for colour and scent. She gave them plenty of manure and they rewarded her with blooms the size of dinner plates.

Young Andreas, her grandson, had fixed a hose-piped irrigation system that kept things surviving the worst of droughts. Here she could lose herself, weeding, hoeing, checking the tomatoes, peppers, zucchinis and the potato crop. There were always jobs to do in her garden, even if she was getting slower and slower at finishing them.

She stood up, hearing the dogs barking. It wasn't the day for the fish van. Perhaps someone was here to see her son-in-law or one of the builders coming to finish off the paving round their new villa. Her eyes weren't so good now and she couldn't see why the dogs were making such a racket.

Yolanda rubbed her gnarled hands on her old apron, wiped her brow and tucked wispy bits of white hair under her head-scarf. She was not in a fit state to receive visitors, not that she had many, since most of her old village cronies were waiting for her in the cemetery.

She secured the gate to her garden and made her way to the parked car, not a truck but a town vehicle. A woman was standing staring at her, tall, thin, in a dress the colour of ripe aubergines, a sunhat covered her face. She was clutching the hand of a young boy as if unsure of her footing.

'Is this the house of Kyria Androulaki, Kyria Yolanda?' the older woman said in halting Greek. She stepped forward and took off her sunglasses and hat. '*Yassou*, Yolanda.'

'*Yassas*,' she replied politely. There was something in the way this woman pronounced her name, not in a Greek way but in the way she'd heard so long ago. Her heart began to race. She looked closely into the dark eyes. Surely not . . . It couldn't be . . . 'Penelope? Is that you?'

They stared at each other, smiling, their bodies had shrunk and aged but the smile, the voice, the eyes, those never changed.

'You came back. I thought, you had died.' Yolanda screamed, her hands flung into the air.

'I thought you were gone too . . .' Suddenly they were clinging to each other, tears, hugs, both trying to speak at the same time. Such a momentous unexpected reunion after all this time.

How long we sat there just holding hands and smiling, I've no idea. So much to say and yet so much left unsaid. We were taken round to a shady pergola dripping with vines and budding grapes where Yolanda sat us down, brought a jug of the most refreshing lemonade and a plate of almond biscuits that Alex wolfed down.

I introduced my family, and Yolanda's daughter arrived with her daughter to greet us.

This is Sarika and Dimitra. I have another daughter in America. She lives in Chicago, a doctor married to a doctor. She's called Penelope.'

I was shocked that she had named her daughter after me. I felt honoured and ashamed at the same time. 'You have photographs of them?'

She smiled. 'Of course, and of my grandsons, Toni and Andreas. My husband died in 1948 in the troubles . . . a widow for many years, but the land has been good to us. And my children too.' She turned to smile at them, then turned back to me. 'And you, you married?'

Lois was quick to come to my rescue. 'My aunt nursed in Africa until she was seventy, didn't you?' Her Greek was basic but she was making herself understood.

'You and I will talk together. There is much to say, I think, and you must all stay and eat tonight . . .'

Lois shook her head. 'Alex and I must go out this evening, but I can pick Pen up later.'

'Tomorrow, then, you will all dine with us.' It was an order.

'Of course, that will be wonderful.'

'My son will drive her back tonight then,' Yolanda declared.

I sat in a stupor of heat and daze, soaking in the view from the farm that now I remembered as if it were yesterday; being a reluctant guest at that joyous party in such dark times; dancing at the wedding that I had been able to attend, tables spread with bright cloths, the music players in the corner, everyone in national costumes and that wonderful moment discovering that Yolanda was the bride. How strange to be reunited once again in the very same place.

Sarika took the others off to see her new villa, leaving Yolanda and me alone at last. We stared at each other.

'Where do we start? I have so many things to tell you,' I offered. 'But they are not easy to say after all these years.'

'And I have things to tell you,' she replied. 'Sad things, you may not want to hear.'

'One thing first, Yolanda,' I blurted. My curiosity couldn't wait a moment longer. 'Was it you who left the flowers on Bruce's grave?'

She smiled. 'You saw them. Sarika takes them every year on his anniversary but this time we put special ones for the anniversary. Was it that . . . ?'

I nodded. 'I knew it had to be someone who knew him. I never dared hope that it was you. I thought you'd been taken in the roundup. I have to tell you . . .'

She reached out for my hand. 'Not now, not yet. Let's enjoy just sitting a while before we dip into those dark waters. You disappeared and I heard you were deported too. I waited for a letter that never came and I thought you'd forgotten us here.'

'Never. I was ill after the war, a breakdown, not myself. I just wanted to forget everything but if I had thought for one minute you'd survived . . .'

'I didn't know what happened to my parents for a long time. I had to put it to the back of my mind, and when the truth came out, how the ship was sunk . . .'

'I was there on the ship . . . I escaped. It's a terrible thing to survive when your friends don't.' There was no holding this back from her now but I was floundering, knowing everything I told her would be painful. But Yolanda was tough and took control.

'Come and see my garden, see what you think of my little paradise. When I am sad or tired of being a widow I sit out there and look out onto the hills that never change. They feed my soul. You must try my thyme honey, the best in the Apokoronas.'

We strolled across, linking arms in friendship, drinking in the joy of this reunion, this reward for me risking the journey back.

How could I translate into Greek that old adage that women of a certain age turn to God or their garden and some to both, I suspect?

We kept to safe ground, talking around gardening, the little victories and disasters that plagued our efforts, the olive harvest, good ones and bad, locust attacks, drought and too much rain at the wrong time. I marvelled at how much she could grow outdoors that I had to grow under glass in England. Both of us were aware that we were tiptoeing around the edges of a murky pool of memories, unsure how much to share, not wanting to break the spell of being together again. What remained of our friendship into old age? I was bursting to hear how she had survived and she was curious as to what I had made of my life.

We talked about her visits to the States to see her daughter. She returned to Salonika, where she was born, only once but she was now as rooted to this place as I now was to Stoken-court. Funny how there were no men in our lives apart from family ties. I talked about my brother and sister and their children, about Athene's early death from leukaemia and how her daughter, Lois, had become so important in my life. How I'd returned to England in bad shape after the war before I pulled myself together and forged a career abroad.

Later, after a delicious lunch from her garden plot, we sat in the shade, exhausted by all the talking.

Lois and Alex made their way home to Kalyves and I was happy just to be sharing this precious time together under the olive tree. I wondered when to confess what I knew, knowing the only way to begin was to dive right in the deep end and get it over with.

'I met your parents. I went to visit them. I just wanted them to know you were well. I hope I did right.'

She didn't look at me but kept staring ahead. 'How did it go? Did they ask after me?'

'They missed you very much. It was hard for them to accept your decision but they were relieved to know you were safe and happy in your marriage.'

What else could I say to comfort her? I didn't lie. I just stretched the truth a little.

'I did come down to Chania but it was too late,' she said. 'They were already looting the Jewish quarter. I lost my baby at five months, a little boy. They hid me in the Red Cross clinic. There was a list of Jews living outside Chania, even those converted to Christianity, and I think they took them all. They came here and ransacked the place, stole the flock, burned the crops.' Yolanda paused. 'Bad, bad times . . . but why were you on that ship?'

'I made a scene. I had false papers. I was deported, but when someone was injured, they sent for me and I was on deck when the torpedoes hit the *Tanais*. We were flung off the ship into the water and picked up by the escort vessel. I thought you were in the hold.' I found myself crying, not wanting to speak further of that night or why I had been spared.

Yolanda fingered her wedding band with a sigh. 'It was a better fate than the ovens of Auschwitz. That is my only comfort – that they were spared such terror. I have only one photo of them, nothing of us together. I've tried to tell my children about them but the young aren't interested, only Penny in Chicago. Would you believe she married back into the faith, to Lionel, so the circle of life goes on? I hope my parents would be blessed by that.'

'You have not seen Etz Hayyim then?' I asked. 'It is beautifully restored.'

'No, I won't go back ever. I prefer to remember it all as it once was. I have no faith now, not in that way.'

I felt the shutters go down. The pain of these memories was too much to share.

'Come, let's go and tell the news to the bees in the field,' she said. 'It's time they knew our story. I'll find you a veil and cover up. We've all the time in the world to share our news.'

Yolanda couldn't take her eyes off Penny. She looked so elegant, straight-backed and lean. Four children had taken their toll on her own figure; her skin was leathered by the sun. When Andreas was shot in the civil war she went into mourning and had never come out of grey or black, as was the custom. She saved colour for flowers and ornaments, the bright woven rugs and furnishings of her room.

Penny looked so bright, and much younger than she did, but they had lived in different times and climates. There was so much Yolanda wanted to know about Penny's life in England, where it rained and was always green, but first she must tell her about Panayotis. She must dig deep into her past and pull out those bits that would give her comfort in the same way she guessed Penny had shielded her from the horrors of her parents' deaths.

So many sorrows and disappointments were soothed by children and family ties. She hoped Penny had a good supply of this too. She kept touching her hand to check she was real and not some ghost that was tricking her mind. She had known old people close to their end who see all their relatives long gone as if they were still living.

They were sitting under the olive tree with the lantern, watching moths flickering to the light, listening to the last of the cicadas as the day cooled. Her son, Toni, and Sarika's husband came to pay their respects, then disappeared to watch football on the television.

Perhaps now it was time to speak of the old days and that visit to Andreas' camp before the ambush. 'Andreas was so angry with me for coming alone and we rowed. I left at first light but the "black cattle", as we called the enemy, were coming up the hill and I hid. I didn't know there were two groups. Andreas's band got the worst of the attack and fled, but the second group caught the enemy by surprise. It was a shoot out and men were wounded in the crossfire. One of them was their leader, Panayotis.'

Yolanda paused. 'I knew who he was and what he meant to you. I was with him and made him comfortable. There was no hope of moving him so I sat with him and tried to speak a little English and he had good Greek. He knew I was your friend. "How is she?" he asked. "Penny?" I told him you were safe with friends. "Ah, Ike and Katrina, I have stayed there, in the hole near Clarence . . . " he said. He was delirious, in and out of consciousness, but suddenly he woke and clutched my hand. "Tell Penny, Bruce's box with Clarence . . ." That is what he said, but it made no sense. He was beginning to struggle for breath and I made him comfortable. He died with your name on his lips, as I pray Andreas died knowing he was in my heart for ever.'

Penny gripped her chair and then put her hands to her head. 'Thank you. I didn't know where he died or that he was killed until I got home to Britain. Though I had a feeling there would never be any future for us.'

'I left the flowers because I knew you would have wanted me to do this. It was the least we could do. He was a good man, full of life, a brave leader. His kind will never be forgotten here.'

'But I forgot him. I was so angry and mixed up. I didn't want
to think about him. I didn't even know he was buried here. I
am so ashamed, but what did he mean about Clarence? Are you
sure that's what he said?'

Yolanda nodded. 'I wrote it down so I would never forget in
case you returned. It's not a name we know, not a saint's name.'

'It was my uncle's name, my mother's oldest brother. He was
round and jolly and spent his life on horseback. His skin was
like creased leather. Good Lord! He meant the olive tree.
Clarence, the old olive tree. I was thinking about that only the
other day.'

Penny was not making any sense as she stood up. 'When I
lived with Ike and Katrina, there was this huge old tree with a
face in its bark. I called it Clarence. Bruce and I . . . He left a
box?' She turned to Yolanda. 'Could it possibly be there after
sixty years? I've no idea where the house was.'

'I do. Ike's house was burned to the ground like all the others
in the district when the enemy retreated into Chania, before the
end. They scorched all the surrounding villages so the partisans
couldn't find refuge there, but I can take you there tomorrow.
You will stay here tonight, no point in going back. We have a
phone: you can ring your niece. Tell her to come back too so
we can all go and see what may be hiding there.'

Penny was too tired to protest. She was lost in thought for
her lover.

'I never got to say goodbye to him and now you tell me these
things. It's hard to take all this in. We're two of a kind, you and
I, our lives so entwined by all these terrible things.'

'And good things, too. We had some wonderful parties.
Come, it's late and tomorrow we'll rise early. Sarika will drive
us to where I think you need to go and we'll take a spade, just
in case. He said a box – I'm sure something will be there still.'

It was hard for Yolanda to sleep with a lifetime of news spinning round in her head. Penny had taken the account of Bruce's

death without tears. She always did put a brave face on her sorrow. To have Penny back in her life was such an unexpected gift. She was right, they were two of a kind, having been through so much together and apart.

She hadn't admitted to the real reason she had gone in search of Andreas or Penny in Chania, and all that followed. To do that she must face one of her own dark secrets in the fight for survival, one only Andreas knew. She'd not mentioned Stavros or those last terrible months of occupation.

September 1944

The bitterness grew in Yolanda's heart from exhaustion and fury as she tried to put back the destruction of the farm and the crops. Clearing debris was backbreaking with little help. They repaired the stone house as best they could and she filled the room with flowers to take away the smell of those thieves and looters.

Andreas came and went, and the coolness between them grew. She wanted to reach out to him but, surrounded by comrades in arms, he was too busy to take much notice of her signals. The *andartes* also came and went for fresh supplies of clothing and food but it was dangerous for any of them to be seen out in the open now.

There were rewards of big bags of rice for information leading to the capture of Kapetan Cyclops and his bandits. There was such hunger, and villagers might be tempted.

The late summer heat lingered, crops withered early, but Yolanda dug deep into her reserves of grief and determination to keep them fed and watered, often carrying water on her back if they were in an arid rocky hideout.

She felt she was being punished for doubting the loyalty of one of Andreas' men and for bringing the enemy to their door to search for her.

Now she kept her own counsel as Stavros returned from Chania. He looked surprised to see her, eyeing her as if she was a bad smell. In turn, she stood, arms folded, hardly acknowledging his heroic return. But she did question him about the fate of the Jews and prisoners in Agia.

He shrugged. 'They went away in trucks. I was lucky to escape. A guard was bribed and, when they were loading us up, he pulled me out of sight.'

Yolanda was not convinced. Why had he come back? Was he biding his time before betraying them? It had happened before, but to prove it was another matter. He knew who she was. Had he betrayed her too? Would the German soldiers come back for her? It felt as if her whole world were falling apart, wondering just who she could trust and who was watching their comings and goings.

Then one morning two scruffy men appeared at the door begging for food; miserable, filthy, foreign strangers. She'd been warned about deserters and she was glad Adonis and Dimitra were now back home so she was not alone with them.

'We are soldiers . . . Germany is finished, no good . . . we will fight with you now,' they stuttered.

Yolanda was careful to give nothing away. She fed them, as was the custom when strangers came to the door, sat them down with the last of the rough wine. One boy was from Yugoslavia, the other from Romania, or so they said. They wanted to go home. 'We make no more war with friends.'

The *andartes* had gathered up a few genuine deserters over the past months. They were useful with information and, of course, speaking German. They were known to the loyal policemen, who would use them to check out any other deserters. This way they'd picked up spies posing as deserters and shot them.

Adonis wasn't fit to take them up to a rendezvous to pass them over so Yolanda said she would run, herself, to Andreas' camp and warn them to expect new arrivals. They wouldn't be allowed near their base camp.

It was another hard trek, making the usual detours and false doglegs just in case she was being followed. It was noon by the time she found Andreas, sitting round a fire, roasting hares.

'I don't know what to do with them,' she explained. 'They say they want to fight. They have very little Greek.'

'Come sit, eat. You did right to warn us. Take them to the old cave on the high rocks and we'll check them out there. Can you do this? Are you strong enough?'

It was the first time her husband had enquired after her health, the first time he'd shown appreciation of all her efforts. She sped back downhill with wings on her feet and, under cover of darkness, with the shepherd Taki pointing a rifle behind them, she escorted them back up to the cliff top. The strangers, cheered by wine and cheese, whistled and chattered along the track, unconcerned about being guarded.

Andreas, Stavros and two other men were waiting to greet them with slaps on the back. 'You are good men, come join us.' They'd done this many times before.

Yolanda was happy to be spending the night with her husband, alone for the first time in weeks. That vixen Anna, who'd ogled him in her kitchen, had disgraced herself by running off with one of his men, against all the rules and custom. They would be hunted down and punished. Yolanda slept with Andreas under his blanket and he reached out for her with desire, making her weep with relief to feel wanted again.

Stavros offered to keep guard on the two deserters as they slept in the cave under guard. A lookout sat up all night watching for any movement that might mean betrayal, but there was none.

In the morning a strange thing happened. The two men emerged silent and sullen, not wanting to talk, gabbling among themselves in German, thinking no one else would understand them. 'We go back now, no stay here. It is dangerous . . .' They looked frightened.

Andreas, sensing something had altered, had them tied up.

'You've seen our faces, you've seen this place. We can't let you go now. Stavros, what did you tell them?'

He shrugged. 'They are spies. They should be shot.'

'Why?' Yolanda snapped. 'Why do you say that?' She sensed they were just two lost boys in need of direction.

'You can't trust men who desert their units. They can turn coat again.' He was staring at the strangers with contempt.

Then one of the men screamed, 'No kill, no kill . . . kill him. He is spy, he is bad man. I see him. You are all spies come to trap us, to kill us . . .' He was shaking with terror. 'He come and tell us go back or he will kill us. We are traitors to the Reich, he said.'

Stavros pulled out his gun to shoot the boy but Andreas stayed his arm. 'Why is he saying this? He has never met you before, or has he?'

'He speaks good German,' the other boy shouted. 'He is German spy. You are all his friends. You are spies.'

Stavros wrenched his arm free and shot the boy, and then turned his gun on Andreas for a second. 'They lie, these peasants always lie to save their skins. They talk rubbish. I am one of you. Have I not served you well?'

Yolanda rushed to the injured man to stem the blood flowing from his chest. 'What did I tell you, Andreas? The boy is speaking the truth. Can't you see he threatened them? They are terrified.'

'Don't listen to a Jew, they lie. She should be with the rest of her kind. She knows nothing.'

'Don't speak of my wife like that. It was you who told me she was dead. Why did you escape that hellhole and no one else did, unless . . .'

Stavros pointed the gun again at Andreas. The other men stood in shock, fishing for their knives. 'You are making a big mistake. It is I who have kept you safe all these months. If it was not for me giving false information, you would be dead long ago. I admire your stand for freedom.' Stavros stepped back, ready to spray his bullets across the men. 'I am no traitor. I have always worked for the freedom of the Greek national people. Can't you see the threat coming? The communists are taking over, allies of Russia are all around us. We nationalists must stick together.'

'So it was you I saw, signalling to the patrol, the day Panayotis died,' Yolanda shouted.

'I give them a little and take a lot. You have to understand, it is for the best.'

Andreas lurched forward. 'How could I have been such an idiot? No, it was you who made me doubt my wife's good instinct, you insulted her people. Was it you who sent the beasts to our door, ransacked our home and desecrated our land. *Why?*'

Stavros backed again and snarled like a cornered rat. 'Why, you stupid fools? You can't beat the might of the master race. You island fools think you can resist without punishment, hide English soldiers without punishment, kill good men before they even land without punishment, and then you shelter these scum of the earth, deserters, give them food and arms against their own comrades. What I do is for the good of the Greek nation. I will not see our country brought down by Russian bears. I was keeping you all safe. You have to understand that.' He was waving the gun in Andreas' face.

Andreas stood firm, his cheeks twitching with rage. 'What I see are good men dead because of you, men tortured, deported, executed. We will take you before the court. We do not shoot before we are sure of our facts.' Andreas stood firm. 'Give me your gun.'

Stavros spat on the ground, then dropped the pistol. 'Do what you like, you are all dead men. It is only a matter of time before they come for you. They know exactly where you are – the tracks to base camp are easy to search – and when they find you they'll take her and send her to the death camps with all the rest.'

Yolanda heard all this as she finished the tourniquet round the boy's shoulder. The shot had missed his lungs and heart. He would live, but her own anger erupted into a blaze of fury at all the treachery of this loud-mouthed fascist. She saw his pistol, dropped on the ground. Kneeling up from her crouched position, she grabbed it, as if to finish off a mad dog, and shot Stavros in each leg, one bullet for each parent.

He staggered backwards in shock. 'Stop that witch!' He was edging slowly towards the rocks as his legs collapsed under him, kneeling as if in prayer. No one spoke, no one helped him as he shuffled back from Yolanda's gun, losing his balance, toppling backwards to the edge of the rock face. He looked down and then up in horror. Yolanda stood above him.

'What are you waiting for?' she screamed. His face was filled with horror at the chasm below him and the look of revenge on her face as she nudged him with his own gun. He was helpless, crippled by pain but he cried out, 'Stop her madness!'

The men closed in on him, forcing him back until he keeled over the edge, his scream echoing around the rocks. Then there was silence.

Yolanda allowed herself a brief smile as she threw down the gun. 'What? Did you think I'd wait for him to talk himself out of this? His kind gave my family no quarter. Take me home, Andreas.'

2001

'How did I do that to a man in cold blood? I think his bones are out there still, unburied and unmourned. I forgot my vows, Penny. I did what I did and I've wondered all my life whether I did right. My work was to save lives, not to takeany.'

They were walking across the fields, checking the young stock as she told her secret, hidden for so long.

'It was the uniform and the brainwashing that created such monsters,' Penny replied. 'I hope I'd have had the courage to do the same.'

'But what if he wasn't a traitor but just a nationalist? Did I tell you that he recognized you from that wedding photo? He kept asking questions about you.'

Penny nodded. 'He was a fascist when I met him, an ardent convert. We went out together for a little time in Athens but I couldn't stand his views. I think he was a menace. I did catch a glimpse of him but I don't think he recognized me then. I ran away to warn Bruce but no one believed me either. I'm glad you told me. I did wonder what happened to him. How did Andreas react to being betrayed?'

'He was shocked and he looked at me with different eyes after that, with respect. They all looked at me with respect,' Yolanda chuckled. 'Especially when I had a knife in my hand.' Her dark eyes sparkled at the retelling of such a drama. 'We began again and it was good between us.'

'Did they come for him?'

'No, of course not, we were never troubled again. The enemy were too busy saving their own skins. But after the war there were recriminations and many partisans were executed by makeshift courts. We had such a short time in peace.

'Andreas went back to the Red Cross and helped with its relief programmes. I never nursed again. How could I when I'd killed a man? But I worked with him, distributing food aid. The Red Cross ships came into the harbour late in '44. They saved many lives with food shelters and medical supplies.

'When I think about that time now, I feel good that I fought back. I didn't stand back and leave it to others to do the dirty work,' she sighed. 'That's what I think now but it's not what I felt then. Time changes everything.'

It was strange waking up in Sarika's villa, with its cool marbled tiles, pretty white-lace cotton drapes, heavy dark furniture and the icon of the Virgin and Child in the corner. I could hear the chatter outside from daybreak. Everyone makes the most of the cool summer morning in Crete.

I lay back, thinking how easily I could've gone home without ever knowing Yolanda was alive. It felt like a dream, and the fact she'd sat with Bruce until the end was a such a comfort to know. If I'd not gone to the cemetery and seen the grave, or to the synagogue . . . It didn't bear thinking about, and now we were going to find old Clarence. I'd thought about the tree only a few days before, wondering if it'd gone for firewood by now.

I had decided in the small hours to change my scheduled flight, put it back for a week. Lois wouldn't mind. There was only the dog to return to and he was safe with the kennels.

How could I leave when we're just getting to know each other again? Life had been tough for my friend, widowed young, but there was a bond between her and her family, with respect for each other. Women were always at the centre of such tight knit Greek families, in the background, but holding real power, and Sarika was growing just the same with her own children.

Nothing was too much trouble for my comfort: how rich a welcome I'd been given. I could hear their loud voices echoing around Sarika's house as I sat on the balcony of my bedroom, staring out at the grandeur of their hillside surroundings and Yolanda's beautiful garden next door. I heard the tinkle of the sheep bells on the wind and drank in the morning scents on the air.

As I dressed I wondered just what this day would bring. I must ask Lois to pack my suitcase when she called later.

We ate a breakfast of white figs and fresh yogurt with coffee, and when Lois and Alex arrived I told them my change of plan. This led to a flurry of phone calls and Mack promised to set all the new arrangements in motion for me. We set off in convoy down the track, winding down a side lane, cutting across the hills until I totally lost my bearings. Then after fifteen minutes we came to the old villa, which had scaffolding all round it.

'They say a Greek footballer has bought it for his family,' said Sarika.

'No, it is a politician,' argued Yolanda. 'Only they have the money.'

'Everything's changed since we're in Europe, grants, new roads, tourism, so many concrete lorries on the road. Where will it end?' Sarika shouted in perfect English.

'What happened to Ike and Katrina?' I asked.

'They went back to America. It was hard after the war and people took sides. Ike took his family back and rented out the land. Then the plants climbed over the house to strangle it,' Yolanda said.

We parked round the back. No one was working on site,

and, apart from the scaffolding, nothing had changed. I could feel myself tensing up. Would the old olive tree still be standing? There were wire fences everywhere. The land was partitioned into sections, some cleared with sheep grazing, others wild and left to run riot, but the olive grove looked as it always had, pruned, tended and the blossom still on the branches.

'Can we go in without permission?' I asked.

'Poof! No one here to see us,' Yolanda dismissed with a wave of her hand. 'Now where is this tree you give name to? You English are so sentimental . . .'

Lois was laughing. 'She still drives a car called Mabel, won't change it for a new model.'

'When Mabel retires so will I. She's been a good friend.' I found my pace quickening, trying to recall how far from the house I used to sit with the children for a peck of peace in that noisy household. Then I recalled how we hid Bluey and his band of brothers not far from the tree.

'There was an ancient chamber, a hole in the ground somewhere close to the tree, I'm sure.'

Alex was racing round. 'Is this it?' He was pointing to a squat trunk, the size of a beer barrel, with swirling bark. 'It's the fattest one, Aunt Pen.'

I stood eyeing it up. 'So it is. I didn't think it could last so long.'

'The olive is the most ancient of trees. They can last for thousands of years. It has one deep root sunk into the earth but to fruit well they must be pruned hard, and this one has, but I see no face in it,' Yolanda laughed.

'I sat here many times and thought of home far away, and it was here that Bruce and I, we talked, and you know . . . But a box? Where would you hide a box? The ground is solid as rock, years of soil and leaves. I don't think we'll find anything here,' I sighed. 'Tell Lois what Bruce said to you.'

Yolanda repeated the story of the box and Clarence, and

something about a hole. 'He was very confused but he called your name. Why are you smiling at such sad things?' she said.

'I was thinking of Bluey and the boys, hiding in the chamber. What if he meant the hole *near* Clarence, the escape hole? When patrols came by, the escapers ran for the hole in the olive grove. It was where Ike hid his oil and grain; no one knew it was there. They said it was haunted by ancient spirits. It was the perfect hiding place. It's not far from here.'

'Is this an ancient burial site?' Lois asked, but no one answered. 'If there is one burial chamber there will be others. How exciting.'

'Oh, don't say that,' Sarika replied. 'No one wants to find such stuff on their land. The government will want to buy the land and dig on it.'

'Careful,' I shouted. 'If the entrance is loosely covered, one false step and we'll be thrown in.'

'Look,' Alex was racing ahead, 'there's a fenced-off bit here. Can I take photos?'

There was a rectangle of barbed wire protecting the entrance. Someone didn't want their flocks crippled or trapped.

Lois grabbed my arm. 'You be careful now. I don't want any broken pelvises.'

'It's buried treasure, Mummy, like Indiana Jones,' said Alex excitedly.

Sarika pulled away the wire, inspected the thick grasses. 'This looks like it, but it is dangerous for old bones. We mustn't wake the spirits,' she said, crossing herself.

'There weren't any spirits sixty years ago, unless you mean all the raki the boys swallowed. We hid them down here, and Bruce too, once.'

'I hope you're right,' Lois smiled as she and Sarika made to pull away the scrub. They lowered themselves down gingerly and then their voices came echoing up. 'It's amazing, just slabs of stone built on top of each other. Nothing here but rubbish and creepy crawlies, and it smells fusty. If we hold your hands you can come down, but no fancy tricks. We could do with a torch.'

'There's a cigarette lighter in the car,' Sarika yelled.

'I'll get it.' Alex was off like a hare back to the truck. I watched him with envy. Once I had raced down here, back and forth, hauling sacks, now I was putting one foot slowly in front of the other, willing myself not to fall in head first. It was dark but there was a gap of stone slab above us letting in a little light. It was as cold as a fridge. These Minoans built well.

'I can't see any boxes,' said Lois as Sarika flicked the lighter on and off into the crevices. 'Someone cleared this out years ago.'

My heart sank with disappointment. What was I expecting to find here? A sign saying 'X marks the spot'? A box would have been checked out years ago and I'd never know what Bruce had wanted me to find.

'Go round the walls slowly,' Yolanda yelled down to us. 'It's just that I remember reading in the newspaper how a shepherd found a package hidden in the stone walls near his hut, documents left by a soldier. I think they found who they belonged to and sent them back to New Zealand. He came back to thank them with his family.'

Sarika kept up the search but the slabs were solid. No one could stick anything into them. *Where did you leave it, Bruce?* I was praying.

'Try the steps,' Lois suggested. They bent down and shone the light among the leaves and rubbish accumulated there. Suddenly: 'Look! There's something under there in the corner.'

We all held our breaths as they ferreted around the corner of the step. 'It's only an old tin, not a box, a very rusty cigarette tin,' Lois announced.

'Let's take it up,' I croaked, hardly daring to hope this was it.

Sarika climbed out first, helped me out, and then Lois came up with her treasure. She held it out for us to examine. It was rusted, the size of a bully-beef tin, battered enough to be what we were looking for. Alex photographed it and all of us standing round looking dazed and pleased.

'It was tucked out of sight. It looks like rubbish to me but it won't open here,' Lois said, taking control of us, stepping up to the mark as she'd done so many times. I felt so proud of her.

'Thank you, thank you. It looks exactly what a man might carry on him. Light and easy to hide, but who knows what's inside?' I was trying to sound casual. 'I don't suppose it's anything special.'

'Penny,' Yolanda was clutching my arm, 'he told me with his last breath to find it. It is for you. We will open it. Be patient, the boys will help us.'

It was hard to contain my emotion. I was impatient, curious and nervous. I didn't deserve such good fortune. I didn't deserve respect. I wasn't worthy of him. All my life I had shut out this time entirely, because I knew I must face the truth of everything, not pick and choose the bits that pleased me.

Yolanda had shared her terrible secret of how she had found the strength to destroy the threat to her future. By executing Stavros, she'd found inner respect, discovered a part of herself she'd not known was there in her 'eye for an eye' revenge.

I had a secret too, one I could share with no one but my own conscience, a secret that had tormented me all my adult life. Must I open that rusty tin hidden in the deepest recesses of my heart before I was worthy of opening the real one?

June 1944

Penny wandered through the streets with Brecht, buying the bare minimum, not wanting him to spend any more of his pay on her: a meal, a few items of essential clothing; that was the extent of her debt to him. But then sporadic gunfire broke out and she had nowhere to stay. She felt so feeble, hardly able to put one foot in front of the other without help. Her limbs were disobedient to her commands as she kept seeing herself flung overboard into the water, and the screams of the dead roared in her ears.

She'd recognized shock many times in others, now she must accept it in herself. She needed rest and shelter, and when Brecht booked himself a double room in a hotel, she'd no will left to refuse to join him there.

It was as if the whole day was leading to the moment when this would happen and for that a debt must be repaid. She'd no energy to protest, to be proud and English about it all. She felt nothing but the urge to sleep away the rest of her life in oblivion.

The next morning she woke alone in the bed. No one had shared it with her. His clothes were on the chair and it was clear he'd slept on the floor. She heard him in the bathroom as she buried her face into the pillow. She didn't want to see his body. It would be tanned, lean and muscled. It would be in keeping with the rest of him, handsome and strong, things she'd noticed about him from the first time they had met. She wondered how well his wound had healed.

He'd made no demands on her and she was grateful that he respected her enough not to claim his due, but it would come, as sure as night follows day, and she would have to allow him to access her body and take from it what he willed.

Brecht dressed and left to check out the breakfast room, leaving her alone to wash and dress. She'd still not uncoiled her hair. It smelled of the sea, oil, stiff with salt, and she'd slept with it pinned tight around her head. It reminded her of where she'd been and who was left under the sea, steeling her resolve, protecting her.

He came back with fresh rolls and fruit. 'Where shall we go today, into the hills or to the coast?'

'This isn't a holiday,' she replied.

'It is for me. Soon I leave Athens. You will find work but first you must rest. You are not fit yet. Did you sleep last night?'

She nodded and picked at her food.

They spent the day out of the city, strolling around, and visited the Archaeological Museum to escape the heat of the day. As they walked around the exhibits, he talked of his visit to Knossos and the excavations. 'Nothing is harmed, everything is as it was.'

She couldn't bear to listen. He was polite, respectful and oh, so cunning, giving her what she really needed: clothes, food, intelligent conversation, pretending that there was no war between them. He was biding his time, waiting for the moment. There was an organ recital in a church still standing, a young German organist playing Bach's Toccata and Fugue in D minor. They sat among the officers listening to the intensity of the soaring music. If she closed her eyes she could be in Gloucester Cathedral.

She slept alone that night, and the night after. He found a train to the coast and an open beach cleared of mines where he swam while she sat watching him racing down into the water. His body was beautiful but the ugly scar puckered his thigh. She had nursed that wound, fingered his leg, taken his pulse, bathed his limbs. She felt a pull inside her she'd not felt before, not since her time alone with Bruce, as if something were coming alive within her, an instinct she didn't want to disturb. That night she hardly slept for the ache, and the fear she was being watched, the restless tossing and turning, the images of his body diving into the sea, the heat of the bedroom, the whirr of the ceiling fan. She felt her mind's resolve spinning out of control.

He was always staring at her, his head tilted to one side when she spoke, the flashing warmth in those iris-blue eyes, and there was a scent on him too, of youth and vigour, a dangerous aroma when she'd been starved of comfort for so long.

How could she look with lust on the enemy? Why was she assessing his broad shoulders and slim hips, the solid muscle of his thighs? What would it be like to be crushed between them?

He was aroused by her, she could sniff it like smoke on the breeze, and it terrified her that there was such unspoken fire growing between them.

'Perhaps you'd prefer to spend today by yourself?' he offered as they sat having real coffee in the square. 'Do be careful, there are parts of the city now where it's not safe for girls or strangers.'

'I'm not a girl and I'm not a stranger. I lived here for years. I worked here. This is my city,' she snapped.

'Not any more, this is a jungle. You could visit your old School of Archaeology?'

Penny shook her head. 'No, too many memories. What are your plans?' She realized suddenly she didn't want him to leave her.

'Nothing much. I have letters to write. It's been such a long time since I saw my family, I am worried.' He told her about Katerina and her accident. She told him about Evadne and Zander and her father's visit. She told him how she ran away to

Athens to get out of Mother's plans for a debutante season and how she'd defied them in staying on in Athens, living a life she could never have achieved at home.

He laughed. 'I ran away too but into the army to get away from my father's demands that I run the estate and become a farmer.' He sighed and looked at her, saying, 'Perhaps a farmer would've been a better choice?'

She did not reply but stared out at the buildings still intact and the bustle of the city.

They walked, and talked all day on anything but Crete and the war. Each day grew closer to the end of his leave. He told her of his decision to go back into active service and the uncertainty of his future, and suddenly she felt afraid for him. Suddenly she knew she cared what happened to Brecht and it terrified her.

That night they ate at Zonar's, as she had so many times before the war, and walked back to the hotel, side by side, talking about excavations and technical drawing, museums and all their mutual interests, and as they drew closer to the hotel she suddenly knew he was not going to ask for payment in kind. He wouldn't demand anything other than her company because deep down he was as afraid as she was of the feelings growing between them. This was territory neither of them had trodden before and there were hidden minefields.

That night she couldn't stand the itchiness in her scalp any longer. 'I must wash my hair . . .' but hard as she tried to soap off the lather, it wouldn't come clean.

'You need something stronger. I'll ask at reception.' Brecht came back with a bottle of detergent.

'It looks like turps,' she cried. 'I shall have to cut all my hair off.'

'Over my dead body,' he said. 'Here, let me help you. Dip your head in the sink and I'll rinse it off for you. I used to do this for my little sister.'

She ducked her head down and let him soap it again and rub the lather slowly around her head, rinsing it. 'Does it squeak yet?' he asked.

'I think so,' she replied, searching blindly for a towel with soap in her eyes. Then she wrapped her hair in the towel.

'You need a comb . . . we didn't buy one?'

'It will have to dry out.'

'My mother used to section off each side and comb it out. Katerina used to scream. She has hair like you, golden silk.'

Slowly he untangled the strands until it fell down straight. 'You dyed it, I see.'

'I had my reasons.'

'I know, blonde Cretans are thin on the ground.'

Penny turned round and unwrapped the towel to reveal her nakedness. 'Is this what you really want from me?' She had to know.

'No, it is not,' he croaked, turning away. 'I won't take what's not given freely. There's been enough of that. I want no payment from you. Who do you take me for?' he snapped, angered and shocked by her action.

'You are a man with needs. It will have been a long time without a clean woman. You bought me everything I have, fed me, sheltered me. How else can I pay you back?' she replied.

'I will find another room,' he said, gathering up his clothes in a hurry.

'Don't leave me. I have no other currency to give you. I'm sorry,' she cried, shocked by her own brazen need of him now.

He paused at the door, turning round. 'I won't touch you even though I find you beautiful and brave and the most wonderful woman I've ever desired. I'd never dishonour you like that. I was brought up to respect women.' He sighed. 'It is late and you are tired. Sleep and I will sit in the chair again.'

'I'm cold, my hair is wet – how can I sleep?' She searched his face, seeing the hurt as he tried to look away from her body.

Without thinking what she was doing, she walked towards him and touched his face, his cheekbones, the curve of his jaw as she felt her breath quicken. 'Brecht . . . I don't even know your Christian name . . .'

'Rainer,' he said. 'I thought you'd never ask that of me . . . I've called you Penelope in my mind for many years.' He was standing over her now. 'Thank you for your offer but I can't do this if . . . you fill my thoughts but . . .' He was looking at her with such longing, like a man who is in love with a woman. She felt a surge of desire rising from her limbs, from her arms, her heart thudding like nothing she'd ever felt before. She could no longer deny such feeling.

She took his hand and sat on the bed. 'I have no experience of this.'

'All the more reason why I should leave now,' he said, pulling away from her.

'No, please stay. I need you. I want to thank you. You saved my life, saved me so many times, why I don't know. Why me?' The tears began to flow and with them such a desire to be held and comforted, to be kissed, and when she found his lips nothing mattered but the taste of wine on them.

He held her and his lips touched her throat, her ears, giving her a jolt of desire. His breath warmed her as he whispered into her ear. His hands felt for her tiny breasts, cupping them as if they were precious china. She smelled the spicy soap on his skin as she buried her face in his chest. They fell down and she let his hands slowly explore her body, stroking her, soothing her loneliness. He fingered her, gently waiting until she responded; the ache inside growing into such a powerful surge of longing and excitement. He slowly slid his body so close to hers and there was no stopping their bodies joining together.

In those never-to-be-forgotten moments when his tenderness met her passion, she knew the power of being a woman.

Her body was satisfied even if her mind was emptied of all consequences of this seduction.

In this moment Bruce was forgotten, her pain deadened. She knew in her heart that this had always been going to happen the moment she stepped into the hotel room, but not as she expected in sullen passive resignation. Without her signals and persuasion Rainer wouldn't have forced himself upon her. This was her doing and hers only.

They didn't leave the hotel the next day but lay in a cocoon of cotton sheets, exploring their bodies, finding the pleasure places she hadn't known existed, giving and receiving. Here there was no war, no uniforms, no past or future, just the sensual delights of lovemaking. She was drunk with sensations, nakedness, relaxing in a far-off place where nothing mattered but the now.

2001

I had sat many nights reliving these memories. Logic accused me of sleeping with the enemy, giving into base instincts, betraying Bruce's memory. When his leave was over, Rainer left me, promising we would be together one day when the war was over, and I believed him. I waited for the letter that never came.

That was when I woke up to the cold reality of this brief wartime affair. I cut off my hair as was done to all female collaborators, claiming it was infested. I applied to become a nurse but no one wanted me. I was destitute and begged for help from the Swiss embassy, which sheltered me and eventually shipped me back home where I collapsed. My father had died and Bruce was dead.

Evadne told me the news one day as we walked through the rose garden. By then I was a living ghost with no feelings or tears, drifting in a nothingness state like a rudderless boat in a sea haar. I don't care to recall much of that dark place.

Now, sitting under the olive tree, I felt a strange sense of calm as if waking from a long dream with a sigh. I wasn't a mad woman. My lips would stay sealed. There are some things so private you can never share them. You carry them alone all your life. Suddenly I understood that grief is a lonely journey but sometimes needs a physical outlet. Ours was a passionate coming-together. I was not coerced. I sought my comfort and gave it too. There was tenderness in our passion, not degradation.

He too was wounded by his time on the island. Rainer was my crime and my punishment, for I have thought of him all my life, wondering if he survived and found his own form of forgiveness. It's hard to be in love when you're on opposite sides. We were two of a kind, and perhaps in another age, had we found each other, who knows? Love has its own landscape and it was in Athens that ours blossomed and withered. That was all.

There comes a moment in your life when you can forgive yourself for your weakness. It came for me when I realized there was more to me than two weeks in Athens with Rainer Brecht. I could forgive myself for not being the perfect upright nurse. I sleepwalked into an affair, exhausted, fragile, in need of protection. The shell I'd grown round myself was torn away, exposed by war. I could've died, but didn't, because of him. I was alive when so many were not. This had to serve some purpose.

I took flight from all of the memories by good works, to compensate, to pay back, to punish myself, even. I felt I didn't deserve a normal family life. I had given into baser instincts. I had let my self-imposed standards down. Yet I was human, no better or worse than others. What happened between Rainer and me wasn't a tawdry affair. It was beautiful and loving, short-lived, and I would not deny it ever again.

Suddenly I felt cleansed. I'd been given the chance of reconciliation in coming back here and the renewal of friendship. I'd been given a gift to go back and see my younger self as others might see me.

I was not always faithless, impatient, childless, 'flaky', as Lois calls people sometimes. The life I had found in Africa was useful and gave me a sense of proportion, for who cannot see such poverty and need, and not despise the current rat race? So no more agonizing, enjoy these precious days left.

It was Lois and Alex's last night and I was staying on. Sarika insisted everyone came for a final barbecue to celebrate the reunion and finding Bruce's tin. We hadn't worked out how to open it safely, having even soaked it in olive oil to release the rust, but the lid was fixed solid.

It was a warm night and the full scents of the thyme and rosemary and mountain herbs filled the air. A table was spread under the pergola, lit with citronella candles. Lois arrived and Mack, all with long sleeves and laced with insect repellent. Across the valley the flickering lights of the villages below us made a marvellous backdrop. Somewhere out beyond lay the winedark sea of Crete.

The women had cooked up a feast of dishes: pork steaks sizzling on the grill, long village sausages, lamb pieces, baskets of thick bread, jugs of oak-barrelled village wine, salads, a chicken and rice pilafi and then ice creams and fruit; enough food to feed an army. I did my best to do it justice and Alex mopped up what I was leaving so as not to offend.

The music was playing in the background, the music of Crete, and the young ones got up to dance the *pentozali* steps and try the faster dances. Yolanda and I made a valiant attempt to join in but ended up just swaying in time to the rhythms.

Just for one night our families were joined together, laughing, joking, toasting each other, '*Yamas*'. Their generosity knew no bounds, but why be surprised? Had I not received such a welcome in the midst of danger and starvation?

It was Sarika's husband who brought me the little tin. 'We have to cut it, I'm afraid, with a can opener. It should be airtight after all these years. Or will you keep it as it is?'

I didn't hesitate. 'Bruce left it for safekeeping for some reason. I think we should open it and I am curious. Let's do it now,' I said, feeling at peace with myself. Whatever it contained would be a link stretching over the years to me, a precious gift. 'Just one thing,' I called out to him. 'I'd like to open it in private, if that's OK?'

'Of course,' he smiled, his dark features, so typical of Cretan

mountain men, crinkling into a smile. 'My uncle remembers
Panayotis in the war. He said he was a brave *palliakari*.'

This was a compliment indeed, linking him to so many brave
men and women who fought so we could enjoy the freedoms
tonight: freedom to complain, to demonstrate or strike, to live
in our cultures without oppression. Long may it continue, I
prayed.

He beckoned me across into the workshop and his bench. 'I've
done it, here, take it.' He'd peeled it back like a sardine can.

Clutching the tin, I made for a quiet corner to open it further,
my heart thudding with excitement. In touching the contents,
I would touch a little of Bruce. Crammed inside the tin, doubled
up, was a slim notebook. As I eased it out I saw it was a tiny
diary with flimsy pages stuck together. It must be Bruce's notebook of his adventures on the island.

My hands trembled, not wanting to tear anything. The pages
were covered in scribbles and little sketches. Bruce had kept a
diary, strictly against the rules, of course. There were dates
scribbled on the top but I would need a magnifying glass to read
the sentences. How frustrating, not to hear him reach out to me
over the years, listen to his accent in my head, but at the back
there was one entry in darker pencil, just about legible. This
would have to do for the moment.

15 March 1944. Sitting in this bloody burial chamber again,
wondering if it's safe to pop my head over the parapet and head
back south. Good to see my girl in Chania. She takes such risks,
I worry she might be betrayed. Now waiting for wireless orders.
Glad P. is safe where she is with N. for the moment. I never
wanted ties with this job but she's so much part of my life here,
knowing she's doing her bit too gives me strength. Thought it
too risky to having feelings but it's the opposite. When all this is
over, I'll buy her a ring.

We fight for the right to have homes and families, to be safe from bully boys with guns, stealing what was never theirs. I'm fighting to get home and start again with the one girl I know will make me happy into my old age. She is so full of surprises. Never saw myself as one of the pipe and slippers brigade, but you can get mighty sick of eating grass and snails, smelling like a sewer pipe. Roll on home comforts one day.

What is risky is carrying this around with me, too many names and places so it can stay here tucked in the can in case it rains in. God how it can rain here . . .

The pages were blank after that, but slipped inside was a crumpled photograph. It was the one of Yolanda and me taken at the wedding. We look young and happy. I could hardly see for the tears in my eyes. Oh, Bruce, what might've been between us had you lived? Now I'll never know, but to have this gift was a comfort of sorts. I clutched it tight while the healing tears flowed.

So you loved me as I once loved you. In reading these pages there's a chance to close the chapter on that unlived life we'd never had together. I'm glad you never knew how I betrayed you, but no more of that, . . .

Tonight was for celebrating, dancing and friendship, and the years left to Yolanda and me to make up for lost time.

There was no shame in keeping my own counsel. My secrets were my own to live with, not burden others. I made good use of our time here, made my pilgrimage, paid my respects to the dead, and now I must rejoin the living, savour the rich aromas of friendship renewed.

I watched Lois, Alex and Mack attempting to dance to the film music from *Zorba the Greek*. All of us had been given a new lease of life by this visit, I mused, as I sat clutching the diary, smiling, knowing those chains of shame, fettering me to the past, were loosening. Now I felt free, free at last to return home to this special island.

I may have lost my lover but I'd found again a place that

would always be part of my heart. In the safety of Stokencourt, I would read Bruce's diary and cherish his memory. Perhaps it was worthy of donating to some military archive when I was no longer around. But time now to look to the present and future. There's always some pressing battle to face when you are old and the clock is ticking away.

I could see a table full of Cretan pastries to savour, music and all the shadowing colours of Crete. It was going to be a long and noisy night, but it was so good to be alive to enjoy it, I smiled as I made my way back to the dancing.

Chania Airport, 2001

Rainer joined the queue for the shuttle bus out to the tarmac landing strip and the early morning flight to Athens. He climbed up the stairs, pausing to take one last lingering look at the hills, feeling the heat and scents already building up. It was time to return north to an empty house, correspondence and his grey life. He would miss the sunshine and the vibrant busyness of his holiday.

The seat next to him was unoccupied, but to his surprise he was sitting across from the mother and boy whom he seemed to have been following all around the island on his jaunts. He sprang up to help them secure their hand luggage in the locker and she turned to thank him. The boy was soon plugged into his game console.

'All good things end. You are returning too?' he asked politely. 'I think you were on the ferry out?'

She nodded. 'Yes, it is over too quickly. Do you come to Crete every year? So many do?'

'No, just once before. It is very beautiful. Pardon me for asking but your mother is not returning with you?'

She smiled. 'Oh, you mean my aunt, my great-aunt, actually. No, she decided to stay on, changed her flight at the last minute. She found an old friend . . .'

'That is good. But she lives with you?'

'Oh, no,' she laughed. 'Heavens, Aunt Pen lives in the

Cotswolds. We live in London,' she replied, looking towards her son.

Rainer was curious to know more. 'My wife and I visited Stratford-upon-Avon and spent many happy visits near Chelten . . . ham, but I forget the names. It was a long time ago.'

'Yes, Aunt Penelope is lucky. Stokencourt is such a pretty village. We often go to stay there.'

Rainer's heart lurched. Did she really say 'Penelope'? No, surely not . . . Would she have been sitting next to him if she'd returned? Could it possibly be that the woman who'd smiled across at him in the café, the woman on the deck at dawn, the woman standing by the grave was Penelope?

He didn't want to intrude, but to be so close and so far . . . He felt he was bursting to know more. 'Excuse me, but I would like to ask. Your Aunt Penelope, was she by any chance a nurse?'

The niece beamed at him. 'Why, yes, all her life. She taught in Malawi, trained up nurses there. Do you know her?'

'I'm not sure but she did remind me of someone. It's a small world and we tourists seemed to end up in the same spots. How strange.' He paused, taking a deep breath. 'Do give her my good wishes.'

'Who shall I say was asking?'

'Doktor Brecht, Rainer Brecht, but perhaps she'll have forgotten one of her patients. It was a long time ago.'

The stewards interrupted, coming down the aisle checking seats as the engine roared into life for takeoff.

Rainer stared out of the window, his heart thumping at this coincidence. Could it really be her? As they raced down the runway and up into the air, he smiled, thinking perhaps his pilgrimage was not over yet. A visit to England in the autumn was always pleasant. Was there just one more piece to fit in the jigsaw of his past before he could rest in peace?

Author Notes and Acknowledgements

The Battle of Crete was fought over 11 days, in May 1941. The island fell but never surrendered. Resistance continued until May 1945. I have tried to respect the timeline of major events and locations in this struggle. One British Red Cross nurse remained at her post until captured; Johanna Stavridi was honoured by the Hellenic Red Cross for her courage. Her story can be found in Eric Taylor's *Heroines of World War II* (Hale) (1991) and Dilys Powell's classic *The Villa Ariadne* (Efstathiadis group, S.A., 2003). The character and background of Penelope George was inspired by the stand made by the late Miss Stavridi, but this story is entirely fictitious.

What happened to the Jews of Chania in June 1944 is recorded in articles and essays *The Jews of Crete, Volume 11 (Etz Hayyim Synagogue, 2002).* There was only one known female who escaped the round-up – the late Victoria Fermon. Yolanda Markos and her family are entirely my own creation and not based on anyone living or deceased.

On board the *Tanais* were Italian prisoners of war, local resistance fighters as well as the Jewish community of Crete. No one knows the exact number of victims who drowned, but there were survivors, some of whom gave their account to an enquiry years later. I have tried to imagine the terror of surviving such a disaster.

Some of Rainer Brecht's wartime exploits loosely follow that of Einer von der Heydte whose account *Daedelus Returned* provided some useful information. Rainer, however, is a figment of my imagination. I have taken liberties with some timings, locations and events for dramatic purposes, but I hoped in doing so to capture some of the brave spirit of the Resistance Movement all over Crete. Any mistakes are entirely my own.

I could not have written this without the help and encouragement of Reg and Daphne Fairfoot of Artemis Villas, Stavros. I also treasure the time spent with Nikos Hannan-Stavroulakis, Alex Phoundoulakis and Anja Zuckmantel at Etz Hayyim Synagogue and the hours we spent in their company as tour guides there. It was at the annual memorial service for the victims of 10th June 1944 that I first heard their tragic history and knew this was something that I must one day try to honour. I am indebted also to Trisha and Mike Scott of Kaina, the Kokotsakis family of Aptera, especially Androniki for her memories of occupation, and Sue Harris-Kokotsaki's translation of Olympia Kokotsaki-Mantonanaki's award winning poem. I would like to thank Dr Don Everly, former Curator of the British School in Knossos, for a wonderful guided tour of the world famous site, Manolis; Sofia and Marialena Tsompanakis, Jeff and Brenda Thompson again for their hospitality and Ann and Graham Bacon for showing us an ancient tomb chamber close to Stilos that made such a perfect hiding place. You will find many relations of "Uncle Clarence" among the ancient olive groves of N.W. Crete.

It was the late Tony Fennymore who escorted us round Chania on one of his Saturday morning city tours all those years ago and unwittingly sowed the seeds of this story. His enthusiasm for all things Cretan was contagious. Once again I must thank my editor, Maxine Hitchcock, and copyeditor Yvonne Holland for their attention to detail and useful suggestions and my 500 Club confidantes, Trisha Ashley and Elizabeth Gill, for their support. Finally, love and gratitude to my husband David, my chef and chauffeur, whose practical encouragement and enthusiasm never wavers.

Some Further Reading:

The Battle and Resistance, Antony Beevor. Penguin. 1991
Inside Hitler's Greece, Mark Mazower. Yale University Press. 1995.
On the Run, Sean Damer and Ian Frazer. Penguin. 2006.
The Cretan Resistance: 1941-5, N A Kokonas. 2004.
The Jews of Ioannina, Rae Dalven. Cadmus Press. 1990.
The Cretan Runner, George Psychoundakis. Penguin. 1998.
Fenny's Hania, Fenny's Crete Publications. 1999.

Leah Fleming. Crete 2012.